FUSE

Illustration by
Mitz Vah

That Time I Got Reincarnated as a SLIME

7

JUL 2021

Rimuru Tempest

That Time I Got Reincarnated as a Slime

That Time I Got Reincarnated as a SLIME

7

FUSE

Illustration by Mitz Vah

YEN ON

New York

That Time I Got Reincarnated as a SLIME 7

FUSE

Translation by Kevin Gifford
Cover art by Mitz Vah

This book is a work of fiction. Names, characters, places, and incidents are the product of the author's imagination or are used fictitiously. Any resemblance to actual events, locales, or persons, living or dead, is coincidental.

TENSEI SHITARA SLIME DATTA KEN volume 7
© Fuse / Mitz Vah
All rights reserved.
First published in Japan in 2016 by MICROMAGAZINE,INC.
English translation rights arranged with MICROMAGAZINE,INC.
through Tuttle-Mori Agency, Inc., Tokyo.

English translation © 2019 by Yen Press, LLC

Yen On
150 West 30th Street, 19th Floor
New York, NY 10001

Visit us at yenpress.com
facebook.com/yenpress
twitter.com/yenpress
yenpress.tumblr.com
instagram.com/yenpress

First Yen On Edition: December 2019

Yen On is an imprint of Yen Press, LLC.
The Yen On name and logo are trademarks of Yen Press, LLC.

The publisher is not responsible for websites (or their content) that are not owned by the publisher.

Library of Congress Cataloging-in-Publication Data
Names: Fuse, author. | Mitz Vah, illustrator. | Gifford, Kevin, translator.
Title: That time I got reincarnated as a slime / Fuse ; illustration by Mitz Vah ; translation by Kevin Gifford.
Other titles: Tensei Shitara Slime datta ken. English
Description: First Yen On edition. | New York : Yen ON, 2017–
Identifiers: LCCN 2017043646 | ISBN 9780316414203 (v. 1 : pbk.) | ISBN 9781975301118 (v. 2 : pbk.) |
    ISBN 9781975301132 (v. 3 : pbk.) | ISBN 9781975301149 (v. 4 : pbk.) | ISBN 9781975301163 (v. 5 : pbk.) |
    ISBN 9781975301187 (v. 6 : pbk.) | ISBN 9781975301200 (v. 7 : pbk.)
Subjects: GSAFD: Fantasy fiction.
Classification: LCC PL870.S4 T4613 2017 | DDC 895.63/6—dc23
LC record available at https://lccn.loc.gov/2017043646

ISBNs: 978-1-9753-0120-0 (paperback)
        978-1-9753-0121-7 (ebook)

10 9 8 7 6 5 4 3 2

LSC-C

Printed in the United States of America

That Time I Got Reincarnated as a SLIME

7

The Jura-Tempest Federation

Storm Dragon
Veldora Tempest

Samurai General
Benimaru

Oracle
Shuna

Octagram Newbie
Rimuru Tempest

Covert Agent
Soei

Instructor
Hakuro

First Secretary
Shion

Second Secretary
Diablo

Goblin Rider Captain
Gobta

Tempest Starwolf/Pet
Ranga

Great Saint
Arnaud Bauman
of Air

Great Saint/Noble of Light
Renard Jester

Great Saint
Litus
of Water

Great Saint
Bacchus
of Earth

Great Saint
Fritz
of Wind

Great Saint
Garde
of Fire

Great Saint/Captain of the Crusaders
Hinata Sakaguchi

Deity
Luminus

The strongest deity in Luminism;
the only one Hinata worships.

The Seven Days Clergy

A legendary band of Western Holy Church advisers, each one an intensely powerful Enlightened. Charged with raising and teaching would-be Heroes.

Great Saint/"Raging Sea" Battlesage
Glenda

Great Saint/"Giant Boulder" Battlesage
Grigori

Great Saint/"Blue Sky" Battlesage
Saare

CONTENTS | THE CONFLICT BETWEEN HOLY AND DEMONIC

PROLOGUE

THE MAGIC-BORN MEMORIAL

That Time I Got Reincarnated as a Slime

Clayman was dead. And when Laplace delivered the news to the group assembled before him, the reaction was stunned silence.

"You lie! There is no way that could happen!"

This was Footman frantically shouting now, but no one could find it in themselves to see things his way. Laplace was always so aloof, easygoing, never one to express any of his true emotions. But his face said it all. This was not the joker all of them knew—he was literally hanging his head in shame before them. It was all they needed to see to know that Clayman was really and truly dead.

"...Last night, the night of that Walpurgis Council, I lost my connection with Clayman," Kazalim ponderously stated as Teare sobbed nearby. "My connection with someone I viewed as my own child. It could only mean one thing for him—death. I hardly wanted to admit it to myself. Even now, Laplace, after what you told us, I am filled with a stubborn refusal to admit it..."

"This was my mistake," a boy with black hair regretfully lamented. "I thought the demon lords were kid stuff. I needed to be more careful. Gather more intelligence and *then* take action."

There were ten demon lords in all, looking down upon the world from atop their lofty peaks. But even in such heady territory, each of them bore different strengths and weaknesses. Clayman's apparently successful application of Demon Dominate on the mind of the demon lord Milim caused him to forget that vital fact—and even worse, led him to believe he could rule over all his fellow lords. It was much too rash of him.

"If you're gonna put it that way," replied Laplace, lightening the mood with a joking tone, "I'm the one who suggested it to the guy. I never thought for a moment it'd turn out like *this*, no, not that it matters now. Plus, you have to admit it—Clayman was too stupid for his own good this time. I *told* him not to let his guard down, but he got carried away with it, and it blew up on him. All there is to it."

"Laplace!" snarled Footman. "You can't speak of him like that!"

"I'm only tellin' the truth. He was weak, he got carried away, and now he's dead."

"Laplace!!"

Letting his anger overcome him, Footman took a swing at Laplace. His fist dug into the cheek of its target; Laplace didn't bother to dodge it. But that was all. Laplace remained where he stood, his eyes swiveling toward his attacker.

"Oh, what, you wanna go, Footman? Well, be my guest!"

He let slip an easygoing smile as he taunted Footman, all but daring him to focus his anger upon him. Kazalim saw right through it.

"Stop it, you two!" she roared, halting them both. "This is a sad occasion for each of us."

"She's right," the boy added. "Why are you playing the bad guy all by yourself here, Laplace? That's not like you. If anyone should play that role, it oughtta be me for hiring all of you."

"Ah…" Now Footman realized it. Laplace was goading him on purpose. "My apologies, Laplace."

"…Nah, it's fine. But you know, pal—and you too, President—you sure are mean, ain'tcha? I *am* trying to be the bad guy here, so how 'bout not letting the cat out of the bag?"

He rubbed his cheek as he continued to complain. And something about the sight was so comical that it really did lighten the mood—if only a little.

Back in control of their emotions, the magic-born discussed what to do next. Wailing about the misfortune of it all, Kazalim reasoned, would do nothing to realize Clayman's goals. Their talks grew sterner, more serious.

"…I couldn't tell you what happened in there, but as the demon lord Valentine put it, Clayman definitely died during the Council. He didn't mention who did it, though..."

"Too bad I couldn't have beaten it outta him..."

"No, Laplace. I am glad to see *you* still breathing, at least."

"Ahh, I was just lucky. It happened to be the new moon, and bein' a vampire, Valentine was at the low end of his strength. We were in a holy place to boot. Lotsa holiness fillin' up the atmosphere. That's the only reason my attacks worked at all."

Nobody doubted Laplace's words. Laplace only managed to defeat Valentine, whose strength was on a par with the Kazalim of the past, thanks to several overlapping factors working out in his favor. Plus, Laplace was second only to Kazalim in brute force. His role as vice president of the Moderate Jesters was no empty title—he had the strength to back it up. That was why everyone in the room so readily accepted Laplace's astonishing victory—and thus, the talks continued, with nobody noticing the lie lurking between his words.

"This is quite the conundrum, however..."

"You could say that," Kazalim muttered. "We lost the base of operations we granted Clayman, his forces, his treasure...everything. A staggering loss."

The boy nodded his agreement.

"Wh-what do you mean?" Teare asked. "Whether the demon lords killed Clayman or not, we still have his headquarters, don't we?"

"I know that Clayman's forces were routed," added Footman, "but we still have every chance to regroup and attack once again, no? We still have Adalmann, that crazed Saint, patrolling the lands. A wight king like him is just as strong as any of us—and the curse you've laid upon him is as active as ever, isn't it, President?"

Kazalim exchanged glances with the boy before slowly, painfully, opening his mouth. "The complex I granted Clayman fell yesterday, in the course of a single evening. That slime, of all people, sent a small assault force to capture it."

"Huhhh?" Laplace reacted.

"No!" Teare shouted.

"You're kidding me!" protested Footman. "So the magic-born I saw on that battlefield wasn't even the full force at that Rimuru's disposal— Ah, wait a minute." He looked up for a moment. "Hold on, hold on, I remember that crystal..."

"Right." The boy nodded. "The images Laplace took— You saw the ogre mages in there, didn't you? I think it's safe to say that each of them alone is a Special A-grade threat in the battlefield."

Footman fell silent, mouth agape.

"...Really?" Teare whispered. Nobody answered.

"Regardless," reported Kazalim, "that slime Rimuru was at the battle. I suppose he sprang that fight upon us as a ruse so he could capture Clayman's quarters himself. For a slime of his caliber, it's not impossible to imagine him breaking through our defensive lines."

Now the rest of the room was beginning to realize just how ominous the situation was.

"Which is why," the boy said, "I think we need to reconsider our objective."

With the majority of their military forces gone, he reasoned, any strategic moves needed to be avoided for now. Clayman's death alone was a serious psychological blow to everybody who knew him. But fortunately, they had not lost everything. They still had resources left untapped in order to spread out the risk, as well as the group they had implanted deep inside the Western Nations. Plus, the political influence they wielded behind the scenes with those two groups was still as strong as ever. Perhaps they lacked physical might, but they had intelligence-gathering experts deployed across the land, laying out feelers to gauge every nation's direction.

To the boy, who had started with nothing and come this far, it was still possible to stage a comeback. And that was why...

"...For the time being, we need to lay low. It's a shame about Clayman, but we don't have enough power to try to exact revenge upon the demon lords. If we want to reach our ultimate goal of conquering the world, I think we need to be patient for now."

His audience nodded their agreement.

"True enough. We've made major strides over the past ten years. Perhaps it planted the seeds of arrogance inside all of us."

"Yep. Hence why Clayman got it in his head to pull all that nonsense..."

"Right. I hate to say it, but doing anything rash right now is likely to make things even worse."

"I hesitate to accept it myself, but I concede it is our best option for now…"

The boy giggled a little as the magic-born all offered their agreement. "Ha-ha-ha! Oh, cut me a break, Footman," he chuckled, patting him on the shoulder. "I've still got all of you—the best cards in my hand. I can't afford to lose you guys over some reckless shot in the dark, too."

This was something he truly meant and also the main reason behind his decision. He needed to be sure everyone was on the same page as him, or else he feared at least one would let their anger get the best of them. Footman knew that perfectly well—and he knew he had to accept it.

"I know, pal. Better to bottle it up inside for now, so we can let it fully erupt later."

He did understand that. Losing his cool and picking a fight with a cadre of demon lords would simply spell the end of his life. He had to accept the boy's reasoning.

The boy, appreciating this, looked at the magic-born assembled before him. "But hey, it's no fun to be the punching bag *all* the time, right? Maybe we won't *do* anything, but we can *say* a lot of things. That slime took Clayman for everything he had, and I think I know how to get back at him a bit."

He gave an ominous little grin.

"How do you mean?" Kazalim asked.

"There is something unusual about that slime," the boy replied, grinning with glee. "In just a few years, he has built up a new, and massive, force. It's hard for me to believe, and in any normal situation, we'd never want to defy him. So let's wait and see a little, huh? And to do that, I've got something I want to deploy."

"Oh, great." Laplace shrugged. "Another little scheme of yours? At least it beats you ordering me to pull off some *other* insane trick, as you usually do. Hopefully I can stay in the audience for this one, thanks."

For now, the magic-born were withdrawing from the public eye, descending into a sort of primordial darkness—sharpening their fangs for the fated day of revenge, whenever it may come.

DEMONS AND SCHEMES

That Time I Got Reincarnated as a Slime

Once we settled on the name Octagram for ourselves, Mizeri and Raine, the green- and blue-haired maids in Guy Crimson's service, prepared an extravagant meal for us all. They were decked out in dark-red maid's outfits, and their kitchen skills, it turned out, were second to none.

As Ramiris told me, the original purpose of the Walpurgis Council was to let demon lords hang out and swap information. As a vestige of this, perhaps, the space we were in featured a separate room…a sort of casual lounge, you could say. Attendance wasn't mandatory, and all the demon lords did their own thing—some left immediately after the meeting ended, some stuck around long enough for dinner, and others whiled away the time by chatting in the lounge.

Me, I went for the food. You don't get a chance like this every day, and honestly, considering how much more overpowered Guy was compared with the rest of us, I wanted to see what his diet was like. The resulting meal was more exquisitely delightful than I ever could've imagined. Each dish was an astounding new discovery, the best of its type in the whole world, and as I lingered over each one in reverie:

Report. Component analysis complete. It is now possible to re-create the recipes black tiger stew, grilled sage rooster, golden peach sherbet, and roast earthensleep dragon steak.

*　　*　　*

I stole all the recipes. Is that mean of me? It seemed kind of unfair, not that I really understood what made them work. *Steal* makes it sound illegal or something. This was just intelligence gathering. These recipes called for meat from monsters rated A or higher, which you don't exactly see walking into town every day. But once I had the right ingredients, I think I would know how to prepare them now.

The feast was rounded out with a bountiful selection of fresh fruit. Six of us were at the table, by the way—me, Guy, Milim, Ramiris, Deeno, and Daggrull. Valentine and Leon had left long ago.

I took a moment to admonish Milim for tricking me as she gorged herself. She was still playing dumb, but I needed to give her a taste of reality. Meanwhile, I had Carillon and Frey promise me that we'd all discuss the future at a later time. Once we cleaned up after the war, I figured I'd be consulted about the upcoming city-rebuild work. This was going to be a brand-new nation, one with Milim at its head, and I intended to approach those discussions so they benefited me as much as possible.

Ramiris was still bugging me about moving to my hometown. I refused her point-blank, of course, but she wasn't giving up. You could see it in her eyes. I figured Treyni would be nice enough to pacify her a bit for me, but I had the sneaking suspicion that Treyni loved spoiling Ramiris more than anything else. It seemed that was practically what she lived for, so I reminded myself not to expect much as I resolved to keep an eye on them.

Daggrull and Veldora seemed to be hitting it off pretty well, and Guy and Deeno were engaged in friendly conversation. I decided to offer all of them some of Tempest's world-famous brandy, distilled from our own wine. Part of my branding efforts, you might say. Spreading the word about how useful a nation we were would oil the gears for diplomacy later. That much is true whether you're dealing with a demon lord or your next-door neighbor.

"Not bad."

"Well, well, look at this..."

"*Hack! Cough, cough cough!* Man, that's got some bite..."

It was maybe a bit too much alcohol for Deeno to handle, but Guy and Daggrull enjoyed it. *So would you* please *not drink all of it first, Veldora?* I had a pretty decent stockpile left in my Stomach, but I didn't store it in there just so Veldora could guzzle it all. And Milim immediately grabbed at the brandy, too, of course. I didn't let her have any. You *know* she'd be an angry drunk. And considering how she tricked me, I had to put my foot down on this.

"And it's fine for *me*, mmmmmm?"

Ramiris, meanwhile, was already preciously cradling her glass, three sheets to the wind in the blink of an eye. I let the frantic Beretta and Treyni deal with her. This was actually good for me. If she stayed sober and undistracted tonight, there's every chance she would've tried following me back to Tempest.

So things were in full swing before long at this feast, and I decided to take my leave before Ramiris woke up from her stupor. It was quite an ending to the Walpurgis Council—not at all what I expected, but I'm glad my worrying was all for naught in the end.

It had been, to say the least, an eventful twenty-four hours. Walpurgis began at the stroke of midnight; by the time we wrapped it up, it was already early afternoon the next day.

In a flash, I was back at Tempest. The trip over there was one thing, but with Dominate Space, the journey back was a snap. And unlike before, my nation hadn't fallen apart in my absence—spirits were high, everything worked fine, and I was tremendously relieved. All our forces had kept their high alert going, just as I ordered. They were all more refined now, contributing to safety on the streets more than ever. I had overlooked nothing. The town's security system, modeled after the police I was familiar with on Earth, seemed to be a decent success.

As I observed all this, a thought struck my mind. *You know, this country's defenses alone could take out a nation or two all by themselves, couldn't they?* Nearly every solder left on defense duty was the equivalent of a B rank, after all. Your garden-variety magical or paranormal beast wouldn't dare lurk nearby.

Overall, the rule of law and order had really taken hold around here. But that made me worry about monsters coming out of the city, potentially causing havoc somewhere else. It might be better, I thought, to check up on that. So I dragged Veldora and Shion back to town, riding on the back of Ranga.

The moment I entered the city, the local residents and patrolling soldiers immediately took a knee at the side of the road, forming a path for me to follow. It was all so expertly choreographed. I had no idea when they learned how to do it. *What's up with that?* I thought—only to find Diablo approaching me from the other end of the path. He gave me a sincere smile, one brimming with joy, as he exchanged glances with Rigurd.

"Welcome back, Sir Rimuru!"

"It fills us with joy to hear of your induction into the Octagram! I am so glad to see you back here safely!"

I appreciated that from Rigurd and Diablo, yes, but...seriously, what's going on here? And how did you guys know I was crowned a demon lord? That had to be the first time anyone used the term *Octagram* in this world, too. I should know—I thought of it myself. The questions just kept piling up. Wasn't Diablo supposed to be out conquering the Kingdom of Farmus right now? Why was he here roping the entire town into doing this little dance number for me?

Starting to feel a little ashamed about all this, I finally decided to ask. "It's simple, Sir Rimuru," the smiling Diablo replied. "We had asked Lord Veldora to keep us updated."

I squinted at Veldora. He immediately averted his eyes. Dude. *Come on, man. I don't know what he's guilty of yet, but he's guilty of something.*

After I put the screws to him a little, Veldora quickly revealed the truth. It turns out that he agreed to play Tempest informant in exchange for three dessert dishes at the next meal—and he held up his end of the bargain, telling Diablo about everything that happened in the Council.

Now it made sense—why they knew about me being a demon lord and about the Octagram name we had adopted. Maybe I should go so far as to praise Diablo for his data-gathering skills. Even if a person was smart enough to consider paying off someone as powerful as Veldora, only a select few would dare attempt it. Of course, Veldora deserves a lot of credit for actually agreeing with that nonsense, but still, I like this kind of proactive behavior. If all parties involved were pleased, I saw no need to harp on it.

Still...

"Veldora, do you even *need* to eat?"

"Wh-what kind of nonsense is that, Rimuru?! It's not a matter of needing to eat or not. I eat because I want to. *You* hardly need to eat, either, do you?"

Gah!

He had a point. I don't have much of a leg to stand on here. Shuna's cooking had improved by leaps and bounds lately, and we had a variety of desserts on offer these days. We managed to perfectly re-create the cream puffs I found in that Englesian café, and we were even inventing things like custard pudding now. The larger array of alcoholic beverages available also contributed to the invention of new taste-tempting treats.

I was having Yoshida, the café owner, help with this, developing new recipes and so forth; he readily agreed, happy to gain access to the drinks we made. "Now," he gleefully said, "I think I can make a lot of things I couldn't before." We already had a few test dishes laid out for our dinner tables; Veldora had tried a few of them during the celebration right after I resurrected him, and the results looked like they honestly shocked the guy.

You sure you should be so easily plied with food like that, Veldora? And all it took to make Milim putty in my hands was just a bit of honey... You know, maybe I could conquer the world with a well-stocked kitchen instead of all these military forces.

As I thought about this, Shion and Diablo were exchanging a few words with each other.

"You *did* serve as Sir Rimuru's guardian, did you not?"

"Of course I did! And thanks to that, now we all know you aren't needed as long as I am around. But what about the task Sir Rimuru gave you?"

"Eh-heh-heh-heh-heh... All is well. I intend to brief Sir Rimuru about it personally."

Their smiles didn't even reach their eyes; the rivalry was still as intense as ever, I could see. If I left them to their own devices, they'd be at it all day.

"Guys, can you knock that off?"

"Yes." Rigurd nodded. "I am sure Sir Rimuru is tired. I believe Haruna has a meal prepared for all of you. We can talk once you are suitably refreshed."

Thanks, Rigurd. I'm loving this new air of authority you're giving out.

*　　*　　*

So I had him lead me through town.

Everyone we passed by was all smiles, ready to go into full-on party mode at the drop of a hat, but Benimaru and his team still weren't back from their mission. The full celebration could wait until later. For now, I could rest in the knowledge that one thorny problem, at least, was solved.

Thus, I decided to sink into my hot-spring bath, enjoy the food Haruna prepared for me, give myself a mental recharge, and then listen to Diablo's report. The battle with Clayman ended in total victory for me, and that just left the establishment of Yohm's new kingdom and our future wrangling with the Western Holy Church to deal with. There would be new negotiations to consider shortly—with the Beast Kingdom of Eurazania, with the Winged Nation of Fulbrosia, with the Dragon Faithful who worshiped Milim—but those all looked bound to end on friendly terms, so there was no need to fret much about them now.

"So," I asked Diablo as I enjoyed some post-dinner tea, "what have you been up to? I asked you to destroy the Kingdom of Farmus and install Yohm as its new king. If you abandoned that job and came back here, should I assume that to mean you need more resources?"

I was back in slime form for the first time in a while, relaxing in Shion's lap as I enjoyed the roundness of her breasts over my head. I think that made my question sound even more serene than I intended. If Diablo needed help, I figured someone like Soei could provide it. We had some leeway again for a change; no need to make Diablo fend for himself.

Shion was laughing above me, going on about something like "Oh, I would say being your tea fetcher is the ideal job for Diablo, my lord. Allow *me* to conquer that kingdom instead!" and so on, but I ignored her. I just couldn't see her as up to the task. It was probably her way of lending Diablo a helping hand, but I wasn't listening—and as it turned out, it wasn't necessary.

"No, Sir Rimuru," he said as he refilled my cup, "no resources will be necessary. Everything is proceeding smoothly and according to plan."

Drinking tea in slime form was a bit tricky, so I simply decided to lie back and enjoy the aroma as I prepared to receive his report. Ahhh, bliss. A bliss that abruptly ended with the next thing he said.

"First, I restored all of them to their original condition. Reducing them to inert slabs of meat was proving rather, ah, inconvenient."

Slabs of what?! What's he talking about? Shion shivered a little, picking up on my confusion. *Wait, was that her interrogation method…? Hoo boy. Better shut my imagination off before things get too dangerous.* I had paid a visit to the interrogation room exactly once, warning her not to "go too far" with the three prisoners we held in there, but…well. I honestly didn't care if Shion killed them, back at that time, so I didn't push the issue too much. Bit late to regret that now, I suppose.

Things were already looking dicey here, but I kept up a brave face, hiding my turmoil as I encouraged Diablo to continue.

●

The first thing Diablo did, as he dutifully explained to Rimuru, was restore Church archbishop Reyhiem and palace sorcerer Razen to health.

This was conducted on the way to Farmus, in two wagons surrounded by a team of mounted guards. Diablo was seated with the three prisoners in one of the wagons—well, "with" wasn't exactly right, because although the wagon could comfortably house six passengers, Diablo was the only visible figure inside it. The other three had been packed inside boxes on the floor. As, well, living slabs of meat.

What Shion had done was render them into a form almost too hideous to describe, something far removed from anything recognizably human. She had done so in tiny incremental steps to ensure nobody died, slowly and repeatedly exposing their musculature to the outside air, delicately scraping the meat off their bones. To put it less delicately, Shion was using those three to help her learn how to filet human beings alive—while ensuring the subjects felt no physical pain at all. This was Master Chef, Shion's unique skill, which pushed them all right up to the brink of death, only to revive them with healing potion so she could start her research over from the beginning.

The sight and sensation of having that repeated over and over, seeing their bodies be disassembled and reassembled—all painlessly—broke all three of them for good. You could see it in their anguished expressions—when you could make out their faces at all, what with all the other exposed guts and viscera in the way.

Returning them to Farmus like this, all of them could tell, was a bad idea. So Diablo began to put together a solution, if rather reluctantly. "What a pain," he groused. "The laws governing their continued existence have been so twisted and warped that healing magic hardly works on them at all." But the experience also opened his eyes to the power of arts and other unique skills, something that goes beyond mere magic. Even with his all-but-complete knowledge of magic and its rules in this world, he had found a new surprise to play with. It delighted him.

Thus, in that wagon trundling its way to Farmus, Diablo successfully banished the remains of Shion's force as it was applied to the three prisoners. Reyhiem was first to be revived, followed by Razen. Diablo had no particular order in mind for this, but when it came time to tackle King Edmaris of Farmus, he stopped.

"Oh, thank you, thank you...!"

It was Reyhiem who found his voice first.

"But enough about us," Razen added. "My king... Please, bring my king back to what he was..."

Diablo rewarded this blind loyalty with a restive glance...and laughed.

"Ee-hee-hee-hee-hee... You, asking favors of me? You understand that the payment for this is dear, very dear?"

There was kindness to his smile—but not a shred of warmth to his eyes.

"Ah... N-no, I..."

Razen turned pale with fear and regret—

—and then he remembered. Diablo, sitting calm and composed in front of him, was not a demon to trifle with. An Arch Demon—or really, nothing even as approachable as that. An Arch Demon would be a threat, enough of one to perhaps spell doom for any smaller nation it pays a visit to. That's how they earned their Special A rating, qualifying for Calamity status. Their magical force made any half-hearted effort at a magic barrier bend to their will. The fierceness of their aura could blow the defensive fortifications of an entire city away in a single onrush. All that, plus magical spells that crushed anything they encountered. Any adventurer who didn't rank at least an A themselves had no chance of handling an Arch Demon—simply standing in front of one would be forfeiting their lives. Even Razen would hesitate to confront one.

But that didn't even compare with Diablo. There didn't seem to be any aura coming from him at all; he looked merely human. Only his eyes were unique. One glance, and they were unforgettable, like golden moons in the dead of night with slashes of crimson red down the middle. It was alarmingly eerie, but otherwise, he was no different from anyone else—meaning he could simply walk right through any fortifications a city might use to block a lesser demon's approach.

If humans had any advantage over demons, it was in knowledge and wariness. Monsters could be intelligent as well, but the smarter they were, the more they wanted to show it off—usually in the form of their aura, which they used as a sort of magicule-driven calling card. That was what made barriers sensitive to such energy surges so effective against them. But what about a monster that hid its aura? A Calamity that just appears, in the middle of the street? Razen didn't even want to imagine that scenario.

A demon smashing through a magic barrier, while regrettable, could at least be anticipated. It'd buy you time to shore up your forces and launch a counterattack. But if that demon could ignore the barrier entirely…anyone could see that it was no laughing matter. Any monster like that would be arch-demon-level or higher. *That* was Diablo, one of the first Primal Demons.

But there was something even scarier than that. That was the fact that Diablo, this ancient and fearsome demon, was in servitude to another master. The master of all those monsters, with the strikingly beautiful golden eyes and silver-blue hair—shining so bright that you could almost see through him. Fleeting, but possessing power beyond anyone's recognition. Someone worthy of being called a demon lord.

His mind was filled with sheer terror as he watched this lord massacre an army of twenty thousand, but when they met later, he felt a different emotion. When Razen was being taken away as a prisoner of war, the way this demon lord regarded him... It was like glancing at a pebble on the road. The moment those golden eyes spotted him, Razen was practically intoxicated. Gone was the pain racking his body, the fear of imminent death. And then he understood. There are things in this world that were never meant to be touched. A voice from the heavens booming "Don't go overboard." It must have warned Razen then. *Don't count on your chances. Taking on a being who counts a Primal Demon among his servants—no wonder your nation has fallen. To a demon lord like that, destroying Farmus single-handed would be too simple.*

Razen remembered it all. Ignoring the lurching and jolting of the wagon, he got out of his seat and kneeled before Diablo.

"Of course I understand. And I hope I can...er, that you will allow me to join you as even your lowliest servant! I swear that my body, and my soul, is yours to utilize. So please, please offer some pity to King Edmaris..."

He was staking all his loyalty on this request. Diablo greeted it with a placid nod.

"Very well. I suppose even someone like you is considered relatively powerful by human standards. I am sure you have your uses. Besides, I had no intention of killing him unless Sir Rimuru ordered me to. I will be glad to free him for you. But..."

However, if the monarch wanted to go back to the way he remembered himself, he would have to work for it. He would need to be shown to the kingdom's nobility, in the horrifying form he was in now, to show to the world the foolishness of bending a bow against the Rimuru Diablo was so devoted to. Razen waited nervously for Diablo to continue, while Reyhiem was too terrified by the oppressive atmosphere to move an inch.

"But I will let this go just one time. Depending on your future behavior, not only your king's life, but the very breath of existence that blows over the land of Farmus may be snuffed out."

He meant it literally. Diablo's will—meaning, Rimuru's will—was to be followed, or else. Razen, and Reyhiem, and even King

Edmaris in his exposed, twisted, boxed-up form all knew the intent behind the statement. All three were fools, but they were not idiots. Whether they liked it or not, they understood Diablo wouldn't hesitate to act on that threat. The only way they could remain alive, it was clear now, was to give Diablo their full support.

"Of course, sir! Give us any order you seek! We will cooperate to the best of our ability!"

Reyhiem threw his head close to the floor in a humiliating kowtow, a mental hair's breadth away from licking Diablo's boots.

"You have our loyalty, my lord!"

And Razen had already made up his mind. Whether the king was safe mattered little by now. The only thing that had kept Farmus, and its royal lineage, safe for this long was Razen's pride in his job. Even Edmaris, in all his anguish and desperation, could see that. Now, Razen had forsaken him—and thus, forsaken Farmus.

But the king knew it was the best choice available. Defying the demon lord meant the destruction of the nation. King Edmaris had two choices left: pledge his allegiance to the demons or attempt a resistance and be cut down immediately. And the good king was not foolish enough to make the wrong decision at a time like this. Thus, for his last official act as leader of the Kingdom of Farmus, he made the right move.

"As the final king of Farmus," he declared, with some reluctance but still loudly and clearly, "I promise I will provide any support you require, Sir Diablo."

Diablo had pledges from all three of them. At that moment, behind the scenes, his Tempter skill was doing its work, ensuring that each one would be in his servitude.

"Don't worry," the demon gently whispered with a smile. "Do what I say, and I will make sure you do not suffer for it."

The land of Farmus was in a state of mass confusion that day. Their lord, King Edmaris, had returned in a shocking state of affairs.

There, in the royal castle's audience chambers, the collected nobility of the nation gasped in horror. There, atop the throne, a box had been reverently laid upon the cushion. Inside was…a cube of meat, a nauseating mixture of geometry and biology with the king's face buried in the center. It was alive, its eyes a tad glassy as it stared out of the box, but fully conscious nonetheless.

"Shogo! What madness is this? Why is His Majesty in such a miserable state?!"

"Hear! Hear! And what of the other two? What happened to our royal armies?"

"And what of Folgen?! What is our knight captain doing?! How could this ever have happened with Sir Razen overseeing matters?!"

Panic spread as the noblemen began to shout over one another, fervently trying to mask their fear. Razen, taking the form of Shogo, could hardly blame them.

. . . .

. . . . . .

. . .

Several days after losing regular magical contact, the people remaining in the kingdom were on pins and needles. Their proud, overwhelming force of twenty thousand couldn't have been defeated, but there was no telling what sort of unexpected events may have transpired. There was no way to be sure if their king was safe, even—more than enough to fill any mind with suspicious doubt.

In the midst of this, Razen had taken Archbishop Reyhiem back home, using a Warp Portal to transport the both of them back to the castle's warp chamber. A passing sentry had noticed their limp forms on the floor early in the morning that day. It threw the palace guards into a panic as they scrambled to identify them—Shogo Taguchi, the otherworlder, and Reyhiem, archbishop and His Majesty's close confidant. The guards helped the latter up, still confused about all this, before noticing the box the boy took great pains to keep safe in his hands.

One of them looked inside, unprepared for the sight. He was an upper officer in the royal guard, known for courage and coolness under fire, but not even he could refrain from screaming in horror. There were strings of some unidentifiable organic matter connecting haphazardly from one section to the other, emitting a rotting stench—a twisted sight, like plucking all the organs out of a body and gluing them back together at random. The sole ruler of the Kingdom of Farmus had been reduced to a sickening creature, and no one could criticize that royal guard for so rudely screaming his head off at him. Attracted by the noise, others went to look for themselves and reacted the same way; the attendants and ministers were all thrown into utter chaos at the transformation of their lord.

Some screamed and sobbed. Some found themselves emptying their stomachs on the spot in fear. Some fainted entirely. None of them could believe this was their king. But this was reality. When they finally dared to come close enough, it was confirmed for good—this truly was Edmaris before them.

"What are you doing?!" one of the ministers shouted. "We must help His Majesty!"

That was the catalyst. At once, everyone sprang into action. The sorcerers who stayed behind in the palace tested out every spell at their disposal. The high-level priests of the Western Holy Church were summoned, each attempting their own healing magic. Faced with this object of primal fear, they tried desperately to restore the king to normal, faces straining at the sickening sight, attempting to keep their wits as they continued their work.

But nothing worked. No matter what they tried, they couldn't save their king.

....
......
...

Now Shogo had regained consciousness. He was immediately called in for questioning.

Razen felt a slight sense of sympathy there, faced with his former comrades. His fealty was squarely with Diablo, and he wouldn't hesitate to betray them now. They would all face their fates alone, based on their own decisions—but Razen felt just a hint of pity for them. All of this was on Diablo's orders, including his feigned unconsciousness. Everything was going to plan.

As Diablo's servant, Razen had received a briefing on what his new master intended to do with this kingdom. He fully understood what needed to be done to achieve those aims. In a word, this land was to become the demon lord's plaything. The moment Farmus was selected as a game board with everyone here as pawns, the history of the country as an ongoing concern came to an end.

But this was not necessarily bad news for its people. When told of the demon lord's plans, Razen felt a broad sense of hope. Already in his mind's eye, he could see the land of Farmus growing more prosperous than ever before. If achieving this goal meant toppling the current system in place, then so be it.

"Calm yourselves! This is Razen inside this body. I have taken His Majesty back to safety, with the kind assistance of a champion to our cause."

"What? You're not Shogo?"

"What happened to...? Ah. Yes, now I see."

"Imagine, Sir Razen inside that impudent snit Shogo's body! This will take some getting used to."

Despite the initial confusion, the people in the chamber were convinced. Razen was, after all, a great magician.

"But you fled the battle? Does that mean our forces...Farmus's forces have been defeated?!"

"What happened after that? You didn't simply march back to the castle because you couldn't eradicate the monsters, did you?"

The noblemen's questions grew to a torrent. They were the leaders of the nation, although many of them secretly (or not so secretly) schemed to use this war as a cover for the profits they intended to make off it. Defeat, and the financial losses that entailed, were unthinkable notions.

"Silence, all of you! We must let Sir Razen say his piece!"

It was the Marquis of Muller who finally calmed the crowd. That, too, was part of the plan. Diablo had made contact with him the previous night via a connection to Fuze, guild master for the kingdom of Blumund. Things were all proceeding just as Diablo had pictured them.

Razen began by explaining how the king would be saved. A native champion named Yohm had apparently negotiated with the lord of the monsters, procuring some of their restorative potion that he would soon bring back to Farmus. Word had already been sent to the gate guards, ready to receive Yohm's party at any moment.

He then moved on to what exactly happened to the Farmus forces.

He did not get very far into the tale before the chamber erupted into shouting once more. All it took were three magic words: Veldora was reborn.

"That—that can't be..."

"That evil dragon's found new life in the monsters' land...?"

"No... I thought Veldora had been eternally banished!"

"There is no time to waste. We must report this to the Holy Church and have them dispatch a Crusader group at once!"

"It's all over! If Sir Razen speaks the truth, we have no means of resistance. The remaining forces in Farmus hardly number enough to put up a new defense!"

"He's right! Bring our knights back here immediately!"

"Indeed. If our magical link with them is cut off, we must send a messenger for General Folgen!"

"There's no time for such nonsense! We must flee this land before this knowledge reaches the general public, or we may lose any chance to do so!"

Chaos and terror reigned. Some professed the need to strike back; others saw fit to abandon the people outright and go into exile. Muller silenced them all with a thundering roar.

"Enough of this! Whether our knights are alive or not, the situation remains the same. Panic will accomplish nothing for us, Sir Hytta. Where do you intend to flee to? That Storm Dragon is a Catastrophe for us all."

The noblemen regained their composure. Calmness returned for a moment, only to be shattered as Razen continued, explaining what had transpired in that faraway land—the sad (and entirely made-up) tragedy of how the entire Farmus force had disappeared without a trace, following Veldora's revival.

The tale made all the present nobility fall silent. Nobody said anything. It was entirely preposterous, so difficult to believe, for everyone. Soon, they began asking Razen questions, attempting to come to grips with the situation.

"S-Sir Razen, is all of that true? We have no idea where any of them are?"

"Indeed. The battle between our forces and the monsters resurrected the sleeping dragon in his domain."

"That, that couldn't possibly be! The Western Holy Church declared him to be sealed away forever! Are you saying that was a lie?"

"No. They were right—Veldora had been extinguished from this world. But the seeds of the dragon species can never be fully removed. They are simply reborn elsewhere. It surprised all of us, though, seeing this rebirth take place so close to us and in such a short time."

"Then what happened to the survivors, Sir Razen?"

"Yes! Is General Folgen still alive? How many forces can we still account for?"

Razen solemnly shook his head. They had all died, thanks to an enraged Rimuru—such was the truth. But he had direct orders from Diablo to describe the fates of every fighter as unknown.

"What is the meaning of this?"

"As I said, I do not know where they are. The knights and monsters that were fighting on that land disappeared once Veldora revived himself. We were all that remained—"

"Ridiculous!"

"Just to be sure, you literally mean they disappeared? Not scattered across the land following a rout?"

"Our supply teams would have been stationed behind the front lines. Surely they must be safe, at least?"

Razen fell silent, eyes closed. Seeing this forced everyone to trust him at his word. The knights were all gone. One of the ministers fell to the ground, erupting in tears. He was the one who asked about the supply teams, in no small part because his son had been sent out on one of them, his first battle experience. Keeping him away from the front had meant pulling all the strings he could, but the effort had been wasted. He had only agreed to his deployment because this was supposed to be a raid, a journey to seize the monsters' assets and kill with abandon. And now this. The despair came so unexpectedly, it made him cry almost instantly.

But even that tragedy was just one in a multitude. Approximately twenty thousand people were missing in action. It was a cataclysmic loss like none the nation had ever seen—and as "missing" as they officially were, nobody expected them home anytime soon. They were as good as dead.

And now all of them had connected that cataclysm in their minds with the revival of Veldora. They had all been sacrificed in order to breathe life into the dragon. To Veldora himself, that was nothing more than a hateful lie, but it was exactly what Rimuru and his advisers wanted. Diablo had just made masterful use of Razen to manipulate the thoughts and minds of the Farmus nobility.

*

Then, as if on cue, footsteps rang out from outside the throne room. Yohm and his team had arrived—with Mjurran as his chief adviser, Gruecith, his main bodyguard, and the sorcerer Rommel, his personal secretary. Taking up the rear was Diablo himself, dressed in his finest butler-style clothing but oozing a very non-butler-like arrogance from every pore. This chamber was not the sort of place someone as low-born as an adventurer could easily step into, but Razen had arranged for a guide to lead them in.

"Sorry I took so long," said Yohm to Razen, "but I think I finally got the big guy to see things our way."

He tried to hold his head high as a statesman, but his street-bred speech habits proved less simple to fix. Turning him into nobility was not going to happen overnight. His attitude alone made the other nobles question him.

"Who on earth are you?! Do you have any idea of your rudeness, commoner?!"

Despite being informed that Yohm's party was here to heal the king, one of the ministers saw fit to chew him out. He was aware of Yohm the champion, yes. Yohm's likeness had been passed around, so the minister knew exactly to whom he was speaking. There was no mistaking his Exo-Armor, either—but none of that mattered to him. This was the royal castle, and the rules of the common streets didn't apply here. Yohm's casual tongue was unacceptable.

This unnerved Razen. He turned a wary eye toward Diablo, gauging whether this tirade offended him or not. If the nobility was not fully prepared for this, Razen would have to shoulder the blame. He could understand the minister's anger—it was a perfectly normal reaction to have, as he saw it—but now wasn't the time for this. He regretted not being more thorough in his guidance.

"Lord Carlos," he intervened, "please wait a moment. This group is the very one that saved us. They are the only ones who hold the key to rescuing His Majesty!"

"What? They saved you, Sir Razen?"

"As the so-called defender of our kingdom, Sir Razen, that hardly sounds like you. What is the meaning of this?"

Despite the noblemen's misgivings, Razen was still the most powerful wizard in Farmus. There was no doubting his powers, and his track record in defending the kingdom from outside threats spread across hundreds of years. His words were not to be taken lightly, and so the nobility sheathed their swords for now. If anything, though, this response was merely a bluff in the face of the mortal danger this nation faced. If Razen had been saved, perhaps there was a way all of them could be, too.

As Razen opened his mouth to answer the question, another voice joined the conversation.

"Allow me to answer that."

It was Reyhiem, the archbishop. He had pretended to be himself just revived this moment to come to Razen's assistance. Relieved, Razen gave him a nod, then turned to Diablo, noticing his expectant smile.

"Yes? How *was* Sir Razen rescued, then?"

"I trust he has already told you about the Storm Dragon's reawakening," Reyhiem began. "The battlefield was intense, vehicles from both sides smashing against one another. Our side outnumbered theirs, but the monsters had the geographical advantage. It was a much harder battle than any of us expected, and there were many casualties on both sides."

His voice echoed across the otherwise silent chamber as he continued, keeping a close eye on Diablo to gauge his response. The chaos on the battlefield was what revived Veldora, and when he emerged on the scene, both human and monster were sacrificed en masse.

"It was all Sir Reyhiem and I could do to keep His Majesty protected," Razen said as he nodded. He was careful to emphasize that there was nothing he could've done to save them.

"Exactly, exactly. We were situated in the rear of the main force, watching in despair as the tragedy unfolded before us. Before the

Storm Dragon, dooming our legions to death and crushing everything in his path, we all said our final prayers. But then, one rose up to stand between us and this merchant of death."

Razen shot Diablo a glance, to which Diablo gave a self-satisfied nod back. It was just the signal he and Reyhiem wanted.

"It was none other than Sir Rimuru, the master of the monsters."

"Indeed, it was. Sir Reyhiem and I were both prepared to die, but Sir Rimuru convinced Lord Veldora to calm his rage."

"Convinced? He actually spoke with the monster?!"

"It would be suicide to stand before the likes of Veldora. Being exposed to all those magicules would kill most creatures."

"How did he do it?"

The nobility was understandably surprised. If Veldora could be reasoned with, perhaps there was a way to keep him from laying waste upon the land. They looked toward Razen and Reyhiem with hopeful expressions. There was every chance that Veldora would spare Farmus, but it would be foolish to idly hope for that to transpire. But what was to be done, then? Nobody had an answer for that. Now that they knew a force of twenty thousand, including the king's personal knight corps, had been literally erased from existence, nobody was reckless enough to suggest confronting the dragon. If they could negotiate with this threat, that was the best solution for everyone.

"You are all aware, I assume, that Sir Rimuru is also the overseer of the Forest of Jura?"

"Or so *he* claims, at least," groused a minister. Diablo greeted this with a scowl that immediately filled Razen with alarm.

"It is no mere claim, Minister," he said. "I have personally witnessed the town the monsters built, and truly, it is more than worthy of serving as the capital of any kingdom. But we can discuss that later. Regardless, Sir Rimuru has the dryads, the guardians of Jura, working alongside him."

As he put it to the nobility, Rimuru used the dryads as a kind of interpreter for his talks with Veldora. That made it all the more convincing. The dryads were well-known for having the power to guard the lands where Veldora slept. They were classified as A rank by the Free Guild's reckoning, and in terms of the danger they posed, Special A wasn't out of the question. If they were serving this monster Rimuru, his powers must be at least as extensive as that. Nobody in the room had a problem picturing it. They were all high-level nobility, and none of them were lazy with their intelligence gathering.

"I see..."

"So making him our foe was a mistake...?"

The ministers recalled how eager they were to invade the monster lands. They hated to face this reality, but it was a headache they all had to deal with now.

"This is ominous," one of them muttered. "If it was possible to negotiate with this dragon, then antagonizing our sole potential inroad was a grave error, indeed..."

The rest of them went visibly paler. There was no way they could ask Rimuru to intervene on their part. At worst, he might even send Veldora over to Farmus to teach them all a lesson.

Then Yohm, summarily ignored up to now, walked to the center of the chamber. Ensuring all eyes were upon him, he began to speak, his voice calm.

"Um, yeah, so listen, you guys don't have to worry about that. When I killed that orc lord, I was working with Rimuru the whole time. He's actually a pretty openhearted guy usually, you know? In fact, he's got a pretty keen interest in working alongside humanity—"

"Oh-ho!" Lord Carlos interrupted him, exercising every bit of his regal pretension. "Then let this man stand in for us and tell him of our demands. We will give you our demands at a later time, so please retire to another room and wait for us."

Class is an onerous thing. Whether a champion of the people or not, Yohm was still a commoner, not even deemed worthy of a knighthood. Many in the room made no secret about how much they looked down upon him. Lord Carlos was an earl, among the most powerful in the Farmus bureaucracy, and the greatest example of how full of themselves the nobility often proved to be. This attitude would not normally be a problem in this chamber, but—again—now was not the time. Already, some of the other nobles were rolling their eyes at Carlos.

"Whoa, whoa, wait a sec. I said he's usually openhearted, but not right now, you know what I mean? You all probably know why."

"What?"

"You declared war on Rimuru's nation, right? Bad idea, my friend. Rimuru lost some of his pals in that battle. He, um— He's pretty pissed off."

"What nonsense is this, commoner?! It is not your place to question the actions of our nation! If you are on speaking terms with Rimuru, that is all we require. It is a champion's duty to intervene for us. You must do something!"

Lord Carlos was acting as haughty as ever, totally ignoring Yohm's pleadings. Yohm had trouble hiding his disgust. *I swear, these nobles,* he thought, taking pains to look undisturbed as he continued.

"Look, can you just listen to me for one moment? From the way I heard it, you didn't send any envoys, you didn't declare war or anything; you just took some otherworlders and let 'em go to town, huh? I went out to mediate with you guys, but when I heard all that, lemme tell ya, I was shocked. But look, I'm a Farmus man. Born and raised. I don't wanna see my homeland get wrecked, so I tried finding a way to calm Rimuru down. Razen over there asked me to."

If the nobility continued to act as despotic as they were, it was no exaggeration to say Farmus's days were numbered. Sensing Diablo behind him, Yohm could physically feel the doom over them all.

Catching sight of Diablo taught Yohm all about what true evil was. It made him realize what a bunch of small-time bandits he and his group really were. *Real* evil doesn't bother to try buttering up the men in charge. They bow down to no one, staying constantly true to their will.

Diablo was on good behavior right now only because he was faithfully following Rimuru's orders. Him acting up right now would have adverse effects on Yohm's future as the new king. Overly punishing the nobles would leave the real problem unaddressed, and if he simply killed them all to shut them up, it'd tarnish the new government's reputation. The most ideal way to handle them was to wait until some of the more rebellious ones made their presences known. That was why Diablo stayed silent, keenly observing them all.

If, on the other hand, the nobility decided to incur his wrath, all that flew out the window. If Diablo decided none of them were worth keeping alive, that would be the end for them, right there. Mjurran and Gruecith, serving as advisers to Diablo, were in agreement on that. Only a very few high-level magic-born could hope to corral someone as powerful as Razen. Diablo was one of them, and if Diablo wanted to take action, Farmus in its current weakened state could do nothing to resist him.

This was much of the reason why Yohm's party was far more nervous about how this meeting in the throne room would go than any of the nobles were.

Razen felt just the same way as Yohm. It was clear that Diablo thought little of human life, and he had none of the hang-ups about noble titles and commoners the rest of them had. They were all equally worthless to him—his treatment of King Edmaris made that blindingly obvious.

If they started flinging insults at Rimuru, master of the monsters, they had no idea how Diablo might react. Lord Carlos, hopefully, would be the only target of his rage. If he wasn't, then all intelligent life might be banished from Farmus entirely.

Razen knew that, and that knowledge made him frantic. Assuaging the panic running inside his head, he tried his best to back up Yohm.

"Lord Carlos, that is quite enough from you!"

"What? You take the side of this scruffy commoner, Sir Razen?!"

"I said, that is quite enough!" he found himself shouting. "I will *not* have you intrude until you understand the situation!"

It was rare for Razen to raise his voice in court. It cowed the nobility into silence, waiting to see what would happen next.

"Listen to me, all of you," he said, mentally recalling the script he was given. "Sir Yohm is telling us the truth. Shogo and his otherworlder compatriots were defeated by the monster army's generals. When our forces tried to overrun our enemies, the Storm Dragon blocked us, sealing our fates. The survivors consist of Sir Reyhiem, His Majesty, and me—us three only. We were held captive, and it was the good word of Sir Yohm that earned us our release."

He continued with the tale, and no one else dared to cast doubt upon it. Soon Reyhiem and Yohm were contributing information, supported by Muller and the Earl of Hellman. Together, they all pleaded their case before the biggest and brightest figures of Farmus politics.

"...So you say that His Majesty was subjected to a curse on the battlefield that put him in his present state?"

"Our lord has offered peace...and the master of the monsters is willing to listen...?"

"Are you saying Farmus, our homeland, has yielded to monsters?"

"Have we any other choice? Surely you don't intend to suggest we continue the battle. We would have the Storm Dragon to answer to."

"No, I..."

The otherworlders, their aces in the hole, had been dispatched by Rimuru's top officials. Veldora was on the move. The Jura-Tempest Federation, an organization they once derided as a rabble of slavering beasts, was—from a military perspective, at least—leaps and bounds ahead of Farmus. Attempting to stage a frontal attack against this foe would be the height of folly. Everyone in the chamber had the same thought—in admitting defeat, the king made the only decision available to him.

Soon, the group had come to a consensus.

"Well, if we have an offer being made to us, why not accept it, everyone?"

The majority nodded their agreement to Muller's suggestion. There were some contrarians among them, no doubt, but none of them voiced their concerns. Nobody seemed to contest the fact that this war could no longer continue.

It was now settled. The Kingdom of Farmus would enter negotiations with Tempest. And with that decided, Diablo finally took his cue.

"Heh-heh-heh-heh... A wise decision," he said as he began to saunter toward the center. "In that case, as promised, I will release your king back to you."

"Who are you?!"

"Pardon me," Diablo proudly stated. "My *name* is Diablo, faithful servant to my leader, the great and powerful Rimuru."

The assembled nobility had little idea how to address this man. Diablo seemed so natural among them that they had trouble speaking up. Only Razen demonstrated any fear of him, for only Razen knew what that name meant. The mere fact the name existed at all; that struck terror into him. *Some things*, he thought as he enviously looked at the audience and sighed, *are better off not being known at all.*

Others, however, regarded Diablo with suspicion. These were the king's own royal guard, stationed by their lord's side and keeping an eye on this interloper's every move. Finally, when he was just about to reach the throne, they stepped in his way—only to be completely ignored, as Diablo continued tracing a path to the gruesome box atop the seat.

The guard was now visibly angered but nonetheless frozen in place. Even if they wanted to speak, none of them could. By the Free Guild's reckoning, each knight in this guard rated an A-minus—not quite a full A but certainly above a B. One could even call them the strongest of Farmus's remaining force, left behind in the castle to keep the rest of the administration well guarded. They numbered a hundred strong, there in the chamber, and none of them could move an inch.

It wasn't anything Diablo actively did to them. It was simple terror. Their well-honed survival instincts told every one of them how much of a danger Diablo was.

"Very good," he said as he greeted the sight with a smile. "No need for anyone to die needlessly, am I right?"

So he continued until he stopped at the box that contained what was left of King Edmaris. Calmly, he took a Full Potion out of a pocket and poured it straight into the container—and without anyone noticing, he simultaneously undid the binding curse placed by Shion on its contents. The resulting transformation was dramatic. The moment medicine made contact with flesh, the king was back, in the robust shape everyone recalled. Diablo's scheme was a roaring success. This king, whose malady had been thought of as incurable by the men assembled, was back to normal in an instant. The attending doctors and sorcerers all yelped in surprise.

"What, what *is* that potion...?"

"It is a Full Potion," he gently replied. "A specially refined creation of my homeland, the most potent of all restorative treatments. We export it only to nations on friendly terms with us."

This introduction was a key part of the plan. The potion, after all, was Tempest's main economic weapon.

Full Potions were only rarely found worldwide, usually dug up from the ruins of ancient magical empires. One sip could perform miracles up to, and including, the regeneration of missing limbs. Only a Revival Elixir—an agent that provided nothing short of resurrection—could outclass it. The recipe for it had been lost over time, although rumor had it the dwarves were frantically trying to re-create it. If it was being actively manufactured, people the world over would seek it.

Diablo had previously heard, from Gabil and others, about how eager Rimuru was to advertise this wonder drug. Unlike Shion, he was an enthusiastic pupil, learning everything there was to know about Tempest in short order. Thus, despite the grimness of the situation, he didn't waste the opportunity to show off a little. That attention to detail made him stand out among Rimuru's staff. It was, in a way, a rather extreme example of Diablo's refusal to compromise on anything he did—one reason why antagonizing him was extremely ill-advised.

Razen and Reyhiem, he knew, were scared that he might massacre everyone in the castle. But nothing could be further from his mind. Doing that would wipe out Rimuru's trust in him. He had been tasked with making Yohm king of this realm, and Diablo wasn't stupid enough to risk that. In his mind, he had a cunning plan—the classic carrot and stick. Careful applications of both would allow him to manipulate the minds of the ministers and noblemen gathered here. He would make them consider it wiser to acquiesce than defy him. And if any one of them was foolish enough to make the wrong decision, he would cleanse the kingdom of their presence. That was the gist of it.

The king was back in human form, much to the astonishment of his slack-jawed audience. To the casual observer, it looked every bit like the Full Potion alone had healed him.

"How do you feel?" Diablo asked.

Edmaris, a tad pale in the face but otherwise none the worse for wear, nodded back.

"Ah... Y-yes... Thank you. You saved me."

This weak reply was half honest feelings, half scripted act. Edmaris was doing Diablo's bidding. Tempter, Diablo's unique skill, was in the same family as Rimuru's own Merciless, allowing him complete control over anyone whose spirit he had sufficiently broken. Under its influence, if King Edmaris ever attempted to defy Diablo's will, Diablo would immediately be informed of it.

As the king put on the clothing hurriedly provided by an attendant and breathed a sigh of relief, Diablo motioned at him with his eyes. He nodded back.

"Now, my liege, I have a message from Sir Rimuru, my own lord," said Diablo.

"I will be glad to hear it, messenger from the monster realm."

This was the first time the king of Farmus acknowledged Tempest as a sovereign nation. It was also a signal to everyone in the room. From this point forward, as far as King Edmaris was concerned, Tempest would be recognized as an orderly negotiating partner—which in turn meant Diablo was the official representative of the other side of the war.

It was as significant a gesture as Edmaris could muster, in an effort not to get on Diablo's wrong side, and thanks to that, any noblemen fostering ideas of revolt were silenced for good. Of course, nobody had any will to continue the war at this point. This declaration was less for Diablo's sake and more in hopes of protecting the king's own countrymen.

"Allow me to give you his statement. One week from now, my lord wishes to hold peace talks between the representatives of both nations here, in this land. Before we sign the peace treaty, you are asked to agree to the following conditions provided by us..."

Diablo took out several pieces of parchment paper.

"You have the right to make your choices about these stipulations..."

After an ominous opening, the document laid out its terms— ostensibly written by Rimuru, but in reality, written by Diablo. Its contents were, to be frank, revolting.

The first article provided was for the king to abdicate and the nation to pay war reparations. The second was for the nation to surrender to Tempest and become a vassal state. The third wasn't even a choice—it simply stated that, if the first two choices were not replied to in the affirmative, the war would continue.

These conditions may not have seemed like they altered the current situation very much. But they did. With Tempest now recognized as a state, Farmus's footing after starting a war without so much as a formal declaration was shaky at best. None of its neighbors would want any part of it, and the Western Holy Church would doubtlessly have their hands full with Veldora. Nobody in the room imagined that any local power would go out of their way to help Farmus.

It was, in other words, blackmail. A threat to raze the land, avoidable only by swallowing a litany of intolerable rules.

Diablo read all the conditions out loud, his haughty voice reaching every corner of the room, the glee evident on his face as he enjoyed the nobility's reactions. When he was finished, he could hear one of the ministers whisper "Ridiculous" in a half wail. This he ignored as he turned toward King Edmaris and bowed.

"...That is all. Please have a response ready for us in a week's time."

"W-wait a moment! That is far too little time for us to work with! At least provide us a month to—"

"Silence. I have a short temper."

"But—but, sir, this is not a matter we can decide upon in the royal parliament. We must summon the regional barons and stage a vote with the entire assembly—"

"I said '*Silence*.' Your logistical issues matter little to me. And I will also suggest not to attempt any juvenile tricks with us. These deadline-extending excuses shall not be tolerated. If there is no reply after a week, we will take that to mean you wish to continue hostilities. I ask you to provide your full consideration of this matter."

And with that one-sided caution, Diablo turned his back on the king and his court. He could hear someone loudly calling him a tyrant, but it didn't bother him. He simply left Yohm and his men behind and walked out alone, his work apparently done for the day.

After he was gone, King Edmaris officially called for a session of the royal parliament, with all nobility required to be present. This was set for three days from now—just barely enough time to bring them all together even with the aid of magic, but such were the stakes. If Diablo's deadline was one week, the nation had to take action. Time was of the essence. The appeal had to be made to them all.

At once, the king's attendants sprang into action. The room echoed with the clamor of activity as they began to prepare for the meeting as Edmaris watched, exhausted.

"Do all of you understand the situation?" he asked his closest ministers feebly. "Before the nobles arrive, we will need to decide on a direction. I will offer my views tomorrow, at another location, and I would like to hear from all of you as well."

There was no doubt that Farmus was hurtling headlong toward its doom. Now was no time for infighting within the bureaucracy. The parliament was going to be a wild, confused meeting, that much was certain—which made it all the more important that everyone was on the same page beforehand.

That, the king thought as he silently firmed up his resolve, *and so we can keep the casualties as low as possible.*

The next day, the king and his group reconvened in another meeting room. These were all trusted confidants, the only exceptions being the Marquis of Muller, most powerful among the court's neutral elements, and his associate, the Earl of Hellman.

Edmaris began by summarizing the events that led here once more, his audience silently listening on. Razen and Reyhiem had already covered this territory, but the horrifying truth of it all still crashed upon the ministers like a tidal wave.

"My liege," Muller asked, "is all of this true? I mean, about Veldora being revived?"

The king nodded. "It is just the way Razen and Reyhiem put it yesterday. But the sole problem I face right now is which conditions must be accepted, out of the three offered. That, and I also wish to deliberate over how to handle future events."

As he implied, nothing should be left on the table in this discussion, and soon, opinions were flying in all directions.

"The Forest of Jura that Veldora protects is a forbidden land. Not even the Eastern Empire has tried to lay hands upon it. It would be a fool's errand to tackle it on our own."

"Too true, too true! There is no path to victory for us. Any further belligerent activity would spell the end of our nation!"

"Indeed. The question, then, is how to approach conditions one and two..."

"I refuse to let us be colonized! How could we let the monsters rule over us when our own positions haven't even been guaranteed?"

"That's not necessarily true. I doubt we will see any further wars, for one."

"Ridiculous! The landholding barons of the kingdom will hardly allow such nonsense."

"It will mean civil war!"

"Which, I suppose, is what the monsters want to see."

"And what of the king abdicating? And the reparations? Have you seen what they are asking for? It will collapse our finances."

"Ten thousand stellars... The equivalent of one million gold coins. A good fifth of our annual tax revenue."

"Outlandish..."

"But think about it. Is that not preferable to the end of our kingdom?"

"That it is. They are honorable enough, at least, not to demand every coin in our coffers."

"So there is nothing to be done but accept their terms...?"

"I see no other way out, no."

King Edmaris listened on in silence as his ministers and nobles deliberated, keeping his thoughts to himself.

Beautiful... As sweet as a young girl, but such an overwhelming presence in person. This Rimuru, lord of the monsters—he is a fearsome demon lord, indeed. Merely thinking about him makes terror erupt from the bottom of my soul.

There was no way the king could ever put his own majesty above him any longer. The fear in his heart made the thought of defying him unthinkable. He had been rendered helpless, a cube in a box, forced to devour his own limbs. He never wanted to experience that again, and now he had to convince the ministers to see things his way.

In his mind flashed images of defeat and the assorted types of torture he had endured—and in between, the monster's town, far more orderly than he had guessed. The birth of a new demon lord and the resurrection of the Storm Dragon. It was all the truth, and Edmaris knew it meant bitter defeat for him. Stained by greed, he had made a terrible error. If he had approached on friendlier terms, perhaps they could've worked together in a far different situation. But the time for that was gone.

No further errors would be allowed.

Diablo advised him that he was free to respond to these three conditions any way he wanted. In other words, his reply didn't much matter. Diablo's goals would be met either way. Instead, the king reasoned, his duty was simply to keep the fallout to a minimum—and that was the approach he took as he gathered his thoughts.

The choice for number three was a given. Further war would mean annihilation, from the king to the lowliest citizen. The second question was more worthy of debate, since it meant the people's lives and livelihoods would be guaranteed. The glimpses he enjoyed of the monster town's skyline were still fresh on his mind. He had even seen adventurers among them, smiling and laughing with their monster friends.

Perhaps it is not so bad a fate after all...

Edmaris enjoyed the fantasy for a moment but quickly dispelled it from his mind. *It could never happen. Nobody would trust in a monster; not unless they saw that city for themselves. I laughed it off as the ravings of a madman myself...*

The nobility had a duty to keep their people safe. If they opted for unconditional surrender and life as a vassal state, it could overturn the entire nation. The neighboring kingdoms would resist, no doubt, and it was doubtful the resolution would pass parliament. A king had the right to force his will upon his subjects, of course, but the assassination attempts would no doubt come along shortly after.

So far, question one offered the most obvious decision. Abdication meant that Edmaris would step down, handing the crown over to someone else, and be made to swear never to wage war again. There was a demand for reparations, yes, and while there was no legal basis for that, it was difficult for him to turn it down. It would lead to a much faster, and cheaper, peace than continuing this war would.

There was no guarantee that the monsters wouldn't pile on more demands later. But with these two in particular, he could tell they had a solid aim in mind.

Diablo had extensively interviewed King Edmaris, and as he did, he made it clear that Yohm would become king of a newly established nation. Edmaris had three children—two girls and one boy, the youngest. His daughters were married off to noble families abroad, which left his ten-year-old son the only viable heir. If the king abdicated now, there was every chance of a bloody power struggle. The king even had an idea of who would aim for his throne—that would be Edward, his half brother and head of the nobility faction in this palace.

Reading that far in, Edmaris could tell what Diablo wanted. He sought to take advantage of this potential power struggle and make the royalists and nobility fight against one another. In fact, this was bound to happen no matter what decision he made. Whatever he chose, Diablo could easily factor it into his own plans.

The king sighed to himself.

...So it just doesn't matter?

And if it didn't, if the results were the same regardless...

"All right, everyone. Allow me to state my views."

Just when the debate was starting to die down, King Edmaris began to speak.

"The nation of monsters calls itself the Jura-Tempest Federation. It is a gathering of assorted species of monsters, all bound together by an overseer by the name of Rimuru. I do not feel it is such a bad thing to join them in this federation..."

"You seek to become a vassal state?"

"No, not like that. I am merely stating my belief that their nation is governed in a surprisingly peaceful manner."

He stopped for a moment, allowing the audience to gauge just how resolute his expression was.

"This war was a mistake. It was not for the sake of our people, but of my own greed. That is why the heavens saw fit to forsake me. The price of that made Veldora rise from the dead and spread the seeds of disaster across Farmus. If I had followed the Marquis of Muller and the Earl of Hellman's advice, none of this would have happened…"

"My liege, please, none of this is…"

"We are unworthy of your great modesty, Your Majesty."

"Thank you," the king said, nodding in heartfelt appreciation. "There is no longer a second chance for us. None. Thanks to Sir Rimuru, lord of the monsters, I stand here before you now. There is no 'next time.' One more incorrect decision, and the flames of war will descend not just upon me, but upon all our people. My pride and honor no longer matter. All I want to do, at the very least, is ensure my people are not engulfed by those flames. What can we do to steer things in a better direction? What will make our people happier? *That* is what I want us all to consider!"

The ministers froze in surprise. Their cold, calculating king, always putting his own profit ahead of everything else, admitting to his mistakes and calling upon his advisers to come up with a better idea. Their shock was understandable. They all looked wide-eyed at their king, reflecting upon their own thoughts. The selfishness within them, as they used pride or whatnot as an excuse to protect their own assets, was now all too obvious to them.

Every last one of them stood up, then kneeled before their king.

"My liege," Muller said on their behalf, "we apologize. We were all foolish. We must seek out a better path…for our nation and for our people!"

The rest of them shouted out their *Hear! Hear!*s as their heads touched the floor.

The talks continued well into the ensuing night, as Yohm and his team were invited to participate as advisers.

"I believe I did a fairly good job of shaking them up," Diablo reported, smiling.

Whoa! Wait a sec! There's so much I could comment on there, I hardly knew where to begin. But I suppose the biggest issue was:

"You *showed* them that thing?"

"I did, sir. I thought it the best way to instill fear in their minds."

Wow. He showed it to them. That...meat cube. Shion acted awfully proud about it, not that I did anything to encourage her. No crap they're scared, man! If this was before my slime reincarnation, I totally would've been blowing chunks. That's the kind of impact that thing had.

Like, this is totally demon lord territory I'm stepping into now, isn't it? I tried to keep a clean image, and now that's being replaced with something downright terrifying. What's done is done, I guess, but still. Mixing the terror with the relief seems like an easy way to earn their trust in us, at least, even if it is an approach the yakuza would use.

I hopped off Shion's lap. Some tea, in human form, sounded good. I needed to relax and switch gears a bit.

"With regards to the peace talks, my lord, I have requested ten thousand stellar gold coins in reparations."

Bpph!!

I spat out all the tea in my mouth. Ten thousand stellars? I mean, yeah, I did ask him to use reparations as a wedge to drive between the king and nobility, but that figure's beyond unreasonable. It deviated so far from reality that I wasn't sure the neighboring countries would see it as fair at all. Bartering was still the preferred method of trade in this world—currency was the norm in population centers like Blumund or Englesia, but over in the farming villages, people could go their whole lives without seeing anything more valuable than a silver coin. In other words, money had a lot more value here than I originally gave it credit for.

One copper coin was about ten cents, one silver coin about ten dollars, and one gold coin about a thousand. That was the general understanding I worked with, but even that only applied in the big cities. In real life, the differences were even starker. For example, your average laborer in the city earned six silver coins a day, 150 per month—around $1,500. In the villages, meanwhile, you wouldn't even make a hundred silvers a year. That's less than a thousand to live off. The economic disparity in this place is nuts.

Of course, there weren't as many diversions to blow your income on. You probably weren't throwing your money around all that much. Really, coinage didn't hold much purpose at all for a lot of people. To put it one way, disparity or not, your living circumstances didn't change that much from social class to social class. And if you consider the lack of any international financial organization dictating the terms of the economy, maybe it was healthier this way anyway.

This meant, perhaps, that right now was our best shot at building an economic superpower. Diablo's a smart guy. When he heard me talking about multiple races sharing one another's prosperity earlier, he immediately connected that to economic domination. We needed a distribution network, one capable of bringing products from low- to high-demand areas, and coinage was a must for that. Taking control of the flow of money would let us essentially dictate the world economy.

There were many local currencies used by the world's nations, but in practice, the coin of the Dwarven Kingdom was the main one in use. It would be easy to build a world economic sphere reliant upon a single currency. I could imagine that being on Diablo's mind as he made his moves.

Getting back on topic, despite my initial impression, it turns out that money in this world was treated more like one copper = $1, one silver = $100, and one gold = $10,000. Ten thousand stellar gold coins, then, meant we were asking for war reparations to the tune of $10 billion. This wasn't Japan. There wasn't as much *stuff* all over the place, no great need for a national budget to be that massive. Thinking along those lines, the figure we asked for was astronomical.

"Don't you think that's going way too far?"

"Heh-heh-heh-heh... No, it is not a problem. I gave them three choices, but there is only one real answer. Question three hardly deserves debate, and neither does question two. The only real decision to make is on question one, and it is from there that their negotiations will begin, I suppose." He then added with a laugh, "As much as I'd like them to go my way on question three, however..."

He was right. There was only one real choice. Would they try to talk us down on the price? Nah, they weren't that dumb. They might ask for payments spread out every ten years, perhaps, if they couldn't cover it now.

"I have no intention of offering a discount," advised Diablo. "Farmus will be forced to give in to our demands. However, I doubt it will ever come to pass anyway. If that amount of coinage leaves their markets, the effects on their economy would be staggering."

Yeah, I'll bet. I knew Diablo was doing this on purpose.

"I suppose what they'll decide to do is force the obligation on some third party."

Oh?

Here was what Diablo pictured. Basically, they'd make a deposit, then pay off the balance with something else. That way, even if the owner of that something else refused to back it up with coin, that was no longer any of the kingdom's business. They'd be off the hook, and if we complained about it, they can turn us away and claim they lived up to their end of the bargain. The approach would only work if you were dealing with a *very* stupid adversary, but if we fell for it, there could be trouble.

"What would we do then?"

"It is all factored into the plan. I am sure we can recover at least a thousand stellars, and that would wrap up the first part of the operation."

Huh? Hang on.

"How do you know we can earn that much?"

"Oh, that? Simple."

To sum up, it was because Farmus simply didn't have much immediate use for the stellars. That actually made sense, if you think about it. With one coin worth six or seven figures, trying to make change for them must've been a huge pain in the ass. It was nothing more than a hoard unless you were engineering some huge deals, and they'd likely figure—in Diablo's estimation—that coughing up a decent number wouldn't affect them all *that* much, day-to-day.

Gold coins were what drove the national budget most of the

time, so the stellars were more like securities, inaccessible under normal circumstances. In a world without banks, you couldn't generate interest off them. So maybe they wouldn't put up much of a fight about them after all.

Well played, Diablo. I was willing to meet them in the middle and ask for somewhere between a hundred and three hundred stellars. About $1 million per victim on our end, plus a little consideration for the roofs and stuff we had to repair. That was the minimum I was comfortable with, so if Diablo thought he could extract a thousand, then I had no problem with going to the bargaining table. A cool billion was still more than enough for anything I could imagine.

Diablo, meanwhile, wasn't content with just that. He was also formulating a plan to trigger civil war inside Farmus. Scary guy.

"What more do you really need from them if we're already recouping our losses?"

"Heh-heh-heh-heh. King Edmaris may be freed, but he is now my willing puppet. He is under the thrall of my Tempter skill, so I can will him to do anything I want, to some extent. In other words..."

With Tempter activated, Diablo had life-and-death power over the king. He couldn't fully take over his consciousness or anything, but Diablo had the right to "will" him dead at any moment. As long as he kept following his orders, all was well, but if he showed any signs of rebellion, Diablo would immediately spot them. He could kill the guy right then and there, and if he understood that, a betrayal just wasn't going to happen. Controlling people with terror is a pretty scary skill, huh? Everything's fine if you don't cross Diablo, but still.

Anyway, that's how Diablo was observing King Edmaris's behavior. As he hoped for, the king primarily deliberated over question one and seemed ready to abandon the throne. He had asked Muller and Hellman to call upon Edmaris to take responsibility for this crisis, but that no longer seemed to be necessary.

I guess Diablo had been building relationships with the royalists in the castle, too—something that deviated from the original plan a little but actually worked out for the better, as he explained it. When Edmaris abdicates, the foundation of power he built goes with him—and with that, it becomes easier to pin the blame for everything on him. "With the Royal Knight Corps dead by your hand," Diablo told me, "there is no one left to protect the royal family. Right now, antagonizing the nobility spells death for Edmaris. He'll have to answer their every need—at least, on the surface."

Nobody was around to speak for the king. The nobles wouldn't hesitate to take advantage of that—which goes into the third party Diablo mentioned. War would be the only thing to come from that. The nobility wanted to make King Edmaris into a sacrifice, and the king was racking his brain for ways to fight back.

So...what next, then? The royalists didn't have an army; they were bound to be pummeled. *How can we avoid that?*

Understood. The best approach would be to bring in Yohm's force and retain a cooperative relationship. This would allow for...

Oh. Right. Yohm's connected with me. Edmaris knows I want him to become king, and if he makes concrete moves toward that...

Maybe an immediate handover of the crown wasn't too realistic, but if we could frame it as Yohm saving the king's life, perhaps it could look like a ruined royal family passing the torch on to another generation.

"So the king's going to take Yohm, and us, as his allies?"

Diablo beamed. "Yes. A very wise assertion."

Oh, I was right?

Having us as an ally would give Edmaris a force that made his Royal Knight Corps look like a bunch of kids. The nobility, carried away and assuming they had an easy win, would be slaughtered at the hands of Yohm the champion.

"So should we give Yohm more resources?"

"We should. Razen, who is also under my command, has been instructed to contact us when the time comes, so I hope I can count on you for that."

That's Diablo for you. He's got all his men at work so he can kick back and relax. He was taking the motto *Be prepared* to its most elegant extremes.

Razen, though, huh? This super-great guy, the protector of the kingdom and all that? Guess that didn't matter to Diablo. But no point dwelling on that.

"So can Yohm beat them, though? What if some other pretender to the throne forms an alliance with the neighboring kingdoms?"

"I am having Sir Fuze and King Gazel pressure their governments not to intervene. I think that is a possibility we can safely ignore. If it does come to pass, however, I will enter the battle myself, so don't worry."

All I could do was nod at his supreme confidence. *Diablo's totally intent on staying behind the scenes, isn't he? Crazy to think he's basically letting all these other people take down an entire kingdom for him.* Raphael was also telling me the chances of an alliance were dim, so I had no complaints.

I gave the kneeling Diablo a pat on the shoulder.

"All right. I'll leave that to you, then. Let me know if anything happens."

"Yes, my lord! I assure you that everything is in good hands!"

∗

So now I had been briefed on the general outline. Just when I was checking up on the little details, Haruna came in with a new dessert—something to accompany the tea, as she put it.

"Oh, is this the green-tea custard?"

"It is, Sir Rimuru. I may not be up to Lady Shuna's quality yet, but I do believe I've improved!"

With a soft smile, Haruna set the plates on the table. Veldora, who had been reading manga without bothering to join the conversation, picked that moment to join me there, as if he'd earned the right.

"Hohh? Some for me, then?"

"Of course, Sir Veldora."

He gave a gregarious nod and reached out for a plate of the eggy treat.

"Sir Veldora," Diablo said as he offered his own plate to him, "here is your promised portion."

"Gwaaaaah-ha-ha-ha! You are a man of your word, Diablo!"

Talk about a cheap bribe.

"You don't want any, Diablo?" I asked, figuring Haruna could always scare up another one, but Diablo bowed politely in response. "I paid my portion in exchange for the information I received. There is no need to be concerned for me."

What a gentleman. A man of his word, indeed. Although I didn't see why custard was worth making such a big deal about. But if that was what Diablo preferred, more power to him.

"Oh? Well, all right. Still," I said, changing the subject, "it's funny how you came back right in the middle of Walpurgis. We must've passed right by each other."

He was gone when I left at midnight, after all. I figured we couldn't have missed each other by much. But:

"Oh, no, my lord. After I was done threatening King Edmaris and his court, I traveled across the Farmus countryside to investigate its financial situation. I wanted to make sure I hadn't overlooked anything in my plans, but then Sir Veldora ordered me back here."

That sounded, um, important. Veldora rose to his feet, almost knocking over his chair.

"I, er, I have an errand to attend to."

"Hold it right there, Veldora."

I rose quickly, grabbing him by the shoulder.

"W-wait! I can explain!"

"No, you can't! Stop getting in the way of people's work!"

I confiscated the custard from Veldora's overeager hands, ordering Haruna to exempt him from dessert privileges for a while. He could cry about it all he wanted, but I couldn't let this pass. I swear, you can never let your guard down around the guy. Maybe it was fortuitous in the end, what with Veldora stopping by Walpurgis and lending a hand, but that didn't matter. If I let this slide, who knew what nonsense could arise next time.

It's a good thing the capable Diablo was around to handle matters, but what if Veldora had bothered one of my other friends with his self-centered requests? It made me shudder. The Storm Dragon giving out orders would mess up the whole chain of command I had

going. That's why I made *damn* sure he checked with me next time before trying anything like that.

Fortunately, Diablo had no other pressing business in Farmus, apart from the peace talks five days from now. He had delegated his authority to others for the rest of the work, so for now he was fine serving me. "As your butler," he said, "I couldn't think of abandoning your side." That made Shion wince, but I had to hand it to him.

So about those peace talks.

"Oh, you think I oughtta attend, too?"

"No sir, I can handle things well enough alone."

I always found it reassuring during high-stakes meetings to have my boss in attendance, but to a born achiever like Diablo, it wasn't necessary. In fact, as he put it, my presence at the palace would crush the nobles' "will to fight"—I didn't know exactly what he meant by that, but I was sure things were safe in his hands.

For now, at least, I felt assured that the whole Farmus invasion thing could be filed into a cabinet in the recesses of my mind.

And then, everything went exactly as Diablo pictured it.

All the nation's nobles gathered at the palace to hold a session of parliament. This one was far more intense than the last, and the king and his ministers looked deeply troubled. Even the members of the anti-royalist contingent were visibly distressed, adding to the electricity in the air.

"We are here today," the king began, "to discuss our campaign to dispatch Tempest. I regret to inform you that the Storm Dragon wiped out our forces on the battlefield. The only survivors were Razen, Reyhiem, and myself. We were defeated."

The explosive report sent shock waves across the meeting hall. The brutal state of affairs in Farmus, as explained by the king, was unbelievable enough, but what he had to say next subjected him to withering criticism from the nobles. Which was to be expected. He was, after all, declaring that he would accept the monsters' conditions and offer them war reparations…to the tune of ten thousand stellars.

"That's madness! One stellar is a hundred gold coins. We're going to gift them a million gold?!"

"Why would we ever pay such a ransom to a horde of monsters? I refuse to let this happen on my watch!"

"And even if we emptied the national treasury, would we even be able to cobble together that much cash?!"

Given the role of stellar gold coins as a sort of physical bond certificate traded among nations, most realms rarely had even a hundred on hand. The land of Farmus was large, indeed, but *maybe* they could scare up a thousand if they wanted to. If this was to be paid in regular gold-coin currency, the logistics behind the delivery gave the nobility understandable pause. If this was a nation they had formal relations with, the debt could be paid with a broad assortment of goods, but those were terms they couldn't offer to a brand-new nation, much less one run by monsters. Either way, it was sure to be a major blow on Farmus's economy.

Diablo knew that ten thousand stellars was an impossible request. Of course the nobles would complain about it. To them, who hadn't set foot near the battlefield, they could never truly understand the threat. There wasn't enough awareness among them that the future of their nation was at stake.

It therefore did not take long before their complaints morphed into a drive to continue the war.

"Indeed, surrendering to their forces would be absurd. We have no guarantee that our adversaries would honor their promises and keep their hands off our people."

"Our only option is to resist to the bitter end. I would gladly stake my pride to say that our forces could easily defeat a dragon that has only just awoken!"

"With Veldora as our opponent, the Western Holy Church will not stand by idly. I imagine the beautiful, talented Hinata will take action."

"Ah yes, the captain of the Crusaders? She is a vixen, a cold and calculating one, but we can always count on her at times like this."

"The Holy Church is known across the land for being Veldora's mortal enemy!"

"Don't forget about the Hero."

"Ah yes, 'Lightspeed' Masayuki of Englesia!"

"Exactly. The strongest Hero of them all, a man who slew his foes before they even knew what happened to them. I'm certain he will show Veldora in short order that Lightspeed is no mere nickname!"

"Yes! That's the spirit! We'll clear those monsters away in the blink of an eye!"

The nobles were growing restless, bragging about all the impossible things they would accomplish. The objective, to them, was theirs for the taking—they just wanted someone else to take it for them. The royalist ministers watching began to feel terribly awkward—it reminded them too much of when the king first broke the news to them. Some visibly reddened as they sighed in despair, while others silently reflected on what their leader must have felt back then.

King Edmaris, to his credit, understood what was running through the minds of the nobles he had assembled. The war hawks were doggedly interested in preserving their own interests and no one else's. They didn't care about Farmus itself, nor the lives or property of the people who dwelled in it. Their supreme, serene confidence stemmed from the fact that they had no intention of really fighting for it.

The king knew it would turn out like this. The landed nobility here had yet to grasp the reality of it all. They had tasted none of the terror; they had no interest in facing the brunt of this menace. They just wanted to stay holed up in a safe place and make someone else duke it out. If it ended in defeat, they would all refuse to be held responsible for it, no doubt.

And maybe they could've gotten away with coasting like that before. Farmus was large, its land giving it several decisive advantages over its neighbors. But that wasn't going to work now. Putting the screws to nearby nations wouldn't accomplish anything—and besides, their foe was a catastrophe-class monster who laid waste to an entire army single-handed.

The nobles' rage continued, most of them shouting for the king to shoulder the blame. The royal family should pay the reparations out of their own pockets; the monsters' demands must be refused; Farmus must prepare itself for total war.

In a way, they weren't mistaken, but they were missing a vital point. Farmus had already lost most of its internal ability to fight—something that, perhaps, they were refusing to believe. When this was pointed out to them, some turned white with horror, while others brazenly challenged any affront. Just as King Edmaris feared, the nobility refused to work as a coherent group.

As the parliament grew more chaotic, Edward, the king's half brother and leader of the anti-royalist nobility sect, chose that moment to speak.

"My brother... Your Majesty! Even if you abandon the throne, you cannot avoid your responsibility! Is a king as proud as yourself truly admitting defeat so easily?"

"...Edward, listen to me. We are pitted against Veldora, the Storm Dragon. My pride, compared with his tyranny, is a mere pile of ashes! You will never see me willing to face such terror again in my life. Or if it is such a matter of pride to you, will you take up the fight? I will not stop you! But I do believe that it will result in nothing but more blood on your hands."

"No, I... My liege, if everything you are claiming is the truth, are you not attempting to flee the nation by yourself?"

"There is no place to flee to, you simpleton! That is exactly why I intend to pay the money and abdicate the throne."

Just as he aimed to pursue the king's responsibility, Edward found himself stunned into silence by his brother's uncharacteristic vigor.

"If I do not abdicate," the king continued, lowering his voice, "then Farmus will become either a colony or a state at war. Are you all right with that? It will mark the end of this nation."

"Ngh... But simply surrendering to this monster force..."

Edward's voice slowed, his mind still refusing to accept the facts. He was interrupted by the timid voice of Lord Hellman, speaking up just as the meeting hall grew quiet.

"May I have a moment? I received these documents in the morning today. Its content is so vital to this question that I wish to share it with all of you now..."

He had on him a declaration from the kingdom of Blumund. In it, the nation reaffirmed its support for the land of Tempest and criticized Farmus's failed campaign. It was, in short, an attack on Farmus.

"Where does such a tiny kingdom get the *nerve*?!"

"As if they would have said anything if we won. They think they can enjoy the last laugh, don't they?"

The bad news for the fuming nobles didn't end there. The minister of trade then reported receiving a similar announcement from the Dwarven Kingdom earlier. This made even the most hardcore of the war hawks demur, their words growing weaker by the moment.

"Blumund may not be a concern, but if the Armed Nation takes action, that bodes very poorly for us. Do you think King Gazel will maintain his neutrality?"

"The issue," the earl reasoned, "is less that and more the power of his words. As a vital trade partner, it would be bad for us to anger their king."

A gloomy silence fell over the meeting hall—only to be broken by a pale-faced soldier barging into the room at a full gallop.

"Sir! We've just received an emergency report from the Guild!"

Despite the fact that a top-level legislative meeting was being held, none of the guards stopped him. That was thanks to the authority allowed by the Top-Secret Vital Emergency Transmission dossier in his hand. The prominent label made even the most contrarian of the nobles fall silent. This level of secrecy was authorized only for Special S-grade dangers; the Free Guild had a deal with the world's governments where impeding its delivery was a crime as serious as treason.

"Give it to us," King Edmaris flatly stated. With a shaky hand, the soldier extracted a sheet of paper from the envelope and slowly read.

"The monster Rimuru, who has named himself overseer of the Forest of Jura, has reportedly declared himself to be a demon lord!"

"What?!"

"That...!"

"It is in fact good news, no? Our nation is saved!"

"Yes, the other demon lords will not take kindly to this. This Rimuru fellow has sorely overreached. He will learn the terror a true demon lord brings to the world shortly."

"And if all goes well, perhaps the other demon lords will defeat Veldora alongside him!"

Cheers erupted from the nobility the moment the messenger paused to take a breath. What the soldier had to say next quickly restored the silence.

"...We have word that, resisting this declaration, the demon lord Clayman challenged Rimuru—er, the demon lord Rimuru—to a duel and lost his life in the process!"

Gasps filled the room.

"...Haaah?"

"Impossible..."

"Where is Carillon, the Beast Master? What happened to Frey, the Sky Queen? Are they simply letting this upstart take over the Forest of Jura?!"

The shock was real. Now their foe was a full-fledged demon lord. But as the nobility questioned what the demon lords adjacent to Jura were doing, the soldier finished reading the missive.

"...Regarding Carillon and Frey, they have reportedly renounced their seats as demon lords and agreed to affiliate themselves with the demon lord Milim. The group is in the midst of restructuring itself, its eight current members naming themselves...the Octagram!"

The anti-royalists fell completely silent. They knew, now, that their adversary Rimuru was part of this new Octagram. Even the royalists, tipped off to this news in advance, looked tense and nervous. No matter how many times they heard it, the report was so difficult to believe that it drove them to silence as well.

It seemed the source for this report was the demon lords themselves, who all signed a directive disseminated to the Guild. There was no questioning its veracity. The demon lords were all so powerful, there was no need for them to resort to tricking the human race to fulfill their needs.

With a slow, solemn voice, King Edmaris spoke.

"Did you hear that, everyone? Veldora is a threat, but this monster Rimuru is another one entirely. A monster beyond all imagination, one who apparently made short work of the demon lord Clayman. Have we had enough debate yet? I have already made up my mind.

I will abdicate the throne. It was foolish of me to proclaim this was for our nation's sake, when I had barely any clue about the foe we prodded. It was my mistake, driven by pure greed. If only I had taken another approach, perhaps they could have been good neighbors to us."

By the king's reasoning, his departure could help build a new relationship. None of the nobles listening to him voiced any disagreement. Now they understood. The only way forward was to do what King Edmaris said.

"Thus, I will leave my post as king...and I wish to nominate Edward as my successor."

"My brother...!"

"What?!"

"Not Prince Edgar?!"

The hall was thrown into chaos once more.

It was a given that Edmaris would give the throne to the sole prince of the nation. That was why Edward was working so hard to make his presence known. He knew Edmaris, his elder brother, had to go, and the opportunity was like a dream to him—even if Prince Edgar was awarded the throne, it was still a golden chance to state his case for next time. The prince was only ten years old, but as long as the king's brother was still alive, he would not have another regent ruling in his stead. If (Edward thought) he could plant the seeds of uncertainty and doubt in the nobility's minds, he could make them think that he was the only viable choice for the throne, at least until Edgar reached adulthood.

Now, that had all been taken care of for him. He smiled in front of the throne.

"We face difficult times ahead," muttered Edmaris bitterly. "Edgar is still too young. He will have trouble overcoming any of it."

Reactions were varied, but a healthy contingent was already convinced. The Marquis of Muller spoke first: "I believe that is the best solution, my liege."

Edward internally gloated at this. If he had the head of the neutral faction's endorsement, there was no overturning this decision. And once he had the throne, this crisis could be deftly handled—such was his conviction. They could find one way or another to delay the payments, buying time to get their neighbors involved and go on the offensive. As the anti-royalist nobles proposed to him earlier, they could even form a cross-humanity alliance of sorts, bringing paladins and Heroes together to fight for the entire world.

And maybe none of that would be needed at all. A new king meant a new administration, and there was no reason why that government needed to follow the old one's agreements. They could declare the debt null and void, and that would be it. If Tempest complained about it, they could just keep pinning the blame on Edmaris, the ex-king.

It was a simple thing, but it was enough to convince Edward. *Heh-heh-heh... This nation will reach new heights of prosperity under my rule.* He smiled broadly, basking in the glow of his newfound power—never realizing that this, too, was all part of the script.

The session proceeded more smoothly from there. Problems were brought up; adjustments were made down to the last detail. By the end of the day, they had a final outline that was approved by unanimous vote for use in the peace talks.

Said talks came all too quickly—as did the signing.

Several days later, the great nation of Farmus, with all its proud history, had signed an armistice and a peace treaty with the Jura-Tempest Federation. On the surface, Farmus had recognized Tempest as a nation, and while formal relations were a ways away, they could no longer flout international law when dealing with them. At the same time, Tempest was not a member of the Council of the West, the Western Nations' primary legislative body, so even if Farmus did stage another invasion, there was little anyone could do to legally stop them.

Tempest had attained nation status only in the most basic of definitions. But this treaty proved, once and for all, that this new country called Tempest could defend itself. It was led by the demon lord Rimuru, who boasted the Storm Dragon as a key ally, and in just over two years, he had laid claim to the entire Forest of Jura. Whatever he was, he was a nonhuman brilliant beyond any human measure. Considering that, no nation dared to open hostilities with Tempest. Compared with the potential profits waiting to be reaped, the projected losses were just too great. It could even knock out the attacking country entirely.

From that day forward, Rimuru began to be treated as an impenetrable leader, a disaster-class demon lord—and thus, without major difficulty, the first part of his plan was completed...

...exactly as Diablo had pictured it.

CHAPTER 2

ROLES TO UPHOLD

That Time I Got Reincarnated as a Slime

Shuna and Soei were the first to return to town the morning after Diablo's report.

"I have returned safely!" Shuna proclaimed, rubbing her cheeks. She had apparently exhausted her magical force in battle, requiring several hours of recuperation before she could cast Spatial Motion. I could just use Dominate Space to pop myself over to where I wanted, but Shuna's relative lack of magicule storage meant she could only tap so much magic per day. Soei could've used Shadow Motion himself, but he waited, thinking it gauche to return first despite being Shuna's guard. Even now, several of his replications were patrolling Clayman's main base—I guess nothing too dicey was happening right now.

"And where's Hakuro?"

"I asked him to clean things up for me," Shuna replied with a smile as Soei averted his eyes. *So they threw all that work on him, huh?* Hakuro, unable to use Spatial Motion, didn't have much recourse if they left him alone. But I dunno, he always saw Shuna as kind of a beloved granddaughter anyway. Maybe he didn't mind that treatment too much.

Currently, he was working with Geld to investigate Clayman's castle, divvy up the war spoils, and command the prisoner-handling process. I gave him an internal word of thanks for handling all that boring follow-up for me. It must be a ton of work, but an amateur like me couldn't offer much help. I think I'll just keep mum unless asked.

Benimaru and the others made it home by that evening.

"Huh? What's our chief general doing back here?" I asked.

"Hee-hee... With the war over, there is no reason for me to stay there forever. So I gave my command over to my talented officers, and we left the scene."

He seemed remarkably invigorated. I guess this means Benimaru let the Three Lycanthropeers handle the rest. I could see the anguished faces of Alvis and his cohorts in my mind.

Those two, Benimaru and Shuna—guess they really *are* siblings, huh? They just pulled the exact same trick on their subordinates. I wish they would learn a little responsibility from someone like me—

Understood. I believe this to be the result of following your example, Master.

I didn't ask you to "believe" anything! Besides, you know that has to be wrong. Did something go haywire in the circuits between morphing from the Great Sage to Raphael?

Negative. Such a phenomenon has not been detected.

Oh, sure. Deny it. I bet *that* part of its logic got *extensively* upgraded. Better let it slide—it's not an argument I'd ever win anyway.

I decided to turn my attention back to Benimaru. "So is Gabil still at the battlefield?"

"He is, yes. He has kindled a friendship with one Middray, a priest in the service of Lady Milim, and they are tackling the post-battle cleanup together."

"Ah. So Geld's in Clayman's castle, and Gabil is outside?"

Even Gabil's lending a hand, huh? Between him and Geld, it was a relief to see all these people handling the practical side of warfare for me. I could really rely on 'em. War, after all, didn't end after you won it. Things got even hairier afterward, especially given how we captured nearly all of Clayman's forces alive. There were untold numbers of prisoners, on the field and in the castle, most of them capable of labor. We guaranteed them all their lives, so we'd have to step up and take care of them. At least they were magic-born, not human, so you didn't have to worry *that* much about upkeep—although even they would get grumpy if you didn't feed them.

Whether someone held a grudge against you after losing a battle or not, the victor was responsible for what happened afterward. Transporting all the POWs from the site at once was a major job. I didn't want them revolting when our eyes weren't on them, so we'd need guards on patrol at all times. Disarming a magic-born didn't neutralize them much as a threat, either. This world had magic *and* skills. Thinking about it, no wonder the take-no-prisoners approach was preferred up to now, huh?

If only there was a surefire way to make them do our bidding…

"Oh, nothing to worry about there," Benimaru said, that easy-going smile still on his face. "I brought them all together and simply, ah, *coerced* them to see things our way."

"Um… Yes. Good."

I instinctively nodded. No need to ask what exactly they talked about, I'm sure. Some of the prisoners must've been around to see Benimaru burn Charybdis to a crisp, and once word got around about that, I doubted too many of 'em would want to try their luck. Besides, the Three Lycanthropeers were there, and beastmen seemed like well-qualified candidates for prisoner management.

"So I guess we won't see Gabil back here for a while?"

"Likely not. He can't use Spatial Motion, so I suppose he will return with the Lycanthropeers."

He'd fly back once things settled down, I imagined. But hang on—

"Wait, the Lycanthropeers are coming, too?"

Why them? They weren't planning on bringing all the sheltered citizens and disarmed prisoners back here, were they?

"Well," Benimaru replied, "remember how Lady Milim blew the Eurazanian capital to pieces? We were talking about housing them in our nation for the time being."

As he put it, the beastmen were hardy enough that they could march all the way over here without complaint. Which wasn't what I was asking about, but…okay?

"We really can't take *all* of them, can we?"

It took ages to set up campsites for the twenty thousand we took in last time. Even worse, Geld and his team of high orc engineers, whom I'd usually rely on for jobs like this, were busy elsewhere. We had some extra land available—space we cleared for future development—but again, organizing camps would be a huge hassle.

"We discussed that with Geld and Alvis," Benimaru explained. "We've decided to divide the prisoners into rough brigades. They'll be sent to a variety of destinations, actually."

Well, *that's* a relief. And it sounded like they were pretty carefully screening each of them. If a prisoner had a village to return to, they were sent off by themselves. Only the beastmen seeking to learn a trade or skill would come to Tempest. Beastmen or magic-born with muscle, meanwhile, would stay on-site and serve under the command of Geld's team, redeveloping the vacant land that used to be Eurazania.

With Carillon stepping down from his demon lord post and joining Milim's side, Eurazania was now technically Milim territory. It was situated south of the Forest of Jura, spread out in the middle of a vast, fertile land, and plans were underway to construct a palace for Milim in the area. I had suggested to her that she ought to move her capital there, since they were building it from scratch anyway, and she instantly agreed to it. No further discussion. That's *so* Milim.

Thinking about it, though, I realized Milim didn't exactly have a...staff, per se. Middray and the rest of the Dragon Faithful were her servants, in a way, but—at least on paper—they merely worshiped Milim; they weren't bound to her at all. Thus "relocating the capital" was an odd way to put it, since she didn't really have a capital to start with, but I guess it doesn't really matter.

Carillon and Frey both readily agreed with the idea, and so we plunged into the construction of a new city. Our funding was provided by Clayman's hoard of gold, silver, and treasure; we had a ready group of POW laborers being organized and assigned work details; and Benimaru and Geld had things going so smoothly over there, I had nothing to be concerned about.

I was constantly amazed at their growth. *Hey, Tamura! Remember me? Your boss, who had to explain everything to you fifty times and you still couldn't do it right? Yeah, I have this entire horde of monsters who do better work than you!*

*   *   *

The way Benimaru put it, we would be housing fewer people in Tempest proper than last time.

"So we won't need to set up any new temporary housing?" I asked him.

"No, I think we should be fine. But it will not only be beast-men; we have magic-born prisoners as well. We had best make sure everyone is aware of that and exercises suitable caution."

"I see," Rigurd said with a nod. "Very well. I will explain matters to everyone."

These guys are *soooo* reliable. I didn't even need to order them around; they could make their own decisions. Wait... Couldn't these guys get along without me by this point? The thought made me feel a tad isolated.

*

One evening, a few days after Benimaru's return, Diablo entered my office carrying a box painted black.

"Our negotiations proceeded as planned, Sir Rimuru. This box contains proof of our peace agreement and one part of the reparations, totaling fifteen hundred stellar gold coins."

Oops. Forgot about that. Today was peace-talks day, huh? He said I didn't need to show up, so forgetting about it wasn't a big deal, really...but I still felt a bit guilty. I felt like everyone else was working hard on this huge work project, and I was just sitting at my desk playing solitaire. Not that I was, but still. I didn't want to be a lonely despot, after all.

Or that was how I consoled myself as Diablo presented the box to me.

"Ah, excellent. That's more stellars than we expected, no?"

He had demanded the outrageous sum of ten thousand. As I found out later, nobody was sure whether ten thousand stellars were even in circulation worldwide. "We can only create one stellar gold coin per month," King Gazel claimed when I asked. "Our kingdom did not begin minting them until a fairly long time after our founding, so I imagine they have some rarity value!" He had a point—there were hundreds of times more garden-variety gold coins flowing around.

And now I had fifteen hundred of them here. Over 10 percent of the entire world's supply. It made my head swim. You could really see how strong Farmus was, being able to scrape this up.

"I guess Farmus really *is* a superpower, isn't it? I'm impressed they collected so many."

"Perhaps. But it seems the majority of this was seized from the personal coffers of King Edmaris himself."

According to Diablo, most of these stellars were the personal property of the king, left in the vaults with no particular use to speak of. They had the backing of the Dwarven Kingdom, were worth loads of cash, and boasted artistic value as well, so they had been the property of the royal family for much of its long history.

"Luckily, King Edmaris's thought process was as I had planned it. With no knights to protect his family, he reasoned, he was bound to lose it all once the nobles clashed with him anyway."

So he cleaned out the royal vaults ahead of time. I see.

"...So does that mean we're gonna have civil war soon?"

"No doubt, my lord," a smiling Diablo replied. "The remaining balance exists in the form of an outstanding loan, but I doubt the new king will abide by that agreement for long."

Taking the potential new king into consideration, Diablo had gone out of his way to have Edmaris's younger brother Edward take the throne, instead of the young Edgar. This was done with Edmaris's agreement; everyone involved felt it was the only way forward. Normally, the former king would be rewarded with a dukedom for his service to the country, but Edmaris turned this down, renouncing his post and becoming a viscount. In this role, he would be shortly moving to a small patch of rural land in the countryside—not far from Earl Nidol Migam's own lands, near the Forest of Jura.

To everyone's eyes, it looked like Edmaris had lost his lust for power. In which case...

Report. The Farmus forces who refuse to pay the remaining reparations will likely move to push all responsibility for this affair on Edmaris.

*　　*　　*

Yep. It was all going the way Diablo meant it to.

"Nidol's domain of Migam is home to Yohm's band, too. This way, they can come help out if anything happens, huh?"

"Indeed, my lord," he replied, still smiling while Shion listened on behind me, scowling. Or maybe not listening. She probably tuned it out once she realized it was all way over her head. But I wasn't talking about her.

Hmmm. Nidol's land bordered Jura's. By country standards, it was midsize, boasting its own Free Guild branch and a fairly decent population. If you were going to start a popular movement, it wasn't a bad spot for it. That's where Yohm was, and he was famous around those parts, hailed as a champion and broadly supported by his people.

"If the new king tried abandoning Edmaris, could Yohm stop him?"

"He could, sir. And having Sir Yohm denounce that new king for his insincerity would no doubt lead to conflict."

So Yohm siding with Edmaris would lead to a pretty natural clash of wills, then. Sounds about perfect. If the new king really did pay off his debt to us, it'd be hard to do much else against him. We'd have to brace ourselves for the long haul, aiming to take Farmus down bit by bit. But Diablo was thinking two steps ahead of me, manipulating the minds and wills of the people to gain his results. In that case, things could very likely start moving in a hurry.

There was no doubt that the new king would try to get Edmaris out of the picture pronto. If the government was able to capture him, our plans would be ruined. Of course, we could ignore that new king and just push on in anyway, but that'd come at the cost of whatever trust the international community has in us. Always have the moral upper hand. That's how the human world worked.

"Well, keep a vigilant watch, all right? Can you manipulate the new king's side without getting too many people killed?"

"If that's what you seek, yes. Allow me, Diablo, to handle it."

So reliable. He's almost scarily smart. If I left it to him, he seemed ready to accomplish well near anything.

"Then do it. If you're short on war funds, you can use these stellars if you want."

I placed a thousand of the coins into my Stomach and pushed the remaining five hundred in his direction.

Fortunately for us, all our wounded were now fully recovered. Apart from paying personal visits to their beds, I wasn't called upon to do much of anything for them. A thousand was almost too much reparation, and we had also thoroughly looted Clayman's home base of its valuables, so financially we were doing pretty damn well, I thought. Much of our newfound fortune would be spent on future urban development, but we had enough breathing room to provide Yohm whatever he needed.

Despite my intentions, Diablo smiled and shook his head. "I deeply appreciate your concern, Sir Rimuru, but it will not be necessary. As laid out in my plan, if you can provide me with a suitable army, the rest will take care of itself. That, or if you grant me permission to wage battle myself—"

"Uh, no, that's fine. I'll give you all the troops you need, so instead of that, I need you to lay low as much as you can, all right?"

I had reason to cut him off. I knew how much of a freaky unknown Diablo was, so I definitely didn't want to use him in the wrong place and expose myself like an idiot. Unleashing him against human armies would be far too one-sided—all it'd do was make people fear us. We'd be further away from a common understanding than ever, and I wanted us to have as amicable a relationship as possible. Besides, we had all the war power we needed. We had no enemies; not in public, at least. Even with Geld's team tied up with engineering work, Benimaru and his army alone would be enough. Farmus, with the majority of its fighting force gone, was not a threat to us.

So I decided to just prepare reinforcements if necessary and use this stellar windfall to invest in the new nation Yohm was poised to build.

This was enough to convince Diablo. "Very well. I will remain firmly behind the scenes."

"Right. You know, Shion, you could learn a thing or two from Diablo."

"What?! When have I ever lost my head and failed to follow your will, Sir Rimuru?!"

I tried to throw a word of advice toward Shion like this now and again. She seriously never seemed to realize she did anything wrong.

Yeesh. I guess that'd be a long-term project, gradually instilling in her mind that going berserk all the time wasn't such a hot idea. It made me heave an internal sigh. Something told me it'd be a while before I could trust her with solo missions.

After finishing his report, Diablo brought up another question, as if it had just occurred to him.

"Sir Rimuru, the Western Holy Church has reportedly tried make contact with Reyhiem, one of my pawns. He has received a summons to visit their headquarters and explain the situation with the hostilities in Farmus. What do you think about that?"

Reyhiem? He was the archbishop of Farmus or whatever, right? Now he was just one of Diablo's faithful dogs, but ignoring a Church summons sounded like a bad idea.

"Hmm... If we ignored them, would that lead to trouble?"

"It would. I think it best to allow him to testify to them, if only to see what the Church's next move will be."

"Yeah... I'm sure they're hungry for info, what with there being just three survivors."

Out of the former king, Edmaris, the court sorcerer, Razen, and Archbishop Reyhiem, it made sense that the Church would want to hear from Reyhiem first. He was the only real candidate out of the three.

"But wasn't the Church monitoring Veldora? Because right now, it's true that he's revived again, but the timeline we're giving is a bit off from the truth. If we lied to them, wouldn't they see right through that?"

"You think so? Shall I have him speak the truth, then?"

I thought about this a moment.

The Church could very well be a monkey wrench in our future plans. Ideally, I'd want to engage them in a way that didn't cause interference between us, but given their flat-out refusal to work with monsters, I didn't like my chances. Not even the Dwarven Kingdom was on very good terms with the Church. The dwarves' habit of treating monsters as equals violated their whole doctrine—but it hadn't erupted into war yet. The two sides were simply ignoring each other.

Should that be what we aim for? I didn't want to trample over a millennium or so of Church doctrine, but I didn't want to unconditionally accept it, either. If they wanted all monsters to die, I wasn't about to lie on my back and wait for the dagger. I had to respect them, and we had to be considerate of each other. If one of us said something the other couldn't accept, it could lead to war, in the end. A deep understanding of each other would be a must, along with a prudent effort to keep away from any potential land mines in our talks.

Of course, that only applies if the other side plays along. Otherwise, we'd just be deluding ourselves into complacency. If the Church branded us a divine enemy, we'd have to resist that—and I wasn't afraid to smash them to pieces, if it came to that.

For now, though...

"Hmm. How about I send them a message for the time being? We seized some magic-image-recording thingies from Clayman, right? I'd like to personally record a message with one of them. We can have Reyhiem take it over there and see how the Church reacts."

"Very well."

"Great! I will bring one over at once!"

Diablo sagely nodded as Shion ran off to fetch a crystal for me.

A few days had passed now, after Diablo reported that Reyhiem had commenced his journey to the Church, but we had yet to hear any response. The reaction from them was muddled confusion, and I could see why. Veldora was back, and there was a new demon lord in town (i.e., me). Figuring out how to deal with us wasn't something they could make a snap decision on.

Well, if they didn't react to me, I didn't mind. For now, I was satisfied with sitting and waiting to see how things shook out.

*

The Three Lycanthropeers arrived a while later, along with a procession in the tens of thousands.

They didn't take nearly as long as I thought. You gotta hand it to these beastmen and magic-born. Just in terms of their core strength, no human could compare with them. With magicules all over this world, they could run on magic when physically exhausted and with their own two feet when magically exhausted. Their marching speed was several times what an army on Earth could manage—and I'm talking about all of them, down to the average beastman on the street. They really *were* bred for battle.

I didn't see Gabil among them. Presumably, he was in the rear somewhere, I thought, as Alvis and Sufia came up to greet me.

"Hmm? Isn't Phobio here?"

"About that," Sufia began. "Phobio stayed behind to tend to the magic-born we took prisoner." He was sticking around while Geld was at Clayman's palace, apparently, to ensure no revolts took place. In other words, they were pushing the boring work on him. Sorry about that, Phobio. But even if Benimaru had bullied him into that role, we did need someone on surveillance. We should appreciate him for working with us instead of pushing the responsibility on someone else.

We had, by this point, fully prepared to accept this crowd. I had worked with Kaijin and Kurobe, our manufacturing specialists, to work out how many people should be assigned to this or that department around town. These were all volunteers with a keen interest in technical work, but we could only accept so many, so we agreed to set up rotational shifts for the more popular work details.

It might be a good idea to build a technical school of some sort around here, I thought as we quietly handled all this work. Someplace where we can provide year-round instruction on what we were doing. It seemed smart to me.

At the very far end of the procession, I finally caught sight of Gabil. "I have returned, Sir Rimuru!" he bellowed from the skies, not looking at all the worse for wear.

"Hey, nice to see you! You put in a fine effort at the battle, I hear."

"No, no, I still have so much to learn. Sir Middray, under the service of Lady Milim, practically pummeled me beyond recognition!"

Ah yes, that dragonewt with the crazy strength. Benimaru mentioned him, too.

"Yeah, well, if he worships Milim, he's gotta like fighting a lot, no doubt. You aren't exactly a wimp—maybe you just aren't used to your newly evolved powers yet. You got a while to go."

I wasn't sure if this comforted him at all, but I said it anyway. He didn't look too chagrined, so I was sure he felt the same anyway.

"Ha! I, Gabil, am prepared to expend every effort to live up to your lofty expectations, Sir Rimuru!"

That statement, and that smile, were all the proof I needed.

After I said my hellos to the rest of his force, he suddenly remembered a sheet of paper that he took out from his pocket to show me.

"What's this?"

"I received this from Lady Milim, my lord. She told me to give it to you."

What could this be? Nothing good, I was sure. She mentioned stopping by again as we said our goodbyes after the Walpurgis Council. But sure enough, there was her childish scrawl, written haphazardly across the paper.

This is Milim! Next time I visit, I'll be bringing along some guys who just can't seem to leave me the heck alone. I want you to teach them everything there is to know about cooking. This is an urgent request, so I figured I'd ask my buddy Rimuru for help!!! Please please please!!!!!

The urgency certainly came through in the message. These hangers-on; was she talking about the Dragon Faithful?

"Uh, did she tell you what this is about?"

"A little bit. I met a member of the Dragon Faithful named Sir Hermes while I was there, and he was kind enough to discuss his following's internal workings with me."

The way Gabil described him, Hermes seemed to have a pretty good head on his shoulders. Not battle-obsessed like Middray at all; more of a free spirit, one who had traveled to the Dwarven Kingdom and Western Nations.

Being in the Dragon Faithful, as he explained to Gabil, meant a life of frugality. "He claimed that the food they present to Lady Milim isn't cooked or prepared in any way whatsoever. Perhaps they share some tastes with us. I've never enjoyed a fish that wasn't best when it was eaten raw, you know."

I'm not so sure you guys have that much in common, Gabil. Lizardmen's digestive systems were probably just built that way. But they knew about preparing food, or at least smoking it, and they had a

few non-fish staples they enjoyed as well. The Dragon Faithful, meanwhile, didn't seem like they had heard of the concept of cooking at all. I doubt they were eating raw meat all day, but whatever preparation they did seemed strictly for the purposes of avoiding contamination and nothing more.

"Uh…okay? I thought dragonewts had the same sense of taste as humans."

"We do, sir, we do! Thanks to my glorious evolution, I have gained the most wondrous, expert set of taste buds. All the bland meals of my lizardman past pale in comparison to the vast cornucopia of delights I can now sample!"

"Yeah, I'll bet. So when you eat a good meal, you know how you kinda want to eat it again later on?"

Gabil nodded sagely, growing increasingly excited. "Yes… Yes, now I see your point! This is Sir Hermes's way of eliminating that Dragon Faithful tradition once and for all, is it not?"

Probably, yeah. Tradition or not, I could read Milim's mind easily enough. If they worshiped her as a god, though, why were they deliberately ignoring her will? That's kind of, um, blasphemous, isn't it? And why can't Milim just chat about this with them herself? Maybe, in her own unique way, she didn't want to rock the boat with them. She knew they were only acting out of virtuous intentions, so she put up with that treatment without complaint.

"In that case, we'll need to give them all the royal treatment, won't we?"

"Oh, absolutely! A splendid idea, I think!"

We'd need to keep it casual, nonchalant, making sure we didn't act all high and mighty. Then they could naturally observe, and learn, what made Milim happy. It sounded like a tougher mission than I first thought. *Better assemble my team and discuss this later on.*

So I instructed Gabil to return to his research in the cave. Vester was putting in a full effort down there at the moment, but we still didn't have a large enough team. Losing Gabil's crew must have been a major blow to their progress.

"Right. I shall be off, then!"

"Yep. We will also consider your reward at our next conference, so I'd like to have you in attendance."

"Yes, my lord!"

Pride filled Gabil's face as he flew off. He must've just remembered that I appointed him to Tempest leadership earlier.

*

A month had passed since Walpurgis, and with all the new people, things were running at a fever pitch around town. In the midst of it, Geld finally Spatial Motioned back. It was the first time I had seen him in a while, and he looked pretty beat-up.

"I…it's good to see you again, Geld."

He heaved a sigh at my pensive greeting. "I have to say, Sir Rimuru, I look up to you more than ever now."

"Whoa! Where'd *that* come from?"

There was no doubting the respect in his voice as he turned his weary eyes to me. I hadn't done anything of note recently, so I had no idea what he was talking about. What happened to him in the space of a few weeks?

"Well…"

The story Geld had for me was a classic tale of incompetence among new hires. He had organized the prisoners into groups, deploying them to this or that allied force. That much went well. After that, he commended these troops in the midst of their surveying and land-clearing work…but certain problems quickly made themselves known.

High orcs had no problem using Thought Communication to chat with one another, working as a team even in silence, but we'd need a different plan with the mix of magic-born involved here. Verbal instructions couldn't be understood—and besides, a lot of the main staff, Geld included, weren't that great at making themselves clear. It's one thing to be capable of something, but quite another to explain it clearly and lucidly to others. Lots of artisans like him faced the same problem.

This meant that as ruthlessly efficient as Geld and his team were, things fell apart when anyone else got involved. The results were boundlessly frustrating to him. The magic-born weren't great fans of being ordered around, either, so even if you carefully showed them what to do in person, many of them weren't interested in meekly copying your actions. Those that were, as Geld put it, still weren't up to his grade of quality. I could see that. More people didn't always mean better work. Put together a crowd of idiots, and all you had was a mob on your hands. That was why education was so important.

"Show them, convince them, let them try, and praise them—only then will a man be moved."

That's a quote from Admiral Isoroku Yamamoto, commander of the Imperial Japanese Navy during World War II, and it's something that I think anyone in a leadership position needs to take to heart. It expertly encapsulates the difficulties of leading and instructing people, and it also shows that people find real pride and meaning in their work only when recognized by others.

Listening to Geld's grumbling reminded me of the more painful moments of my office job, in my previous life. Work staff who never listened to you, people down the ladder who tried hiding their mistakes, bosses who attempted to push the blame on someone else. It wasn't wine and roses for me back then, either. A lot of good memories, too, but get me started on the bad ones, and I could go all night.

And whenever I had it really rough:

"All right, Geld! Let's have a drink!"

I slapped him on the shoulder. Rewarding the staff for hard work was part of any boss's job, and one way to do that was to let them vent their grievances and work out everything in their system. I needed to pay special attention to Geld, given how much responsibility he felt for his work—and so we drank the night away, while Geld aired out all his pains and concerns and I carefully listened.

I planned to assemble the leadership for a conference the next morning—but before that, I called Hakuro over for a private chat, contacting him via Thought Communication the previous night. I traveled to his quarters at sunrise.

"Sir Rimuru," he greeted me, almost choked with emotion,

"coming over personally to see me..." He didn't look as tired as Geld.

"Sorry to put you through all this grueling work."

"Oh, not at all, not at all. We've sifted through the prisoners now, so my job is almost done. I have to say, though, Geld has it far worse. I finished transferring leadership over last night, so there's no need for me to go back over there, at least."

"Geld... Yeah, sounds like he had it tough. After I contacted you yesterday, he and I drank for a while, and it sounds like he's got a lot on his mind, you know? Like, up to now he's been able to just shut off his brain and focus on his work, but directing prisoners on the job site was a huge challenge for him."

"Indeed. He would have it easier if he was willing to compromise on matters, but he was always far too serious-minded for that."

As Hakuro explained, it would've been easy to use force to corral this motley band of magic-born, coercing them into following commands. But if you do that, you can't expect a top-quality job to result from it. You'd have to *settle* here and there, and as an artisan, those results wouldn't be enough to satisfy Geld.

"I have something else to report to you, Sir Rimuru..."

But to Hakuro, that was Geld's problem. He turned back toward me.

"What's that?" I asked.

"Clayman, as you know, ruled over what was called the Puppet Nation of Dhistav, a land where the majority of people are in the slave class. These are entirely dark elves, no other species, and well over a thousand of them were tasked with maintaining and managing the castle grounds alone."

"Right. So?"

"Well...as they described it to me, Dhistav used to be home to a kingdom of elves..."

Elves? The denizens of the Sorcerous Dynasty of Thalion descended from elves, too, didn't they? Is there a common ancestor here? Maybe not—we're talking pretty well out of the way, geography-wise.

"...and remarkably enough, some elven ruins remain in the land. The dark elves described themselves as keepers of their graves."

"Oh?"

Grave tenders? Over what sort of graves? Elves had life expectancies of who knows how long, besides.

"So you're saying there are these well-guarded, untouched ruins from an ancient kingdom just lying around?"

This was big news to me. Ruins like these were dotted all over the world, often raided by the hunter-gatherer adventurers who made treasure hunting their line of work. Most of them didn't have a very good time at it. Only a precious few ruins had been discovered at all, and those that were had already been picked clean a while ago. But if there was a brand-new cache of ruins to explore and exploit...

"Hakuro, I'm classifying this discovery a state secret. Don't tell anyone about this for the time being—not until I go there and survey things for myself."

"Yes, my lord," he said quietly, nodding. He must've understood how vital this could potentially be.

If I had to guess, Clayman derived much of his riches from the things discovered in these sites. He had to. That would explain all the Artifacts and magic items Geld told me they recovered. But does that mean we should just...you know, take them over?

I decided to hold off on judgment for now. The secret seemed to be safe with the dark elves; word wouldn't get out unless we wanted it to. This was demon lord territory, forbidden lands that no adventurers dared to approach. Better to go slowly on these ancient ruins—trying to overextend ourselves to all of them at once was too likely to backfire.

✳

Everyone was now seated at our main meeting hall. I surveyed them all from my specially made slime seat.

"Um, right. Hello, everyone. As some of you already know, I have been promoted to demon lord!"

""""Congratulations!!""""

They all shouted their tidings to me, happy and excited whether they knew or not. I was just as happy. I had safely weathered a major storm.

"It was a long journey, indeed, yes," Rigurd observed, "but we have finally made it." *Uh, Rigurd, it hasn't even been two years since we met, right?*

Rigur, meanwhile, was crying like a baby. "Truly astounding! Seeing our leader become a demon lord fills me with so much emotion..."

Shion sneered at the crowd like this was all inevitably going to happen. "It is the start of a new era for Sir Rimuru!"

Though, really, it was an emotional time for me, too. The only problem left was essentially the Western Holy Church. If I could handle them, it'd be easy street on the way to creating the ideal environment I'm looking for.

Brimming with confidence, I continued my briefing, going over what we decided on at Walpurgis.

"Ah, right. I didn't mention this, but it's been decided that I'm the official ruler of the entire Forest of Jura region. I don't think this really changes much, since it's already been that way for a while. It just means that, you know, if someone invades the forest—not that they would—we'd be fighting back under my own name. Also, should we formally declare our rights to this territory, do you think? Or are we safe just leaving it be for now?"

As I spoke, the looks on my leadership grew more nervous. Some of them appeared downright terrified. *What? Did I say something bad?*

"Um... The whole forest? Truly?"

"Uh, yeah?" I replied to Rigurd.

"Are you serious?" Benimaru gasped. "Including everything on the other side of the river?"

"Errr, probably?"

He was referring to the Great Ameld River that flowed across the forest, dividing it in two. The other side bordered lands under the influence of the Eastern Empire, a place we still had little to no connection with.

"Is that a problem?" I asked.

"Not a problem for us," Benimaru replied after some thought, "but I don't believe the area past the river counts as the dryads' domain. So far, Sir Rimuru, you are recognized as overseer only of the lands that the dryads themselves have built up. To the denizens beyond the river, the advent of a new demon lord would likely prove to be quite a headache."

He smiled the whole time—savoring the thought of mowing down any rebellious factions over there, no doubt. That was...um... no. Bad idea.

"If you asked me," Kaijin rebutted, "this is an astounding development. The demon lords have formally agreed that you have rights to all the forest's natural resources, if I'm understanding this correctly. This includes anything that anybody takes from it, over on the other side. That's big news, pal!"

It's like he was reading my mind. He was right. It didn't strike me as anything big at first, but it had the potential to explode. As Kaijin explained to me, people had been harvesting the forest's resources on the sly for a while now. The dryads were willing to let it slide to some extent, but given the general state of lawlessness past the Great Ameld, it was common for people to take wood or produce or whatnot from Jura to the Dwarven Kingdom, making a living off the sales. There was no regional authority to seek permission from, nothing stopping them—but now, if they wanted to do that or live in the forest, they needed my approval, and they'd have to march over here to get it.

"Um... Oh crap, does this mean we're gonna get *more* people here?"

"I think it does," Shuna said, a serene smile on her face. "Now that you're an approved demon lord, anyone who fails to come here and pledge allegiance to you could be legally branded a rebel."

Her opinion had to be shared by much of Tempest, I figured. But why require permission after who knows how many years of living here? That sounded like needless bureaucracy.

"Well, why worry about that now? I mean, if they're already residents of the forest..."

"No, no," countered Rigurd, "a demon lord is, in a way, a projection of pure power. It is something to be proud of. To a goblin, you understand, a high-level magic-born is something of a divine presence."

"Exactly," Gabil added. "Some of these uncontacted residents may seek the protection of the demon lord; others may go on with their lives without recognizing your authority. They have the right to make that decision for themselves. But even among the lizard-men I used to be with, the protection of a demon lord would have been a literal gift from the gods. Defying one was unthinkable; ignoring one, the height of folly. Compared with the risk of anger-ing the local demon lord, it would be wholly typical for them to come and greet you instead."

And as Shuna put it, failing to acknowledge me could even put you under suspicion. If you got attacked for it, you had no right to complain. Not that I'd want that, though. And besides, what if you're a monster who's never heard of me before? How would you even know?

"At the very least," Gabil said, "the lizardmen are coming to see you, I assure you. My father has already been told of your ascension!"

Wait. When did they decide to do that?

"You mean Abil? He's coming?"

"He is! He told Lady Shion about it as well. Ah, he is count-ing the days before he can see you in all your demonic glory for himself!"

This was starting to sound big. Really big. The lizardmen were one of the larger-size races in the whole Forest of Jura. If *they* took the pilgrimage to see me as a given, I assumed that went without saying for any species weaker than them. And I'm sure the process would be pretty casual for anyone familiar with me, but if not, they might be showing up on my doorstep trembling with fear. I'd just look like the latest local despot to them; they might freak out over making one false step and being annihilated or whatever. *Maybe there's something we could do to make this whole process a lot more...chill?*

Still, though...

"Ha-ha! I'm sure Sir Rimuru would expect nothing less!"

I peered down at the triumphant-looking Shion. If she knew Gabil's father was going to show up, why didn't she bother tell-ing me? And I really didn't appreciate that grin on her face. She didn't care about this visitor at all. I swear, she looks like the perfect executive secretary on the outside, but if you want her to actually *do* the job, forget it.

Ugh. Just leave her be. I mean, I'm glad she enjoyed hearing praise for me (even more than I did), but I knew she'd take any criticism from me the wrong way, so...

To sum up, once word got around about my demon lord-dom, I'd have a parade of visitors beating a path to this town, most monsters preferring to request my protection instead of risk my wrath. We'd have a hell of a lot of visitors to deal with soon, in other words.

We would have to conduct a cross-forest survey shortly, seeking out the intelligent races. This wouldn't be a problem in areas where I was already the acknowledged leader, but anywhere else would be an uphill climb.

But if we were gonna be busy with that anyway...

"Hey, I was just thinking—we gotta spread the word around the forest about my ascension anyway, right? So why don't we turn it into some really big ad campaign and use it to unveil this town to the whole world? It'd be easier to make everyone come over here than go reach out to all of them, I think."

"...How do you mean?" a confused-looking Rigurd asked me, so I went into some more detail on the idea I just came up with.

Really, it wasn't anything difficult. This town, the capital of Tempest, was starting to become more well-known among the monsters in Jura. Koby, and the kobold merchant caravans he led, were doing a great job spreading the rumors wherever they went. At least a few people must've been interested in visiting, and I was just thinking now was a good time to expand our population a little. The beast-men hanging out here would complete their education and return home soon enough; we'd need to make up for those losses, and if we were gonna keep up the teaching effort, then the more students, the merrier. Our food situation was steadily improving, and we definitely had the room for more people.

If anything, we were starting to face a shortage of workers. There were all these ideas, all these projects to explore, but not enough people to throw at them. A big, lavish unveiling could be just the thing to attract more of them. They'd come to pledge their fealty or whatever, they'd learn about the town along the way, and at least some of them would consider a permanent move.

Two birds with one stone. In fact...

"Plus... You know, we've all been on pins and needles the past little while. Why don't we kick back a little bit? Let's hold a big festival to start this off!"

We'd set up a specific time for the meet and greets with me, and we'd stage a city-wide festival around these to fete them with. That way, I wouldn't have to spread the meetings out over weeks and weeks. There'd be a huge feast, too—I still had Milim's request filed in the back of my mind. It'd be a chance for all of us to take a breather, show off what we've done, and get everything wrapped up in one fell swoop.

"A festival…?"

"Wonderful! Truly a wonderful idea!"

"Let's do it! It will be a magnificent event!"

My associates were up for it, at least. The town was getting experienced with this, what with the monthly feasts we already held for ourselves, and our developments in the realm of food and drink were growing more complex and large-scale by the day. Expanding on that, and allowing everyone to join in, sounded like a lot of fun.

"This will kind of be *my* public debut as well, so let's make it the biggest one we can!"

""""Yes, my lord!""""

There were no objections. The budget? Ah, no need to worry about that. Rigurd would figure out something. We were flush for the moment, and a little indulgence wouldn't put a dent in that.

Things proceeded quickly after that; I guess those words held a lot of sway with people. Suggestions and feedback filled the hall, much to my silent surprise, and before I knew it, we were extending invitations to dignitaries the entire world over. Was this a little hasty? Monsters were one thing, but were we okay inviting *human* heads of state as well?

We had a hot spring. We had ample accommodations, including a state guest house worthy of handling the highest of nobility. Haruna and her crew had already impressed super-celebrities like Archduke Erald and King Gazel. I think we ought to be fine. Even if it took shuffling the dates and locations around, or at least stepping up our security, this could be a great chance for the world's leaders to get to know me.

The overseer of all these people (i.e., me) had just officially become a demon lord. I could see why people wanted to celebrate that. I used to be Japanese, and Japanese people *love* their festivals. I figured I needed to really go all out with this and teach everyone what a real party is about—that and show them what a friendly demon lord I was.

With a promise to hammer out the festival details later, I concluded my report. We followed this up with reports from the rest of my main staff. I had a grip on everything, but not everyone on the team knew what everyone else was up to—and maybe I'd learn something new myself.

Diablo, in particular, had a completely different view of the world from me. It was like he didn't know what common sense was. Small trifles to me could be huge, world-changing matters to him, it felt like, and if something like that came up, it'd be difficult for me to handle that alone. That was why I set up these regular info-sharing reports.

Rigurd kicked off his briefing by stating that our merchant partners had begun returning to town. Our numbers were trending upward again, likely because Fuze was spreading the word that things were safe now.

Beyond that, none of the other nations were making any particularly noteworthy moves. My ascension seemed to alarm many of them, but for now, they were likely waiting to see how Blumund and the Dwarven Kingdom would respond.

We also had word that Elmesia El-Ru Thalion, Her Excellency the Emperor of the Sorcerous Dynasty of Thalion, had expressed a personal desire to open formal relations with Tempest. I could practically hear her whisper "so build a highway linking us already" underneath those words, but there's no doubting what a useful support they'd be to us. Her statement, propagated by magic to all world leaders, had apparently led to much consternation.

"It can be said," Rigurd happily closed, "that all our relations are fulfilling their sworn duty and working hard on our behalf across the world!"

Next came Soei. I had left him to investigate a lot of things, so I figured he'd have the floor for a while.

This included the preliminary setup for the highway between here and Thalion, the advance surveying and so on before we put shovel to dirt. I had already worked out the general route from my bird's-eye view over the forest, so Soei was sent out to check for nearby monster villages or other construction obstacles.

This was something I had him do for the roads to Dwargon and Blumund as well; it was pretty important work. You didn't want to omit that stuff, unless you wanted trouble later. So far, the monsters impacted by the roads had been cooperative with us, so there were no major problems to speak of, but you never knew when we'd have to eminent domain someone out of their ancestral homes or whatnot.

Very few of them would defy my will, me being demon lord and all, but I didn't want to act *that* much like a tyrant, so I had to be careful. It'd be easy to just push them away by force, but I wanted to avoid that if I could. Coexistence was my creed, and that applied equally to humans and monsters. Hopefully I wouldn't run into any issues this time, either.

I wasn't in this to demand anything from the monsters I ruled over. Anyone who wanted my protection got it, but otherwise, I didn't want to interfere—well, unless they lived right in the middle of my projected road. But I wanted to avoid pointless conflict, so if they were willing to negotiate, so was I. I'd be happy to make all the moving arrangements for anyone displaced, should I need to. After all, any village near this road was bound to become a resting stop, a lively place filled with inns and taverns and travelers going to and fro.

It wasn't all going to be smooth sailing, but it'd make for a better life for the natives. That's how it worked for the previous two highways, and hopefully it would once more.

"I did not find any hostile monsters present on or near the projected route," Soei began. "When I explained Sir Rimuru's plans to them, they all provided their ready agreement to me."

Ah, good. I'm glad he made it clear we weren't kicking anyone out of their homes.

"That's great. In that case, make sure you wrap up the surveying and other work by the time Geld's free again."

The rough on-site investigation work was already complete. If we didn't find any more safety concerns after this, it'd be time to send our engineers over.

"Well, one moment. I did discover one issue. The Forest of Jura is in your jurisdiction, Sir Rimuru, but the Khusha Mountains lie on one of its borders. The area is filled with high peaks and treacherous canyons, and at the higher altitudes, there is said to be settlements populated by a long-nosed tribe known as the tengu. That is information from the local populace, so I found it difficult to dismiss entirely."

In the lands southwest of Rimuru, the capital and central city of Tempest, there was a mountain range that spread out across the shores of Lake Sisu. These were the Khushas, an area that high orcs had migrated to in the past; a southern branch of this range was also home to the former demon lord Frey's castle. It was noted for its beautiful, extended rows of towering peaks, many of which were treacherous and all but untouched by living creatures.

The current plan called for a highway to be built right up to the border with Thalion. There was a midsize town there situated between the mountains that would serve as the terminus. We wouldn't need to go through the Khushas themselves. So what was Soei worried about?

"What's the big deal about that?"

"The tengu are said to be friendly, but at their core, they are a warmongering race. Even the demon lord Frey avoided direct conflict with them. I would suggest seeking her advice about this…"

Technically speaking, Soei advised me, the Khusha Mountains were outside the Forest of Jura and thus not our territory. It wasn't Frey's, either, making it independent, unclaimed land. I could've just used my demon lord powers to beat them into submission, but maybe it'd be better to zip over and explain matters to avoid future trouble. In their eyes, they might see me as a greedy demon lord trying to expand his territory.

Soei sounded disappointed at having to leave the decision about this to me, but I actually thought better of him for it. I was so proud of him for not forcing the issue and trying to work with the tengu himself. He was careful like that, and that made him endlessly helpful for missions like these.

"All right. So should I go and—?"

"Ah, one moment. If that's the issue, let me head over."

Just as I hoped to get this wrapped up quickly, Benimaru stopped me. Whenever he casually volunteered for something like this, it always alarmed me a bit—but he was right. I left the matter to him.

"You've seemed rather friendly with Lady Alvis as of late, my brother. I would hope you are not volunteering merely for the chance of a tryst with her?" Shuna commented.

Huh? Benimaru and Alvis were *that* into each other?!

"What does she mean, Benimaru?"

If Shuna was telling the truth, this was serious.

"You misunderstand her, Sir Rimuru. Shuna, enough of your nonsense."

He acted unperturbed enough. It didn't seem like he was lying to me. But let's face it. Benimaru was a good catch for any woman able to capture his attention. Anyone could see that.

"Don't worry, Sir Rimuru. Whether Benimaru is here or not, you will always have me!"

Oh, great, more of Shion's nonsense.

"Huh? What are you talking about?"

"Heh! Falling for Alvis's trap and ready to abandon our nation, are you?" Shion continued. "Well, go! Do whatever you like!"

"Shion, how on earth are you interpreting things *that* way?"

I could see veins throbbing on Benimaru's head. I mean, yeah, I was kind of jealous of him, too—two years, and I still didn't have a girlfriend to speak of—but I didn't think he was gonna go elope or whatever. Shion's imagination was a fearsome thing, indeed.

"Yeah, I really doubt that, Shion."

"You heard him, Shion. Sir Rimuru, you do trust in me, yes?"

"It's not a matter of trust by now. You're one of my closest partners."

There wasn't a cell in my body that questioned Benimaru. He couldn't be less like my old coworker Tamura, except in how they'd both found a steady date before I ever did. But I could deal with that later.

This whole conversation was getting ridiculous. "Right. If we keep talking about this, Shion's imagination is gonna run wild on her. Benimaru, I'm assigning this job to you!"

"Yes, my lord," he replied with a fatigued nod. Yeesh.

Still, Benimaru was the right man to serve as my proxy here. He was second in command only to me, and I doubted he would under-estimate any adversaries he came across. I wasn't expecting hidden mountain settlements on the Thalion border, but considering the future, it was better to work everything out with them sooner or later—and Benimaru's better than me at that stuff.

∗

There was one thing I had yet to hear about.

"Can you tell me anything about the changes in our monster eco-system, Soei?"

I had asked him to investigate trends among the monsters in town and along our highways. A lot of residents were practically brimming with magicules; the air was pretty dense with them by now, which was exactly how you got mystic beasts—they'd spon-taneously manifest from pools of the stuff, and the more that were created, the more likely at least one would be harmful to us. Beasts like these necessitated a constant patrol around the forest. They were a threat to humans even at D rank or below, so we needed to be hypervigilant with those guys. If one ranked B or so showed up, that required immediate attention.

Rigur, as head of our security department, was the main man in charge of handling them. His team was experienced now, and even the newer ones could provide able service after several weeks of training. They patrolled the highways, ensuring the merchant wag-ons could ply their trade in peace, and they did a good job at it—for now, no problems had been reported. But they couldn't cover the entire forest, so there was no telling where a new, and powerful, creature might be lurking.

Soei had informed me that it wasn't worth worrying about much, which was puzzling. What did he mean by that? Like, we could live safely alongside them? If they didn't harm us or the travelers, then sure, I could accept that. Any monsters intelligent enough to be negotiated with were free to live out their lives, but you just never knew when a new menace, like the A-minus-ranked knight spider Gobta tangled with, might rear its ugly head and start defending its territory.

That's why I was concerned with the forest outside of the highways and other areas we had populated. Those places, it seemed to me, were more likely to house these potential threats. Soei had his Replications looking into this for me, so I was pretty sure he at least had an inkling by now.

"I did not discover anything particularly problematic," Soei coolly replied to me. "If I had to name one, it would be the saber grizzly I chanced upon in the forest's northwestern reaches, but I safely dispatched it."

Hmm. Nothing problematic?

Report. A saber grizzly is equivalent to an A-minus rank, similar to the knight spider.

What?!

"Whoa, that's, um, that's nothing a normal adventurer could take on!"

I couldn't hide my shock. He made it sound so commonplace that I didn't pick up on it at first. No merchant would be able to travel in areas with freaks like those nearby. They'd be a danger even to Gobta and his patrol teams.

"Uh," Gobta grunted, picking up on my concern, "is that for real, Soei? 'Cause I don't really wanna deploy anyone new and untested to places where *they* are. It'd be dangerous."

"I wouldn't worry. You spoil them too much anyway, don't you?"

"Heyyy! Wait a minute! Maybe *you* wouldn't worry, but to us, if we let our guards down, we're goners!"

"Then go to Hakuro," Soei blithely replied as Gobta kept whining. "Just have him train you harder. You'll be fine."

Hakuro nodded at this like it was plainly obvious. I felt kind of bad for Gobta, although his reaction piqued my interest. He himself didn't seem too scared of a saber grizzly. The magicules coming off him seemed to be higher than before; he was probably on the higher end of the B rank by now. But there's a pretty big jump between B and A, I figured...

Hey, Raphael, I'm not misreading Gobta's power, am I?

Understood. When Unified with a starwolf, the resulting growth in fighting level cannot be measured in numbers.

*   *   *

Ah. All right. Yeah, I think that Unification was an A-minus. And with Gobta head of the goblin riders, maybe a saber grizzly wouldn't be a big issue for him. And didn't he mention success-fully defending himself against an attack by one of the Clayman squad leaders? Between Hakuro's training and his own experience, he must have been improving, in his own way. He didn't *look* any different, but maybe Gobta's a force to be reckoned with?

I smiled a bit as I reflected on this. "Now, now, I think Gobta's got a good point. Just because *you* can handle it doesn't mean the whole world can, Soei."

That was meant to defend Gobta a bit, but I also wanted to remind Soei not to try solving all his problems alone. If the more power-ful among us use themselves as a yardstick, that'll bring a world of pain upon anyone who can't live up to that. It'd also make things more inefficient for the powerful themselves, burdening them fur-ther and ultimately leading to their ruin. I spent a few moments explaining this to the team, mixing in a few real-world examples.

"…I understand. I did not think carefully enough."

Everyone is different. Soka and the rest of Soei's team were tal-ented enough to satisfy his harsh demands, but it took a special group of people to do that. I appreciated his apology, but I hoped he kept that fact in mind somewhere. The same could be said of Beni-maru and Hakuro; I wanted them to be a bit more broad-minded in how they raised the new generation. Geld and Gabil, on the other hand, thought a great deal more about the people under them, so I had less concern about them. Hopefully everyone could learn from them. It'd make for better relationships all around.

Meanwhile…

"Although I should say that training Gobta and the rest is a great thing. You gotta make sure they're prepared for the unexpected!"

Hakuro gave a sly grin as Gobta hung his head low. Sure, not everyone advances at the same rate or to the same degree, but train-ing itself is never a bad thing. It's just like going to school—it's bound to help you later on.

Convinced that Gobta was on the right track, I went back to the main topic.

Just as I feared, we were starting to see new, and dangerous, monsters born in the forest. Our patrol teams had potions on them if worse came to worst, and the starwolves were astonishingly fast on their feet, so I'm sure they could flee easily enough. But I can't expect our upcoming visitors to act the same way.

"If we have all these magicules pooling together, that's going to create more unusual monsters to deal with. It'll be too late for us if they kill someone. We need a plan of action."

We could try stricter patrols, but that wouldn't address the root of the problem. We'd have to keep that up forever, stressing all of us out. Unless we identified and removed whatever was creating these dense clouds of magic, I'd have to keep worrying about this for all time.

So now what...?

As I pondered over this, a helpful voice called out from an unexpected place.

"In that case, why don't we place anti-magic barriers over the highways?"

It was Vester. Kaijin immediately stood up to reply.

"And you know, pal, we just finished up the perfect device for that." He grinned at me. "A fully automatic, barrier-producing magic generator!"

*

I knew he had been working on a few things in secret. But really? An automatic magic generator?

Apparently, this was a device that automatically kept any magic spell going, as long as you told it which one. A major innovation, it sounded like, kind of an advanced version of the inscription magic–driven tools he had invented before. I guess Kaijin and Vester, chagrined at how useless they were during the whole barrier crisis we had, stepped up to try developing this. These guys are amazing. Making a working model in such a short time... What are they, geniuses?

Turns out, though, this wasn't just a couple of dudes working in a garage. Gabil was pitching in during his spare time, as well as Kurobe (who wasn't with us at the moment). Even Shuna was helping out. In a way, we had some of the world's greatest magic wielders coming together for this project. It was kind of epic.

Kaijin had long been devoting his days to research, leaving forge duties to Kurobe. I'm sure it wasn't *just* research, what with his duties as head of Tempest's production department, but still.

As he explained to me, the automatic magic generator utilized the magicules naturally floating in the air. He figured we had tons of those around us right now, and that there had to be a way to harness those—hence the idea. The Prison Field covering the town worked by purifying the inner space of its magicules, absorbing them. In much the same way, monsters took in magicules from the air and produced magic crystals from them. They had researched these natural processes, analyzing how they worked.

Another thing, one I had already mentioned, was that this nation was unnaturally full of magicules. We were all projecting pretty heavy auras even when we tried to hold them back. Even in a regular cave, the density could be enormous in areas, enough to give birth to a whole gaggle of B-plus creatures. It was all just too weird for this country. Kaijin and his team had tried to figure out what to do about this for a while, it seemed.

"So if we use this automatic magic generator, we can create anti-magic barriers?"

"We sure can," Vester confidently stated. "And that's not the only thing!"

They were both grinning ear to ear now. I could hardly believe these two used to be at each other's throats. But anyway.

"What other use is there? I thought the barriers were the point."

"Heh-heh-heh... Get this, pal! This generator includes a mechanism that collects and gathers magicules from the atmosphere. We can use this to lower the density of magicules in the air!"

Whoa! Really? I had to restrain myself from shouting with glee. *That's exactly the solution we were looking for!*

"It definitely is, Sir Rimuru," Vester said. "But it's not without its drawbacks. It requires a certain magicule density to work; otherwise, it is too inefficient."

"Not that we have to worry about *that* around this town, huh, pal?"

I nodded my agreement. It wasn't a problem worth considering.

"So basically, these devices will suck magicules from the air and automatically create barriers for us?"

"They could, yes, but eventually they'll run out of local fuel and fizzle out. That's why we've set it up so you can refill their magical energy stores."

As Kaijin put it, the area around Tempest had more magicules than it knew what to do with, but the closer you got to the Western Nations, the sparser they became. It'd be a problem if the barriers disappeared without anyone noticing it, so the devices were set up to generate magic based on its previously loaded stores as well.

What was the fuel source? The crystals made from magicules collected from the air—in other words, magic crystals. Normally, these crystals would be too inefficient an energy source to use for fuel as is. Unlike the magic stones crafted with secret Free Guild technology, magic crystals were neither uniform nor stable. Converting them into magic energy would cause a good 90 percent of their magicules to dissipate into the atmosphere.

Magic stones were better, and thanks to the Great Sage, we had a fully optimized conversion spell driven by inscription magic. It didn't require any magic stones at all, as long as the potential output exceeded the energy needed for recovery. The technology we developed back before we could just buy all the magic stones we wanted was still paying off big-time today.

Now, they reported, they could generate the magic with a minimum of loss, providing the desired effects even with the 10 percent of a magic crystal normally available for use. What's more, the "wasted" 90 percent wasn't gone forever—it just went back into the air, ready to be used again. As long as the required density was there, it was virtually a perpetual motion machine.

And we could use these things in other ways. For example, how about creating a whole bunch of magic crystals, sending them to the Free Guild, and having them converted into magic stones? Then we could operate these things even more efficiently. The most important use, however, was paring down the magicule density around us. Less density meant few monsters and magic beasts to worry about; fewer great hordes of creatures stomping around. The number of unique monsters that might pose trouble for Gobta's team could potentially be reduced to near zero.

Truly, a wonderful invention. A perfect match for one of our nation's most unique quirks. I could envision a future where we couldn't live without it.

"You know," Kaijin cheerfully stated, "I think we've also found a lead in extracting the energy needed to convert them into magic stones. For that, though, we're gonna need some dedicated equipment. It's gonna be too hard with what we have now, so that's why we looked for a way to use magic crystals as is."

First, they found a way to make crystals from the magicules in the air; then they developed that tech further; and *then* they theoretically learned how to make them into magic stones. But while the stones I purchased in Englesia helped them out a lot, they led Kaijin and Vester to the conclusion that producing our own was an uphill climb. I think I remember hearing that the process required a dedicated factory filled with large-scale equipment. It was complicated, high-level work, and while they had the theory worked out, applying it was a different matter.

Well, nothing worth going crazy about. If we could use magic crystals anyway, there was no need for haste. Besides, using those crystals for fuel proved to be a lot easier than expected, they told me. All they had to do was rewrite the formula for the relevant inscription magic, and *boom*, they had a working magic circle.

"And what's more," Vester excitedly continued, "these automatic generators can cast magic besides just barriers!"

Impressively, they could handle quite a few more spells, although there were restrictions. Just place the relevant magical inscription on a magisteel disk, pop it in the device, and you could conjure up all kinds of things—a bit like a record player, except it ran on magic crystals instead of a power outlet. I remember telling them about media playback devices like that, but I had no idea they'd leverage that knowledge into something magical like this.

If they could miniaturize it down to CD-player level, maybe we could even make them portable. Or how about the opposite, creating larger models for tactical-level magic deployment? The possibilities seemed endless. For the time being, though, the generator was a rectangle a bit over three feet long on each side and half as deep. Kinda big. Heavy, too—enough that it took some serious muscle to lift. If we could keep them stocked with magic crystals, though, there wouldn't be any need to physically move it at all.

Vester's proposal was to nestle these devices within the heavy stones we used to pave the highways, setting each one to maintain a magical barrier. They could carefully measure out the life span of each one, having the daily patrol teams replace the crystals to keep the barriers going—although no replacement was needed if the local magicule density held up. As long as nothing was amiss, the devices could just be checked up on regularly and otherwise left alone.

It seemed like a pretty smart plan to me—easy to use and adaptable to a wide variety of functions. By their calculations, one generator every six-ish miles along the highway would guarantee a safe refuge across the whole area. We had patrol stations every twelve miles along the roads, so it wouldn't add much to a patrolman's daily duties.

"So what about the magic inscriptions?"

"Heh-heh-heh... Dold's already got the prototype done. We'll have Kurobe work out the manufacturing process for the generators, so at this point, pal, we're just waiting for the word go."

"My team has largely completed the education I've been giving them, so we're holding fewer classes at the moment. I have some free time to work with, and I would love to take this job on, if possible!"

Vester's eyes were burning with anticipation. Research wasn't enough for him—he wanted to see these devices humming along for himself. And so did I. It looked like they could solve our magicule problem while improving highway safety. I saw no reason not to add this to our highway planning.

"Okay, Vester. I want you to begin tomorrow!"

"Leave it to me, sir!"

He smiled, elated. Glad I could rely on him. I intended to have the high orcs left in town help with the installation. The devices were ponderously heavy to a human being, but just a bit of a lift for a monster. It'd be far more efficient that way.

I figured that adjusting the ranges of each barrier to match the path of the highway might be the biggest challenge remaining. Vester laughed that concern away, but before he could go into detail, the friendly atmosphere was shattered.

"Gwaaaaaah-ha-ha-ha! Once you complete that network, I can release as much mystical energy as my heart desires!"

"No you can't, dumbass! You'll kill half the populace if you do!!"

I couldn't help but yell at him for that. I *really* didn't need Veldora's crap right now. Vester's smile turned into an alarmed, pale frown.

"I wouldn't advise it, no," a disturbed Benimaru replied. "*We* might be able to handle it, but the rest of the city? I doubt it."

"Indeed," added Shuna, "even if we moved Sir Veldora off-site, the force of the blast would likely affect us in one way or the other."

Yeah, no duh. Even the sealed-off magicules leaking out made it impossible for most people to be near him. If he started shooting out his mystical force willy-nilly, we'd be awash in corpses.

"Aww, but...I've been holding it in for so long... It's wearing me out..."

"Deal with it," I snapped back.

"...But why doesn't holding yours in bother *you* at all, Rimuru?"

Huh? Well, why d'you think?

"Me? I just shove it all in my Stomach."

Ever since Rigurd suggested it, I had been bottling up my mystical force and pushing it into my Stomach. By this point, it was an instant transfer, preventing any of it from leaking out at all. Ascending to demon lord status boosted my magicule stores a fair bit, but it also upgraded Predator to Belzebuth, Lord of Gluttony, which vastly expanded my Stomach storage. Thanks to that, I had no desire to unleash my mystical force at all.

"You must remember," Diablo advised me, "that perfectly blocking one's mystic force is intensely difficult. Even Sir Benimaru and his family are allowing a tiny amount to leak out."

"Yes," Veldora said, nodding meekly. "You are an observant demon, Diablo. Come on! Tell Rimuru more about how hard this is for me!"

Diablo then explained how the demon races are particularly gifted in the handling of magic and mystical forces. That gave them perfect control over such powers, but even from that perspective, Diablo was giving Veldora an A for effort. With all the energy stored inside him, Diablo reasoned, keeping it under control was a Herculean act.

"Is that true, Veldora?"

"Yes! Yes, it is! I've been holding it in ever since you taught me how to, and I want to go blow it up somewhere!"

This, uh, might be kind of a big deal. He wasn't set to pop right this instant, but if we didn't take action, we might have a disaster on our hands. If he busted all of that out without warning, we'd have acres and acres of wasteland—and with all these freaky powerful monsters and creatures dying en masse as a result, that could lead to the creation of another Charybdis. Talk about your Catastrophes. Whether he meant it or not, Veldora was seen as a mortal danger to the world for pretty solid reasons.

"All right. I'll think about that, so hold it in for a while longer, okay?"

"Very well. I can manage that well enough, still. But try to be quick about it!"

Good. Still, does it always have to be like this? I solve that magicule-density problem, and an even bigger one immediately replaces it? I let out a soft sigh. You just never know what life's gonna throw at you.

∗

Soei had finished his briefing, and before long, so had my other main leaders. But just before I was ready to adjourn:

"Could I have the floor a moment, Sir Rimuru?" Geld raised his hand, looking concerned.

"What's up, Geld? If you've got something to say, go right ahead."

He didn't seem *that* troubled last night. It probably had to do with the magic-born prisoners, the source of all his recent stress. I wanted to help him if I could, but...

"I was hoping," he began, "to tell my fellow orcs about your ascension to demon lord. Would you mind if I traveled to the villages of my countrymen, practicing my Spatial Motion as I did? Things appear to be calm across the land now, so I may perhaps find other comrades interested in serving you."

Come to think of it, he's been so hard at work here in town that I don't think he's had the time to visit the high orc villages. I had been hearing about improvements he made to our food situation, but beyond that, I honestly hadn't been giving him much attention. *He deserved this*, I thought. But:

"Geld, if you find anyone willing to join us, I'd like you to send them to this town first."

"...Why is that, sir?"

"Well, I appreciate your interest in adding to your own forces, but I think it's important they complete their education here beforehand."

That was my backstory. High orcs like Geld could use Thought Communication to instantly get up to speed on work duties. That was a massive advantage to them and one of the reasons Geld was such a major contributor to our cause.

"But we could begin work at once... Between building these highways, constructing Lady Milim's castle, and everything else, you need labor that can move as quickly and fluidly as your own arms and legs..."

Which, by Geld's logic, meant the more high orcs around, the better.

"No. We have all those prisoners to work with, don't we? So you go lead them and build them up for me."

"But..."

"Geld, I know what you're thinking. Your suggestion *would* be the most efficient way, I won't deny that. But I want you to aim higher."

"Higher?"

"Yes. There's no doubting that Thought Communication is an incredibly useful thing. It cuts down on mistakes, and there's no reason to deliberately shut it off. But if we give preferential treatment only to races who can use that, what happens to the prisoners? Are we just gonna have them mopping floors and doing other menial tasks?"

"We..."

The suggestion seemed to help Geld reach the same conclusion I had. Going forward, we clearly needed more workers. That's why we had to train those prisoners now, while things weren't too rushed. That's the iron rule of business—work when you have to; train when you don't.

Plus, if I let Geld practice favoritism with his own species, that could lead to all kinds of discrimination I really didn't need around here. I was aiming for a paradise enjoyed by a diverse number of races, so there was no way I could allow that stuff. We were at a vital turning point in a number of ways.

"Also, Geld, you're definitely a talented commander. I think if I put you in charge of this diverse group of magic-born, that'll polish your skills even further."

"I...?!"

"Our construction schedule is full, certainly, but there's no need to panic. Just use the experience you've built and lead them with your own words. And..."

I took out a sheet of paper and handed it to Geld.

"This is...!"

"I want to leave this construction job to you. That's just the foundational blueprint, but I firmly believe you're up to the task. Are you up for it?"

"Sir Rimuru..."

This blueprint was for a gigantic structure, one I had been crafting here and there in my spare time. I showed it to Milim and the rest, too—Frey was impressed with how high it went, while Carillon rumbled his approval of the sheer majesty of the thing. Milim, meanwhile, simply loved it. This meant that all the guests who'd stay here would have no problem with it...although, this was an investment in the future, provided de facto free of charge to them, so I didn't want to hear any complaints anyway.

The building was inspired by what I saw in Englesia and my drive not to lose out to them. I was picturing a skyscraper at first but changed my plans after I thought something more original and suitable for this world was in order. That was what I was leaving in Geld's able arms.

Not that we'd be hands-off, of course—Geld needed some follow-up from me, lest the weight of the job crush him. My eyes turned to Kaijin; he smiled back. Smart of him to pick up on a slime's gaze. But maybe I should've held this meeting in human form; not everyone can notice that so easily in my regular shape.

"Leave it to us, pal. I'll give Geld all the backup he needs, and I'll take Mildo along, too, so you can have him handle your little city planning project, huh?"

"What about your current work?"

"Ah, that'll be no problem. Our research has settled down a bit, and we're educatin' the next generation. I think I'm safe leaving town for a while."

Good. My small concerns were being whisked away by bigger issues—ones I was far more excited to tackle. No way Geld would mess this up.

"I'm sure you'll be fine. Let me see you handle this and grow even stronger than before. I'll be happy to talk things over if you have any problems, though, so don't get too worked up about it, okay?"

"B-but…!" Geld looked frozen, his back nailed straight up. "With a job as large as this one, what if I fail at it…?"

"It's fine, it's fine! Even if you do, that's still gonna be vital experience for you. Nobody's gonna die doing this, and it's not like it'll cost any more than a typical city if it goes haywire on us, right? We can always earn it back."

He was serious-minded, he always put in a full effort, and he always took responsibility for his actions. That was why I had to say that. It'd have the opposite effect on someone lazier and less motivated than him, but it was just the advice Geld needed right now.

"Yeah! He's right! I mean, look at me! Last time—"

"Last time you did what, Gobta? Mind coming to my office later to tell me in detail?"

"Gehh! Was this whole thing a trap for me?!"

Ugh. Gobta always wants to show off like that. At least he helped Geld loosen up a little.

"Heh… Heh-heh-heh-heh. Thank you, Sir Rimuru. I suppose I was so afraid of failure that I let the little details overwhelm me. Please, allow me to take this on and live up to your expectations!"

"Good to hear. You've got the job!"

It *was* good to hear. Geld gave me a refreshed smile, his mind clear of concern.

"Why does he get all the attention?" a clearly jealous Shion asked.

"It's the right person for the right place," I replied. "You have your own work, don't you?"

"Ah yes. Cooking!"

No, you idiot!

"Mmmm… Well, we all have a few things on our plates, but in your case, I wouldn't say cooking is one of them."

I tried to be as indirect as possible. If she had one single job, I suppose it'd be protecting me and this town. I mean, she had her own good points, too. We're all good and bad at different things. No need to freak out about it.

"But look, Shion," Benimaru said, getting ready to end the conversation, "you have an almost unfair amount of strength, enough to even beat me depending on the circumstances. So when I'm gone, please keep Sir Rimuru safe and sound, all right?"

*

Our reporting was just about done. I could have wrapped things up there, but while we had the chance, I figured we'd listen to an update from Diablo about his own work.

"Very well," he said with a respectful bow as he began.

His update on worldwide trends and how they influenced us was the same as Rigurd and Soei's. He must have picked up on the same info, but a little confirmation was always nice. It'd all tie in with establishing Yohm's claim to the throne eventually.

He also told us about Yohm, the man who would be king. He had no education on how to act like a noble, much less king, so there was no way he could negotiate directly with all those high-borns. Instead, Edmaris, the former king, had joined Diablo's cause and was in the midst of providing a crash course to the guy. Sounded good to me. With Diablo watching, I doubted the former king would try any funny stuff. Depending on how things worked out, it might be pretty neat to befriend Edmaris and take advantage of him. That would probably help Yohm out as well.

So as I listened to Diablo brief the rest of the room, I made a mental note to go see this man Edmaris for myself sometime.

The new king, to no one's surprise, was lurking around behind the scenes.

"It'll be a while before he makes any moves, though, right?"

At least several months, I figured, before he could regroup his forces and take real action. But Diablo disagreed—or at least had an answer well beyond my own imagination.

"Heh-heh-heh-heh... I would like to have this done sooner

rather than later, so I am taking measures that will encourage him to hurry it up."

"Huh?" He was smiling at me again. "Do we need to prepare for something?"

"No problems there. I have let Sir Benimaru organize the forces we will deploy when the time is right."

"Yes," Benimaru casually replied, "we are all set to go there. One force that will mingle with the general public and make its presence known, and one force operating in the shadows. Both are ready for action. The selection process was quite a pain, actually. Nearly everyone volunteered for this mission."

They all seemed so informal about it, like they were figuring out what time to meet at the park for a picnic. *It's a little more important than that*, I thought...

"However," Diablo said as his smile faded, "there is a... I wouldn't call it a problem, but something that does concern me slightly. I didn't report it since it was not worth reporting at the time, but Reyhiem has yet to return."

Ohhh, right. I thought I was forgetting something. I sent a rather pointed message to Hinata, and I still hadn't received a reply.

"That's the archbishop we let travel to the Holy Church to report to them, right? Did he not make it or something?"

"No, he had reached the Englesian capital accompanied by my agents, crystal ball in hand. There is a preset transport gate there that leads directly to the Church headquarters in the Holy Empire of Lubelius, so he should have arrived safely."

The road from Farmus to Englesia was a two-week journey by wagon, hugging the coastline the whole way. Adding Lubelius to the trip would tack on another three weeks or so—but this world has magic. Between the two nations was a pair of transport gates, special magical pathways. Go through one and traverse the alternate dimension inside, and you can travel from one end to the other in an instant. Only a small handful of elites even knew about these gates, but Reyhiem, as an archbishop for a large nation, would likely be one of them. No doubt he had access, too; once he entered Englesia, he reportedly made a beeline for the capital.

He had absolutely used the gate there. The greater demon Diablo summoned to tail him said so himself. The city had a barrier over it, so a greater demon breaking in could cause a furor, so he simply watched Reyhiem go inside the gate and reported it back to Diablo.

"And he hasn't left the capital since?"

"No. We've kept the city under watch, so we should be briefed once he does emerge from it..."

...but that hadn't happened yet. Reyhiem must be stuck in the Church. I began to fear the worst.

"Did they kill him to shut him up, maybe?"

"I have not detected any such thing as of yet. My Tempter skill can seize the soul of anyone it has thrall over the moment they die."

If there was no soul to harvest, he must still be alive. I was starting to get a little scared of Tempter, but never mind that.

I imagined Reyhiem would've been safe in Lubelius's capital, what with the Temple Knights undoubtedly guarding him. But he still wasn't back. The Church's inquiry could've just been taking a while; maybe this wasn't cause for alarm yet, but it did bother me a little. But hey, if he's alive, then fine. As long as they didn't kill him and blame us for it, it's all good.

"So we still don't really know what the Western Holy Church is up to?"

"No sir. They may try to interfere with my plans, but at the moment, it is difficult to say. I will be sure to remain on high alert and deal with whatever we discover."

"Good. A little daunting, though. There's too little intelligence to read the situation very well."

If we had enough info, I could've just left it all to Raphael, besides.

"My apologies, my lord," Soei stated, looking frustrated. "Attempting to infiltrate Lubelius is, sadly, a dangerous proposition..."

"Oh, no, no, you're fine! Pushing yourself too hard never accomplishes anything!"

If we were going to sneak into the nerve center of the Holy Church, sworn enemy of monsters, Soei himself would be our only candidate. Even then, if Hinata was there, I'd be sorely anxious for him. Soka and the others wouldn't have a chance; they'd be discovered and executed in short order. I had strict orders in place not to go overboard with this kind of thing.

Still, though…

"You think we're gonna be enemies now?"

The message I recorded painted a picture of—in so many words—putting the whole ruckus from before firmly behind us. I taunted them a tiny bit, too, but hey, I needed to have a little fun, right? …Or not? Maybe that was a bad idea, but it was out of my hands now. No undo button to press.

The overall message was friendly, though, so I was pretty sure that's how they'd take it. Hinata was intelligent enough to make the right decision, I believed. If she opted to live alongside us without hostility, that'd be the most ideal thing.

For now, outside of the Octagram, the Church was the biggest threat out there. The Eastern Empire seemed kinda fishy, too, but they were unlikely to take action for now. If the Western Holy Church could do the same for us, Diablo's plans were all but accomplished already.

"That is a thorny question," Benimaru said. "Personally, I would prefer to have this dispute firmly settled, rather than leave any grudges behind."

I appreciated his feedback, but if we were defeated, it was all over, so let's keep it peaceful, okay?

Shuna gave me a thoughtful look. "You know, Sir Rimuru, we were attacked while you were fighting the Saint Hinata. These attacks were undoubtedly timed, and someone needed to plan that out in advance. Plus, Clayman himself hinted at the presence of someone behind the scenes…"

She helped me recall someone I really shouldn't be forgetting about. The big man upstairs.

"'Him,' huh?"

"Yes," said Hakuro, bitterly nodding. "And now that we know this someone exists and is trying to entrap us, we will need to consider his upcoming moves as well. Now is no time to let our guards down."

"No," Shuna said, nodding with the crowd, "no time to let anyone escape our attention."

"Yeah… And if that guy's involved, Hinata might take action, too."

But something didn't seem right to me. You know that feeling?

The suspicion you're overlooking something? And then it struck me all at once—this thing eating at me.

"...Say, what if Hinata didn't attack me on her own volition? What if she was asked by someone or ordered to?"

"How do you mean?"

"Given the timing," Shuna asked as she traced my line of thought, "isn't it clear Hinata is connected to this other person?"

That only strengthened my suspicion.

"Well, honestly, I really don't think Hinata was taking orders from someone, but what do you think? Even if she was connected to that someone, d'you think she'd take orders from him?"

"""""?!"""""

I heard a couple gasps from the audience.

That woman didn't bother listening to a word I said. Why would she listen to a request, or *especially* an order, from anyone else?

"Good point, pal," Kaijin replied. "She's captain of the Crusaders; who would she ever take orders from? The only one *she'd* ever listen to is the god Luminus herself. I mean, everybody knows that not even the Church leader can corral her; am I right?"

If Hinata answered to nothing but divinity, that put her at the top of the Church ladder. That eliminated the "operating on orders" idea.

"Yeah, you see? She sure didn't listen to *me* at all. I really can't imagine her taking orders."

Which meant, if you looked at it the other way, if we could convince Hinata fighting was a bad idea, we didn't have to clash with the Church at all.

"Orders from no one, huh?" mused Benimaru.

"So," added Shuna, "the attack timing was just a coincidence?"

"Or something the Church took very keen advantage of," Diablo muttered—a very demon-like theory, but it made sense. I couldn't imagine Hinata being taken advantage of, but it was still a possibility.

"Perhaps Diablo is right, and someone was inspiring Hinata to do what she did. The mystery mastermind may be involved, too. But..."

"But you doubt said mastermind was in a position to order her around?"

"Exactly," I said, nodding at Diablo.

Benimaru closed his eyes, considering my suggestion. "So this mastermind drove Farmus to action, manipulated Clayman, and tried to destroy our nation. But he didn't have that kind of free control over Hinata, then...?"

"Does that mean, Sir Rimuru, you don't expect any moves from the Western Holy Church at this time?"

"That's the thing, Diablo..."

I couldn't answer his question.

From her point of view, it should've been clear to Hinata that we, and the Church, should avoid being enemies. I clearly stated that in my message to her—I didn't want to oppose them at all, and since we had a disaster-class threat in me and a catastrophe-class one in Veldora, Hinata couldn't be stupid enough to take on Tempest. Just look at the stakes; she would accomplish nothing. Even if she won, all she'd earn from it was more fame, and that wouldn't nearly make up for the massive losses the Church would face. It just wasn't sane to wage war if you had nothing to gain from it. Hinata didn't like listening to people, but she had to see that, at least.

But I still had my concerns. There was this certain annoying dragon thing next to me mumbling "Luminus... This god's name was Luminus? I feel like I've heard that before" and so on, which kept interrupting my train of thought, but I still had my concerns.

"Hinata told me that we were a 'bother' to her. That's because the teachings of the Holy Church—of Luminism—dictate that life alongside monsters is impossible. But that might not be the whole story..."

Why did Hinata call us a bother? Because Luminism refused to acknowledge us. But if that was the only reason, it just didn't seem rational of her—or to put it another way, it wasn't like Hinata at all. There had to be something else. And while this is the exact opposite of what I just said, what if there *was* some mastermind behind it all? Someone besides Hinata, who also sees us as a bother to their plans? What would that someone want?

Report. There is an increased possibility that multiple motives are at place. All these events are interconnected. However, it is estimated that they are not all occurring by the will of a single entity.

*　　*　　*

Um, meaning...?

Understood. Considering the nations, people, factions, and other factors involved, several goals can be categorized. These goals may seem to match one another at first glance, but several contradictions are present as well. It would be unnatural to unify everything under the banner of a single mastermind.

So it's not just *one* mastermind. That's the core of it, and hearing it that way, it made sense.

Clayman was being controlled by another part of the cabal, then? Ah yes. That did make sense, if you thought about it. They simply worked together for a common goal; Clayman wasn't following any specific orders or anything. Maybe they were just giving each other little suggestions or shoves in the right direction. In fact, Hinata might not have been involved with him at all.

It *did* seem more natural to assume more than one player was running around. Plus, if these factions changed, some players may no longer want to put up a fight. That's how international politics worked; it wasn't something that operated on passing emotions.

So...

To Clayman, we were nothing but a bother—but at the same time, he tried to take advantage of us. He would've loved it if Hinata and I knocked each other out.

To Farmus, I, as overseer of Tempest, was a bother. They didn't want to destroy us; they wanted us to fall under their rule. They hoped Hinata would take me out and would've loved it if she had.

So where does Hinata's heart lie? In terms of being a Luminism adherent, she wasn't about to ignore a monster nation.

These were the three frames of mind that drove the whole situation—and in the end, I fled from Hinata, Farmus retreated, and Clayman died. Which brings us to now.

The situation that attracted these masterminds in the first place had changed. Clayman was gone, and the "person" behind him must've been busy reconstructing what little fighting force he had left.

Would this guy still want to directly fight me?

*   *   *

Understood. The possibility of taking such action is likely low. If the mastermind's powers exceeded Clayman's, he would have become involved well ahead of when he did. Even if he was preserving his own powers this entire time, involvement would mean little by now, after such a grave strategic defeat.

So there's no reason to come after me. Not like this guy in the shadows would decide to go reveal himself now, long after the fact. Whether he wanted to make a comeback or not, he knew a frontal assault on me definitely wasn't the way to do it.

What about the other factions?

King Edmaris was off the throne, his ambitions crushed. The new king was doing…something, and there were those among the administration who certainly wished us harm. We were a bother to them, no doubt, and there was a good chance they hadn't given up on taking us out of the picture. But Diablo was watching them. If they were trying to become a new mastermind, they were sure taking their time with it. I doubted they were a threat, although you couldn't declare them down for the count. Maybe someone among them was hiding a darker, more sinister aspect. This is why dealing with human beings is such a pain sometimes.

The Western Holy Church was being completely opaque. Judging by Reyhiem's missing-in-action status, things must've been pretty chaotic in there. Was Hinata struggling to cope with this, too? If she didn't have a clear and present reason to oppose us, there wasn't much reason to take action. But what if she *does* take action? It'd mean something was forcing her hand.

Report. It must not be forgotten that there is a high possibility of multiple people working in the background.

Yeah. Good point. And if there were, whether Hinata wanted it or not, things could keep on moving forward. Guess optimism right now wasn't such a good idea.

"Perhaps, because there are multiple interests at stake here, we should work on the assumption that it is not solely Hinata's decision to make?"

Diablo must've arrived at largely the same conclusion I had.

"Well said, Diablo. I was just about to say that myself."

It was Raphael who saved my ass, of course, but no need to reveal *that* much. Maybe Diablo's a hell of a lot smarter than I thought? I was using Mind Accelerate to rev up my brain a million times ahead of normal, and Diablo had arrived at the same conclusion at roughly the same time. Without Raphael, I'd be eating his dust.

"Heh-heh-heh-heh... In that case, we had best keep a close eye on the Western Holy Church's meddling this time, as well."

He pretty much was already, I knew, so maybe the warning I was about to make didn't really matter. Still, the rest of my team deserved to hear it.

"We might just be making a big mistake, though."

"How so?" Benimaru asked. The rest of my cabinet was watching me closely, too. I definitely needed us all on the same page here.

"Like Diablo just said, there might be more than one 'man upstairs.' Chances are that the current status quo is the result of multiple interests working on the same playing field. This time, too, different players are after different goals, so we shouldn't assume our opposition is all gonna act the same way, you know?"

My team nodded their approval. If that explanation was enough to get my point across, *they're* pretty damn quick on the uptake, too. Except for Gobta, given how he was napping at the moment. That was almost a relief to see. He's still getting punished later, though.

"And you think these multiple interests are linked with the one Clayman spoke of?"

"I don't know, Benimaru. But we can't decide on anything yet. Working on unfounded assumptions when there's not enough data is dangerous, I think."

I shrugged. Being in my slime state, it just looked like a few ripples pulsing across my body.

"That'd make sense, though," Kaijin added, convinced. "Like, if Hinata was moving based on obligations, not necessarily orders."

"Heh-heh-heh-heh... In that case, I will investigate further. It was the merchants who provided Edmaris and his ministers with their information, but thinking about it, that should have raised my suspicions."

That struck a chord.

"Hang on. The merchants...?"

"Is something bothering you, Sir Rimuru?"

"Well, I mean, Farmus invaded us to boost their coffers. War has a way of moving money around, and you always have people trying to profit off it. Maybe some of the merchants are working behind the scenes to get a piece of that action?"

"I see..."

That was another point we'd overlooked. Our enemies might not be vast nations with huge armies at their control. Ultimately, both now and in the distant past, it was greed that led to animosity between peoples. And as long as money could be exchanged for power, the merchants needed to be monitored as well.

I leaped off my seat, taking human form and surveying the audience. Then I began to hand out orders.

"Shuna, examine the account books we recovered from Clayman's castle and see which merchants were frequent visitors."

"Yes, my lord."

"Diablo, pin down some of Farmus's civil servants and figure out which merchants they have the closest ties with."

"At once, my master."

"Benimaru, I want you to double-check your selections for the force we're sending as Yohm's reinforcements. They'll need to be prepared for anything."

"Not a problem."

"Rigurd, I'm leaving you in charge of town. We're going to hold a festival for the ages, so get the place prepared for it."

"No need to tell me twice!"

"Geld, don't worry about any of what we just talked about. Just focus on your own work. If we get in serious trouble, we'll come to you then, so just trust me for the time being, okay?"

"Of course. Nobody in this realm would ever distrust you."

"Hakuro, you assist Benimaru. Gabil, work with Rigurd. Rigur, shake down our entire security system. We need to be prepared for all the races we'll be hosting soon!"

"On it!"

"Yes sir!"

"All set!"

"And, Shion, um... You be my guard! Yeah, that!"

"Absolutely!"

Clearly, I was on a roll. I gave Ranga a pat on the head as I smiled, satisfied. *This should work; everyone can handle their own business now.*

"And what of myself?"

"Oh yeah, uh, Veldora, stay out of everyone's way."

"It shall be done!"

I doubted it. Him, I'll need to keep a personal eye on. Oh, and...

"Gobta, I know you're tired out, but come see me in my office."

"Gahh!"

Seeing my smile first thing after I shook him awake must've spooked him a little.

Ah well. Even after becoming a demon lord, these meetings never seemed to change very much.

HINATA
SAKAGUCHI

CHAPTER 3

THE SAINT'S ANTICIPATION

That Time I Got Reincarnated as a Slime

On that day, the world knew true terror once more. Veldora, the Storm Dragon, was reborn.

It had been formally revealed by the Western Holy Church, not long after the Guild announced the most recent missive from the demon lords. They had gone from ten to eight, forming an Octagram, and this alone was enough to spread chaos worldwide. It wasn't long before the kings of all nations were faced with vast, headache-inducing changes in the world situation—changes that would continue for days on end.

The Western Holy Church itself was experiencing unrest like none in recent memory.

Several days after Hinata Sakaguchi's battle with Rimuru, contact with Archbishop Reyhiem was cut off as he accompanied his kingdom's military deployment. He was required to submit regular reports, and if those reports were missing, something must have been going wrong with the Tempest invasion.

When informed of this, Hinata immediately decided that a personal visit to Tempest was in order. But just as she did, she received a divine missive to guard the cathedral instead. Veldora, the Storm Dragon, was the reason. Thus, despite expecting her Crusader forces to assemble before her shortly, she was prevented from deploying when she wanted to.

Exactly who this proved to benefit the most was a question

worthy of debate. An unprepared Hinata challenging Veldora to a duel would surely result in defeat. If she was aware of the dragon's presence, however, and could devise a lucid strategy for invading Tempest, that nation could very well be taken while Rimuru was still absent.

Tempest was Hinata's ultimate goal, not Veldora, and with the powers she had on tap, she could have made simple work of it. The ball was in her court—but only if she gave due consideration to Veldora's subsequent moves and Rimuru's own reactions to them. Either way, though, both sides managed to avoid the worst for themselves.

●

It was a city enveloped in a calming light, a holy metropolis protected by a divine barrier.

This barrier had been the subject of research over many years, adjusted and perfected until it boasted the highest level of protection in the land. It prevented all outside enemies from invading, dutifully fulfilling that obligation for the past thousand years. It was, in a way, the personification of the prayers of everyone who lived inside it. It could even block out the sun itself, automatically adjusting the light levels inside the bubble as needed—brighter by day, dimmer by night. The temperature inside was kept at a near constant all year, producing cooler summers and warmer winters, while the compartmentalized farmlands inside could produce seasonal crops at almost any time.

It was a utopia, one whose residents never had to worry about starvation. Every child received a level of compulsory education, and every adult was provided with a job. Its society had achieved complete harmony, its paradise monitored by the law and order that ruled over it.

This was Lune, the Holy City, capital of the Holy Empire of Lubelius. The day after the last Walpurgis, Hinata was walking the path toward its main cathedral. The surrounding air was pleasantly warm, tempered by the solemnity of the atmosphere. This land was a bountiful one. No one starved; there were no beggars at the side of the streets. Everyone was provided a suitable role, carrying it out to the fullest. They all awoke to the same bells and slept at the same time. The more capable of the laborers assisted the less able. And all was managed in perfect harmony, guaranteeing the happiness of every citizen that lived and breathed inside.

It was an ideal, equal society, one granted under the name of their god, and the city spread out before her eyes was the completed, physical form of that ideal.

Hinata observed the faces of the people passing by. They were all smiles, each looking calm and serene. But something concerned her.

To her, this holy land was truly the ideal city. It was her lofty goal to make the Western Nations, and eventually the whole world, a peaceful, war-free society. She craved a land where the strong no longer had to prey upon the weak to survive. Reality, however, was all too bleak. The Kingdom of Englesia and the Holy Empire of Lubelius were far, far too different from each other. It made Hinata doubt herself every time. The freedom of Englesia, the harmony of Lubelius. Two nations that seemed to contradict each other in every way, from their political systems to their core principles.

And nothing made the difference as stark as the looks on the children in each land. She could hear some of them near the educational facilities built adjacent to the cathedral. A few of them, perhaps late for class, were running down the pathway toward the building, the faster ones pulling the arms of the laggards. It was a common sight, certainly not cause for alarm. But Hinata could spot the disparity present in the picture.

What was Englesia like? She recalled what she saw there. It was morning at the time when she spotted children smiling as they wriggled past the school gate just before the morning bell. Anyone caught dawdling before it was closed would no doubt face a lecture from their instructors shortly. Here, though, those who made it in time taunted the stragglers, beaming proudly. Now what would have happened if they tried running hand in hand, like in Lubelius? The answer was clear—they'd all wind up late, facing the headmaster's wrath. She knew this was a silly yardstick to make comparisons with. The kids could avoid all this if they just woke up a few minutes earlier. But she couldn't stop thinking about it.

Where was the difference? Were the faster kids bullies? No. They picked on the slower ones, but there wasn't any air of superiority involved. Even the stragglers flashed embarrassed smiles back at them. Even with those stern headmaster lectures, they still seemed to be having fun with their lives. But what would happen over on Lubelius? All the children running to class wore the same expression. That calm, serene smile of satisfaction, just like the grown-ups. That total disinterest in competition or personal expression; all the same face.

A fully managed society can provide happiness, but it cannot provide freedom. They were all equals, carrying out their appointed tasks, the haves providing ample support to the have-nots. This land's people fully completed it.

That was Hinata's goal—creating an equal, conflict-free society. A world where no children would ever be abandoned by their parents, where everyone was allowed to live in happiness. It was an ideal, Hinata knew, not a realistic concept. But whenever she felt ready to give up on it entirely, the sheer idea of Lubelius presented itself to her. Competition bred conflict, and competition did not exist in this fully managed society. It was, in other words, Hinata's ideals put to action.

The Holy Empire of Lubelius's political system was fairly close to communism. With their "god" the head of state, they had established total equality among all members of society. This god was the Papacy, the organization that represented the Holy Emperor.

Communism's greatest weakness was the unavoidable presence of a ruling class above everyone else. The government was forced to sing the praises of equality while actually maintaining a hierarchy in practice. If corruption began to rot the upper class, it was difficult for the masses to rectify that. It would lead to unequal distribution of goods, expanding the disparity.

Divinity was Lubelius's solution to this problem. The Papacy was, by definition, a superior existence from the very beginning, so inequality among the people would theoretically not become an issue. The rulers, of course, handled matters like diplomacy with other states, but under their god, all were equal. It was a con, yes, but a con that had served as reality for the Holy Empire over a millennium of history. It had served as an ideal like none could before it, and there was a good reason for it…

...Luminus, the god ruling over all of this, was actually the demon lord Luminus Valentine.

Luminus Valentine, the absolute monarch, the flesh-and-blood demon lord, the Queen of Nightmares and ruler of night—and the only adversary Hinata had ever lost to.

✳

In front of an absolute ruler, all people held equal value. To Luminus, this concept of a fully managed society was akin to a farmer taking care of his livestock. But this was exactly why the whole utopia worked at all.

As vampires, Luminus and her kin didn't tear people apart to live off their flesh. All they needed was a little blood to ingest, using the life force inside it to sustain themselves. The higher the vampire's rank, the less of this blood they needed as they lived their eternal lives.

It was said the blood of those they preyed upon tasted sweeter the happier the donor was. Compared with other nations, people had it pretty good here. If a donor gave up a *lot* of life force at once, that would be a problem, but Luminus placed strict prohibitions on that. Thus, order was fully kept in this nation, since the lower-level vampires had no way to defy the will of Luminus far above them. Everything was equal, far more so than the Western Nations could ever manage.

It was what made Hinata believe in the equality ever present in Luminism, using justice as her credo when she joined the Church. Now she was one of its most fervent missionaries, believing its core tenets to be absolute. As a paladin, tasked with providing equal salvation to the people, she wanted justice to prevail with anything she did.

Shizue Izawa, her teacher, was far too lax by comparison, and the structure devised by Yuuki Kagurazaka, the boy from the same land as her, was too fantastic a dream to be treated at all seriously. It simply handled issues as they arose, failing to offer any real preventative measures. Seeking to improve oneself was a laudable endeavor, and she had kind words for the Free Guild's cooperative approach.

But given its reliance on fees in exchange for work, equality seemed like a lost cause with them.

Thus, Hinata left the tutelage of her teacher. Shizue told Hinata to count on her if she ever lost her way, but that wasn't going to happen. That would be depending on her too much. If she kept depending on Shizue, Hinata vaguely thought, it'd ruin her.

....

......

...

The only thing she could rely upon in this world was her own power. Thus, Hinata sought the kind of power that nobody else could ever hope for.

She had a natural fear of carrying anything precious with her, lest she lose anything else. She didn't deal with other people; power was her only desire. She had become a paladin a mere year after joining the Western Holy Church, then its corps captain less than two years later, building up what was lauded as the most powerful Crusader group in history with her own two hands.

But the higher she rose through Church ranks, the more she saw what it really was. And then she found what lay at the essence of Luminism. The Holy Emperor Lubelius was actually a vampire by the name of Louis. Even more shocking to her, this Louis was the elder twin brother of none other than the demon lord Roy Valentine. Conspiring with a demon lord to retain your power—nothing could have been more ridiculous, more contemptuous of its people.

It enraged Hinata when she learned of it—enough so that she went into the Inner Cloister alone to purge both Roy and Louis. The resulting battle left her with mortal wounds, forcing her to lie there and wait for her death. There she was, with her little sense of justice, her weak power, unable to save anyone. The "benevolence" of choosing whom to save, because you can't save them all. It seemed so comical, so pointless to her.

Heh...heh-heh-heh... So much for me. The weak are always doomed to die weak. But at least I rid the world of one obstacle...

But even so...Hinata believed she didn't make the wrong decision. She reduced the amount of evil in this world; she had nothing to be ashamed of. That, by itself, left her satisfied.

As her sight grew dim, Hinata could hear the sound of light

footsteps. She thought it was her mind playing tricks on her, but then a clear, refreshing voice serenaded her.

"I could hear this racket in my own bedchamber. What are all of you doing?"

Before her was a radiant young girl with silver hair. Her heterochromatic blue-and-red eyes shone eerily, coldly looking down on Hinata and the others on the floor. The aura floating around her was on another level, making Louis and Roy—whom she had just fought to the death and beyond—look like children.

...?!

Hinata, face-to-face with death, was overwhelmed by her presence, this beauty beyond all human comprehension. This clear, transparent presence, so far away from her.

She had the dignity of the upper class, the air of someone used to ruling over others. Good and evil seemed like trifles when presented to her. And as if to prove that:

"And you two think you can die and leave me behind?"

The waves of force emanating from her revived Roy the demon lord and Louis the emperor, despite the lethal blows Hinata knew she'd landed. It was a supernatural power, one Hinata had no knowledge of.

It's over... Everything I have done...

Despair filled her heart, as the flame of life began to flicker away—

"And you as well, human. You will not be allowed to die with that pride in your mind. What is justice? Justice is not about crushing evil. Who do you think you are, deciding whether I engage in evil or not? There is no such thing as a justice that can satisfy all forms of free will. It is arrogant to think you can do otherwise. Am I wrong?"

The words beat against Hinata's eardrums as a warm light descended upon her, saving her life. There, as her wounds seemed to magically disappear, the girl spoke.

"You have one week. If you are powerful enough to defeat my closest confidants, you can certainly overcome the Seven Days Trial. Only then will I seriously deign to engage you."

She took the trial. She completed it, Usurping the powers of those she studied under to obtain superhuman strength.

And then, wagering her life for the attempt...she lost to that young girl, Luminus Valentine, and capitulated to her.

....
......
...

But even with that defeat, the sword refused to break. Instead, it grew more flexible, stronger—and with it, Hinata was reborn, as a divine sword, the right hand of divinity, the slayer of all travails.

To Hinata, the presence of Luminus was all that mattered. Luminus was the key to an equal, fair society, and losing her would mean the destruction of all order. Maintaining a utopia required constant effort and resolve, and along those lines, Hinata was a double-edged sword. If Luminus ever became the enemy of humanity, Hinata would have to slay her with her sword. It seemed impossible, but she was resolved to do it. That was why now, even today, she continued to put herself up to the trial.

∗

Soon, Hinata had reached her destination. There, waiting for her, was Louis, the Holy Emperor who was now a kindred soul. He had unbelievable news for her.

"My brother died last night."

Last night.

Hinata had chased off an unknown intruder in the cathedral that night. She was meant to meet with someone else, but after Luminus's missive made her cancel all that, she changed her plans. That, fortunately, allowed her to end the night without dirtying the holy lands with anyone else's blood. Or so she thought.

"You're joking, right? Roy is a demon lord. He was at the Walpurgis Council."

"I speak the truth, Hinata. Roy returned earlier than Lady Luminus, and the intruder you let escape ran into him first."

"No. That intruder fled the moment he saw me. He was so fast that I wasn't able to give chase, but..."

"Indeed, perhaps you thought it was just a diversion. Lady Luminus charged you with defending the holy lands, not with killing intruders. That is the job of our Imperial Guard, as worthless as they have just proven themselves."

"The guard that I'm chief knight of. But Roy, being killed by someone on that level? Who's the worthless one now?"

She laughed boldly, right in front of the Holy Emperor—Roy's elder brother.

Luminus Valentine was the true demon lord, the twin brothers Louis and Roy her close confidants. Louis ruled the external world as its Holy Emperor, while Roy ruled behind the scenes as demon lord. Luminus, meanwhile, governed over everything as a god.

This was the world they had pursued. It was also why Luminus preferred a policy of insular government, locking herself inside the Inner Cloister and never revealing herself in public.

Roy, serving as her demon lord representative, had been more than powerful enough to sit alongside the other nine at the table. Simply being born a vampire made him the equivalent of a B, ranking-wise. His muscular strength, durability, reaction time, and everything else were several times better than what a human could muster, and his race gave him a multitude of excellent skills, including Steel Strength, Self-Regeneration, Shadow Motion, Paralysis, Charm, Coercion, Transform, and more. There were few vampires in the world, but even among the so-called high-level magic-born, they were a head above the crowd in fighting ability.

Louis and Roy were elder noblemen, both in the service of their leader Luminus since ancient times. Their powers were monumental, it went without saying, and Hinata was fully aware of that. Having fought them both once, she had no doubts. This only meant one thing: Whoever last night's intruder was, they must've been unbelievably powerful.

"...But it doesn't really matter, does it?" Hinata whispered. "As long as Lady Luminus is safe. Not that anyone need worry about her..."

Not even Hinata could fully gauge the depths of the demon lord Luminus. She was beyond all imagination, a supreme being that served as both an ideal goal to reach and a potential opponent sometime in the future. It would be impertinent for Hinata to even bother worrying about her.

Roy, meanwhile, was worth about as much as a pebble on the

street. Not to offend Louis, but it didn't really matter whether he was killed or not. He was weak, he died, and that was that. As far as Hinata was concerned, that was his own fault.

"It does matter. We let Roy exercise his violent streak as a threat to make people adhere to Luminism. With him dead, there is a chance people's faith in our creed may dwindle. The evil dragon Veldora is alive once more, and yet, the Forest of Jura still remains stable as well."

"You have a point…"

Hinata could guess why. It was that slime she let slip through her fingers. This, she had no excuse for. It was fully her mistake, and nobody was more aware of that than she was. It was her choice to let last night's intruder go, but that slime, Rimuru, she wanted eradicated from the world for good. She couldn't help but praise him.

I can hardly believe he managed to escape that place. I knew you were a careful one, Rimuru, but that was nothing I could have imagined…

"…I can't speak about the dragon, but I imagine the forest is stable because of that slime, Rimuru, I let escape."

"Mmmm. I conducted some of my own investigation, and it has been confirmed that the Kingdom of Farmus's forces have been annihilated. Counting the time back from Veldora's resurrection, it had to be the work of that Rimuru. Quite an adversary for you, wasn't he?"

"I suppose the moment I saw him, encased in that Holy Field, was the best chance I had of defeating him."

"You didn't give him some discretion, perhaps, after he claimed to be from your realm?"

"Of course not. Lady Luminus's aims are incompatible with that slime's. I know where he's coming from, and leaving him to his own devices would only wreck our plans. That's why I chose to ignore what he had to say and instead tried to destroy his town…"

"So the angels will be moving soon enough."

"They will. They're safe for now, but if they keep developing the town at that pace, they absolutely will."

"That would be distressing. We aren't ready for them yet. I'd like to ensure that our victory in the next Temma War is absolute."

"I know. We need to tear those angels limb from limb, and that's why we can't afford to speed up the timetable."

Louis nodded.

Whenever the cities of the world developed past a certain level, the angels began to attack them. Why, nobody knew, but their actions followed a set recognizable pattern. When it happened, countless numbers of innocents died—and to combat them, Hinata had expanded her forces and devised a way to knock them completely out of the picture. Her proselytizing for Luminism was also a way to help people work together, making their harmonic cooperation a palpable force to work with. That, she believed, was the best way to follow the will of Luminus, her god.

Rimuru's behavior was getting in the way of that—and now that she knew Rimuru was the cause of Shizue Izawa's death, she had personal issues with him. There was no reason at all for her to cut him any slack. With him were his monsters—intelligent, rational, and understanding of humans. It pained her a little to involve them in this, but Luminus called them her enemy, and her will was the law.

Victory in the Temma War was of utmost priority, and to earn that, Hinata wouldn't hesitate to do what must be done. She was cold, pragmatic, and above all a rationalist.

"But perhaps your failure will turn out well in the end."

"What do you mean?"

"The Western Nations will likely band together to deal with the threat in the Forest of Jura. With Roy gone, what better foe to unite the human race against?"

"...Do you think so? I doubt it'll go that easily."

But did he have a point? Maybe, Hinata thought, it was a good thing after all. A stable Forest of Jura was what they wanted, and if they sought to live alongside humanity, that was all for the better. But if Rimuru really did massacre the Farmus force, he was clearly a threat they couldn't afford to overlook.

Still...

"You know the Eastern merchants who brought me information. We were planning to meet last night as well. If it weren't for Lady Luminus's order, I wouldn't be here right now."

"Oh? Rather good timing, then."

"Almost too good, isn't it? Those merchants were trying to use me. If you think about it, maybe keeping Rimuru alive and present was the right answer, not to make excuses."

But the nail that sticks out gets hammered down. They may have survived the Farmus invasion, but the resurrected Storm Dragon was bound to attack Rimuru before long. Plus, Rimuru was calling himself a demon lord, apparently, which invited the rage of the other ten and earned him a ticket to last night's Walpurgis.

"I would imagine so. Until we are fully ready, I'd prefer to use that land as a bulwark against the East...assuming Rimuru survived the Walpurgis Council."

"Right. Do you think he'll make it through?"

"Lady Luminus will return soon. We will know by then."

"Having to tell her of Roy's death is a depressing thought."

"She'll be in a bad state, I'm sure."

"She was a lot kinder to him than I ever was..."

"Mmmm. I suppose I'm not very kind myself. My own brother is dead, but I don't feel sad about it at all."

Hinata just shrugged at Louis. They stopped talking, waiting for Luminus. Before very long, a herald arrived.

"Stand back! Lady Luminus has returned!"

In a flash, the cathedral became a hive of activity—and soon, Hinata and Louis were going to face a conversation they never expected to have.

∗

Now they were at the Inner Cloister, a sacred mountain looming in the center of the Holy Empire of Lubelius. The Holy Church headquarters was at the foot of it; proceed straight through its grounds, and you'll find the Holy Temple, which houses the cathedral that connects to the mountain's entrance. Beyond it and up the path, the Inner Cloister loomed ahead.

This was the holiest and most forbidden place in all of Lubelius, even more so than the Holy Emperor's official chambers.

Relaxing there was the demon lord Valentine—or rather, Luminus—as she recounted the previous night's events, clearly peeved.

"So that's all of it. That annoying dragon simply insists on getting in my way at every possible moment!"

Hinata's first reporting of Roy's death only added to her anger.

"Such a stupid child," she murmured in reply, betraying no emotion whatsoever as she entered the Inner Cloister, just as regal as always. She seemed coolheaded enough as she described the Walpurgis Council, but when she reached the point where Veldora revealed her true identity, her well-defined, beautiful features reddened with anger. It was overpowering to her audience as she let out all her pent-up emotion.

"And look at Roy, too! I could've revived him as long as I was within sight of him, but noooo..."

"My brother is happy, Lady Luminus. That is all that needs to be considered—"

"Silence! This sounds like I practically led Roy by the hand to his death!"

"No, my lady. It is my brother Roy's fault for failing to live up to your expectations."

"But..."

If any one factor was involved, it was bad luck. Everyone in the Cloister knew it wasn't their fault.

"I apologize," Hinata said. "I let that intruder go, and Roy..."

"So be it," replied Luminus, face tightened as she looked at her and Louis. "You merely followed my orders. I am the one who deserves the blame. But we don't have the time to mourn for him now. The dragon is revived, and we have a new demon lord in Rimuru. That is the undeniable truth, and we must decide how to handle it."

"Yes, my lady."

"I understand."

Hinata and Louis nodded. This question would decide the entire direction the Holy Empire would go in the future.

"I would like to defeat Veldora for you," Hinata offered.

"Hinata," Luminus coldly replied, "you have grown stronger, yes, much stronger than when you fought me. You are well past the Seven Days and on your way to equaling my level. But even if you can defeat the demon lord Rimuru, you will never defeat Veldora."

"She is right, Hinata. That is how fearsome a presence the dragon is. A true Catastrophe."

Louis, who was there for that dragon's previous rampages, agreed readily with Luminus.

"He is that powerful? But didn't the Hero seal him away?"

If a human did it once before, Hinata reasoned, it could always happen again. Luminus and Louis immediately brushed it off.

"Look, Hinata. That dragon is a form of natural energy in itself. Perhaps you could use magic to quell a raging gale, yes, but that dragon has its own free will. It cannot be cut with a sword or affected by magic. When he flies into a rage, the shock waves will ravage the earth, far more so than any of our puny magic."

The thought seemed to genuinely dismay Luminus. Louis nodded in agreement, his face pale as if he had just recalled an ugly memory.

"It was truly a nightmare," he said. "Ah, that ever so beautiful Nightrose Castle, turned into an unrecognizable pile of ashes..."

"Don't remind me of it, Louis. That castle was the culmination of vampire knowledge and science, and now it exists only in our memories. There is no use in craving what we cannot have."

"Quite true."

The exchange taught Hinata just how dangerous this Veldora was. *But...if it comes to it*, she quietly swore to herself, *I will kill him*.

Then she realized something else. The whole reason the Inner Cloister was atop this holy mountain. It was to prepare for a potential Veldora attack, wasn't it? So she could constantly observe the skies and stop him before he arrives. Nightgarden, the main city in the Holy Empire, was located entirely underground for that reason as well—to prevent dragon invasions, to keep the casualties to a minimum in a fight. That was how wary Luminus was of this Storm Dragon.

"Hinata, please restrain yourself. I do not wish to lose you, too."

And if Luminus put it that strongly to her, she had no option but to nod back.

Now, her mishandling of that encounter with Rimuru was sticking in her throat like a sewing needle. Labeling him a monster and ignoring his attempts at conversation were both mistakes. Not in terms of what her faith taught her, or so she wanted to think, but still, her actions had led directly to this current situation. If that was what the Eastern merchants had wanted, then Hinata had fallen for it hook, line, and sinker.

How distasteful. Giving me that information when they knew exactly how I would react. Or perhaps they have an informant of their own?

It was hard for her to believe, but Hinata could imagine someone in the Church working with those merchants. They may know all about their preparations for the angels by now—and maybe that was why they pointed her in Rimuru's direction, to take him out for them. A mole in the Church had to be something for consideration—but for now, such a thought had to be left to simmer. There were other problems to deal with.

"Very well. But...what will we do about Rimuru now, as demon lord?"

"We have no choice but to let him be. The Church has yet to declare him a divine enemy yet, fortunately."

"No, but..."

"Is there a problem?"

"...There is. I fear the city and highways the monsters are building could cause the angels to invade more quickly."

"Ah yes, there was that. Having those little insects flitting around is annoying enough, although making the demon lord Rimuru and the Storm Dragon Veldora our enemies would be much worse. But if they attract more attention for us, they'll become the angels' main target, I imagine. Either way, not much point thinking about it now."

To Luminus, the angels were all but worthless. Hinata, understanding that, voiced her agreement.

Beyond that, there was another problem:

"There is also the fact that their town... It turns the concept of monsters being humanity's common enemy, one of Luminism's core tenets, on its head."

The question made Luminus visibly scowl. She mulled it over a moment. This was no longer an easily quashed threat, but if they let their religious tenets be defanged like this, they would lose their validity—and their appeal to the masses. The faith they had spent the last thousand years building would be lost, and that could not be allowed to pass.

"Perhaps," Louis suggested, "he could serve as a useful accomplice for us? As an evil demon lord?"

It was a thought he had shared with Hinata earlier—let Rimuru serve as a propaganda heel, much like how Roy acted as demon lord. But as Hinata expected, Luminus was less than enthusiastic.

"That could not happen. Rimuru, this new demon lord... He just wants to have fun living in his own little nation. That's all. He's going right up to our faces and declaring that he'll give the humans all the protection they want. Because he *needs* their help. He said it himself. *'Anyone who gets in the way of that, whether a person or a demon lord or the Holy Church, is my enemy.'*"

She let out a forlorn sigh.

"If only he wasn't mingling with the human race all the time, Louis, that would be such a good idea," she said with frustration.

And Hinata realized, once and for all, that Rimuru wasn't lying. He really *was* a transfer from another world. But it was too late to act on that.

She was fully aware that she had acted on incorrect assumptions, fueled by her lack of interest in listening to others. It was a bad habit, and it just blew up in her face big-time. At least nobody seemed to know that the god Luminus was the same person as the demon lord Valentine yet. If worse came to worst, only her own life would be forfeit.

"For now, then, all we can do is sit and watch."

"You're right. Simply hold ourselves as we always do. No brash moves. The more excuses we make, the more we may entangle ourselves. Our only responsibility is giving our faithful across the world the truth—Veldora, the Storm Dragon, is back."

"And what about Rimuru?"

As Hinata brooded, Luminus and Louis were already deciding on their future policies.

"Yes... Well, Rimuru seems the sort of leader open to political exchange. We could deceive the Western Nations easily enough. Are you fine with that, Hinata?"

It was a question, but Luminus meant it as predecided policy.

"...I am."

"Would he bear a grudge against you?"

"...A little. I did try to kill him."

"Ah yes, you did. But Rimuru is not stupid enough to hold that against us to the point of becoming enemies."

Such was the will of Luminus—a leader who didn't even mind if Rimuru knew her true colors. But Hinata was unconvinced.

"...I will keep that in mind," Hinata said, attempting to hide her real thoughts as she left.

✳

A little over a month passed. Hinata spent it tirelessly at work. Her paladins were busy building a line of defense against Veldora, while the Imperial Guard was out gathering intelligence for her. Those merchants from the East, once a vital part of this spy network, could no longer be trusted, and so she decided to rely only on info she could personally gather herself.

Now it was time for the empire's monthly conference between both major groups of the Papacy—the Crusaders, the paladins under Hinata's direct control, and the Master Rooks, the Imperial Guard forces serving the Holy Emperor. They were both the pride of Lubelius, with Hinata Sakaguchi standing at the very peak.

She served as the conference speaker—Hinata, chief knight of the Master Rooks and captain of the Crusaders, not to mention the strongest knight in the nation. A high seat was prepared for her; all the other attendees' chairs were situated in a semicircle around her.

To her right were six people representing the Crusaders. First was Vice Captain Renard Jester, known as the Noble of Light, a paladin with a soft, plaintive expression. Next to him was Arnaud Bauman of Air, the man lauded as second strongest only to Hinata. He stood head and shoulders above the rest of the troop leaders, serving as a sort of assault-team specialist for the Crusaders.

Following Arnaud were four other commanding officers: Bacchus of Earth, a large brooding man gifted at smashing his magic-infused Holy Mace into his foes; Litus of Water, a beautiful healer and elementalist who employed the holy spirit Undine on the battlefield; Garde of Fire, a tall knight and conjurer who wielded his flaming Red Spear; and Fritz of Wind, a magical fighter as talented in wind magic as with his twin swords. He was a tactical trickster, a rarity among the high-minded Crusaders he served alongside. Fritz never wore his uniform up to the prescribed code of perfection, but no one admired and respected Hinata as much as he.

Each of these commanders led a team of twenty or so paladins, while Arnaud served as their overall leader. The five seated here were the best among the hundred and ten or so paladins, and there was no doubting their talents.

Contrasting with them, on Hinata's left side, were the Master Rooks, a much more ragtag assemblage in a motley variety of uniforms and armor. They numbered a mere thirty-three but still formed their own division, for each one was a powerhouse in battle—rooks, as the Holy Emperor proudly called them. They all ranked at least an A on the charts, and a few of them were even champion level, a Calamity on the threat scale.

A few were particularly notable. There was "Blue Sky" Saare, who looked like an innocent boy but was older than anyone else in the room. He was the chief knight of the Imperial Guard before Hinata took the role.

Then there was "Giant Boulder" Grigori, Saare's right-hand man, whose Impervious skill granted him astonishing physical resilience. His muscles were his weapon, and they were harder than most types of metal, making him an impregnable fortress of a man.

Last but not least was "Raging Sea" Glenda, who was newer to the fold than Hinata but had made a serious name for herself in recent years. Notable for her spiky red hair, she was a wild woman, an ex-mercenary whose fighting skills were still veiled in mystery. Only Rama, the person who had ceded his post to Glenda after she defeated him, knew about her full strengths. This trio was known as the Three Battlesages, and they sat together opposite the six paladins.

The nine were all literal superhumans, far beyond the framework one would think the human body could provide. They all were certified Saints, a sort of complement to a demon lord, and with Hinata, they were collectively known simply as the Ten Great Saints.

Whenever a person engaged in grueling training in one subject or another, they would occasionally evolve into a higher form of existence upon completing such a trial. Accomplishing this made them Enlightened, greatly extending their life span and transforming their physical bodies into something like a half-spiritual lifeform. They were released from flesh and blood, in other words, and thus the amount of energy Enlightened individuals could work with was enormous. Their brute and magical strength was powered up to levels beyond compare, letting them be the equivalent of potential demon lords.

They were the guardians of humanity, the servants of divinity who evolved the *correct* way—even if this was only by the standards of certain people.

They all sat there quietly, awaiting Hinata's arrival. Several paladins were stationed behind each commanding officer, the rest of the two divisions remaining on their feet in their assorted gear.

Soon, the heavy door creaked open.

"Sorry to keep you. Let us begin."

With that, the meeting commenced.

✳

Behind Hinata, shaded by some bamboo blinds, the Holy Emperor Louis was taking in the joint conference at his seat. But just as proceedings were set to begin, Saare immediately threw them into disorder.

"Whoa, whoa, where do you get off being late? Not only did you fail to keep Veldora from waking up, you even let a new demon lord be born. And you're the fool representing us? If this is a joke, I'm not laughing."

Even though Hinata was the acknowledged leader, not all her soldiers were particularly enthusiastic about the orders they carried out. Saare, having lost his position as their leader, was the head of the anti-Hinata faction.

Over the past month, both divisions had been sent off worldwide by Hinata on a wealth of missions, bringing back assorted intelligence and confirming that the rash of recent cataclysmic events were all connected. The ascension of Rimuru, the Storm Dragon's revival, the Walpurgis Council, and the recent turbulence in the Kingdom of Farmus—all these happenings had their origin in Hinata reaching out to Rimuru, and Saare wasn't shy about implying as much.

"You are being rude, Sir Saare," a bemused Renard coldly stated.

Arnaud nodded to his fellow paladin. "He's right, boy. If you have an issue with our captain, I'd be happy to work it out with you."

"Oh," Grigori fired back from his seat next to Saare, "you fancy-pants knights wanna start a fight with us? Awfully pretentious of you, considering you only act that way around opponents polite enough to lose on purpose!"

"What?"

"You seem interested in a quick death."

The meeting had grown almost immediately intense. Hinata took the opportunity to cool it down.

"Enough foolishness. Now's not the time for allies to be squabbling with each other. Saare, if you'd like to take my place up here, you're welcome to my seat anytime. I'll need to test you out first, though, keep in mind."

That was enough to bring silence back to the room. Her words went beyond mere frustration and well into the realm of murderous intent—if they kept carrying on, she was fully prepared to start slashing away. The audience was smart enough to pick up on that. It was rare for her to show that much emotion, forcing even Saare to admit that any more prodding would be dangerous.

Instead, he just glared at her in frustration. "Pfft! I'll keep that in mind."

He had already lost to her once—a battle he never should have botched. In his eyes, Hinata was the clear underdog, but the results proved the opposite. The memory of that day kept him from making any unwise moves. Until she could probe and reveal the secrets of Hinata's strength, he knew victory would never be his. So he did her bidding for now, uninterested in waging a war he couldn't win.

With Saare calmed down, the joint mission finally began.

"Reporting," said Litus, freshly returned from field work around the Forest of Jura. "The forest was a perfect picture of peace. Despite Veldora's resurrection, I spotted groups of merchants entering and exiting the area."

The caravans from Blumund were streaming into the Tempest capital of Rimuru on a near-constant basis. The nation's trademark healing potions were hot sellers, but merchants were also standing in line for rare goods like silk fabric and weapons made from monster-derived components.

"How is that working? Are they engaging in trade with the demon lord?"

"We should think about Veldora first. The records say he is

extremely belligerent, causing a swath of destruction wherever he goes, but I haven't seen any sign of that yet."

Hinata raised a hand to wave the questions off. "Let us hear the report to the end."

"Very well. I spoke with the merchants, and they said the kingdom of Blumund had declared full and open relations with Tempest. This includes a security guarantee, and Blumund's citizens are allowed to come and go as they please. The highway connecting them to Tempest was also kept in neat and clean order; even the animal droppings are briskly disposed of. There was no sign of monsters nearby, and overall, I believe this security agreement is legitimate and active."

"Did you travel down this highway?"

"Yes. I wanted to see it for myself, so I disguised myself as a traveler. There are peacekeeping sentry posts at regular intervals along the road. When I reached town, I found it to be far more advanced than I expected. The concentration of magicules in the air was understandably higher than normal, but it was still below levels that would affect average people. It gave me the impression that Rimuru, true to his word, really does seek amicable relations with humankind."

"...I see. And what about Veldora?"

"Well, yes, about that..."

"What is it?"

"...I was unable to confirm his presence. Entry into the Sealed Cave was forbidden, and I failed to find any other spots the dragon might be lurking in."

"Hmm."

Hinata gave a placid nod to Litus as she finished her report.

"If we can't confirm Veldora's existence," Fritz asked, "could the news of his revival be a mistake—?"

Hinata shot him a look to silence him. "Luminus's divine missives are never wrong. At least we are surer of Rimuru's activity now. Let us move on."

She kept the meeting going, having each attendee report on what they saw and heard, ensuring everyone had all available information at hand before they began to debate.

"So things were tranquil from start to finish during my time in

Englesia. If their rivals at Farmus were to fall, I believe they would take the opportunity to expand upon their current power."

The briefings continued. Master Rooks members had free rein to visit the Western Nations, as well the right to give orders to the Temple Knights stationed within their borders. They outranked even the local Temple captains, after all, and while they customarily acted only on orders from Lubelius (for the sake of maintaining a simple chain of command), the Master Rooks could command them directly in emergency cases. This allowed them to operate practically above the law in the west, obtaining even some classified information with ease.

This was one difference between them and the paladins. The latter enjoyed similar unfettered travel access to foreign countries, but they were barred from giving orders to the Temple Knights. The organizations were two different entities, although some Temple Knights later moved on to become paladins. It was up to Hinata to utilize the pluses and minuses of both groups, deploying them where they would help the most.

Saare's turn came at the very end.

"Listening to all these reports," he said, "I think I'm starting to see what Hinata is trying to find out. My turn's next, and I'm guessing my report's supposed to be the clincher, huh?"

"That's right. I gave that job to you because it's the most important one. I'd appreciate it if you got on with it."

"Ah-ha. Well, the current news from Farmus… King Edmaris has abdicated the throne, and on the surface, it appears that the transfer of power has taken place peacefully. But Edward, the new king, is busy assembling an army of talented mercenaries, and in response, the nobility is starting to get frantic, too. It looked to me like the signs of a looming civil war."

Despite reports of Rimuru's ascension being all over the news in the Western Nations, Blumund's trade with Tempest was giving that whole nation a shot in the arm. Meanwhile, things couldn't be more chaotic in Farmus. The nobles were working in a hundred different directions, many of them trying to shore up their military might in a hurry. Some had even made inroads with the Western Holy Church and the elders that led the Council. It wouldn't be long before the swords came out. The impact on the people was already enormous—prices rising, distribution falling behind. Losing twenty thousand troops had even led to a government-mandated conscription. Amateur soldiers wouldn't be much help in battle, but Farmus was so cornered that they had no other choice.

It all pointed in the same direction: civil war. The surrounding small kingdoms had no consensus on how to respond to this, but all of them were on high alert against Farmus, smelling the tension in the air and fortifying their borders to ensure they didn't get involved. They all expected the fateful day to come before long.

"...That alone, of course, isn't enough information to make a conclusion on whether the demon lord Rimuru is involved with this."

"True. So?"

"So I went down the list of everyone King Edward made contact with. Important Council leaders; Free Guild management; some merchants from the East; even our own soldiers. He's been busy."

"Is he trying to shore up his military?"

"Bingo. That's exactly it, Hinata."

"Well, it's settled, then. This new king has no interest in paying war reparations of any kind. No demon lord would let that slap in the face go unchallenged, and I doubt Rimuru is foolish enough not to expect that from him."

"Hmm. So do you think this is all part of our new demon lord's plans?"

"Yeah." Hinata nodded.

It's almost funny how all the pieces are falling into place. Based on what we can infer from this, it all seems to be gearing toward some kind of predestined conclusion... Someone's definitely pulling the strings from the sidelines.

The more she heard, the more convinced she became. Who was it? There could be just one answer—Clayman, that swindler who skulked around the Western Nations for years, was gone, and the only one who could even begin to imitate him was Rimuru, this new member of the cast.

I don't like this. You can't let your guard down around him. He's intelligent enough to lay out these thoroughly prepared strategies. Maybe he really was *Japanese once...*

Looking back, as she calmly reevaluated Rimuru, this was all caused by her believing those Eastern merchants in the first place. They had built a relationship of trust over several years, and she completely fell for the line she was given. It was a fatal mistake, and she regretted it—and the worst part was that *most* of the intelligence the merchants gave her was accurate. Only when the topic turned to Rimuru did the truth start to bend a bit. These little lies that were impossible to independently confirm, and Hinata had let them trick her. If she had believed Rimuru, back when the two of them were at the same location, maybe things would have developed differently. But, she reasoned, she couldn't dwell on the past.

Then she noticed something about Saare's report that interested her.

"Saare, you said Edward made contact with merchants as well? What did they tell him?"

"Mm? Why do you care about the merchants? The demon lord painted a picture for us to fall for, and that's that, right? I think what we need to talk about is our future direction. What steps should we be taking right now?"

"We do need that, but I still want to know. Tell me."

"Pfft. I thought money was the only thing those merchants ever talked about."

"Not so. They just have an instinctive habit of turning the conversation toward whatever will make them money. One of them got me, too, so you all need to watch yourselves. So what did you learn from them?"

"Huh. That's pretty impressive, if they managed to use a woman as calculating as yourself. Hmm... I can't really think of anything in particular they said. Oh, hang on... There's a commercial zone in the area you covered, right, Glenda? Merchants from the East and West intermingle in there. Did you hear anything interesting?"

Saare may not have liked Hinata much, but he was still loyal to his mission. He knew and acknowledged her talents—the leadership that helped her craft the Crusaders out of a ragtag bunch of knights. She was merciless against the monsters; she put everything on the line to keep people safe. Somewhere in his heart, he appreciated that. That was why he followed all of Hinata's orders to the letter, never hiding anything he learned from her. He may have had a few ideas on how to seize his position back from her, but he had no intention of dragging her down. He believed in the meritocracy, and for better or worse, he was earnest in everything he did. Hinata knew that as well.

Glenda, meanwhile…

"Well, as far as I know, there wasn't anything suspicious going on."

…had no problems telling barefaced lies. As a mercenary, she was well versed in navigating the underworld, experiencing untold amounts of mortal danger. Something about the tension in the air smelled like good money to her. Faith was one thing; making a profit was another. That was how Glenda worked, and while people saw her as a devout Luminist, that wasn't the whole truth. What Glenda really wanted was the power that Luminism had across the world. Sometimes it was money, sometimes intelligence, sometimes war power; but Glenda needed it all. Her current position gave her open access, and she never, ever wanted to lose it.

This was why she was hiding things from Hinata, including a meeting with merchants from the East in the very commercial zone Saare mentioned. She had also made secret inroads with one of the Council elders. She paid them money, and in exchange, they would spread false rumors around for her. Not now, but when the time was right for her.

For the time being, she couldn't afford to have Hinata questioning her motives. Hinata was cold, unforgiving, and merciless to her enemies. She never left herself open to attack at any moment. But at the same time, she was open-minded, almost soft on her allies—or, to be more exact, Luminists. To her, fellow followers in her chosen faith were like family. That was extensively clear to Glenda. That softness let Hinata forgive Saare's back talk; that softness made her fail to notice the people trying to betray her. And soon, Glenda thought, that softness was going to cost her the position she had worked so hard to achieve.

"If you're that interested, though, I could give it a more thorough look through, Captain."

"Will you? Thanks. Just don't let the merchants fool you, all right? Don't let your guard down."

"Sure thing. I got a few connections, so I should be able to get some details."

Glenda had the bad habit of making promises to Hinata without giving them much real thought. She had no idea her ready agreement let Hinata read fairly deeply into her mind.

Taking a moment to carefully observe Glenda, Hinata sighed to herself.

She must really think I'm that stupid. Perhaps she's under the mistaken impression that I'm soft on my people?

If that was true, she thought, then it really was a pity.

Glenda had one thing wrong—Hinata wasn't one to think of her companions as *that* important. She considered them pawns to play for the sake of Luminus, and *that* was why she treated them so preciously. They all belonged to Luminus, and she wasn't allowed to waste them.

The Crusaders she had raised to serve as her arms and legs had absolute faith in her; they were basically Hinata's personal militia, and she trusted in that faith. The knights of the Imperial Guard, on the other hand, often engaged in intolerably selfish activity. She let it slide only because they, too, had faith in Luminus.

Saare was the epitome of that, mouthing off at Hinata and trying to rebel any way he could. But both she and Saare knew this was just a front. He was a whiner, but he always followed orders—which, in a way, made him a breeze to handle. Plus the fact that Saare didn't know who Luminus was. Not just him, either. Nobody besides Hinata was aware that the god Luminus was an actual person.

...I almost feel bad for them. They have no idea, just as I didn't...

Glenda had real ambitions. She had looks, talent, and an abundance of confidence. *She must really believe she has what it takes to topple me,* Hinata thought. She might even be trying to curry favor with Louis, the Holy Emperor, for the cause. She didn't know he was a vampire, so it was only natural that she'd try buttering him up for the sake of pushing Hinata away.

Well, she's free to do what she wants...but...

But if she was betraying the cause, that was another matter.

Hinata never voiced a word of complaint about what the divisions she oversaw did—as long as they never crossed her or Luminus. But with a suspected traitor in their midst, Glenda's behavior was turning problematic. Hinata didn't intend to hold a purge right this moment—for all she knew, someone might be taking advantage of her—but she needed to be on her guard.

...I'm starting to see a breakdown in discipline. Maybe it's time to teach them a lesson and set them back in line.

The thought depressed Hinata. But there were more urgent issues. She mentally switched gears and spoke.

"All right. Everyone has given their reports. I trust that everyone understands the current situation now."

"Yes," his assistant Renard said. "The resurrection of the Storm Dragon has had less of an impact than expected, the only casualties so far being the deployed Farmus military. However, since this is likely a cover story spread by Rimuru, the real number could be zero."

"If that's how it is," added Saare, "I want to hear from Archbishop Reyhiem, who survived it. We know Veldora's back, and I'm intensely curious about what happened on the battlefield."

"I thought so, too. I've already called for him. He should be here soon..."

Hinata had already contacted Cardinal Nicolaus, directing him to bring Reyhiem to her. He was there for the defeat and probably saw Rimuru with his own eyes. Besides, given the several days' worth of apparent time between the advent of Veldora and Farmus's defeat, the rumors going around the neighboring states about Veldora destroying all those forces were pretty unlikely. As a survivor, Reyhiem's testimony should be extremely useful. He was supposed to arrive this morning but was apparently behind schedule.

"I look forward to it. I can't wait to hear what he has to say."

"Maybe he knows something about Veldora, too."

"There were rumors of the demon lord Rimuru negotiating with Veldora and calming his rage," Arnaud added, "but I'm not sure what to make of that one, either. He's revived, yes, and he's been lying low so far, yes. With that in mind, it seems rather plausible."

Everyone nodded at this. Silently, they had all concluded that the Storm Dragon and the demon lord were involved with each other. In that case, Hinata saw no reason to hide what Luminus already told her.

"...Yes. That much is true. I can say to you now that among the missives I received from our lord Luminus, there was one about how Rimuru is controlling the Storm Dragon. As a result," she said, "we must not lay hands on the demon lord Rimuru at the moment. Please bear that in mind."

"Y-you mean...?"

Hinata stood up. "I'll be blunt," she said in her most authoritative voice. "In this instance, we must remain undercover. None of our dealings with this demon lord must come out to the public."

This was, in essence, an order for everyone to keep their hands off Rimuru. It surprised them all.

"What?! You want us to simply ignore all the theatrics he's pulling over in Farmus?!"

"Demon lords are untouchable as a rule, yes, but only in the public eye, if you recall. They're no match for any of the Ten Great Saints!"

Saare had a point. Humanity wasn't totally helpless against the S-class threat of the demon lords. They had built up enough force to fight back with, if necessary, and those were the Enlightened classes, the Ten Great Saints being among them. Arnaud, Renard, and Grigori could each defeat a Special A-ranked foe, Hinata thought, and even among the Ten Great Saints, Saare was outclassed only by Hinata in force. Against a demon lord, Saare wouldn't be that much of an underdog. You almost never saw storybook-style one-on-one duels in real life anyway, but if it turned out that way, she figured it'd be a close battle. If it was Clayman, that Western Nations sneak, the odds were even in Saare's favor.

However, that only applied to the would-be demon lords, those strong enough for the role but not yet ascendant. Against a *real* demon lord, none of the Ten Great Saints had a chance in the end. To Hinata, who knew Luminus intimately, that much was obvious.

And Rimuru, too...

Farmus, and other nations its size, were home to extensive systems that summoned large crowds of otherworlders and raised them to be fighters. Many criticized it as a violation of human rights, but when faced with the common threat of human-destroying monsters, real needs tended to get in the way of noble intentions. Their numbers included Razen, the royal sorcerer who reincarnated himself all the way to magic-born status, and the late commander of the Farmus Royal Knight Corps, Folgen. That mammoth amount of force was directed straight at the demon lord Rimuru, and they lost.

Between that and Luminus telling Hinata the tale of how Rimuru killed Clayman instantly, nobody—Ten Great Saints or not—held a candle to him. Not unless they evolved further, in the real meaning of the term, and became *true* Saints. Like Hinata had.

Right now, if all ten took on Rimuru at once, everyone except Hinata would lose. She didn't want to see them waste their lives on the effort. Plus…

"You know, though… We have both this demon lord and the Storm Dragon to deal with now. There is no doubting that any wrong move might lead to further chaos."

As Renard calmly pointed out, Veldora was cooperating with Tempest. Lubelius could plunge all its forces into Tempest, and there was still no telling who would win.

"But we cannot allow the demon lords to do whatever they please in the domain of humans!"

Grigori's shouting brought the heated debate back to silence. It was, in a way, a summary of what every attendee was thinking to themselves. All eyes turned to Hinata. She remained calm, unaffected, as she looked back at them.

"The missives of Luminus are absolute. We are not allowed to defy them."

"Come on! Is she telling us to let Farmus be razed to the ground?"

"No, Litus. That nation's main problem is the upcoming civil war. Its people, not its nobility, must be protected. You need to pay close attention to the area, ensuring none of the sparks affect the people of Farmus or its neighbors."

"Meaning?"

"We may see some changes in heads of state, but interfering with that would be meddling in internal affairs. That's the excuse they always used whenever we tried putting an end to their otherworlder summoning projects, as I'm sure you remember. It's worked before for them, and they all but assume it'll work again."

Hinata even let out a smile as she coldly laid out the facts.

"In that case," Grigori asked, "should we just sit here and tolerate whatever Rimuru cares to do?"

"Yes. We should. The demon lord has declared his disinterest in hostilities with the human race, and there is no further reason for us to be hostile in return. Archbishop Reyhiem of Farmus was part of the invasion team, and I myself attempted to defeat Rimuru. We have both failed. And now that he likely sees us both as enemies, I'm not sure there is another option for us besides keeping quiet."

"But those are the mistakes of the Western Holy Church—and of yourself! It is not the mistake of Lubelius!" Grigori bellowed.

Hinata stood strong, her smile turning frigid. "Exactly. And that is why you need to stay hands-off. If worse comes to worst, I will declare that it was the arbitrary decision of the Western Holy Church to act against him... In other words, me."

"Wha?!"

"Lady Hinata!!"

The paladins voiced their objections as Hinata addressed the Master Rooks. Even Saare found himself unable to answer.

"Calm down. I doubt he wants to wage war with us as well."

The statement offered no comfort.

"C'mon, Hinata, you really trust him that much?" Saare asked.

"I know this sounds unlikely from someone who tried to kill him earlier, but yes, I think we can trust him. He told me himself that he's also an otherworlder. I ignored it at the time, but it seemed he was trying to avoid conflict with me."

"An otherworlder?! So he was reincarnated as a magic-born, like the demon lord Leon?"

"No. According to what he said, he died on his home planet and was resurrected as a slime on this one."

"Are you kidding me?"

"You should know how much I dislike jokes, Saare."

"Pfft. But I've never heard *that* pattern before. There are cases of people being reborn, yeah, but that's just a matter of retaining your memories from your previous life. But crossing worlds while doing it...? Maybe, but..."

"I haven't heard of it," Renard said, consulting his own memories.

"But what are even the chances of being reincarnated as a slime?" Arnaud asked. "I mean, what if that happened to you, Litus?"

Litus's well-defined face twisted into a grimace. "I wouldn't want to imagine it. If I can't even speak the language, how could I explain to people what I'm thinking? Given the literacy rates around the world, I'm not sure I could even convince people that I'm not a dumb animal. Slimes aren't *supposed* to talk."

No speech, no arms or legs. Even if you shared a language, you wouldn't be able to use it. Thinking about it, Litus even began to pity Rimuru a little.

"Yeah."

"True..."

"I had dismissed his talking as the ravings of a monster," Hinata said, "but I think he was probably telling the truth the whole time. At this point, I do feel I was a bit needlessly rough on him."

If Rimuru wasn't lying—if he was trying his hardest to be honest with her—Hinata realized now that he probably hated her guts for not making even a perfunctory effort to communicate.

"Well, who can blame you?" Saare reasoned. "He's a monster."

"Yes," Renard said, "and our faith forbids contact with them."

Both of them likely would've done the same thing Hinata did in that situation. Their faith did not deal in gray areas. Lending an ear to a monster was unthinkable, and if Hinata *did* do that, it would lead to serious questions.

"Plus, I was told that Rimuru was the one who killed my master..."

"What do you mean?"

"I've talked about it before. Those Eastern merchants were using me. They told me that the monsters were transforming into people to eat their way into other nations—forming their own country and tricking the ones around them. They also said Rimuru, the named monster leading them, killed my master. I immediately resolved to kill him."

Saare dejectedly shook his head. "And you let him get away. Maybe that's not such a bad thing now, huh...?"

He was right. By this point, it was clear this tip Hinata picked up from the merchants had given her nothing but trouble. She knew it, and she also knew that no matter how her encounter with Rimuru ended, she'd still be dealing with tons of fallout.

"I tell you, though, he has a natural talent for fleeing. And now he's a demon lord. He's undoubtedly evolved, so taking him on again couldn't be a good idea."

No one objected. The missive was given; there was no use trying to argue this on religious grounds. They would have to make an attempt at reconciliation.

"So what are you going to do?" Renard asked.

"I can't do anything," Hinata calmly replied.

If this was a human being, she would readily risk her life to fight him. But if the demon lord Rimuru wants to build relations with other countries, Hinata was ready to silently accept that. She had no intention of turning her back on the will of Luminus. *If Rimuru's actions start diverging from his words, on the other hand, that's another matter.*

"Then what if Rimuru sees you as his enemy?"

"Yeah, you did try to kill him. Now that he's got a bunch more power, maybe he'll try to get back atcha, huh? I wouldn't blame the guy."

Hinata brushed off the concern. "I told you—I'll just say it was all my own selfish decision. But before we engage in any hostilities, I want to try going over and talking with him. If need be, I'll give him an apology, too."

She made it sound so casual, the way she put it, but nobody in the joint meeting could let this pass.

"That's crazy!"

"It's incredibly dangerous!"

"The demon lord might set a trap to kill you when he has the chance, Lady Hinata!"

"Yes! And even if he doesn't, what if all his legions of monsters descend upon you?"

"Calm down. I'm not saying I'll simply waltz over there tomorrow. I need to make sure I correctly understand Rimuru's mind-set first..."

But as she attempted to simmer things down in the room, Hinata personally didn't expect much of a problem. The reports all painted Rimuru as a pretty softhearted person. In her brief experiences with him, she saw nothing that made her question this. If they could both speak frankly with each other... It was a selfish hope, she knew, but it seemed worth pursuing.

It was hope, however, that could never be fulfilled. Among the tangled desires of so many players, all at the mercy of their own motives, things were now moving in a worse direction than even Hinata anticipated.

There was a knock on the conference-room door. "Come in," Hinata curtly replied, assuming it was finally Reyhiem. The guards on the other side obliged, opening the heavy door, and inside strode exactly the man she expected—Cardinal Nicolaus, one of her most trusted of friends, and a nervous-looking Archbishop Reyhiem behind him.

That much had all been scheduled in advance. But it was the group filing in behind them that made Hinata's eyebrows arch upward. The Seven Days Clergy was here.

(Good to see you again, Hinata.)

(Are you in good health?)

(What are you looking so surprised for?)

Hinata couldn't hide her astonishment. "Why are all of you here...?" she unconsciously whispered. The normally staid cardinal was looking nervous himself, and Reyhiem was white as a sheet.

"Who are these guys, Hinata?" Saare asked.

"S-silence, Saare!" Nicolaus hurriedly replied. "You are in the presence of the Seven Days!"

Nicolaus sat up straight, startled. "...The Seven Days? The ones of legend?"

"Exactly," Hinata admitted—and when she did, everyone in the room stood up and saluted.

The members of the Seven Days Clergy were all wise and well trained, surpassing the realm of Enlightened and charged with training the next generation of Heroes. Their existence was the stuff of legend, shrouded in mystery, and they never went out in public, content with being discussed in the context of fairy tales. Not even the paladins knew about them—only a few directly interacted with them, including Hinata and Nicolaus. One had to be at the very top of the Western Holy Church to be introduced to them.

This was the group that administered the Seven Days Trial undertaken by Hinata, a test to help determine the next Heroes and champions of humanity. This responsibility made the Clergy a vital part of the Church.

But Hinata hated them. They were top-level advisers to the Church, ordered by Luminus to oversee the organization and educate its staff. However, before Hinata took up her post, the Crusaders were an organization in name only. To her, it was sheer negligence.

Looking back, I should've stripped them of their powers when I had the chance.

Hinata's unique skill Usurper worked in two ways. One, called Seize, took away its target's skills; the other, called Copy, let her learn them for herself. During her Trial, she thought of the Clergy as legendary contributors to the Luminist cause, so she naturally exercised Copy to learn from their powers and improve herself. One could call her an apprentice to the Clergy along those lines... but the Seven Days were not having it. They shunned Hinata for daring to rise above them, interfering with her in any way they could find.

This was a crafty group, one that had lurked in the darkness of the Church and called the shots for an untold amount of time. But there was nothing productive in their actions. And once she took the Trial and realized that, Hinata immediately judged them to be useless relics, took their skills, and left. Now she was using what she learned to train Arnaud and the rest of the division commanders.

I wonder if that's why Luminus had me take the Seven Days Trial in the first place...

If she did, she had to hand it to Luminus. Such incredible wisdom. To her, the Clergy had plainly abandoned their mission to train the next generation, instead focusing on covering their own backs. But if Luminus let them dodder on, there must have been a reason for it. That was why she never defied them. Not in public.

Once everyone was seated again, Hinata addressed the group.

"So may I ask what brings you here today?"

(Hee-hee-hee! No need for alarm.)

(No, no. Archbishop Reyhiem here has brought back some information about the demon lord Rimuru, has he not?)

(We were simply interested in hearing about it ourselves.)

The voices echoed around in her mind. The Seven Days Clergy used Thought Communication to answer her. She sized them up again.

There were three of them present—not the entire contingent—and in her judgment, these were the most corrupt ones out of the entire group.

Among them was Arze, the Tuesday Priest who governed fire. His force was like a disposable lighter compared with Shizue Izawa's. He had nothing to teach, and Hinata didn't even need Usurper to complete his trial—but for some reason, he must've assumed she was incapable of Seizing his skills. That made him look down at her constantly, which rankled her.

The other two present, Dena, the Monday Priest, and Vena, the Friday Priest—Hinata couldn't guess at their motives. Helping Arze out, probably.

What a chore. Luminus ordered me to make this as quick and painless as possible, too...

Hinata grew nervous. Rimuru already had a poor impression of her. If she let this Clergy get in her way here, she might never be able to reconcile with him—but as long as she didn't have a bead on their goals, she had to focus on Reyhiem. She turned off her mind as she lent him an ear.

"I was foolish," Reyhiem began. "We challenged a foe that was fearsome, far too fearsome for any of us. He is a demon lord, beyond a shadow of a doubt. Through our own foolishness, we have engineered the birth of a new demon lord!"

His memories of the event put him into a frenzy, his eyes bloodshot and his voice raised to a near scream. He continued, recounting the events that led to this birth—his misguided deeds, all laid bare without omission. It wasn't on someone's orders; he was being driven by the compulsion that he simply had to do it. He needed absolution for his sins, if he ever hoped to be free from his pain and forgiven by his god.

As he told the story, the paladins began to murmur among themselves. The sheer force of this adversary, beyond all common sense, made it hard for them to contain their composure. Neither an anti-magic barrier nor a long-range, magic-specific defensive wall was enough to stop these monsters—not even a holy barrier could mount any defense against those flashes of light.

But Hinata stayed resolute. Based on Reyhiem's testimony, she surmised it was an attack involving concentrated sunlight. And as if to back up that theory, the Seven Days Clergy began to provide their own commentary.

(Hmm. Perhaps this is sunlight magic, the kind Sir Gren was always so gifted at.)

(Light-bending magic? Wouldn't an anti-magic barrier shut that down?)

(And Gren's didn't have that much force to it.)

Gren, the Sunday Priest, was head of the Clergy, his magic commanding light. One of his spells concentrated sunlight in a similar way, and while the Clergy was on the wrong track with their theories, if they and Hinata had the same impression of this, Hinata assumed she was right.

Idiots. It's not directly bending the sunlight with magic; it's reflecting the light off something else to focus it into a beam. Otherwise, a barrier could've easily blocked it. Were water and wind elementals cooperating with him, then? But that would take a lot of complex calculation...

But she had nothing to fear. Once she knew the trick behind it, it was easy to counter. Just put up a protective film to diffuse the heat and scatter dust in the air to refract the light, and the threat was neutralized. If sunlight was the only thing it harnessed, the attack was full of holes to exploit. To Hinata, the attack was worthless.

As far as I can tell, he was using his scientific knowledge from the other world for that attack. No wonder people here couldn't deal with it. They couldn't even understand it. Using it to poke holes in their magical defense was smart, though. Not a stone unturned...

It took a lot of computing power to engineer that attack, as well as multiple ongoing spells at once. That was a serious threat, but now that Hinata knew what it *really* was, it didn't seem that fearsome any longer. But Hinata was making her conclusions too quickly. Reyhiem wasn't done talking. There was more... The main course, in fact.

"One moment. That mystery attack was a dreadful thing. Sir Folgen was helplessly killed; Sir Razen could do nothing against it. Nearly ten thousand of our finest knights were felled by it, I think. But..."

He paused here, nervously swallowing, sweat running down his head, trying his best to hold back the terror.

"...The real horror came after that. The next moment, the battle-field went completely quiet.

"Some were unconscious, fatally hurt; others were wounded and screaming on the ground; still more were healthy but wandering around, scared out of their wits. The cacophony they all created together set the battlefield to a frenzy. And yet...the very next moment," Reyhiem said, "all the noise was gone."

"What do you mean?"

"I mean exactly what I said, Lady Hinata. At that moment, the surviving members of that twenty-thousand-strong force died. Only three remained alive: Sir Razen; Edmaris, the king of Far-mus; and me. Seeing it made me lose my sanity. I was so stricken with fear that I fainted."

At Reyhiem's tale, a similar silence fell over the holy cathedral. A single monster killed a force of twenty thousand in an instant. The truth of that could hardly be commented on in words. And amid the solemn tension, everyone was recalling the same legend in their mind—the tale of a single person laying waste to an entire city and becoming a demon lord.

Then Hinata recalled something Luminus herself told her.

The precursor to the Western Holy Church was launched a good dozen centuries ago—likely longer, but that is as far back as the records exist. Its people, however, had first moved here two millen-nia ago, driven away after Veldora destroyed their kingdom. The dragon's strength and immortality put them beyond hope; trying to engage it would only add to the dead.

To the vampires that called this place home, Veldora prancing around and destroying humanity would lead to food shortages. The purest of high-quality vitality could only be obtained from human beings, and while Luminus and her family were safe, this was a matter of life or death to the lower-level vampires. Thus, Luminus was forced to come up with their current co-op approach to protecting humanity. She rescued them, really, and now they worshiped her as a god.

And it was all the fault of Veldora on the rampage. He was worse than any natural disaster, a threat impossible to prepare for—a Catastrophe. That classified him as Special S on the scale, something humanity just couldn't deal with...but he wasn't the only large-scale destroyer of worlds. The only creatures in the Special S rank right now were the four dragons known to exist. But that's only the public story. In mythology, meanwhile, there were records of two demon lords exacting a similar campaign of death and madness. These were Guy Crimson, Lord of Darkness, and Milim Nava, the Destroyer. Demon lords all got an S rank, but there was disparity in these rankings. Some creatures, like these two, could be rated Special S behind the scenes—and as Luminus explained, it happened when a potential demon lord was awakened by engineering massive destruction, taking in the souls of the resulting dead. Evolution beyond imagination would result.

The term *demon lord* technically referred to the *true* ones who underwent this evolution, and even then, it could take place across several levels. It left some demon lords as powerful as dragons, and Luminus wondered if Guy and Milim had evolved beyond that. Even Luminus, as a true demon lord, had no chance against them. "If I fought Milim," she told Hinata, "maybe I could outwit her. Maybe it'd be a good fight, if it came to that. But I'd never win in the end." And what about Guy? "Ha! It vexes me terribly, but it would be hopeless. He's in his own world."

Someone as self-confident as Luminus, whose powers Hinata couldn't even begin to fathom, describing Guy's force as belonging to another dimension. It made Hinata think—about Guy, and about Milim, who actually faced off against him once. It was hard to imagine.

That's what the Special S ranking was for. If all of humankind banded together, maybe they could deal with such a monster—but even that was wishful thinking, because it assumed the presence of a Hero in the human ranks. There was no Hero right now, and thus no chance.

Plus, the current lineup of demon lords—the Octagram—was on its own level of danger, Rimuru included. Luminus believed Rimuru was still in the midst of awakening, and Reyhiem's words were more than enough to back that up.

*　*　*

Soon the others began to recall the story of the true demon lords, those fearsome presences. They were not revealed to the public lest panic resulted, but they were real, and they were threats.

When the first dragon lost its power, it showed no signs of regenerating itself for some reason. Out of the other three, one had been sealed away until just recently, but now he was back and supporting Rimuru—a demon lord who massacred a force of twenty thousand by himself. This was comparable to what those other two demon lords did long ago. The structural destruction wasn't there, maybe, but the number of souls he obtained had to be staggering.

A heavy silence filled the room. It was clear nobody wanted to admit that a demon lord, in the real meaning of the term, had been born. There was an overwhelming difference between a potential demon lord and a *true* one, and everybody in the room understood that.

Finally, it was Hinata who quietly broke the silence.

"I see. So we should assume the demon lord Rimuru has been awakened…"

The words cut like a sharp knife through the silence, lighting a fire under those who could no longer tolerate the stillness.

"I suppose we should. Now what? If we leave him be, he'll become a threat beyond anything we can handle, won't he?"

"Calm down. Rimuru is a former human. If he seeks to live alongside humanity, there shouldn't be any need to fight him."

"Right. We need to see how he reacts."

"But we know for a fact that he mowed down twenty thousand knights without hesitation! He is clearly a threat. Are you sure we should simply believe him…?"

That final comment from Renard summed up everyone's thoughts. That's how many wars begin—the mind playing tricks, stirring fear of a potential opponent. That was true enough even among the human race; if the adversary was a demon lord, it was going to be hard to trust him. It wouldn't be an issue if that adversary could be hunted down at any moment, but Rimuru was growing more powerful at a rapid pace. To the paladins guarding humanity, and the knights serving as the Holy Emperor's blade, they needed to entertain the idea of tackling him before he grew truly impossible to handle.

But Hinata stuck to her guns. "Silence, everyone," she firmly stated. "The missive is absolute."

Nothing anyone could say would change her mind. As captain of the Crusaders and chief knight of the Imperial Guard, she guided the hearts and minds of the Holy Empire of Lubelius. She had to be a model for every citizen, a firm leader for those who served under her. Her mind would change only if it did so within the will of Luminus. That was what made her so unwaveringly resolute.

And with that, the joint session would end, everyone returning to their intelligence-gathering duties. Or so it should have—but evil has a way of appearing from the most unexpected of crevices.

✳

(Ah, Reyhiem, did you have any other *messages* for us?)

Just as Hinata was going to end the meeting, the Seven Days Clergy finally spoke up. It seemed to jog Reyhiem's mind, as he took a crystal ball out of his pocket and reverently handed it to Hinata.

"I—I actually do have this. It's said to be a message from Demon Lord Rimuru to you, Lady Hinata..."

"A message?"

She accepted it, eyeing it with suspicion. A message from Rimuru was likely something she couldn't afford to ignore.

This crystal ball, provided by Reyhiem at the prodding of the Clergy, was a highly valuable magic item. It allowed anyone to record moving picture images, making it a useful way to transmit messages. It also saw use in international negotiations, seen as a more trustworthy piece of evidence than a written letter.

Regardless of where Rimuru managed to procure one of these, Hinata immediately tried playing it back. Given all the dignitaries on-site, it could be a great chance for everyone to see what Rimuru looked like.

But that wasn't the end of it.

The image showed a beautiful girl, but it wasn't a girl. It was the demon lord himself. His face, reminiscent of Hinata's teacher, Shizue Izawa, looked at the viewer coldly, without emotion. The sense of presence he had came across at full force through the video image.

Hinata blinked at it. *What a surprise. Like a different person from a few months ago...* Her eyes met with Rimuru's in the image. Was that a coincidence, or...? She began to realize just how nervous she was. Rimuru, a fellow countryman. A softhearted demon lord. Maybe her sentimentality was making her underestimate this threat. Logically, she knew that. And as if to back up that suspicion...

"I'll take you on. You and me, in a one-on-one duel."

That was the entire message. So incredibly simple; no room for misunderstanding. Everyone viewing it took home the same message: *Rimuru is enraged. He killed Clayman for getting in his way, and Hinata's up next.*

For a change, even Nicolaus looked perturbed. "Wh-what should we do, Lady Hinata?" But before she could answer:

"Lady Hinata, your orders! I will gladly lead a force to crush this demon lord's ambitions!"

Arnaud, ever the hot-blooded military man, pushed the issue. The debate was now in full swing again.

"Come on," chided Saare, giving Arnaud an astonished look. "You're a master swordsman, sure, but don't you think your brain could use some work?"

"...What?"

"Didn't Hinata just spend the past half hour saying 'hands off'? We touch him, and the other demon lords aren't gonna take that sitting down. Plus, if he's a fully awakened demon lord, it'd be even *more* ill-advised to prod him. I think we should just chill out and accept our opponent's request."

"He's right, Arnaud," Litus said, nodding in agreement. "If we have Veldora to deal with as well, we have no chance of winning. Victory would only come with losses that would be impossible to take. If the adversary seeks a duel, better for all of us if we have Hinata accept it."

A full clash of forces would result in what had to be staggering casualties with no guarantee of victory. Having the most powerful knight in the Holy Empire take the lead instead seemed far more palatable. If anything, the idea filled Saare and Litus with optimism. There was no doubting Hinata's victory now.

Hinata, meanwhile, weighed her options.

Arnaud's offer of a full battle force was out of the question. Getting her nation involved would escalate into the total war that Litus feared, likely dragging in the other Western Nations and developing into a world war. The masses they swore to protect in crises like these would turn into a severe disadvantage; it would go against the desires of Luminus. Veldora, too, was a menace. In terms of keeping losses to a minimum, Rimuru's offer of a duel couldn't have come at a better time.

But:

How should I take this...?

It gave Hinata pause. Looking back, she was extremely lucky she hadn't invaded Tempest without fully grasping the situation there. She had Luminus's great wisdom to thank for that. If their opponent had ascended to true demon lord-hood, things like the number of soldiers on the field no longer held meaning. No matter how tenacious they were, unless they met a fairly lofty bar, they were useless. The disaster that befell Farmus was proof enough of that.

But...no. When Rimuru fought Farmus, that must have been *before* he ascended. It was their defeat that generated the "necessary" number of souls for the job. He had wiped out twenty thousand without even being awakened.

What a monster, truly...

Reflecting on her battle with Rimuru, she didn't think he was capable of something like that. Perhaps he had been restraining himself—but now, he wanted her dead, no doubt.

But if he hated her, why go through the trouble of challenging her to a duel for revenge? It seemed unnatural. If he felt Hinata and the Western Holy Church were a thorn in his side, it was a strange time to act on that impulse. If he was foolish enough not to see that, he wouldn't be going through all this undercover skullduggery against Farmus.

Perhaps there was some other reason.

It's unnatural of him, yes. Has something changed? Did the ascension to demon lord come at the cost of his humanity?!

Acquiring that much power at once would crush any human

being's soul. She saw for herself how much trouble Shizue had containing Ifrit's berserk force. It'd easily drive anyone mad—especially if he was now a *true* demon lord.

…But maybe not. He'd have no reason to ally himself with the human nations, then.

Luminus told her that Rimuru swore to keep humanity safe. If his human heart was a thing of the past, his declaration to build his own city no longer made sense. There wasn't enough information to work with, Hinata thought. Her Measurer skill wasn't producing any answers. It seemed like the truth was still hidden somewhere.

Besides, this whole crystal ball gambit was weird in itself. It could store many hours of footage if necessary, but his message was only a few seconds long. She couldn't shake the impression that some ulterior meaning was lurking behind it.

Plus:

The Tuesday Priest just let on that he knew Rimuru had something for me. Why?

Reyhiem had filed his report. He hadn't said a word about Rimuru's message. But Arze had asked him "Did you have any other *messages* for us?" and Hinata had picked up on his unnatural choice of words. The seeds of doubt were beginning to bud in her mind, although she swallowed them up and refused to let them sprout upon her face. Instead, she simply continued measuring her position, letting no stone go unturned.

Unfortunately, there was just too little data to work with. She could try crunching the numbers and guiding herself to a solution like she always did, but it wasn't leading her anywhere this time.

"Ah well," she concluded with a sigh. "If he's calling me out, I suppose I'll have to go explain matters to him in person."

If Rimuru wanted it, she wasn't that hesitant about a duel. But was there really no chance to talk things out? She wanted to be fully sure of that first. If she could meet with him, she'd have her answer. It seemed smarter than just fretting to herself.

Either way, if this is what it's come to, it's up to me to settle it.

"It is too dangerous!" Nicolaus frantically protested. "There is no need for you to come out yourself! Not with the barefaced malice he clearly has for you!"

It wasn't enough to make Hinata change her mind. "We'll never know that for sure unless we work out his intentions, will we? Plus, there is my apology to think about. Isn't it wiser to meet with him once and try talking matters over?"

She had hoped this would put an end to the debate. But once again, as if waiting for the right moment, the Seven Days Clergy spoke up.

(Heh-heh-heh. That is your decision? Very well!)
(May the protection of the god Luminus safeguard you.)
(The demon lord Rimuru is a threat, yes.)
(But even if your talks turn sour, there is no need for concern.)
(You certainly have what it takes to defeat him.)
(But, Hinata, you are forgetting something.)
(Indeed. The presence of that dragon.)
(I fear not even you could defeat such a menace!)
(Do not overestimate your strength, Hinata.)
(No attack would ever faze that dragon.)
(But take heart, Hinata.)
(We will leave you with this.)
(It is called the Dragonbuster!)

Ugh. Can they be any more shameless about it? All I said was I'd talk with him, but they're already pushing me into trading blows. And their goal is to have me take care of Veldora, right? Or is it...?

The Seven Days Clergy was a band of ex-humans enjoying Luminus's personal approval. Their faith was strictly for her. Hinata could understand if they wanted her to eliminate a dragon Luminus was so clearly concerned about...but she already knew that wasn't the only motivation. They were afraid. Afraid that Luminus's affections would turn away from them and toward a new prodigy. That was why they were so unenthusiastic about training the younger generation. Why they actively schemed to eliminate anyone in their way.

Those fools. They mean nothing but harm for Luminus...

But Hinata did nothing to defy them. That was Luminus's decision, and Hinata was in no position to take action. Instead, she retained her calm.

"I will gladly accept it," she intoned as she took the Dragonbuster from Vena, the Friday Priest. He and his co-conspirators gave her satisfied nods.

(I hope things go well for you.)

(If worse comes to worst, that sword shall protect you.)

(And if the effort ends in failure, the responsibility will fall on your shoulders.)

And with that, the Clergy took their leave.

"Lady Hinata…"

The paladins attempted to plead their case. She waved them off, turning a quick glance toward Louis behind the curtain.

"All right. You have your assignments. This joint session is hereby adjourned."

The Three Battlesages sat there, tongues silenced despite whatever they had to say to her. The paladins meekly accepted it, respecting their leader's choices.

Hinata awoke from a light sleep.

All that self-absorbed reflection on her memories must have made her fall asleep. She could detect the aroma of coffee as her consciousness began to focus. Nicolaus, ever so gallantly ingratiating himself with her, could be seen preparing breakfast in the adjacent room.

"Ah, are you awake?"

This was Cardinal Nicolaus Speltus—a man who, Hinata felt, was best described as unusual. He was a trusted adviser of the Holy Emperor, the supreme leader of Lubelius, which put him at the very peak of power in the land. But when dealing with Hinata, he was as steadfast and loving as a puppy.

"Come, breakfast is served. Would you like to eat?"

It was almost comical. Hard to imagine someone like him preparing breakfast for another person. To anyone else who knew him, Nicolaus was a devil in a Saint's mask.

"Yeah. Thanks."

Nicolaus happily nodded back.

It was the first meal Hinata could honestly say she enjoyed in a while. Her work had barely given her time to sleep as of late—but now it was coming to an end.

"…Are you leaving?"

"Yeah. That's my job."

"But it was I who ordered Reyhiem to come here..."

"And I'm the one who let you do so without comment. You don't need to concern yourself about it."

"Is there any way to convince you...ah, not to?"

"Enough already. Stop worrying. It's not guaranteed to be a fight yet."

...And if it was, it wasn't guaranteed to be a defeat. Hinata still had a trick up her sleeve—not some silly Dragonbuster, but something much loftier, nobler. Besides, Luminus had personally told her to restrain herself.

She had zero intention of dying. If it came to blows, whether Rimuru was ascended or not, she believed he was still a defeatable target—for now. There was nothing to worry about. She wasn't 100 percent sure of victory, but she had a lot of experience with taking on targets bigger than her. Plus, she even had more than one ace up her sleeve. It was such a lovely morning. It didn't need to be marred with such gloomy talk.

"It'll work out fine, Nicolaus. Like it always does. You don't need to worry about a thing."

She smiled—a small, gentle smile. The first one with no careful calculation behind it in a while.

A PRIVATE CHAT

That Time I Got Reincarnated as a Slime

The kingdom of Seltrozzo was a small realm, nestled along the northern coastline between Englesia and Farmus. It was currently providing the stage for a clandestine meeting that would change history forever.

"So how did it go?"

"Just as we figured. Our cover's still intact."

"Heh-heh-heh... That witch may have a sharp mind, but maybe she's nothing too scary after all."

"I wouldn't be so sure. Strength-wise, there's no downplaying it. She's the best in the West."

"Indeed. Ill-advised artifice is powerless against brute force. I would recommend all of you to never forget that."

Here, in a large, firelit room in a realm kept cool all year by the blowing sea breeze, the Five Elders had gathered. Their dress was ornate—some crafted with Tempestian silk, still a rarity to obtain. It was inlaid with anti-magic Artifacts, providing a full defense against any unexpected strikes. It spoke volumes about the group's financial backing.

The room had, of course, been fully sealed off from the outside world, reinforced and designed to withstand magic up to the nuclear level. They even had stout, A-ranked knights standing guard in the middle. All of them were seated in a row, and with them was Glenda, the wild beauty with the spiky red hair—the Raging Sea, one of the Ten Great Saints and Three Battlesages.

Her main source of employment came from these Five Elders, the Council's powerbrokers.

One of them, clad in a loose white outfit, had eyes as sharp as a hawk, his presence dominating the room...were it not for the charming, doll-like little girl seated on his lap. She was maybe not quite ten years old, her hair a silky blond, her lips a light shade of pink. At first glance, it looked like an old man babysitting his granddaughter, as much as the sight clashed against its surroundings. But nobody brought it up. They let the man do what he wanted, as if this was a given—for that man was Granville Rozzo himself, head of the Rozzo family and mediator of the Five Elders.

The Rozzos of the Western Nations were a family of rulers. Seltrozzo was their exclusively owned domain, and family members could be found among royalty in Farmus and Englesia as well. The establishment of the Council of the West was largely the result of their tireless efforts, and while Council seats were theoretically selected by its member nations, most were taken by those under the patronage of the Rozzos. Their power extended far beyond their diminutive borders, outclassing entire nations on the international stage. They could safely be called the de facto rulers of the Western Nations. It was even their funding that let Yuuki Kagurazaka establish the Free Guild.

Granville was their leader, and nobody here was going to criticize the leader's behavior. He gave the girl on his lap a reassuring pat on the head as he solemnly spoke.

"Very good." A thin smile came to his lips. "But Sir Damrada, I fear your lies have been uncovered, haven't they?"

This was in reference to Glenda's report that Hinata had discovered she was being taken advantage of. The question was addressed to Damrada, dressed all in black and covering his face with a broad, umbrellalike hat. He, too, held himself like high nobility, although his clothing was rare in these parts. He was not from the Western Nations.

"Heh-heh-heh... I don't see a problem with that. We may have lost Hinata Sakaguchi's trust, but we earned a great deal in return—*your* trust, my good man Granville."

"Ha. You say that, even though the East has come here to spread division in the West and make money off the ensuing weapon sales. Then the Empire will wait until we're exhausted to take action, yes? Trust hardly comes into it."

"Well, well, well. I should have expected such fine insightfulness from you, my good man."

"Are you denying it?"

"No point in doing so, is there?"

"Heh. How kind of you to say. But back to the main issue."

"Yes."

"We both agree that Hinata needs to be eliminated, am I right?"

"Of course. It goes without saying that Veldora, the Storm Dragon, was the Empire's greatest impediment to its western expansion. Now they say he has been tamed by the demon lord Rimuru. Whether that is true or not, it is safe to say now that the dragon can be negotiated with. That opens an opportunity for us. The next issue is the threat of the Western Holy Church. They are the glue that holds all these nations together, and with that, the Empire's full strength would not be enough to seize the West."

"Oh? So we hardly merit notice from you?"

"I don't mean that at all. All five of you are intelligent and understanding of your interests. After the Empire takes over the West, I hope we can continue to work together to control its economy."

"Work together? Are you asking us to lead the Empire directly to our doors? Don't make me laugh."

"Heh-heh-heh. The Empire is a powerful thing, you know. It will be difficult but not impossible. Are you opposing us?"

"Such insolence from a mere weapons merchant!"

It was Glenda who finally took verbal offense to this. She took out an unfamiliar weapon—a pistol—from her clothing and pointed it at the merchant.

Damrada was unfazed—and not because he was unaware of what that weapon could do.

"Heh-heh-heh... A pistol?" He sounded less than impressed. "I'm surprised to see them here, in the West."

"Oh, you know what this thing is? It doesn't seem to bother you too much."

"Of course I know it. Do you think the West is the only place one can find otherworlders? And remember, I deal in weapons. It

is my job to be familiar with every type of weapon out there. The one you are pointing at me is common in my lands. They are being manufactured in great quantities."

The Five Elders couldn't hide their surprise at Damrada's disinterested explanation.

"What? In great quantities?"

"You Eastern traders are shrewd, indeed…"

"Truly, there is no telling the strength of the Imperial forces. It may be no match for monsters, but against a person, this weapon is all but unstoppable."

Damrada was not a man who lied. What he *did* do was take advantage of the way he was interpreted, leading people to misunderstand his words. Anyone who dealt with him was advised to be on their guard, and if you dissected his sentences, it was clear to see the malice dripping off them. Here, Damrada was giving them a warning—better to work with the Empire, not oppose it.

"But you're right. We *are* understanding of our interests. And as you say, it is best to put our heads down and work together for now." Granville's solemn voice restored order among the elders.

"Are you sure about this, Sir Granville?"

"Enough, Glenda. Our goals were the same from the beginning. Now is not the time for hostilities."

Glenda did not challenge him further. Granville's decisions were final. And Damrada had a lot to listen to, in terms of what it meant to everyone involved. He was the powerful leader of a weapons trading firm, much like the Rozzos, who earned political rule through their financial power. If the situation was different, they would be in more direct competition with each other. But not now.

"Heh-heh-heh… Well said, my good man. That may not always be the case, but for now, we are comrades."

"Indeed. Farmus and Englesia achieve balance by retaining their own powers, and I do not wish to tilt the scales. It is unclear what motivation Rimuru has for toppling Farmus, but I do *not* want that land to be ruled by a demon lord."

"I can understand that, yes. It pains us, as well, to lose the trade route through Farmus from the Dwarven Kingdom. The demon lord Clayman was a valuable trading partner to us, and I cannot say I appreciate Rimuru defeating him. I will be glad to work with you. So…"

He paused.

"So you want us to handle Hinata?" offered Granville. "No need to worry there. We set a trap for her, and she's already stepped in it. Now all we have to do is rile Rimuru into taking care of her for us."

"Yep," added Glenda. "No doubt about it. Hinata saw Rimuru's message, and it sent her marching right to Tempest. Now we just have to turn that demon lord's anger toward her."

"I am glad to hear that. But why are you so intent on eliminating Hinata? I would think a Saint like her would be more useful alive than dead."

Damrada turned toward Granville, attempting to decipher his feelings on the subject. Granville laughed him off.

"Heh. It's simple. That woman is too strong. It is no exaggeration to call her the strongest knight in the West. The magic-born Razen, Grand Master Yuuki, "Lightspeed" Masayuki—she stands above even those champions. You understand that, and that's why you're trying to use us, no? Am I wrong, Sir Damrada?"

"Heh…heh-heh. Yes, she is truly frightening. Too much to handle, you would say? And that is why you want to take this piece off the board. It makes sense."

The two of them exchanged a nod. As alike as they were, one nod could communicate much between them. Thus, without any further discussion on the topic, the group moved on to determine their work assignments.

Damrada promised to eliminate the demon maneuvering behind the scenes in Farmus. He ordered Glenda to set the Temple Knights stationed in the nations surrounding Farmus to action, also promising to work with the new king, Edward, and chase down the Rimuru-aligned faction supporting Edmaris. Then he would spread rumors that Hinata was traveling to Tempest to defeat Rimuru, pinning him down and making it impossible for him to send reinforcements to other lands. As long as they could take care of that demon calling the shots, it would be easy to make Yohm and his band disappear. And by that time, Rimuru would have no choice but to defeat that troublemaker Hinata.

"But what if Hinata Sakaguchi actually defeats him?"

"That could be helpful to us as well. But don't worry. Rimuru is not like the other demon lords. He is a dangerous element, one we will have to take care of sooner or later, but with Veldora on his side, killing him would be ill-advised. We have other plans in motion."

"Heh-heh-heh... I will leave that in your talented hands, then."

"Certainly. Just don't mess up how you deal with that demon, all right?"

"I need no reminders," Damrada said. "I am sure the Western Holy Church has demon experts on their side as well, but the East has a much more extensive organization for that. Not even an Arch Demon will be a problem for it."

"Very good."

"In that case, I had best be going."

Granville nodded as Damrada gave a small bow and left the room.

Only the Rozzos and their bodyguards remained. Once they were sure Damrada was gone, Glenda let out an exaggerated sigh.

"Malice! That is all that merchant gives us. Treating us like children... It drives me crazy!"

Granville gave a cold look at the door. "Heh... Don't be that way, Glenda. Even with that attitude, we've been treated with the greatest of respect."

"But, Sir Granville..."

"Glenda," he calmly chided, "you don't know who those people really are. Hinata knew them well enough, yes? Merchants of death, peddling weapons behind the scenes. She let that slide because they were useful to her out in the open, but if she knew their true nature, she would never associate with them."

"Their true nature?"

"Yes. They are part of an underground organization known as Cerberus—and Damrada the Gold is one of their leaders."

The rest of the elders nodded in agreement. They knew who they were dealing with, which was why all five were in attendance. Glenda could understand their concern.

"Huh. I've heard of that group... How they rule the underworld in the East, and so on. No, challenging them wouldn't be a great idea, huh? I look forward to seeing what they're capable of."

She flashed a wild grin as Granville nodded at her and stroked the blond hair of the girl on his lap.

"Heh-heh-heh... This may not go so easily for you, Damrada. The demon you are dealing with is no *mere* Arch Demon."

There was real mirth to his laugh. His research showed that the demon was so strong that not even the magic-born Razen would be a problem for him. It was a good chance to test out the skills of Damrada's group, but they needed to consider what to do if he was defeated.

"If it comes to that, I could step up..."

"Hmm. I imagine he won't be a problem for you, but just in case, I'd like to get the other Battlesages involved as well."

"Yes. Good point," another elder said.

"The demon lord Rimuru needs to be weakened in any way possible. A demon that dangerous must be addressed at once."

"And even if we fail at that, we need to do whatever it takes to ensure the victory of Farmus's royal force."

"Yes," said Granville. "That demon cannot make any grandiose moves. If he throws his power around on the public stage, it will be harder for him to keep other nations from talking. The more dangerous the threat, the more terrified politicians you'll find screaming for his head. You know what your job is, right, Glenda? I want you to use Cerberus to check that demon's movements."

If Damrada and his men could kill the demon, then great. If they couldn't for some reason, he was helpless anyway, surrounded by hostile royalist forces. It'd be easy for Glenda and the ex-Battlesage Rama to rub him out personally, but as long as they could keep the demon from taking action, mission accomplished. Yohm's force could never take on the federated forces of Farmus's new king.

To achieve this, Granville saw fit to take every possible precaution and bring Saare and Grigori, the other two Battlesages, into the mix. Their formation needed to be rock-solid.

"You got it," Glenda said with a proud grin. "Glenda Attley is on the job."

Having a family name despite not being nobility was unique in these lands. It was because Glenda was not from here at all—she was an otherworlder summoned on the sly by Seltrozzo, or really, the Rozzo family itself. She was an ex-mercenary who learned military tactics during a stint in the foreign legion of an undisclosed nation, and her skills, honed by her worldwide travels, were exemplary. She wielded the unique skill Sniper, which let her handle all types of guns and projectile arms with ease, and she was also a gifted combat fighter and assassin, using a knife as her weapon of choice.

She was a born predator, one whose faithfulness to Granville was etched into her soul when she was summoned. In her eyes, even Hinata, Lubelian survivor of ten years of warfare, was a mere child. Glenda had a war-torn upbringing in her world, and a planet where a woman can be top of the heap just by gaining a little power at age sixteen or seventeen was a paradise compared with the hell she went through. But that, sadly, was based on the assumption that this world was fair to all its people. It wasn't, in reality. That was why people prayed to gods, after all; it was in the teachings of Luminism. But even after attaining a position in the Three Battlesages, she had forgotten about that.

"Right. In that case, I will have Blood Shadow stir Saare and Grigori into action. Make sure you do your part as well."

Blood Shadow was the Rozzo family's darker side, a group of battle-hardened fighters who were open to any type of work given to them. It was familiar to many otherworlders, Glenda included, bound by contract to fight for the sake of the Rozzos.

Glenda nodded. "You're going to use them? All right. All for the sake of the family...and my freedom."

"Mmmm. You may go."

With Granville's order, Glenda left the room, a fire burning in her eyes.

The fire in the hearth burned a shade of red, crackling to life as it grew brighter.

"Is all of this good for you, Maribel?"

"Yes. Very much so, Grandfather. Deploying this group will prevent both of them from taking action. Rimuru will be too busy dealing with Hinata to help Farmus, once the Western Nations intervene to put an end to the civil war—in the name of Edward, of course. Then he'll be indebted to you, won't he?"

"That's exactly right, Maribel. And I refuse to allow anyone to mess with the sandbox we rule over!"

Were it not for the demon lord's shadow cast over the Farmus conflict, he could have given support to both sides and turned the fight into a stalemate—but that had the potential of gifting Englesia too much power. A single force dominating over the land was not the will of the Rozzos; instead, Granville maneuvered to retain an ideal balance.

"For the Rozzos," the blond, lovable Maribel said, "the world!"

""""For the Rozzos,"""" everyone else shouted back, """"the world!""""

This was the center of the world—a world that the Rozzos sought to bring completely under their rule. And under the cover of the Council of the West, this desire was beginning to take real shape. To grow steadily—and grow large.

CHAPTER
4

THE SECOND
CONFRONTATION

That Time I Got Reincarnated as a Slime

The highway to the Dwarven Kingdom was complete, and we had a timetable in place for the road to Blumund—but I just kept getting busier and busier. We needed to establish a new highway to the Sorcerous Dynasty of Thalion, and Milim and her people needed an entire city planned for them.

There was a ton to do, and in the process, we were also developing a massive festival and hatching a scheme to conquer the Kingdom of Farmus. I knew becoming a demon lord would put a bunch more stuff on my plate, but this was pushing my workload to the absolute limit.

And in the midst of all this, I received terrible news from Soka: Hinata Sakaguchi was on the warpath, and she was headed straight for me.

As Soka stood there, panting as she reported back to me, I brought a hand to my head. I was planning to inspect our forges today, but instead, I canceled that and headed to my office so she could fill me in on the details.

Apparently, she told me, Hinata was traveling totally unaccompanied.

"Alone?"

"Yes," she said, looking straight at me. "Nanso reported from his viewing post outside the Lubelius barrier that he didn't see anyone leaving the holy city. Only Hinata, who you told us to keep an especially close eye out for, was seen in Englesia."

Soei's guidance had turned her into a master of espionage. If that's what she said, it had to be true.

"Wait a moment!"

Then Toka, another guard under Soka's command, jumped out from her shadow.

"We've detected new movements."

"What happened?"

"Four paladins have appeared to join Hinata, Lady Soka!"

"Just four?"

"Yes sir, but all appear to be very powerful. They used some kind of magic to shake us off their tail almost immediately."

Toka looked chagrined as he gave us the news. Hmm. What was that all about? Did she leave without telling anyone, and they came running after her? Seemed doubtful. Were they staggering their deployment in anticipation of being watched? No, they'd be a lot more careful if those were their tactics.

I couldn't say, but I had to hand it to Hinata. Always one step ahead of me. Shrugging off anyone who'd drag her down and attempting to strike us with only the best people she had? Maybe she thought that anything less would just get in the way.

So...

"I guess Hinata wants to fight us, huh?"

I didn't want to think about combat with her very much, but it'd all come down to the actions she chose to take. I doubt I'd lose to her that easily now, but I couldn't trifle with her. I was hoping my message would open her mind to the thought of talking things over, but...

"That's unclear. She was carrying this odd-looking sword, however, so I doubt she is coming on friendly terms."

Hmm. She's armed, huh? Well, being armed was a given in this world, and it's not like she would've marched to a demon lord empty-handed. It'd be rash to assume this meant she was in a fighting mood.

"I don't know... That's not enough to make a decision."

"The Crusaders were fully armed as well..."

"Oh, really? Like, full-on?"

"Yes! Full-on, sir!"

Hmm. Full-on. Well, with those paladins joining Hinata ready for battle, I had a feeling a fight was coming up. It disappointed me. I was no fan of combat here. The move indicated that we were a thorn in her side, and she wanted a way to deal with it. But what did she want after that? If we didn't try to understand each other, then one side would have to be eliminated. It'd be a huge, life-and-death struggle.

If Hinata declined to talk to us, we'd have to force our will on her in any way possible. She refused to look at the matter from our perspective; she refused to lend an ear to our words. I can't really call that the high road, in any real way. Didn't Hinata get that? She had never really listened to me since we first met, but I didn't think she was *that* close-minded.

Was her Luminism the cause of it? Maybe she didn't see why a monster like me deserved to be listened to. I'm sure her faith served her well in many aspects; it was important to her, but I wasn't so sure blind belief was in her best interest. Anyone living in modern-day Japan would feel that way, given all the blood that's been spilled in the name of religion. It's important to use your eyes and ears—and think with your own head. Otherwise you're just shutting off your mind, right? It's stupid.

Regardless, it was up to her to use the information she had at hand. What would she decide on? How would she act? That was all her problem. If Hinata decided to be hostile to us, I was ready for it.

Bad news always comes in waves.

I shook my head, trying to readjust my thoughts. "Oh well. I'll gather my staff and work out a plan…"

With Hinata potentially attacking soon, we couldn't afford to be idle. Even if there were only five of them, those guys were nothing to sniff at. Whenever a demon lord was defeated, it was almost always by a Hero and their handpicked companions. I hadn't set out to become a demon lord myself, but now that I was, I wasn't going to sit here and let myself be defeated. We needed to decide who'd tackle those four paladins while I engaged Hinata.

Then Diablo appeared, a rather somber look on his face. "Sir Rimuru, I have a report," he said, having trouble getting the words out.

"What's up? Do we have a problem?"

It had to be that. Diablo's usual confidence was nowhere to be found.

"Yes, we do."

"What is it?"

"Reyhiem is dead. I am unsure of the cause, but he was likely killed. He was in perfect health the last time I saw him, so it was either an accident or murder." He paused, looking apologetically at me. "This was my fault, Sir Rimuru. After all your concern about him being silenced..."

I did say something offhand about that, didn't I? I didn't think it'd actually happen.

We had no idea what had taken place; it all happened inside the barrier that covered the Holy Empire of Lubelius. Given the situation, however, Diablo seemed pretty convinced that he was killed. Things were starting to seem far more serious.

"There are rumors spreading around Farmus's neighboring nations," he bitterly continued. "They speak of a demon scheming to kill the archbishop. Someone is using magical means to disseminate the news, and the Temple Knights have been deployed in response. Once they are finished preparing in a few days, I believe they will join the forces of King Edward..."

This was not at all part of Diablo's plans. In fact, it could have a seriously adverse effect on them. And of course it's all happening just as Hinata goes on the move. No doubt about it—

Understood. It is thought that everything is connected.

Yeah, even I can see that. Did Raphael think I was so hopeless that I wouldn't, or what? *Come on! Heh-heh... Raphael can be such a pain sometimes.*

But this was the last thing I needed. The Holy Church hadn't marked me a divine enemy yet, but that was probably just a matter of time now. And once the official decree was sent out, it'd be impossible to avoid all-out war. They aren't gonna say "Oops, our mistake" and take that back.

So I ordered Soka to assemble my staff. All I wanted to think about was developing my nation. That no longer seemed possible.

It was time for an emergency meeting—all hands on deck, except for Geld.

"Are you sure we shouldn't call for Geld as well, Sir Rimuru?"

"Yeah. He's working hard on his project for me. This is a problem between Hinata and me. Whether it turns into a fight or not, we don't need a huge army."

This wasn't some frantic border defense. It didn't seem right to counter a team of five with our entire military. I mean, with the huge gaps between the weaker and stronger inhabitants of this world, numbers didn't seem to even mean anything a lot of the time. The paladins coming our way would each be ranked an A or higher, so we'd need our main team on the front lines to fight back.

Besides, calling Geld and his entire team back here would be a logistical nightmare. I could use my transfer magic to bring them back, but it'd take too much time to get them were they needed to be. We would need someone to watch the prisoners, too; we couldn't afford to be haphazard with that.

Accepting my reasoning, my staff sat there and listened to Soei relay the situation.

"All right. First, a party of five led by Hinata, captain of the Crusaders, is traveling toward Tempest. Her companions are all high-level Crusader troops, and they successfully eluded the attempts of Soka's team to track them."

Soei's briefing sent murmurs across the audience. Soka and her team were all A level or so, too, and they still couldn't keep up. That showed the kind of threat we were dealing with. They probably would've managed it if they were up in the air, but flying would make them too conspicuous. They were right not to push their luck, and thanks to the alert network we had built around town, Soei was already staying abreast of Hinata's progress. Information is key to any strategy, as was making ample preparations so you didn't have to freak out later.

I had to hand it to Soei, though. His intelligence-gathering skills were phenomenal. Hiring informants to feed him data, disguising his own Replications to send out on the field... I had taught him a bit about the ninjas from my world, and he'd plainly been developing that in his own style. I had called him my "shadow," and it turned out he was an incredible fit for the job. Between that and the practical instruction I had Fuze give him, he was a professional spy by now. If everyone could take the weird Earth stuff I told them and leverage it to *this* extent, I'd never have anything to worry about.

Soei was training and educating Soka and the rest of her team, too, even using locals to gather information for him. By this point, he could handle all of that without me directing him to. Seeing him there, providing his briefing like it was his duty, made me feel proud.

"The Temple Knights in the Farmus area are being deployed to the border areas of its neighbors, effectively forming a ring around the nation. They are moving quickly, in small groups, and I believe they number over thirty thousand. Their mission is to destroy the demon, and they do not appear interested in meddling with the civil war itself. If this keeps up, however, we cannot expect much support for Sir Yohm from any of the powerful nobles in and around Farmus."

Diablo grew notably paler. He had picked up on this same information, though, and it didn't seem to surprise him. There was no doubting which "demon" was being referred to, and he was probably dying to know how word got out about him.

Thirty thousand, though… Funny how all these knights from the surrounding nations—a few hundred here, a few thousand there—could turn into such a big force. That couldn't be ignored, and they could also be indefinitely supplied from the villages. If this turned into a war of attrition, Yohm's side would have the disadvantage.

"…However, the kings of Farmus's assorted neighbors are not following the Western Holy Church's lead. None of them have mobilized their armies. It would seem the Church has its own internal factions as well, which complicates the chain of command in the area. It would be easier to grasp the situation if we had a better idea of their internals…"

Soei shook his head, a little ashamed at the information lacking in his report. *Yeah, they're kind of a mystery group, aren't they?* Even Yuuki claimed not to know much about them. Plus, the Temple Knights seemed to be lower on the totem pole than the Crusaders.

"We should have asked Reyhiem about this," a dejected Diablo commented. He was always pretty self-sufficient, never bothering to ask for feedback from someone he saw as lower than him. That came back to bite him here.

"Exactly! This is your failure, Diablo. It'd be better for all of us if someone more *experienced*, like me, took command!"

Shion preyed upon the chance, of course. She must have hated seeing the "new guy" get a big job like that. And as ready as he usually was to fire back at her, Diablo remained silent this time. *Ah well. Maybe I'll ask her instead.*

"...Actually, Shion, if I let you handle the Farmus invasion, what would you do?"

Maybe—I mean, it's not impossible—*maybe* she actually had a decent strategy in mind.

"I would lead an army into the kingdom and kill everyone in the noble classes, Sir Rimuru!"

Maybe not.

"No! No, all right?! You dumbass!"

If we killed everyone in the ruling class, the power vacuum would lead to a complex, multisided civil war. Without someone to support, you'd have all kinds of would-be warlords vying for power. The best way to keep casualties to a minimum was to retain the current system, replace the figurehead up top, and slowly let the new one take hold. That was why I had the more intelligent Diablo handle this. Shion just wasn't up to it.

"No...? All right."

Even she must have realized how foolish it was. She fell silent, standing up straight behind me. I wish she hadn't bothered to say it if she was aware of how stupid it'd make her look, but I wasn't sure she really wanted Diablo's job anyway. Or maybe this was her way of helping Diablo put this behind him.

Either way, Diablo was still my man for this.

"Look, Diablo, everybody makes mistakes. Not even I thought Reyhiem would get himself killed. Plus, is it really that big a deal you've been found out?"

"Wha? But, Sir Rimuru...? With all this talk about a demon on the loose, I could hardly..."

His concern mainly seemed to be about getting relieved of his position in this drive.

"Listen. When you make a mistake, it's vital to think about how you can make up for it. Anyone can just throw it in and say 'I quit' if they mess up, all right? That's the easy way out! And besides, the general public already knows Yohm is connected to me. You're a demon, but you're also a member of my staff. Who cares what people around Farmus are saying? What matters right now is who killed Reyhiem, right? If we can prove it wasn't you, then we're all good. You don't have to dwell on it that much."

I'm literally a demon lord. Of *course* I'm going to have a demon or two on my payroll.

"You're right," said Shuna. "And I doubt you wanted to replace him with Shion anyway."

"You're wrong, Lady Shuna! If it were me, I would turn the Kingdom of Farmus into a wasteland of…"

Shion's voice trailed off as Shuna gave her a withering stare. Those eyes were just too sharp for her to deal with.

"…He wasn't going to," Shuna continued in her strong but stern voice. "I appreciate your encouragement, Shion, as clumsy as it might have been. We are all part of Sir Rimuru's staff. We cannot allow small mistakes to plunge us into depression."

"Lady Shuna, you are making too much of this demon's meager talents. As first secretary, I was simply teaching this upstart about the gravity of my post!"

The sneer she gave him had a little bit of shame tossed in. Maybe that *was* meant as encouragement. A little hard to follow, but that's Shion for you. Shuna picked up on it better than I did. Sometimes that dunderhead can be really smart.

"Well," Benimaru said, "there you have it. The need for reinforcements will depend on our strategy. If worse comes to worst, we'll bring Geld back, and I'll take the front line."

Numbers didn't concern him very much. What did was how they were going to use their forces. There wasn't a trace of doubt on his face; he looked like he was ready to take on every Temple Knight on the planet. I was glad I could trust him.

"So you want me to continue with the current plan…?"

"Of course, Diablo. I'm gonna have my hands full with Hinata, so it's your job to handle the Farmus takeover. I'm the one who gave you permission to send Reyhiem out in the first place. I'm partially at fault, too. So I want you to see this to the end for me, all right? Or is it starting to look like that won't be possible? In that case..."

"Oh, no, not at all! You were kind enough to give me this work, Sir Rimuru, and I hope you will let me take it to its conclusion."

"Can you do it?"

"Heh-heh-heh-heh-heh... Of course!"

"Good. I know you can make up for this."

Diablo nodded, his ease and confidence returned. He ought to be fine now.

"Sir Rimuru," Shuna said as she smiled at this, "I have a suggestion."

"Oh? I don't hear suggestions from you very much. If you want to say something, go right ahead."

"Why don't we try seeking the advice of Adalmann? He was part of the Holy Church, albeit several centuries ago."

Adalmann?

Understood. Adalmann is the wight king who defended Clayman's castle...

Ohhh! Right! The undead guy Shuna made friends with. I think he's just a regular wight now, what with his power gone. He looked totally wowed when we met, going on about how much of a god I am or something; I guess he's the type to go all-in on an idea once it creeps into his head. If he was part of the Church, maybe he knows something about its inner workings. Things must have changed between now and then, but there's no harm asking.

"That's a good idea. Let's bring it up with him."

At the moment, Adalmann was working with Gabil, handling research and security duties down in the Sealed Cave. I sent a Thought Communication Gabil's way, ordering him to send Adalmann up at once. He was with us in seconds, using teleportation magic to whisk himself to our meeting. Even as a wight, he apparently could still cast the magic he learned during his living days, and it was pretty high-caliber stuff. In terms of magicules, he may only rank a B, but you couldn't afford to downplay his strength too much. *He's intelligent and magically gifted enough—maybe I should give him some better work.*

Of course, he was basically a walking skeleton, and his force of undead was weak against sunlight and incapable of speech. You could communicate with them, more or less, but work around town might be a little tough. *Let's think about that later, then.*

Regardless, it was time to listen to him.

"...Being granted with the tremendous good fortune of an audience with you, my lord, is the greatest honor that—"

"Enough!"

He had been heaping praise upon me the entire time I was thinking about him. I was ignoring it, but it didn't seem to be ending anytime soon, so I finally yelled at him to shut up. Pretty intense guy. Shion liked him ("You have potential, I see!") and Diablo gave him an approving smile, but the rest of my staff were a little put off by the display.

"That's good for now, Adalmann," Shuna said. "We all know you are happy to see Sir Rimuru, but we are short on time right now, so please go on with your business."

Thanks, Shuna. If it wasn't for you, he might start openly praying to me next. With that kind of dogged faith, no wonder he was so strong. It kind of made sense.

So on to Adalmann...

It turns out that he was actually a Holy Church cardinal, one of the highest positions in the whole bureaucracy. Lubelius wasn't a real powerhouse of a nation at the time—the Church wasn't the juggernaut it is now—but we still learned a great deal from him.

First, he told us that the Holy Empire of Lubelius is a religious state with the god Luminus at the peak. The Holy Emperor was considered the official spokesperson for this god; her identity and appearance was unknown. The imperial throne may or may not be passed down from generation to generation, but Adalmann, at least, never saw that happen.

The nation's day-to-day operations were handled by the Papacy, the main ruling authority. In Adalmann's time, the entire Western Holy Church was merely a division of this Papacy. "The Church began strictly as a missionary group to spread the good word about Luminism," he explained. "It had no standing army at all."

However, due to the danger involved with their field work, the Papacy formed the Temple Knights, working out agreements with

the world's nations to build troop stations in their area of activity. They all welcomed the Knights (especially since the Papacy was paying the tab) and promised to cooperate with them. Protecting the Luminus faithful from monster threats also helped keep the general public safe, so their generosity was understandable.

As these relationships with foreign countries grew, there naturally began to be friction in certain areas. That created a need for the Master Rooks, a division that worked under the more direct control of the Holy Emperor. "I call it a division," Adalmann said, "but in the beginning, it was a small handful of people. They all boasted tremendous strength and had the right to give orders to the Temple Knights. As a group, they pledged their loyalty strictly to Luminus and the Holy Emperor—even the most powerful consuls in the Papacy could no more than 'request' their services, not order them."

These consuls were the politicians of Lubelius. If not even they could order this division around, they had to be powerful, indeed.

"By the way, my friend Alberto was invited to join this division once. He turned it down so he could serve as my aide in the Holy Church. The Holy Emperor rewarded him with the title of acolyte."

His jawbone clacked up and down in a show of what I assumed was pride. Alberto was the death knight that gave Hakuro all that trouble, if I recall. He was now just a skeletal fighter, but between his sword skills and possessing a monster's strength, he'd give anyone a run for their money.

"However, I understand that things are quite different around the group now."

Oops. Adalmann still wasn't done talking.

According to him, the biggest difference was the power the Church had acquired; their Crusader paladin corps gave them a much greater say in matters. Papal consuls were now largely picked from the Holy Church's cardinals, putting them in a much safer position than before. The Seven Days Clergy had a lot to do with that.

When Adalmann was there, this Clergy also worked as consuls, enjoying powers second only to the Holy Emperor. They were ordered to rebuild and shore up the Church's position, and the changes they enacted created the Church structure we know today.

This Seven Days Clergy sounded kind of fishy to me, though. It sounded like they were the ones who tried to run Adalmann and his friends out of the Church, and he was clearly still no fan of theirs.

Although the Crusaders performed few noteworthy feats under the Clergy's direction, Hinata's training had helped them grow into the strongest of knight corps. This was how Lubelius had acquired both the Master Rooks and the Crusaders for itself.

"You seem to know a lot about this, Adalmann. Weren't you in Clayman's domain by this point in time?"

Adalmann gave this question a clacking laugh. "The demon lord Clayman saw the Western Holy Church as his enemy. He feared its power to make war and gathered as much intelligence as he could about them. I was a leader in their bureaucracy, so even if he didn't accept my feedback, he still provided me with the information he had."

That made sense. Clayman's near-obsessive wariness had unexpectedly helped us out.

"Please, my lord and savior Rimuru, be careful. Lubelius is home to a group of Enlightened known as the Ten Great Saints, a cabal that even Clayman was afraid of. I must advise you not to let your guard down."

He also mentioned the Three Battlesages, a group within the Master Rooks that was also Enlightened class. This trio, along with six commander-level knights and Hinata, formed the Ten Great Saints. An Enlightened was a human with powers on the same level as a would-be demon lord, and if they had ten of those, no wonder they kept Clayman awake at night. It seemed pretty likely that Hinata's four companions on her current journey came from this group. Bringing regular soldiers along would just guarantee their deaths; better to presume that the top brass would be knocking on our door. Plus, if the Temple Knights were being mobilized, it was safe to assume the Master Rooks were, too, along with the Three Battlesages.

"My lord, please allow me as a former Church cardinal to attempt to reason with this Hinata woman! I will gladly convince her to abandon her faith in the Church and turn it toward you instead—"

"Ah, wait, wait. I don't need any of that, so you can go."

I put a stop to Adalmann before things got any weirder. In a way, he was even worse than Hinata—once his mind's made up, there's no derailing it. Talking with someone like him rarely results in anything useful.

"I see... A wonderful idea."

"Heh-heh-heh-heh-heh... Ah yes, there is always that approach!"

And of *course* Shion and Diablo loved it.

"What are you two idiots talking about?! If we try to pull that crap on her, things are gonna get even *more* complicated!"

Talk about being cut from the same cloth. I was starting to wonder if they actually liked more than hated each other.

✳

With Adalmann gone, it was time to return to the topic at hand. We had all the info we needed—now to devise some actual policies.

First, I wanted to have some kind of throwaway piece I could use to gauge my opponent's power. Who would work for that...? I could sense Veldora eagerly staring at me. *No, Veldora, not you. That's too much.*

"Veldora, you—"

"Ah! Finally, my turn in the spotlight? At your service!"

"No, Veldora. I want you to man our last line of defense."

"Whaaaat?"

"Did you hear me? The last...line...of defense. Doesn't that sound cool? You're the only person I could imagine for the job."

"Mm, of course, of course. I thought so as well!"

He nodded proudly. Great. Good thing I could corral him before he went berserk on me. *Veldora would never lose in battle, but sending him out just wouldn't be the right thing to do*, I thought. I hadn't given up all hope of talking things over with Hinata, so I couldn't just whip Veldora out at first sight, or even as primary backup.

With Veldora placated, it was Benimaru who spoke next.

"First, I will announce my assignments for Sir Yohm's reinforcements."

Mm. Good. Benimaru was turning into quite the commander. He had gained a lot of experience in that previous battle, and unlike Shion, he wasn't letting it get to his head any longer. Now he could correctly analyze the data at hand and determine the differences between the two sides. I was still the commander in chief, but by this point, he was better suited for the job than I was. I mean, hell, I didn't really want that work anyway. *Let's hope that Benimaru can grow into the role.*

With his loud, deep voice, Benimaru announced the assignments. The reinforcements would consist of one hundred goblin riders, led by Gobta; four thousand troops from Benimaru's Green Numbers, along with a hundred members of Team Kurenai to lead them (the remaining two hundred Kurenai members would stay back to protect the town), and a hundred fighters from Gabil's Team Hiryu. That was a force of 4,300 in total.

"...That is all. This will mean fewer troops guarding the town, but we have lycanthropes among our fighters now, as well as Sir Veldora, so I don't anticipate that being a problem. Any feedback?"

"Whoa! Uh, me?!"

"Is there a problem with that, Gobta?"

"Nnnn...no."

Benimaru's eyes were enough to clamp Gobta's mouth shut. Doofus.

"Hakuro will be the supreme commander of this force, but don't worry. If anything happens, I will use Spatial Motion to back you up at once. Just keep in mind that there's a good chance I will be fighting Hinata Sakaguchi myself. This might make it impossible to contact me, so try to follow Hakuro's orders as closely as possible!"

"Understood, sir," said Hakuro.

"It shall be this battle, this very battle, where my name will shine!" cried Gabil.

"Yeah, yeah, all right...," murmured Gobta.

Hakuro and Gabil were raring to go. Gobta frankly worried me a little, but he had a knack for working through crises, so he ought to be fine, I think. Maybe.

"Hmm. I still worry, though. Ranga, are you awake?"

I addressed Ranga, currently sleeping in my shadow. He spent almost all his time in there lately, in part to guard me, but his magicule energy had been expanding in the weirdest way. He probably needed more exercise.

"Will I be deployed, Master?"

"Yep. I need to get you running around now and then, you know? Follow Gobta and keep him safe!"

"I shall! A little wake-up exercise would be very kind to me."

Weird. I was getting the strangest feeling that unleashing this guy was gonna be seriously bad news. For our foes anyway.

"Oooh, yeah, if Ranga's joining me, I'll be totally fine!"

Now Gobta was showing some more enthusiasm. *Looking out for number one, aren't you?*

"Ranga, don't take any reckless risks. And try not to kill your opponents, all right?"

"It shall be done! Lady Shion has taught me how to restrain myself!"

"Um, great..."

Now I was *really* worried. I thought he was just spending all day sleeping in my shadow, but he was doing that, too? Having Shion as his teacher filled me with anxiety, but hopefully it'd work out fine. *We've got potions, I guess.*

Benimaru offered no objection, although his eyes indicated he thought I was spoiling Gobta. Thus, with a delighted howl, Ranga curled up next to Gobta. *Let's just hope anyone who crosses him lives to tell the tale.* I almost wanted to wish my opponents luck.

We had our force assignments. Now we had to discuss the reinforcements Farmus's new king was receiving.

"So, Diablo, tell me how you intend to proceed."

"Thank you, sir. I was expecting reinforcements, but thirty thousand is well beyond my projections. My original plan assumed a force of approximately ten thousand fighting for Edward."

His new plans began with having Edmaris send a letter to the new king once he began moving these troops around, asking him to explain his actions. Edward was no doubt planning to shift responsibility for the reparations to Edmaris, and I wanted to keep that from happening. The new king would no doubt say that any agreement Edmaris signed was null and void. That wouldn't pass muster with the Council if Farmus was part of it—it barely did with us, in fact.

No, his plan likely involved executing Edmaris and reneging on his promises to us. We'd then be angered enough to stage a military operation, and then the Western Nations would join together to resist us—that kind of thing. To prevent that, Edmaris had been rescued by Yohm's squad. He was lying low in Migam at the moment, which was just what we planned. Yohm had a force of about five thousand over there, and the original plan called for us to teleport 4,300 more to Migam for him. That's not a huge difference, but the psychological effect—the terror of having a brand-new army appear out of nowhere behind the first one—would turn the tables during battle.

But now that Edward had started assembling reinforcements, we couldn't use that. If we waited for him to get his whole force together, we'd be faced with a four-against-one disadvantage in numbers. The sooner we acted, the better.

"It seems to me," concluded Diablo, "that Edward is waiting for reinforcements he can use to strike Edmaris's domain."

The plan at this point had been to defeat Edward in one decisive battle or another, then have Edmaris endorse the champion Yohm as king instead of reclaiming the throne.

"Currently, Edward has access to a force of twenty thousand," Soei commented. "Give him three more weeks, and the full force of forty thousand will be assembled. That's more than enough to take Migam, as weak as its rear guard currently is."

So the longer we wait, the worse things will get. But if we go all out right now, it's going to be full-on, blood-soaked war. Farmus had already lost twenty thousand troops; a dragged-out war would cause untold damage.

So what then...?

"...This is just the worst. We could always just give up on this, you know. If I forgive the remaining debt they owe us, we can avoid war that way, right? That'll eliminate the whole pretense for fighting us in the first place."

"We can't! If we do that, Sir Rimuru, you will look like a big pushover!"

"I wouldn't want that, no, but we've already profited from this big-time. Wouldn't it be easier if we just stepped on the brakes and waited until after we've handled Hinata to deal with it?"

As far as I was concerned, we were paid more money than I ever expected to see from them. Cutting our losses now would still put us way ahead, and I felt that waging a war on two fronts would be too risky by comparison. Shion did have a point, though. Demon lords have a vested interest in being feared.

"Heh-heh-heh-heh… Abandoning this plan would be unthinkable. Sir Rimuru, you are willing to let me handle this, yes?"

"Yeah, but I don't want people to keep dying on my watch, whether they're involved with it or not…"

"That will not be a problem. If that is your will, sir, then it is my duty to abide by it. It will be a simple task for me."

I was seriously considering calling the whole thing off, but Diablo hadn't given up at all.

"What are you intending to do?"

"I will find the culprit," he quietly replied. "The evildoer who tried to pin the crime on me."

Wow. He's pretty angry.

"'Destroy the demon,' they say?" He gave me a little grin. "Well, if they want me eradicated, I will gladly serve as their opponent. Somewhere, among this thirty thousand, there could be someone involved with the culprit. I will give them a *gentle* interrogation."

Uh-oh. There wasn't a shred of gentleness about that. And Diablo sounded like he was ready to take on thirty thousand Temple Knights by himself. Better rein him in a little bit—

"I see," Benimaru said as I stewed over this. "If you came out to engage them, we'd have nothing to worry about. But don't kill any innocents, all right?"

"There is no need to remind me. I will never defy Sir Rimuru's will."

"Fair enough. In that case, Hakuro, can you suppress the new king's soldiers without killing any of them?"

"It shouldn't be a problem. It would be easier to stage a surprise attack to end things quickly, but that would provide no training for us."

"True. Gabil, we're going to need a great deal of potion."

"Certainly! I will be sure it is ready."

Huh? Um, hello? I was being left in the dust.

Shion smiled at me. "Looks like the Farmus invasion is in good hands, Sir Rimuru."

"Uh, yeah… Yeah. Good luck, guys…"

""Yes, my lord!"" they all replied.

With that, the conversation was over. Couldn't argue with that.

✳

I didn't like how that was handled very much, but either way, our discussions shifted over to the next issue—who would handle Hinata and her party.

"So about the party of five," Benimaru said, looking at me. *All right. Time to take the initiative on this one!* ...But just as I was about to speak, Soei suddenly stood up.

"Sir Rimuru," he said in a strained voice, "we have an emergency. The Crusaders have begun to move..."

The room fell into a panic...or at least, I did.

"Is something up with Hinata's team?"

"No. Hokuso, monitoring Englesia, reported to me that he sighted a hundred mounted knights departing at this very moment..."

"What?!"

"They are half a day behind Hinata, but at this rate, they will catch up with them before long. They are headed in the same direction, at least, so it seems fair to assume they are coming our way."

Hinata was moving along at a regular, unhurried pace, although her four paladins had used magic to catch up at full speed before slowing back down. There had reportedly been some dispute among the group when they rendezvoused, but they remained together, a team of five bound for our city. They were still in Englesian lands, headed toward Blumund, but only at a relatively slow speed. If those hundred knights wanted to catch up with them, they could—however, instead of using the highway or another commonly used route, they were reportedly more likely to abandon their horses and take the old path into the forest instead.

"So they aren't trying to meet up with Hinata?"

"Their motives are unclear. It will take no less than two weeks for Hinata to arrive, and the knights behind her are likely going to take about the same time."

Soei, who was as confused about this as I was, ordered his force to tail them. We would just have to wait for further reports. Out of the frying pan and into the fire, huh? Except I had the impression we hadn't left the frying pan at all. I really didn't like this, but no point whining about it. Things were rapidly changing.

My staff began to debate among themselves. I listened in, thinking over my options.

There were five Enlightened to deal with, Hinata included, plus a hundred paladins doing who knows what. This hundred was far more of a threat to us than the twenty thousand members of Farmus's military—hell, Hinata alone was way worse. That's just the way things worked in this world. Strength in numbers meant nothing against strength brought to loony extremes. No matter how many nameless Mohawk-wearing punks you lined up in a row, they weren't going to beat the Fist of the North Star.

I wasn't planning to go out there alone. That seemed kind of suicidal to me. So...what?

"Why not just kill them all instead of fretting about it?"

I probably don't need to say who suggested that. Life's so *easy* if you never use your brain at all, isn't it? Just focus on the results; don't think about whether you can or can't do something. Of course, that's probably how she earned that freaky unique skill of hers, but still...

"This would be exactly the kind of thing we could call upon Geld for," Hakuro noted.

"Ah, he has his own tasks to deal with," reasoned Benimaru. "We must handle this ourselves, unless there is truly no other recourse."

I hated to hear that, but they had a point. Should I really be so stubborn about keeping Geld out of this? I mean, we're only talking a hundred or so people. There was no point deploying a massive force against it; it was already clearly something only our strongest people could deal with.

If I was going to handle Hinata, someone else needed to keep the other four down for me. It'd be great if Hinata agreed to my one-on-one offer, but taking on five people at once by myself was way too risky.

Understood. It will not be a problem. The sole concern is the subject Hinata Sakaguchi.

*　　*　　*

Um, that's kind of the problem here, man! Are you feeling all right? You're starting to seem a lot less reliable than the Great Sage was.

...

The whole reason I was stewing over this was because I didn't want to have anybody killed. If I went with massive numbers to tire out the paladins, victory was assured, but it'd result in tons of casualties. We had all kept ourselves alive and well up to now; it'd be ridiculous to stop that streak now.

But...this was Hinata we were dealing with. She's *seriously* bad news. I focused squarely on running away the last time we tussled, but if I had truly tried to fight her, I almost certainly would have been dead. Even though she wasn't even giving her full effort.

Right now, I was the only one of us who could give Hinata any kind of challenge, and if it was a one-on-one duel, I didn't think I'd lose. If she was paired with her paladins, though, I couldn't be so sure. Striding in with too much confidence could get me killed. Those hundred other paladins were another issue, too; how should we handle those? If she just wanted to talk with me, she wouldn't have taken this many people with her. And given how she was going out of her way to avoid notice, you'd have to be silly not to be alarmed.

"Wait!" Veldora suddenly belted out. "I know! How about I just *happen* to test out my dragon's breath when they arrive? We'll simply pretend it was a misfire and I wasn't aware anybody was near me!"

"Can you shut up one second? You're the final defense line, and I mean the really, *really* final one, all right?"

I swear. He was like a bratty kid sometimes. If Hinata *did* want to talk, and we pulled a stunt like that, it'd blow the whole thing. There was no telling how much damage that breath would cause, either. It was too scary to think of. It'd be happier for everyone, us included, if he stepped away from the battle. His plan did make sense if we were in this to kill, but I had to know for sure what our opponents wanted first. We couldn't leave them to their own devices, though, because a few paladins were all it'd take to build another Holy Field over me. They had to be watched but not killed.

Paladins were positioned as the guardians of humankind, protected by the elemental spirits. In this world, monster-based mayhem was no laughing matter. It was a daily threat to one's life. The paladins Hinata trained grew up knowing that fear, as they patrolled the villages and frontier towns they offered their free protection to. Many people owed their lives to them. The Crusaders held a special place in the hearts of those survivors, along with Luminism. Their strength was top-shelf, each one ranking an A or above, and we'd take serious casualties in a frontal assault.

But that wasn't the problem. Killing these knights, these fighters with the hopes and prayers and anticipation of the weak and helpless heaped upon their shoulders, would undoubtedly be the source of untold headaches to come.

If it wasn't for Luminism's stance that monsters were the common enemy of humanity, maybe we could've talked this out. I hadn't abandoned that hope, but I couldn't be too confident that this attempt would work out any better than the last one. To them, we were simply evil, and they didn't negotiate with evil. And I could understand their thoughts. Some of them must have survived their own villages being destroyed, their parents being killed. Being tricked by the wrong adversary meant the loss of life—not just theirs, but those of everyone who needed protection behind them.

Even now, there were wild monsters causing havoc everywhere. Their numbers had gone down in the lands around Tempest, but in other realms, they were still appearing from the woods and going berserk. If we wiped out the paladins, who would keep the countryside safe then? If you think about it that way, I wasn't so sure we should just wipe all these guys out.

If Hinata had just opened up and *talked* to me last time, there wouldn't even be this whole misunderstanding. Sadly, though, she didn't. Because I'm a monster. She was stubborn like that—stubborn enough that, even after that message I sent, she brought a whole force along with her.

Concern. Some factors seem unnatural about that. There is likely a high possibility this paladin activity goes against Hinata Sakaguchi's desire.

*　　*　　*

Huh? So there is *room to talk, then?*

If I put my foot down and declared her an enemy, there were a million and one ways I could defeat her. But as long as I didn't know what they were up to, it was all but impossible to figure out our best move. There were a few reasons for that, but if I had to pick one, I guess it just comes down to the fact that I didn't want to kill Hinata. Shizue was worried for her, too, and now that I had taken on her will, I didn't want to resort to violence.

Ugh! And this was all because of how headstrong she was. So annoying.

Either way, though, if talks failed, we wouldn't avoid a fight. If that was how it turned out, we were at a disadvantage, really. We were dealing with an anti-monster expert, nobody we could afford to trifle with, and I was certain that I wanted to avoid casualties on either side.

We would need to assume the worst in our approach, no matter what they did. If talking didn't work, I wanted it to be a duel between Hinata and me. That was exactly what my message said, so that shouldn't be a problem. They might be considering a more full-on battle, but if they were, they were gonna do it on my turf.

If we could spring a trap or something on them, that could buy time enough for me to defeat Hinata. It was a pain to think about, but it had to be done.

"All right. I've got it sorted out. We need to consider the future here, and along those lines, I want to do our best to avoid killing any of the paladins as well."

That was the direction I wanted to go with—assuming talks failed, of course—and it ignited some more debate among my staff. It'd be a terrible waste if we took casualties of our own in an effort to avoid hurting them. We had to work out the best possible approach, and the surest way was for me to beat Hinata and break the paladins' morale. As a result, our primary focus was earning as much time for me as possible.

"So why don't we just slash 'em all up and silence them that way?"

"..."

"I was joking," Shion said with a cough. *Is she really all right? The way she acts alarms me almost as much as Veldora.*

"Basically," she continued, "you want to maintain the battle, without killing any paladins, and without losing anyone on our side. In the meantime, you will defeat the enemy's leader. Am I right, Sir Rimuru?"

"Yeah. That's what it is. I'm glad you get it."

Oh, so she *did* follow me. I was seriously worried for her sanity for a moment there. And if she got it, I was sure the rest of my staff did. But just when I breathed a sigh of relief, Shion confidently beamed at me.

"In that case, I have an idea!"

Uh-oh. I began to feel anxious, for reasons I couldn't put into words.

"...What is it?"

"There just happens to be exactly one hundred members in Team Reborn, the group I lead. They would certainly be up to the challenge. I'd like them to engage the paladins!"

She looked defiantly at me.

"What are you, crazy?! Team Reborn's only about a C-ranked threat level! They're *not* gonna be up to the challenge—no!"

I wanted to know where Shion's confidence came from. They may have matched numbers-wise, but in terms of strength, it was like night and day.

"...There are some issues with that suggestion, yes, but I think it would be an effective idea."

Surprisingly, it was Benimaru who defended her. Everyone in Team Reborn had the extra skill Complete Memory, which made them hard to kill with regular attacks. It was unlikely, he said, that our foes would break out their worst, most soul-crushing attacks on the first salvo against a weaker force. As he put it, their weakness "would put the paladins off their guard, giving us a hole to plunge through. If buying time is what we're looking for, they might actually be well suited for that."

He was starting to convince me. If the paladins didn't have any way of directly attacking the souls of their foes, Team Reborn would even be at an advantage. It could make things a lot easier than if we sent any other force their way.

"Benimaru is right!" Shion bellowed. "And also, Sir Rimuru, I have been carefully training them all. They have successfully acquired Cancel Pain, of course, and they also resist poison, paraly-sis, and sleep. When it comes to tenacity, at least, they won't lose out to anybody. Hakuro said so himself."

Hakuro was nodding at her. It must've been the truth, but *I thought I'd check to be sure.*

"How did they acquire those resistances, by the way?"

"Well…"

Her reply surprised me. Apparently, she asked Kurobe to make them all weapons that inflicted their targets with status ailments, then had them use those weapons while training against each other, building up their natural immunity. They were largely immortal, so they'd never go easy on their sparring partners, and it was so hard to knock them out entirely that battles tended to last forever with them. In the simulated fights they carried out, it was more a matter of "whoever's left standing is the winner."

"And if Team Reborn is in danger, Sir Rimuru, I can send Team Kurenai in to help them out. Are you up for that, Gobwa?"

Benimaru was talking to the large, attractive-looking ogre guarding the door for us. She came over to me, kneeled, and bowed her head to us both. This Gobwa was the squad leader of Kurenai, apparently. She must've been a goblin at the time I gave that name to her, but you'd never believe it now—at this point, she was an elite officer, dressed in a striking scarlet-red uniform.

"Sir!" she said, puffing out her chest. "I have been training our squad just as hard as Lady Shion has. Please allow us to serve your needs on the field, Sir Rimuru!"

Her eyes were sharp, giving her a strong presence. She was also an A rank, maybe higher, which made her at least as strong as Soka. *I guess Benimaru's been raising some real talents of his own.*

"They may not be an even match for the paladins," Benimaru said, "but my fighters are talented, indeed. Two of them could engage one of the paladins long enough to allow Team Reborn time to escape."

"Don't be ridiculous! My team can neutralize the paladins all by themselves!"

They started bickering. Both of them were certainly ready for a fight, at least. Maybe it'd be worth leaving this job to them.

"All right. Shion, I accept your offer. Gobwa, you handle the rest."

"Y-yes sir! Gladly!"

Gobwa's cheeks reddened as she replied. It must've been exciting for her, which was fine by me. It'd be more ideal if I didn't need to use them at all, but regardless.

"Remember, Shion, don't send them out until we're sure that the talks are a nonstarter, all right?"

"That's fine! But if our foes make any suspicious moves..."

Yeah, that'd be a different story. I forgot about the need to interfere with them in advance, lest they toss a Holy Field our way.

"If they try anything funny, don't be afraid to hold back then. Check with me via Thought Communication first, then take action!"

"Roger that," Shion replied, giving a satisfied nod as Benimaru ordered Gobwa back to the door.

∗

So we now had Team Reborn assigned to delay the Crusaders and Team Kurenai providing emergency backup, about three hundred people against a hundred paladins. I was happy with that. Now we just had the question of who would handle the four saint-class paladins accompanying Hinata.

First off, who among us was powerful enough to handle them? By my estimation, the group included Veldora, Ranga, Benimaru, Shion, Soei, Geld, Gabil, Diablo, and me. Hakuro had the sword skills to keep up as well, although his magical strength wasn't quite up to everyone else's level. Shuna... I wasn't sure. A magical fight was one thing, but against a close-range expert, I didn't like her chances. The Ten Great Saints were reportedly on a level with a pre-ascended demon lord or Orc Disaster; that'd be a lot to ask from Shuna.

So counting Hakuro, ten people. I was handling Hinata. Veldora was out of the question—I didn't want him going out of control on me, so he could focus on town defense. I mean, for all we knew, there could be yet another enemy force on the move that we hadn't noticed yet. We needed our defense to be as solid as possible. Geld, meanwhile, I didn't want to bother if I could help it.

I wanted to have Diablo, Ranga, Hakuro, and Gabil focus on Farmus, not this fight. Which left:

"So the only people I have free are Benimaru, Shion, and Soei, huh?"

Ideally, I'd like one fighter per adversary, but I was short one body. So now what?

"I will join the battle, of course," Benimaru said. This was exactly why he let Hakuro lead Yohm's reinforcements. I couldn't have him miss this one.

"I will stay as well," Soei added. "My Replications can handle my intelligence duties well enough, and Soka and the others are proving fairly useful by this point."

"Me too!" shouted Shion. "As your secretary, Sir Rimuru, I will forever remain by your side—"

Report. If there is an Enlightened-level fighter among the hundred paladins, attempting to buy time with them may prove impossible. It would be safer to devote some of your war power to them as well.

Ohhh. Yeah, there's always that concern, too. Thanks for the actual useful feedback! I knew I could rely on Raphael.

"Hang on, Shion. There's something I want to ask Soei first. Do you know if there are any Enlightened among the paladin force, separate from Hinata?"

Soei closed his eyes for a few moments. "My apologies," he replied. "All of them are at least an A rank, but none particularly stood out from the pack in my perception."

With monsters, it was pretty easy to figure out, what with the way they let their aura hang out all casually. The stronger they were, the more you could *feel* it from them. But with (for example) Hinata, she didn't feel different from any other human being. I couldn't pick her out at all, which was what made her strength so surprising. Ah well. We'd find out quick enough in battle anyway.

"Just in case, I want Shion to monitor the group of paladins. We'll have her command both the Reborn and Kurenai groups. Is that all right, Benimaru?"

"If that is your decision, it is not a problem at all, Sir Rimuru. Soei and I can each engage two of Hinata's companions."

Talk about confidence. To Soei, this all seemed perfectly natural.

"One moment, Sir Rimuru," said Rigurd. "Perhaps this would be a good opportunity for me to join in? I am content with arranging our political system around town, but even I want to smash some heads sometimes!"

"In that case, I, too, am available," added Shuna with a smile. *Look, you aren't suited for close-quarters combat, all right? It's gonna be too dangerous for you.*

"And so am I. I don't want Gobta to hog the spotlight forever!"

Now Rigur was throwing his hat in the ring. He and Rigurd were both past the A rank, but neither was anywhere near demon lord status. It would be throwing their lives away.

"Hang on, hang on. I think this is a little too dangerous for you all."

"But we don't have anyone else, do we?"

"With us involved," Benimaru said, "that will be more than enough."

"Perhaps," countered Rigurd. "I know your team is powerful, but it would be best not to underestimate our foes, wouldn't it? Allow Rigur and me to take this responsibility..."

The debate was starting to heat up. All this worrying might be for naught if a fight didn't break out in the end, but I wanted to tackle this with as much confidence as possible. If we were going to pull out all the stops with this, maybe we should call back Geld after all, just for that one day.

I was pondering this as I tuned out the endless debate my staff was having when there was a loud noise on the other side of the door.

"I told you," I could hear Gobwa say, "we are in the middle of a meeting—"

"Yes, and we want to be part of it!"

"Stop being so belligerent, Sufia. Come on, lady, all we want is to repay a favor we owe him, okay?"

It was Sufia and Alvis, two of the Three Lycanthropeers. The door was finally opened to them.

"Hey. Sorry to barge in. I saw that bony dude runnin' around just now, but what's up with that? We wanna join in, too, Sir Rimuru."

"Demon Lord Rimuru, please forgive our sudden visit. Sufia is being rude as usual, but we truly to seek to support you. Please, allow us the chance to repay the favor you gave to us."

The two of them were in front of me, kneeling. Well, not *directly* in front of me, since Gobwa was still trying to drag them out by the ear. Benimaru raised a hand to stop her, finally allowing them to approach—but now it was Diablo standing between them and me. Benimaru seemed to trust them as well, but either way, a few people here were kind of antsy about them being close to me. Diablo, in particular, eyed them with open suspicion. If I ordered him to, I'm sure he would've chopped off their heads in an instant.

Sufia and Alvis contrasted starkly with each other, but on this point, they were two beastmen of the same mind. They pushed their way in here, knowing it would offend, and asked me to let them help out. The cold treatment from some of my staff was something they seemed to expect.

"Benimaru, Diablo, both of you, step back."

"Understood."

"Yes, Sir Rimuru."

As they returned to their seats, I had chairs set up for Sufia and Alvis. After a few moments to ensure everyone had calmed down, I continued.

"So you want to help us?"

"Yes, Sir Rimuru. We are dealing with some of the Ten Great Saints here, right? It seems you need someone to stop them in their tracks, and we want to be the people who do that for you."

"Yes! Combat's pretty much the only thing I can do, y'know. We'll never be able to repay our debt to you otherwise. Please, use us freely!"

I thought about this. Force-wise, this was not a problem. But if either of them got hurt, how would I ever explain it to the (ex-) demon lord Carillon?

"Are you sure you can volunteer for that without Carillon's consent?"

"Of course! Lord Carillon is always quite tolerant of things like that."

"And our lord seemed concerned about repaying his debt to you as well, Sir Rimuru. If we don't step up here, I am sure he would lecture us about it."

Hmm… Frankly, I appreciated this offer a lot. Having these two around would put my mind at ease quite a bit for the battle.

"I agree," Benimaru added. "I believe we can trust them."

"When I'm gone," Shion asked, "will you be able to eliminate anyone getting in Sir Rimuru's way?"

"Absolutely," Sufia casually replied. Those two did seem to get along pretty well with each other—and I wasn't hearing any no votes.

"Can you do it?"

"You can count on us!"

"Thank you for your kind words!"

I hated to rain on Rigurd's parade when he was all revved up like this, but I needed someone to lead the people in town. When it came to fighting, I didn't have complete confidence in him, either. But with Sufia and Alvis on our side, we couldn't be much better prepared for Hinata and her forces.

It was hard to call what we had cobbled together a "strategy," but either way, we had something to work with. Now my staff was discussing the details with one another, checking to make sure there weren't any holes in our plan.

I closed my eyes and tried to guess at Hinata's behavior again. Raphael's calculations told me this approach was the most likely way to avoid casualties. You could say that I had nothing to worry about, but I was still hung up on a couple of issues.

One, this whole thing would be so much more in the bag if I either gave up on conquering Farmus or called Geld back here. I was going through with this anyway for reasons I suppose you could call purely egotistical. That was why I had to aim for a complete, flawless victory.

If Hinata agreed to talk, then fine. If not, we'd duel it out, one-on-one. We were fully prepared for that scenario, albeit with one considerable pitfall: What if I lost? Then everything would be meaningless. Raphael seemed to have little doubt about my victory, but if I blew it, that would tank this entire operation. Could I really trust Raphael's calculations? I had a suspicion that Raphael tended to err on the side of overconfidence, and it wouldn't be the first time, either. It believed too much in me—it wasn't overrating my chances, was it?

I couldn't banish that thought...but I had to do this. *That's how it's always been, and that's how it always will be. Whether I fully believe in myself or not, all my friends certainly do. I just have to stop wavering and press on.*

"I'm going to say this one more time. If, at any point in this battle, it looks like we'll have trouble keeping ourselves afloat, I want you to immediately focus on annihilating the enemy. The lives of our allies have to take first priority. You need to understand that all this means nothing if any of you get yourselves killed. I expect everyone to make it through this alive, just as we always do. Dismissed!"

""""Yes sir!!""""

If we were too reluctant to pick off a paladin, and it got one of our friends killed, it'd make all of us look silly. I wanted to be sure everyone was fully aware of that. Seeing them all voice their agreement, I reciprocated with a satisfied nod.

Now to wait and see what Hinata tried.

●

The journey to Tempest was proceeding along well for Hinata.

A quick trip through the transport gate was all it took to go from Lubelius to Englesia, but from there, she had to do it the normal way—and without any replacement horses, so frequent rest breaks were a must. She was used to marches like this, so she kept her own gear to a bare minimum. One horse and a sleeping bag, which she kept filled with emergency rations, a pot, and so forth.

The trails weren't blocked by snow or anything, but the seasonal weather still precluded her from making this trip with haste.

She had rendezvoused with four of her paladin subordinates soon after departing. It had been a surprise at first, hearing hoofbeats from behind and spotting four familiar faces—Arnaud, Bacchus, Litus, and Fritz, her paladin commanders. Renard, the vice captain, was holding the fort while Hinata was gone, and since having all the commanders away from Lubelius at once was not an option, they drew lots and picked Garde to stay behind.

"...What are you doing?" she had asked them.

"We would ask you the same question, Lady Hinata. Attempting to get a head start on us?"

"A head start on what? I am merely going there to talk."

"Oh, come now. You know, you sound less than convincing given how clearly you are equipped to wage war."

"Yes! And we have no interest in standing atop your sacrifices. Our glory comes only when we serve under you."

"Indeed. And besides, that message didn't insist upon you traveling alone, did it?"

Hinata rolled her eyes and sighed. "I know, I know. But this is a demon lord, all right? I'm the one who riled him up. This is *my* problem. You have neither any responsibility nor any involvement in it. Return to our homeland at once."

But Arnaud and the others ignored the order. She was eventually forced to say "Whatever" and allow them to join her.

The road this band of five chose was maintained, but it had seen better days. Inns were sparse along the way, and at this time of year, no-vacancy signs were a frequent sight. They would be forced to camp out, and even though they weren't running into monsters, camping out in the cold of winter with nothing but emergency rations took its toll on Hinata and her companions.

By the time they reached Blumund ten days later, they had exhausted a worrying amount of their strength. They decided the time was ripe for a night indoors, for a change.

*

"This town has certainly changed," Arnaud said after the five of them each rented their own room and assembled down at the dining hall.

Hinata felt the same way. Litus had said as much in her report, but seeing it with her own eyes made the difference exceedingly obvious.

After changing and resting up a bit, they decided to go explore town. The markets were packed with people, despite the winter weather, and all sorts of strange and unfamiliar merchandise was available. The backward country atmosphere Hinata felt the last time a mission brought her here was now considerably weaker.

"And did you see the people? So much more variety to the clothing around here now. Some of them had the kind of fancy outfits you normally only see in Englesia."

"Yeah, and those weapons and armor... I think some of it is monster-derived. Real high-quality stuff circulating."

Arnaud and Bacchus had trouble believing their eyes. Hinata could see why. It wasn't up to the standards they enjoyed as paladins, but everything they saw was almost *too* upscale for a small country like this. And all the merchant stalls! In a world where many shops closed for the winter season, the sheer number they saw was an extreme rarity. If they were open, that must have meant customers were around—and *that* must mean that, even in winter, this little backwater town was entertaining large numbers of merchants and adventurers.

"Is this Tempest's influence at hand?" Fritz asked, gauging Hinata's response as he did. All this development must have come after trade relations were opened up with Tempest. That was the only reason he could think of. It also meant that large numbers of people in this town were not only ignoring the teachings of Luminism, but actively flouting them.

"All this prosperity," whispered Litus, clearly shocked, "by doing business with a *demon lord*?"

Hinata, deep down, had to agree with her. This wasn't normal. For *him*, though; for someone like Rimuru who came from the same land as her, maybe this wasn't so strange at all.

For example, the menu on the wall of this dining room.

"Have you decided?" an attractive waitress asked them.

Hinata was ready for her.

"I'll have the ramen, please."

"The ramen! That's been gaining an audience lately. It comes in miso, shoyu, and *tonkotsu* flavors, each available in a lighter or thicker broth. Do you have a preference?"

Six types in all. This wasn't some misunderstanding. Ramen, here, definitely meant the meal she was familiar with.

"*Tonkotsu*, please, on the thick side. And one side of *gyoza* and rice to go with that."

"Excellent! You certainly know your food, ma'am, if this is your first time here. And you guys?"

Her companions watched in awe as she ordered without hesitation.

"Um... The same."

"M-me too..."

"Yeah."

"And I, as well."

None of them knew what any of it was, so they just followed their captain's lead.

"Lady Hinata, could you tell us what this...ramen is?"

"You *do* know, right?"

"Yeah. It... Well, it might be a tad difficult for you guys to eat."

""""What?!"""""

Tension raced across the table.

"Don't worry. I only think it will take some practice before you can eat it correctly."

Hinata was just worried about the chopsticks. Did Arnaud and her other compatriots know how to use them? Did anyone in Lubelius, for that matter? Her friends, meanwhile, were now scared Hinata had made them order something on the level of monkey brains.

After a short wait, the bowls came out. It was ramen, no doubt—a nostalgic sight for Hinata, a totally unfamiliar one for the rest of the table.

Brushing her hair back with one hand to keep from dunking it in the soup, Hinata picked up a pair of disposable chopsticks, snapping them apart.

They're even the kind you break... Is this what they're focusing on?

Could Tempest really popularize chopsticks so quickly that they were already spreading to their neighbor countries? It unnerved her a bit, but the steaming ramen in front of her diverted her attention.

She put her hands together in a small prayer before picking up a *renge* ramen spoon off the stack and sampling the soup. It was definitely *tonkotsu* pork broth, on the thicker side. She had no idea where they got the dashi soup stock from, but it perfectly re-created the heavy, flavorful taste she remembered.

Then she picked up some noodles, brought them to her mouth...
and half spat them back out.

"Are you all right?!"

Arnaud stood up. "Was it poisoned, Lady Hinata?!"

"Quiet. Just calm down and eat."

Hinata picked up some noodles again—this time, placing them
on her spoon and blowing on them a bit first. She wasn't used to
food served at this temperature. It was almost cutesy of her, especially given her usual frigid demeanor, but she was too focused on
the noodles in her mouth to care.

Good body. Good taste. The savory broth had soaked into the
noodles well. It was excellent. She never thought she'd taste this
again, but it was a perfect re-creation.

Silently, Hinata concentrated on her meal, Arnaud and the others
carefully watching her every move. Soon, they tried imitating her.

"...Agh! Hot!"

"Mmmm! Wow, what is this?!"

"The soup's great, too!"

"Incredible! I've never eaten anything like this before..."

They were struggling mightily with their chopsticks as they
challenged themselves to the ramen, but their reactions were like
nothing Hinata expected. To them, whose diets revolved around
the staples of hard bread, salty soup, and fresh salads, this ramen
opened up an entire new universe of taste. It was a revolution for
their taste buds.

And look at this rice! This rice they ordered simply because
Hinata did. It was a perfect accompaniment to the ramen, growing
sweeter in the mouth the more you chewed on it and filling your
stomach in the most satisfying way. And the *gyoza*... Oh, the *gyoza*!
The contents spread across your mouth when you bit into them, the
aroma wafting all the way up your sinuses. It was a symphony of
flavor, played by a large variety of ingredients and performing in
exquisite harmony with the rice.

"This is so good!" Arnaud half shouted. "I can't believe this!"

Compared with the portable rations of the last ten days, this was
heaven. It wasn't long before a single *gyoza* dumpling remained.
Fritz's chopsticks began to drift toward it...only to be deflected
away by Hinata's with a dry *tssh!* sound.

"That's my prey, Fritz. I wanted to save it for last. No stealing."

Fritz felt a shiver go down his spine. She was playing for keeps.

"S-sorry, Lady Hinata. It was just so good, I couldn't help myself…"

"You could always order another plate," an appalled Hinata replied—and right on cue, her four companions began shouting for the waitress. But then, tragedy struck.

"Oh, I'm sorry, guys, but that was the last of our supply for the day." The waitress delivered the devastating news. "You know, this ramen is actually a new offering from us. We only started serving it last week…and just between you and me, I heard it got its start as a fervent request from the demon lord for his dinner. There's a merchant named Sir Mjöllmile who's one of the bigger names around this town, you see, and he purchased this ramen directly from the demon lord himself. Can you believe that? It's not selling that well yet—it's pricey, and there's kind of a learning curve—but once you try it, you just can't get enough!"

Considering this was "just between you and me," the waitress was loud enough to be clearly heard across the entire dining hall. The act fascinated Hinata; no doubt she was instructed to advertise it to her regulars like that. Building a faithful base of repeat customers would allow them to create more of it in bulk, establishing it as a full-fledged product. She could spot a few people in the hall curiously eyeing her table. Watching her consume that bowl so expertly probably made them want to try it themselves.

She took in the last of the soup as they chatted.

"Thanks. That was very good."

Hinata paid for the meal and stood up. Her companions, seeing this, scrambled to slurp up the remainder of their soup.

"No rush. I'm just going back to my room. Also, here's a word of advice: If you drink all the soup, too, you'll gain weight."

Litus was the only one who stopped eating.

"Huh? But… You did…?"

"I'm naturally skinny."

And with that warning, she left. She could feel Litus's hateful gaze pointed at her, but she was too happy and sleepy to turn back around.

"Let's go."

The group was back on the road the next morning, fully rested and recharged. They would need it, because navigating the treacherous roads into the Forest of Jura took a lot of willpower.

Hinata was all smiles as she set off with them, but it wasn't long before that enthusiasm evaporated.

"What's all this about?"

"This is so easy, it almost bores me."

"Yeah, and just look at this highway! It's as neatly paved as the streets of the Englesian capital. This is crazy!"

The surprise around the party was understandable. The road was paved in stone, not a single puddle of water to be found. It was even lightly banked around the turns, and gutters had been dug on both sides. The winter weather hadn't frozen the path at all, ensuring the easiest possible journey.

"I don't even think there are any monsters nearby. There weren't too many out in the open forest, either…"

Litus, who had staged a short expedition into the unexplored woods, couldn't help but be astonished. She was right—the barrier deployed over the entire highway was a shock to see in action. Magical devices had been installed every six or so miles to power it, preventing any nearby monsters from wandering the roads. This made the journey vastly safer, and they saw more passing merchants traveling down the road as they pressed on. Those merchants must've been responsible for breathing so much life into Blumund right now.

"If they've devoted this much time and effort to constructing a road like this, I wonder what we should expect to find in the monsters' homeland up ahead."

Nobody responded to Arnaud. He was just stating what everyone else was thinking—and they all wanted an answer just as badly.

"That merchant said you could take this highway mounted easily enough. He was right."

"Yeah. I thought our horses would be a bother in the forest, but I suppose we had nothing to worry about."

Hinata had heard reports about the large-scale construction project Rimuru was carrying out in the forest. Seeing it for herself, however, made it hard to hide her surprise. The Forest of Jura, so forbidding to humans for so many years, was now as accessible as a city park.

So the party proceeded along for a while, until they spotted a group of hobgoblins riding wolves up ahead.

"Did they notice us?!"

"Hold it," Hinata calmly said. "I don't think so."

She was right. They could hear laughing. It sounded like the hobgoblins were merely chatting among themselves. It was a straight path ahead, so they had noticed Hinata's party, but they just waved and approached in a friendly manner.

"Hello! We haven't seen you before. You don't appear to be merchants—are you adventurers, then?"

"More or less, yes."

"Ah, very good! I wish you good luck on your mission. Now, I'm sure you'll be just fine, but there are a few things I need to warn you about."

The hobgoblin changed his tone, then outlined the rules all travelers needed to follow on the highway:

> No garbage dumping.
> No fighting on the highway.
> Use the drinking fountains located every six miles on the highway when camping overnight.
> For added safety, take advantage of the patrol stations located every twelve miles on the highway.
> If you have the money for it, inns are located every twenty-five miles.
> If you see anyone in trouble, report it to the nearest patrol station.

...and so on.

"Also, you'll see a glowing stone tablet every six miles, but please don't touch them. Breaking them will lead to severe penalties."

It was those glowing stones that kept the barriers running, he explained. They were these little glowing spots among the flagstones forming the road, which also helped travelers find their way in dark nights.

All in all, the rules went into so much detail that the party could hardly believe they were enacted and enforced by monsters.

"All right. Thanks for letting us know."

"Oh, it's fine! You'll see people like us patrolling the highway, so let any of us know if you run into trouble."

With that, the hobgoblin security detail darted down the road, leaving a dumbfounded Hinata behind.

"Um, Lady Hinata…"

"Hold it. Can you remain silent for a little while? I need to think about something."

Arnaud and the others obeyed. The party traveled in silence for the next hour until they stumbled across a drinking fountain—on the exact mile marker the hobgoblin said they'd find it at. These markers, located at every mile along the highway, began at zero on the western entrance to Rimuru (the capital) and counted upward from there. Each one provided quick guidance on how much farther the nearest water, patrol station, and inn was.

Hinata, recognizing these from the trips she had taken on Japan's expressways, immediately saw the value of these markers in a pinch. If you needed help and weren't sure whether to keep going or double back, these provided instant guidance on what to do. It spoke volumes about how much this highway's designers cared about traveler safety.

It's worth noting, by the way, that "miles" did not originally exist as a unit of measurement on this world, but Rimuru ignored that and simply used a system he was already familiar with. The inns were spaced every 25 miles based on the assumption that the average person could walk a little over three miles in an hour and manage that for eight hours a day easily enough. Merchant wagons went about as quickly as a grown person on foot, so as long as you weren't in too much of a hurry, it was easy to organize a trip that gave you an inn to rest in every night.

Clearly, someone had devoted a lot of thought into designing this. There was no doubting it now. Rimuru obviously craved interaction with the human race.

*   *   *

The journey beyond Blumund went far more comfortably than the one before it. The drinking fountain the party found themselves at was just that—a clean source of drinking water, available to anyone for free. It was almost a dizzying sight to them. Seeing the very modern-day planet-Earth concept of free water applied to a forest as hazardous as this one made most of the party wonder what Rimuru could possibly have been thinking.

These fountains were paired with cooking pits and cleared-out grassy areas for those putting up tents nearby, complete with benches made of sawed logs and roofed areas to get out from the rain. It was a campsite, just like any one you'd find off your local highway.

Between this and everything else, the Forest of Jura—once seen as a forbidden holy sanctuary by the rest of the planet—was now calm and accessible enough for just about anyone. This forest that was supposed to be crawling with all kinds of horrid monsters; the kind of place where if you were an adventurer ranked B or lower, one false move could spell death.

This wasn't the domain of human beings. It was an Eden for monsters. And developing it to the point that it was open to anybody... Hinata hadn't even entertained the concept. It wasn't a matter of whether it was possible or not—it was just beyond her imagination, and probably that of fellow otherworlder Yuuki Kagurazaka, too. All that effort they had expended protecting humanity from the threat of monsters, and he made it look *this* simple?

You've got to be kidding me, Hinata thought grudgingly to herself. *Now at least I understand what Yuuki mentioned to me.*

She recalled a meeting with Yuuki at one of her favorite cafés in Englesia. They regularly met to exchange intelligence, and this time, the topic of Rimuru came up. Apparently, Yuuki said, Rimuru was earnestly serious about creating and developing a nation of monsters—and not only that, but he was sending out feelers toward the Western Nations, in hopes of getting friendlier with them. And that new brandy cake they were enjoying at the café? Readily available for purchase from Rimuru, who had invested in producing a wide variety of fine liquors.

"He's like nobody else out there," Yuuki had laughed as Hinata took little bites out of her slice, savoring each one. "It's like he does it all and makes it look easy, you know? And he's got insight way further into the future than I do. I think that's why he's putting so much effort into bringing little treats like that cake into this world."

He warned her that hostilities with him would be ill-advised—which in turn suggested the Free Guild was siding with him. She let that slide without comment at the time. But now:

...*He was right,* she thought as she watched some merchants gratefully taking advantage of the fountain near her. *There's no way he'd focus on these little things unless he really* could *"do it all."*

Two hours after leaving the fountain, they sighted an inn, the last of seven built along this highway. Hinata's party decided to spend the night here, and before long, they were situated in the dining hall.

"All right," she said once they were seated. "I want to hear your feedback. What do you think of what we saw today?"

Arnaud, representing the rest of them, spoke first. "If I...may be honest with you, Lady Hinata?"

"Go ahead. That's what I want to hear."

"Judging by this highway alone, I think the demon lord Rimuru must be an incredibly gifted leader. The sense of security his patrolmen give this road must attract all kinds of travelers. I can't see much of a future for the businesses lining the route through Farmus."

"Indeed," rumbled Bacchus, "monsters are not the only threat out there. You have bandits targeting merchants; you have illness; you have the potential for injury; you might break an axle and be stranded. Such things happen often, and having more people up and down the highway can do much to keep people from worrying."

"True," replied Litus. "If you're someplace where you can expect help if you need it, that really puts your mind at ease."

"And you can save money," Fritz added, "because you no longer have to hire a personal guard detail. That alone... It's big."

The praise for Rimuru was glowing all around.

"He seems to be more devoted to his rule than a lot of the barons you see out there. His title might be demon lord, but if that's what he is, he's a damn benevolent one."

"Yeah. There's a lot we could learn from him. Including a few things our leaders in Lubelius would be advised to implement."

"I'm just glad the divine-enemy declaration never came down."

"Now we'll just have to see if he's willing to accept your apology, Lady Hinata."

Hinata nodded her agreement. "I'll have to be as heartfelt with it as I can. If he still wants to duel with me, I'll have to accept, but..."

But she had her doubts. Why would he seek a duel at *this* point? Whether he forgave Hinata or not, she didn't see why it called for another fight to settle. Rimuru just didn't seem to be the kind of person to show off his newfound demon lord power like *this*.

Even with those doubts in her mind, Hinata's journey continued apace. They took advantage of an inn on the seventh day as well, and this one was already as ornate and luxuriant as any you'd find in Englesia. There was even a vast public bath, the perfect place to soak after a long journey.

What's more, these inns always had at least a few people recruited from Blumund working for them. Trading money for services was still kind of a novel thing for the monster staff, apparently, so her party often saw a human employee providing on-the-job guidance. It was, in a way, an ideal cross-species relationship, and it was more than enough to make Hinata see the need to reconsider Luminism's teachings.

They would arrive at Rimuru, the capital, the next day—and with that, an encounter with the demon lord himself.

I hope we can work this out with words instead of swords...

She knew it was a selfish thought, but Hinata really meant it...even as a vast web of intermingled bad intentions schemed to prevent it.

Hinata, still trundling along, was due in this evening, according to the latest report from Soei's team. She had spent two weeks on this journey, making zero use of teleportation or other magical means to speed things up.

"Thank you. It's so vital to have this sort of intelligence early on. Keep it up."

"This is nothing," Soei said, quietly accepting my praise. "We will redouble our efforts."

He's literally a shadow. I mean it. And when someone as handsome as he is pulls that off, you can't be jealous of that. He looked great.

I should note, however, that when he gave me an urgent report from the inn Hinata first stayed at, he suggested poisoning her to "take her out of the picture sooner than later." I gave him a few not-so-nice words about *that* idea. It still felt to me that Hinata was here to talk, not fight, as much as we still needed to remain on guard. Something about the way she stayed at every inn along the way, totally unhurried, seemed almost *too* bold to me.

"Could this be a diversion?" Benimaru suggested. A diversion? Was she deliberately drawing attention while that separate force launched a surprise attack? It was possible, I guess. This *was* Hinata we were dealing with. As coldhearted as she was, I'm sure no method of securing victory was below her.

"What are the hundred other paladins doing?"

"They continue to lie low along the old path, sir. If we hadn't spotted them just when they departed, I'm not sure we would have noticed them at all."

These guys, meanwhile, were in full-on military mode. Hinata was looking more and more like a lure. Either way, though, we couldn't relax. Shion already had her force deployed; if these paladins made any moves, things would start happening quickly after that.

"Given Hinata's strength, her serving as a lure wouldn't be strange at all. I'm the only one who can handle her—even now, Benimaru, you'd probably be in over your head. If I had to guess, I'm willing to bet she thinks she can beat all of us together."

"Heh. That's quite a lot of confidence, believing such nonsense even after she knows you. I could only call it foolish," Soei said with a thin smile, although to me, *that* assertion was the foolish talk.

But who knows? She would only know me from before my ascension, but I knew just how capable she was. Looking back, it was blatantly clear how easy she was going on me back then.

"We better not let the paladins fan out, then," noted Benimaru. "If they build a Holy Field, that will put us at a huge disadvantage."

Soei nodded at him. "True. If so, we will need to contact Shion out on the field and try to have her eliminate them as soon as possible…"

He paused mid-thought and then told me the one thing I didn't want to hear:

"Sir Rimuru, we're detecting movement. They have attempted to fan out and cover the four cardinal directions around town, but Shion has intercepted them. Battle is reportedly underway."

So Hinata chose to fight. Ah well. If she wants to be my enemy, I've got a plan for that.

●

Putting the inn behind them, Hinata and her companions prepared for the day's journey ahead. They would likely reach the capital of Rimuru that evening, and the tension was written on everyone's faces.

"Well, here we are. I don't know if we'll actually see him today, but be prepared, all right? Even if this does end in a fight, I don't want you laying a hand on him."

"But—"

"That's an order. There's no further point to being hostile toward the demon lord. I'll go in, I'll take full responsibility for all this, and then we'll talk things over—"

Before she could wax poetic about her desire for peace, she was interrupted. An emergency message had just been magically sent to her.

(…nally, we connected to… You hear us, Lady Hi…? The Three Battlesages…en route to…)

It faded in and out, but the urgency and the identity of its sender—Cardinal Nicolaus Speltus—were both obvious. Something must have been jamming it.

Hinata tried to send a message back—(What is it? What happened?)—but she could sense the transmission dissipating into the air before it got far.

(Beware the Seven Days…)

And with that final message, Nicolaus's presence disappeared. Something must have happened, Hinata realized.

Was he trying to send a message to me over and over before he finally succeeded? Maybe whatever happened, happened well before now. But the Three Battlesages are joining in...? Wait, were they part of the chaos in Farmus?!

The blood drained from Hinata's face as she crafted another magical transmission, this one pointed at Holy Emperor Louis.

(What is it? That's a rather poorly formed spell you used. Has something gotten you flustered?)

The emperor sounded serene as usual. That was a relief to Hinata.

(Yes. No time to explain. I'm just going to ask this right out: Did you order the Three Battlesages deployed?)

(What? I did nothing of the sort. Did they?)

(Yeah, I didn't think you suddenly took an interest in human nations. I was on orders from Luminus to keep them on standby, and they're not the sort of people to work on their own volition. Something's going on.)

Louis's main interests in life were Luminus and the city of Nightgarden. This was why Hinata called the actual shots around Lubelius. The Battlesages weren't afraid to voice their discontent, but Hinata's orders were always followed. It was hard for her to imagine them choosing now, of all times, to defy her.

So yes, something must have happened. Or someone was feeding the Battlesages a line.

Seven Days...?

She was now sure about the bad feeling in the pit of her stomach. Immediately, she resolved to return home. A little transport magic would help make up for lost time. She really wanted to be fully refreshed and ready for the potential battle against Rimuru, but now was no time to whine about that.

But the clock was already against her.

(Yeah, it looks like it. I'll need to—)

An audible *thunk* of dull pain ran across her head as her link with Louis was cut off. Some kind of force field covered the area around her, blocking the casting of magic. As it did, she could sense a large battle unfolding not far away, making the very air shimmer.

"Wha...?! Is that...Renard?!"

Arnaud, watching over Hinata, quickly expressed his surprise at these sudden events.

"Let's go!"

Things were moving fast—and not in a good direction. She hadn't even encountered Rimuru yet, and the situation was rapidly deteriorating. Unease filled her mind as she ran at full speed for the battlefield.

●

Hearing that Hinata was making contact with someone, I chose to block her signal. Once I did, she reportedly began running for the battlefield at full tilt. That would nip in the bud whatever she was scheming.

Now, though, it was certain.

"That was Hinata's doing, huh?"

"It would appear so," replied Benimaru. The way she immediately changed tactics once she knew we were on to her... Shrewd as always."

"Well, let's follow the plan. Hinata and I are gonna work this out, just the two of us."

"Roger that! I will let no one interfere."

"Yeah. Keep the paladins at bay. Let's move!"

""Yes sir!"""

With a quick, reassuring nod to Benimaru, I turned into my human form.

"Good luck to you!"

Shuna waved as we all set off—Benimaru, Soei, Alvis, Sufia, and me. Bracing myself, I cast Dominate Space and popped over to Shion's location before Hinata could reach it. I appreciated her holding her own out there, but against a pack of Crusaders, Team Reborn would face an uphill climb...

...or so I assumed; and sometimes, I assume wrong.

I had no idea what was going on. I thought I was going out of my head. How did *this* happen?! The sight before me made me completely lose my sense of speech.

What was I seeing? Well, it was Shion, arms folded in front of her, issuing orders to Team Reborn. That much was fine—part of the plan. It was the way they fought that was the problem. In a good way, it was completely unexpected.

"What in the...?! Our attacks don't work on them!"

"These aren't undead! What is the meaning of this?!"

The paladins sounded just as shocked. The one who asked that particular question would never receive an answer, as a Reborn member took him down with a quick dagger strike. The Reborn had used his own body as a feint to land the attack, making the most incredible use of his immortality.

But I knew it couldn't last. The paladins would regroup soon, and then it'd be a one-sided match...or so I thought.

Again, my predictions were turned on their head. Less than three minutes later, our foes were almost at the breaking point.

As I thought, the paladins *did* rally, successfully closing the distance between them and Team Reborn without a challenge. Given the difference in core strength, they must've figured being immortal wouldn't be enough to make them unbeatable. So they attempted to pin them down instead—but it didn't work. Slash 'em up all you want; the Reborn guys immediately heal, something the paladins couldn't manage. As soon as they fell, they were quickly bound up by the Team Kurenai members on standby, ensuring they were out of the fight.

"Hee-hee-hee!" said one of the Reborn, a small child, as she half taunted one of the captured paladins. "Y'know what? This knife has this superstrong sleep medicine rubbed all over it! The moment we land a strike on you, we win!"

I wasn't a huge fan of her spoiling the whole trick, but ah well. She's just a kid.

Report. The subject Gobwe is older in years than the subject Gobta.

Dude. Really? Man, I have the *worst* trouble telling these monsters apart. I know Gobta's evolved way past from when I first saw him, but looks-wise, it was that exact same dopey face. So should I expect some kind of breathtaking transformation from him in the future?

Either way, seeing this tiny girl lecture a paladin before my eyes almost made me chuckle a bit. This wasn't an uphill battle at all. If anything, for Team Reborn right now, it was a pretty steep *downhill* one. Unless the paladins were careful enough to bring an antidote along or had a natural skill to resist poison, there was no resisting this sneak attack. It'd only work once, of course, but damn, was it effective.

Still, it was rapidly coming to an end. There were yet more paladins in the group, and they weren't going to let up now. Trickery like this wouldn't work so easily against such over-whelming force—and now that they'd seen how the trick worked, we couldn't expect an encore performance. The only reason Team Reborn could land those little nicks and cuts was because the paladins let their guards down after ripping them to shreds, after all.

Still, those nicks and cuts had successfully knocked half of the enemy out of the battle, and that was more than praiseworthy. Talk about overachieving. Now to return to the original plan, which called for a protracted battle of attrition as the paladins— No, I was being proven wrong again.

Shion gave the figures in front of her a signal with her chin. It was targeted at Gobzo and Gobwa, who looked at each other, then Shion, incredulously.

"You wish for us to join in?"

"Aren't *you* going to join?!" Gobzo asked. "'Cuz if it's just us, I don't think it'll be easy to beat those guys!"

"No," Gobwa explained, "I think it's all right if we don't win, as long as we can buy some time..."

"Huhhh?! I thought we were ordered to win at all costs!"

Gobwa, standing guard by the meeting-hall door, knew what we had discussed in there. Gobzo didn't and was totally floored by the news. Something wasn't adding up here, was it?

"Um," Gobwa asked Shion, sensing Gobzo's disquiet, "during our strategy meeting, we were supposed to be on standby, weren't we...?"

Yeah. They were. I *thought* something was weird about it. Good to hear my mind isn't playing tricks on me. But Shion wasn't having it. "What are you fools talking about?!" she roared. "We have victory within reach; can't you see that?! Securing victory against a stronger foe is how you can climb over the wall to the next level! You're being given a golden opportunity! You should thank me for this!"

I...wasn't sure if I agreed with these statements. Victory was within reach, but our foes were stronger? A bit contradictory, isn't it? But Gobwa was convinced, a twinkle appearing in her eyes as she smiled defiantly.

"Yes. Yes, you're right. Allow Team Kurenai to seize this opportunity!"

Gobzo, meanwhile...

"Uh, ummm... Isn't that, like, ignoring orders or something?"

It took a lot of guts to ask Shion that question, but Shion immediately shot him down. "You're still here?! Either you do what you're told, or you'll become the test subject for my latest kitchen delights. Is *that* the decision you wanna make?!"

The threat was all too real to Gobzo. Whether he was convinced by her arguments or not, he dove straight into battle.

...I can't say he was wrong. But it was weird. The way the other two framed it, this was now all Gobzo's fault. Gobwa, as befitting one of Benimaru's fighters, was always ready for a scrap, which made it easier to convince her. Gobzo, despite his slack-jawed look, was a far more honest, upright person. Unfortunately, that often drove him to say things he was better off not saying, which always blew up in his face. Maybe he had it coming sometimes, but if he did, he never realized it. Still, he seemed pretty content overall, so I opted not to intervene.

"...Are you sure this is all right, Benimaru?"

Benimaru shrugged back. "No, but playing it by ear is sometimes a necessity in battle. Shion, in particular, has a keen instinct for this. She gives orders like that because she senses victory, I think."

True. I had gone for a more passive approach, asking them to buy time because I thought they couldn't win—but if we could neutralize this threat with no casualties, no need to go easy.

*   *   *

I turned my attention toward the battlefield.

Things were really starting to ramp up. Team Reborn was taking on the remaining fifty paladins, two team members per opponent with one Team Kurenai fighter providing backup. In a full-on battle, Kurenai fell behind the paladins in strength, but not by an insurmountable gap. The paladins were ranked A, but the lower end of A, while Team Kurenai was about as close to A as you could get without crossing the line. With the right support, it could actually turn into a decent fight.

Plus, Kurenai had backup on-site, substituting in if one of their team fell or was growing exhausted. We had all the potion we needed, so the cycle could keep going semi-perpetually.

"What a powerhouse they are," marveled Alvis. "Imagine, *another* force of that caliber serving your nation?" Her eyes were not pointed toward Kurenai, but Reborn—battle hardy (immortal, you could say) and ready to fight for as long as it took.

"Yeah," Sufia replied with a nod, "they're trouble. Not even decapitation can stop 'em. I bet they'd give us a workout."

They had high praise for Team Reborn, and even I was fairly surprised. The paladins, meanwhile, had no backup support. *If this keeps up, we might even have a chance at this.*

"Yeah, I wasn't really planning for this, but..."

I vaguely nodded back at them.

Shion, meanwhile, licked her lips as she appreciatively watched the battle unfold. I caught a glimpse of the wet sheen on the tip of her tongue. She turned toward me, sensing our presence, and gave us a broad grin. It was hard to imagine it, really, given the mask of terror she gave Gobzo a second ago.

"The plan is working, Sir Rimuru!"

"What are you, nuts? This wasn't the plan at all!"

"Your praise is such an honor, my lord!"

"I wasn't praising you..."

"Now, I must go!"

With that, she planted her feet on the ground and took off like a bullet, leaving me in the dust.

"Uh, go where...?"

She was like the wind, using her extended senses to weave effort-lessly through the twisty trees. The elemental spirits infused her body as she zoomed headlong through the forest.

Upon reaching a clearing, Hinata encountered five high-level magic-born. They had spotted her coming, but their eyes were focused on a much more faraway sight. Following their lead, Hinata spotted her people, the noble paladins, facing what could soon become a bitter defeat.

She painfully sighed, holding in her emotions. The defeat didn't anger her. What did was the way this whole thing broke down into hostilities so quickly. With battle underway, negotiation could no longer be hoped for. Whatever kind of internal subterfuge was going on with Hinata's side, that wasn't Rimuru's problem.

Rimuru, meanwhile, just stood there, watching the battle as calmly as Hinata. Both of them were quietly thinking to them-selves, gauging the forces of their opponent.

On Rimuru's side were four powerful magic-born, plus a woman in a suit emitting an eerie aura. The two women in front appeared to be lycanthropes, former servants of Carillon, judging by the reports. It seemed likely they were part of the famed Three Lycan-thropeers, of the former Beast Master's Warrior Alliance; their mere appearance drove run-of-the-mill magic-born away from them.

But the other two figures lined up with them were no pushovers, either. On one side of the lycanthropes, there was a dashing fig-ure with red hair and two black horns. On the other was a young blue-haired one with a single white horn.

"The Three Lycanthropeers?" Arnaud promptly whispered to Hinata when he caught up to her. "And are those ogres... No, ogre mages?"

Hinata kept her eyes on them. "No. They're oni."

"Oni?"

"I've heard of them. Monsters whose magical powers put them on the level of regional gods. Some pagan religions even worship them as deities, I read."

"Yeah. They're part of the evolution ladder up from ogres, but only a very few of them ever reach that level. But here they are, right in front of us. Consider each one to be a Special A-ranked threat."

This was demon lord territory, and they were uninvited guests. Arnaud and the others were all too aware of that. Hinata, meanwhile, was worried that even Special A might be selling them short a little. That red-haired one, in particular, seemed to have more force than a would-be demon lord. If they ever came to blows, she would want Arnaud and at least two other commanders on her side—but they had four magic-born, and there were only four Crusader officers to go around. That couldn't be a coincidence; Rimuru must have arranged the numbers that way.

And then there was the demon lord himself. His presence was overwhelming, nothing like their previous encounter.

"I'll take you on. You and me, in a one-on-one duel."

The words flashed back into Hinata's mind.
Yeah... Yeah. You wanted a duel with me, didn't you? Because you didn't want any distractions?

If that's what it came to, she at least wanted him to take her life and spare her soldiers. No— She wanted him to win, and win overwhelmingly, then accept her apology.

In secret, without telling a soul, she prepared herself.

She noticed the female magic-born in the suit begin to move, letting out a concussive wave of force as she flew toward the faraway Renard. Rimuru was there, watching her go—and when he was done, ever so slowly, his eyes turned toward Hinata.

Their eyes met.

●

Oh, brother. I mean, seriously, oh, brother. But everything was still within what we predicted. No issues so far.

So I turned around. Hinata was standing there, looking cool, collected, not even out of breath. She must've been watching the battle, just like I was. Her gaze met mine. We just stood there a few moments, staring at each other. I finally spoke first.

"Well, Hinata, now you've done it. I imagine you don't need to be reminded, but this is my territory. The moment you staged military action within our borders, that was enough to make me assume you're hostile. I'm a nice guy, but not nice enough to allow you to strike at us first, you know?"

...Which, well, if we got into a "who shot first" argument, then the truth was murkier. But that doesn't matter! We were guaranteed to lose if they launched a Holy Field, so of course I was gonna send Shion out ahead. If Hinata started whining at me about that, she was barking up the wrong tree.

"Yes," Hinata calmly replied, "that much I can tell. I have no idea why Renard disobeyed orders, either."

Talk about shameless.

"Oh, sure. You killed Reyhiem so you could pin the blame on us, didn't you? And now Farmus's new king has all the momentum in the world behind him."

"Killed Reyhiem...?"

"Yeah. Archbishop Reyhiem. You called him back there, remember? All I did was give him that message for you. Nothing else."

For just a moment, Hinata looked thoroughly confused, but beyond that, her expression was a mask of indifference. Her cold eyes drilled into me, sizing me up. She may have been beautiful, but that only added further polish to that numbing look.

"Oh... I see," she whispered.

"You did get the message, right?"

"Yes. I did."

"And this is your answer?"

"Well...not exactly, but you wouldn't believe me if I said that, would you?"

Not exactly *how?*

"Oh, I could. But before that, you have to order *them* to cease hostilities and return home."

I pointed at the pair locked in combat with Shion. She looked where I was pointing, then softly shook her head.

"I don't know if I can. I think it's going to be over before I step in."

Good point. That was...Renard, right? He was the strongest dude on the field, and Shion wasn't holding back against him. And someone else, too—not quite as strong as Renard, but still up there. I assumed they were both among the Ten Great Saints, but Shion was taking them both on, letting her inner monster shine. *Geez. If that's how thick it's gotten, we don't have much choice except to let them duke it out till they're done.*

It peeved me a little to accept Hinata's excuse, but I didn't think she'd be able to satisfy my conditions.

"What are you talking about?!" one of the younger knights shouted with resentment before I could speak. "If Lady Hinata calls our forces back, what will happen to her? You're the one who called her here; how do we know you won't do anything to her?!"

Sounds like they had no intention of talking this out from the beginning...

"Silence," Benimaru replied. "The only people with permission to speak here are Sir Rimuru and Hinata Sakaguchi. *You* were not called here. Know your place."

"What?"

The knight was unfazed. The next instant, a flash of swords erupted in front of Benimaru. One of them, belonging to the knight called Arnaud, was breezily deflected away by a casual swipe from Benimaru's blade.

"Not a killer blow, was it? A smart choice. If you were intent upon killing me, you'd be on the ground right now."

"I didn't want to get in the way of Lady Hinata's negotiations. I was just prodding you a bit, although I wasn't expecting you to react. I don't want you to have the wrong idea."

"The only one with the wrong idea is you."

"Heh-heh. How about we continue this conversation away from the action?"

"Very well."

Arnaud gave him a smile, although I could see a vein throbbing over his temple. *He can dish out the trash talk*, I thought as they walked off, *but he certainly couldn't take it.* Out of the four members of Hinata's entourage, that Arnaud guy was undoubtedly the strongest. That was why Benimaru chose to take action. Perfect. I was certain Arnaud would occupy him well enough without any murder involved, just like I liked it.

Hinata just watched them go, rolling her eyes instead of trying to stop him. She must have noticed that Arnaud was no match for Benimaru, but she let him go anyway.

"All right," Alvis said, "you all could use some entertainment, too, no? I would be glad to occupy your time for a while, so we don't get in Sir Rimuru's way."

"Yeah," added Sufia, "I've always wanted to test out the might of the Ten Great Saints!"

They set off. Maybe this was their motivation all along; I don't know. Sufia *was* kind of a war maniac like that.

"Let me join you."

"Very well... I'll take you on."

The four tramped off. All that remained was Soei and the lone female paladin.

"Shall we?"

"I suppose so," she said, no doubt reading the atmosphere on the field.

This, um, wasn't exactly what I had planned. I mean, they didn't have to physically march off like that. Except for Benimaru, those three pairs acted more like they were pairing off for dates than fighting. *You don't* have *to exchange blows, guys. Sheesh.*

Besides, I'm fighting a woman myself. The most beautiful one, no less. Not that I'm getting much enjoyment out of it.

...All joking aside, we were now left fully alone. I suppose this was inevitable.

It was time for my rematch with Hinata.

CHAPTER
5

HOLY AND
DEMONIC
COLLIDE

That Time I Got Reincarnated as a Slime

The battle began.

Renard was the vice captain of the Crusader forces, commanding them as they caught up with Hinata on her journey. He himself wasn't a paladin, exactly—he was a Holy Wizard, a master of sorcerous magic. That was a special class, one that only those who mastered elemental, aspectual, and holy magic could claim to be.

And yet, Renard was just as adept with a sword, using his own to lead several missions. Even hiding his Holy Wizard side, he was still laudable enough as a paladin to serve as a commander and eventual Crusader vice captain. It all came down to his talents—those beautiful sword skills. If Arnaud's sword was a blunt weapon, Renard's had a softer touch. Both were exemplary fighters, but Arnaud had a slight edge, thanks to the tenacity that never failed him in battle. In a knockdown drag-out against a formidable monster, beautiful technique was often less important than brute force. That difference earned Arnaud the crown among his peers.

But thanks to that genius-level magic skill, Renard had proven himself more than worthy as a spellcasting swordsman. His physical technique wasn't quite up to Arnaud's standard, but if he fought in a more standard magic/sword hybrid style instead of hiding the sorcery like he usually did, he was just as phenomenal a talent. In fact, as Renard himself gauged it, he could probably outclass Arnaud in strength.

To a paladin, however, one's proficiency in aspectual magic wasn't really part of the evaluation. It was more of a given, with some paladins even capable of fusing their own elemental spirits with aspectual magic to launch powerful spells with no casting time. Aspectual magic, by itself, took longer to cast than spirit magic—and while it was often more powerful, in close-range combat, speed was the most important priority.

Renard was no exception to that maxim, hence his focus on sword skill. True strength, as he saw it, lay at the end of his quest to master the blade. Adding holy elements to his almost divinely quick thrusts allowed him to slice though pretty well anything, as he saw it.

This thought was with him ever since an experience that still rang vividly in his mind. Back when he was a student, he studied abroad in a small nation that fell under the threat of the demon lord Valentine. It was Hinata, freshly ordained as a paladin at the time, who came to the rescue; and in a word, she was strong. A single swipe of her rapier obliterated waves of teeming monsters. Even demons several times a human's size were helplessly mowed down. Hinata's arrival saved that nation's people from the desperation they faced, and ever since then, Renard found himself attracted to the charms of the sword.

Even as he polished his spirit magic skills, he constantly recalled Hinata's rapier in action, attempting to emulate her in his daily training. Once he had gained a mastery of magical arts, he returned to his academy in Englesia, learning about aspectual magic as he awaited a chance to move to the Holy Empire of Lubelius. This was a difficult task for outsiders, but his adherence to Luminism and proven skills as an outstanding talent earned him a nod from their government.

He pounced on the offer, even though it meant cutting ties with his family. Upon completing the move, he took up holy magic and earned a spot as a trainee paladin. The spirit he forged a pact with was affiliated with light—as pure and unblemished as the soul of the one they called the Paladin of Light.

*   *   *

After joining the paladin guard, it took comparatively little time for Renard to become Hinata's personal aide. He took the initiative to volunteer for any mission, no matter how reckless, and the results he provided his newly adopted nation made his qualifications eminently clear.

Hinata could count many people as her rivals: Arnaud and Fritz, both of whom arrived at the same time she did; even Cardinal Nicolaus, who was just as coldhearted and crafty as Hinata herself. As for her admirers? There was no way to even begin counting them. Being an aide to such a paladin was a source of boundless pride to Renard.

And yet…

(Renard, there is something I want you, and only you, to know.)

Right after Archbishop Reyhiem's sensational murder, Renard was beckoned by the Seven Days Clergy. There, he had an unspeakable truth revealed to him.

(Hinata, you know… She was *involved*, shall we say, with the demon lord Valentine.)

(We were about to kill Valentine, you see, but before we could, he revealed that to us as he begged for mercy.)

The revelation made Renard's head go blank. Hinata, this woman he looked up to so much, in a liaison with Valentine. It meant she was pulling the wool over his eyes this whole time. If it was true, it was a betrayal the pure-minded Renard could never allow. It seemed impossible that the Clergy, these great heroes, would be lying—but it seemed just as impossible that Hinata would deceive her own paladins.

Perhaps, though… It is true that Valentine has been inactive as of late. Lady Hinata should be more than powerful enough to slay him, but she's shown no interest in that at all…

Hinata had enough force to dispatch Valentine—Renard was sure of that much. The Battlesage Saare's briefing made Hinata's victory all but assured in his mind. She must have her own motivations, of course…but the thought still troubled Renard.

The Clergy continued:

(Of course, it may have been a desperate lie from Valentine. But that's not the end of the story, you see.)

CHAPTER 5   HOLY AND DEMONIC COLLIDE | 239

(As hard as it is to believe, we have seen signs that she has attempted to connect herself to the demon lord Rimuru.)

(Would it not be unthinkable, normally, to see someone like the good Archbishop Reyhiem killed in this holy land?)

"But...!" Renard's mind was a whirl of confusion. "But Lady Hinata's faith is more stalwart than anyone I know. How could she betray us, to say nothing of our god?"

(Yes, there's the rub, Renard. We, too, have our suspicions about that.)

(But perhaps it is the other way around. Perhaps it is Hinata who is playing an intricate game against us—and Luminus. We cannot call it an impossibility.)

(There is one way we could settle these doubts for sure...)

"Wh-what is it?!" Renard half shouted, accepting the bait.

The Clergy was silent for a moment before continuing. (If we tell you, there will be no turning back.)

(This is not a question we can afford to make into a public matter...)

(Not until we prove Hinata's innocence.)

But Renard's mind was already made up, led expertly into the trap the Clergy laid for him with their words.

"I accept the risk. I promise I will prove to the world that Lady Hinata is innocent!"

(Mm, yes...)

(You will help us then, Renard?)

(It will likely be a dangerous task.)

Renard simply looked on, waiting for them to continue.

(Defeat the demon lord Rimuru!)

(Do that, and we will have our answer.)

(If Hinata is connected to him, she will no doubt stage a desperate rush to stop you.)

This was enough to throw even Renard's confidence.

"But... But Veldora...!"

This response was what the Seven Days expected.

(Do not lose your resolve.)

(Calm yourself and think.)

(Has the evil dragon *truly* awoken? Don't you think all of that is simply wishful thinking?)

This reminded Renard of a key fact. The only people who claimed to know firsthand that Veldora was back were Hinata and the Holy Emperor.

"So you are saying Veldora remains asleep?"

(That is highly probable.)

(Not even Reyhiem personally witnessed the dragon, as we understand.)

(It may even be the case that Hinata is deceiving the Holy Emperor himself.)

A whirlpool of doubt began to spiral around in Renard's mind—just as the Clergy wanted.

(And Hinata has already encountered Rimuru once.)

(We believe that was the moment when she fell under the demon lord's spell.)

(If she has been doing Rimuru's bidding ever since...)

The scales in Renard's heart began to tilt. *Yes*, he naturally began to think. *Hinata needs to be saved. And I am the only one who can save her.*

"Indeed. Yes, I am sure you are not mistaken! Lady Hinata would never willfully deceive us. If she is unwittingly doing someone else's bidding, that would clear her of any doubt on your part, correct?"

The Seven Days Clergy nodded their heads solemnly.

(It would. If you are able to do so, there would be no suspicion.)

(But it will be dangerous!)

They seemed to be testing Renard's resolve. They didn't need to.

"Then please, allow me to take on the task!"

His mind was made up. Hinata needed his salvation. And if she *had* been deliberately lying to all the paladins that served her...he wasn't afraid to strike her down, should it come to that.

(Very well. It shall be yours to handle.)

(Your resolve is strong, we see.)

(Do us proud, Renard!)

Thus, he set off, in direct violation of Hinata's orders.

＊

By the time he was inside the Forest of Jura, Renard's suspicion had grown to indisputable fact in his mind.

Veldora resurrected? Nonsense. There were far too few magicules in the air to make that an even remote possibility. Which meant that Hinata had most likely betrayed all of Luminism—a fact that Renard hardly wanted to consider, even as he continued his undaunted advance.

And then, just as he fanned out the troops under his command and attempted to launch a Holy Field, he was attacked by monsters, as if they had waited for that exact moment to strike.

"Could it be that Lady Hinata has sold us out...?" his companion, Garde, asked. "That she learned of our actions and tipped the demon lord off to them?"

(If Hinata is connected to him, she will no doubt stage a desperate rush to stop you.)

The words of the Clergy rang in Renard's mind. But now was no time for measured thought. He instantly sent the order to fight back, and with that, the battle was on.

Their enemies were stronger than expected...but as it turned out, he had not seen them all yet. Just as Renard was beginning to sense his position was in danger, out came the oni—those detestable, nightmare-like presences—falling out from the sky. They hit the ground, crushing it like an explosion and sending plumes of dust into the air.

"We got some big fish here," observed Garde as he readied his spear. Renard nodded back at him, then calmly gave his orders. Apart from the two of them, there were four paladins nearby, the rest of the force engaged with other monsters. In a moment, these four finished their preparations as ordered. The entire group was enveloped in light, forming a powerful defensive barrier—spiritual armor, the ultimate in protection for a paladin.

This armor came in the form of holy mail, light as a feather and imbued with the power to summon the spirits each paladin had forged a pact with. This granted them unfettered access to these spirits' powers, and what's more, the evil-quelling abilities added to their weapons neutralized all resistances in their foes, letting them strike for damage at every opportunity. All of this consumed a great deal of energy and thus could not be manifested for very long, but with it, the paladins were the true natural enemies of all monsters.

Readied for battle, the four paladins spread out in all directions, focused on their targets. They would be deploying a simplified Holy Field, and not a moment too soon, because the enemies they detected ahead were almost uncannily powerful. In particular, the magic-born standing before them had a gigantic amount of magical energy, like none he had seen before. It was an A rank—and on the higher end of that scale. Not Rimuru himself, no, but likely one of his closest associates.

It was, in Renard's mind, an appetizer before the main dish of the demon lord. He wanted to end this fast so he could move on to the biggest fish in the pond—and so he opted to leave nothing on the table for his first strike.

"Launch the Holy Field toward the target!"

But his lack of foresight would cost him. The order was laid out before he had a full grip of his adversary.

The four paladins sprang into action, deploying the holy barrier. The execution was perfect—nothing could have broken out of it from the inside. But it was not complete, a quasi-barrier with a short range and less of a weakening effect on monsters. It could prevent a foe from taking action, but could it fully block attacks from beyond the barrier? That was an open question.

This barrier was deployed in the shape of a pyramid, about fifteen feet to a side, but it left open the possibility of the target launching a large-scale spell before all its magicules were banished. In such a case, perhaps the attack could reach outside the barrier after all. That was one reason why most barriers were built to be much larger than this. But to be fair, even this quasi-barrier could fully prevent magicules from crossing over. It was a paladin's killer move, one that not even the higher-level magic-born could break through.

Thus, Renard ordered his team to deploy the barrier, keeping a careful eye on all of them. The purifying light surrounding them wouldn't be enough to kill a target like this, so a stout defense was a necessity. They could attack the foe from the outside—but they'd need to be sure what he was first. If it was one of the rarer types that could deflect damage, care would be required to avoid a massacre. They couldn't afford any mistakes.

As the paladins wrapped up all their preparations, the dust from the landing finally dissipated. There, in front of them, was a single monster, a slender, tall female with long, purplish hair tied back. On her forehead was a single horn, jet-black in color, and the strange suit she wore struck the curiosity of anyone who saw it.

Her violet eyes turned toward Renard.

"My name is Shion, *first* secretary for Sir Rimuru. My leader has the following message for you: Choose between submission or death. I am sure you are all intelligent enough to know what those words mean. Drop your weapons and surrender to my forces at once!" she declared haughtily.

The monster calling herself Shion gazed down like some sort of deity as she spoke. Her emphasizing the word *first* was noticeable across the whole of the wood.

Renard sized up his foe, judging her abilities. He had thought her magicule count put her in the high As, but now even this seemed like folly.

"A terrific sight. Special A…or perhaps she could even become a demon lord, if everything came together just right."

Judging by the horn, she was an advanced member of the ogre family. An ogre mage or maybe higher— *An oni*, Renard thought, *a mere hop, skip, and jump away from demon lord.* And a *named* oni—definitely a Calamity of a threat, or worse. Disaster, even, should she ever take that plunge into lord-dom. At least one oni of the past, he knew, held a force that was divine in nature, giving them control over nature itself. They were less monsters and more lower-level gods.

He was plainly right to have his team treat her with extreme caution.

"Hmph! Sorry to disappoint you," Shion calmly replied, "but I am no god, as much as I may resemble one. I am an oni, and something tells me that you think I'm a lot nicer than I truly am."

Niceness is something nobody facing Shion would accuse her of right now. They had no idea what made her entertain that notion, but really, it was just Shion's way of warning them.

"An oni? Perhaps there is not much difference, no, but it matters not to us. Divine or not, you are nothing but an evil monster in our eyes. The only god in our dictionary is the one god Luminus!"

This was the core tenet of the Holy Empire of Lubelius, and it was not to be defied. They would never recognize another god, even one with some degree of regional support among the people. If they do not declare themselves to be gods, then fine, but if so, they must be destroyed. Plus, this was just a monster. No matter how much power it wields, there was no need to go easy on a minion of a demon lord.

It was this belief that made Renard respond the way he did. Shion's retort to this was entirely unexpected.

"I don't care about your god! You have your choice, now give me your response!"

Submission or death. The non-offer rankled Renard deeply.

"Silence, evil beast. The world shall be purified of unclean creatures like yourself!"

Enraged, he ordered his paladins to launch a Holy Cannon barrage. One of the few offensive spells in the holy-magic family, it worked on the magicule level, dissembling the particles to rob monsters of the very essence that formed their bodies. On a human target, it would merely knock them unconscious with its force; on a monster, it would wipe out their very existence. While it didn't work on targets imbued with holy elements, monsters were particularly weak against it, for unlike the natural elements of earth, water, fire, and wind, the "darkness" element was incapable of canceling out the "holy" element. Without angelic holy magic, it was impossible to block the Holy Cannon.

Accepting Renard's order, the paladins went on the attack, firing bolts of holy energy from all sides toward Shion. But she just stood there serenely, the massive blade in her hands deflecting all the energy away. Then, with a dejected why-don't-they-listen-to-me expression, she turned to Renard once more.

"Is that your answer? If you refuse to submit, then that means it's time to die!"

Even Renard was shocked. But he wasn't about to submit to this. Whether this was some local god or not, she was already inside the Holy Field. All they had to do was keep that barrier going, wait for the target to falter under it, and strike the final blow.

But even as he thought that, Renard had to offer Shion praise for her masterful sword skills. She had to be at least a bit weakened by now, but the speed of her moves was every bit a match for his own. Not even he could hide his surprise.

That blade, whatever it was, had the ability to deflect holy energy, which was *extremely* unusual. Given Holy Cannon's magicule-corroding effects, any demonic blade offered up against it should have disintegrated into dust. But that large sword looked as fine as ever.

Then one of the paladins handling the barrier and offense let out a pained groan. A Holy Cannon bolt had struck him.

No! Can anyone even do *that?!*

Renard was shocked. Here she was, apparently taking this holy energy within herself, focusing it on her sword, and literally firing it back at her foes. From a common-sense perspective, it was absolutely impossible, requiring precision on the level of single instances in time—and Shion was pulling it off without breaking a sweat.

Hurriedly, he stopped the attack. The paladin, fortunately, was still conscious, albeit rattled. They would just need to stay calm and figure out another approach—but this move had rattled them all. Attacks going through a Holy Field and striking them were beyond their imagination, an unthinkable circumstance for any paladin. Renard had to bottle it all up as he pondered his next move.

Shion, for her part, was alarmed (or really, annoyed) that she wasn't seeing the full effect she intended. She had made a clean hit on that paladin, but the damage was negligible. It made her realize that whatever this attack was, it was much less effective on humans than monsters. She had underestimated her foes, and now she was inside this barrier—a clear mistake.

But she was expecting this from the start. She had her own ideas about this, and if anything, this was exactly what Shion wanted.

This binding force was something akin to the Holy Field Rimuru warned her about. It was similar in nature, and the magicule count inside it was beginning to fall. Soon, before very long, Shion's own force would be affected—and the Spatial Motion she surreptitiously tried out a moment ago was blocked.

Still, this had all been factored into her plan.

"Hey... Hey." She suppressed her anger as she forced a smile. "Surrender now while I'm still being nice to you."

It was incredibly haughty of her, not to mention nothing that'd ever shake the will of a paladin, but she was dead serious about it. That, of course, didn't come across.

"Fool!" Garde shouted back. "Enough of that bluster! You can't do a thing, locked inside that barrier!"

This howling did nothing to ease Shion's frustration. She was almost ready to explode—and given how short her fuse usually was, she thought she was doing an exemplary job at keeping it together. It may only be a matter of time now, but still, Shion continued trying to reason with them.

"Look, I'm being fully honest when I say that Sir Rimuru ordered me to avoid killing you as much as possible. Right now, I can promise you that I won't hit anyone—in fact, I can even let you try some of my famous cuisine! A wonderful idea, wouldn't you agree? This is your last warning. What'll it be?"

Her proposal was far too haughtily given for anyone to accept. The Holy Field's effects only accumulated over time as it purified the magicules caught inside. No magicules means no magic, no mystic arts, no divine force, no magical manipulation, and nothing that impacted the laws of nature. Only the special skills one may or may not have escaped its effects. To the paladins surrounding her, Shion's bluster merely sounded like a barrage of poor excuses.

But it must be noted that the Holy Field was *not* a defensive barrier. It wholly shut off all magicule interaction but offered no resistance to objects or blunt physical energy. If you triggered an explosion inside the barrier, for example, it'd still send a shock wave and shrapnel outside of it. The paladins, fully aware of this, were approaching this battle in full armor for a reason.

"We in the paladin force," Renard replied even as he failed to fully calm his anxiety, "do not negotiate with monsters. I see no need to discuss matters with you further!"

That was enough to push Shion's patience over the cliff.

"Well said! Have it your way, then, and prepare to be subdued with a maximum of terror!"

Then she smashed her blade to the ground. The force of it ripped through the air, filling it with dust and rocks once more. She grabbed bunches of them at once, hurling a fistful at the knight in front of her.

"Ah...?!"

A single moment—and then a mighty roar, as a small explosion erupted in front of the paladin. The thrown rocks collided with the knight's shield, pulverizing it into scrap metal. The force of it was astounding. *This* was her in a weakened state. If it wasn't for the Holy Field, things would've been even worse.

"Don't let up! Focus on your spiritual armor!"

"Yes," Garde added, "keep it up! Consider this a demon lord we're facing!"

The hapless, defenseless paladin hurriedly rebuilt a shield of light for himself, as Shion balled her fists and stared at them all. Undoubtedly, she meant that to finish him off, and seeing it fail enraged her all over again. The gap between that and her apparent intelligence and good looks was hard to swallow.

But at this point, even she had to realize this was going nowhere. Swallowing her anger, she spoke to Renard once more.

"I have an offer."

"We do not negotiate with monsters. I just told you that."

"Just listen to me. Like I said, I have orders not to kill you—but as part of that, I need to show you how much more powerful we are than you."

"......"

"I tried to go easy on those stones I threw, but that's far more difficult than it sounds. If I go any further with you, I think I might wind up killing one or two of you—"

"That's a bluff!"

"Don't listen to her! This is a monster tactic, meant to throw us into confusion!"

Shion smirked upon seeing the paladins' instinctual response. "Ah, good, I'm glad you're catching my drift here. So my offer..."

"Don't let her deceive you," Garde interrupted. "Let her sweet words enter your ears, and—"

Then, for just a moment, he felt something intensely hot around his right ear. Then came the impact, followed by the sound of the air being ripped apart behind it, rupturing his eardrum. Perhaps it was only his regular mental and physical training that saved him from a concussion.

"Wh-what was...?!"

Turning toward Garde, Renard was shocked to find a large tree behind him torn away from its roots, sending splinters flying as it tumbled to the ground. It made him forget how to speak for a moment.

"Ah...!"

Garde, blood dripping from his ear, realized what had just happened. Shion had tossed another stone—in essence, that's all it was. But the fist-size stone she chose had brushed past Garde's head at supersonic speed before smashing into (and through) the tree. She hadn't missed her target, of course. That ear *was* her target, and she nailed it.

"Do you even need your ears, if you don't bother using them? Now shut up and listen."

The paladins did as they were told.

"You freak of nature..." Garde cursed her under his breath, but he couldn't will himself to move. Even Renard realized by now that Shion had to be listened to. A direct hit by one of those could potentially kill one of his men. Not even spiritual armor was a bulwark against all physical force. With Shion's full strength now demonstrated, they had to admit that this wasn't a bluff at all—if she could fire bolts off faster than Garde the Battlesage could react, it was doubtful the rank and filers could fare much better.

Yes. Hear her out. The longer this dragged on, after all, the weaker she would become. Renard's choice was clear.

"All right. Let's hear your say."

Shion gave him a satisfied nod, smiling defiantly. "Good. Listen to me. I want all of you to hit me with the most powerful attack you have. I promise you that I'll take it squarely with my own body. If I stay standing, I win, and you submit to my forces. Sound good?"

Renard gave the utterly confident Shion a look of disbelief. Then a small doubt raised itself in his mind: ...*Does she really not want to kill us at all?* Because that was exactly how Shion had been acting this whole time. What for, though...?

But Renard didn't have time to think about it. Garde, half-deaf, was already pointing his rage at her.

"All right. We'll take that offer. Men, sync up your spiritual force

with me. Renard, you take control of it! That monster's too dangerous to keep alive!"

Hearing his own name, Renard snapped out of it. "W-wait! We
need to talk it over a—"

"Silence! Let's do it!!"

The other paladins began to pool their forces together as
instructed, a torrent of holy power right at the apex of the Holy
Field. This was then reduced to pure magical energy, amplified by
an injection of Garde's own strength. Without Renard's guiding
hand, the force of these four paladins would fall out of control.

*The midst of battle is no time to wallow in uncertainty. She deliber-
ately requested this from us. She can't complain about what comes of it.*

If she wanted their full strength, he wanted to stake his pride as
a paladin to provide it. Calling this a cowardly move—six fighters
piling up against one—would be a cop-out. Against a monster, victory was the only thing that mattered.

"All right, Garde. I'll guide it."

"Right! Here we go! Infernal Flame!!"

With a spiritual force that blazed like a pyre from the underworld, Garde controlled the towering flames. This was an ultimate
form of spiritual magic, borrowing the powers of an elemental
lord for the job. It was more power than Garde could control by
himself, and now it was all being slammed down into Shion's body.
It was even more powerful than Nuclear Cannon in terms of heat,
a pure wave of destructive energy powered by the spiritual particles
that formed magic itself.

As for Shion's response:

"Hee-hee-hee! That certainly fit the bill! Not the attack I was
expecting, but so be it. This ought to be the best way to strike fear
into your hearts!"

She beamed with glee as she readied her enormous blade. The
next moment, she mercilessly cut right through the Infernal
Flame—a side effect of her Master Chef unique skill.

Although Shion's behavior usually indicated no rational planning whatsoever, she had been utilizing multiple skills to produce
this moment. First, she invoked the extra skill Multilayer Barrier to
protect herself, keeping All-Seeing Eye and Magic Sense active
to probe her opponents for weaknesses. Then, using Master Chef's

Optimal Action skill, she read the flow of those heat waves in a single, natural motion, cutting through them to avoid the direct attack. That, of course, didn't mean the attack failed to burn her skin off and put her in a terrible state. Ultraspeed Regeneration, however, made that no sweat for Shion. Her skin instantly began to fix itself up, returning to normal in the blink of an eye. As brash and reckless as her actions seemed, they were all based on sane, even laudable, logic.

"A promise is a promise. Surrender to my forces and release this barrier."

Nobody found a ready response to Shion's declaration. The paladins just nervously glanced at Renard and Garde. Seeing such unrealistic sights in rapid succession froze their brains. Their pride as paladins had just been crushed.

Only Garde remained unconvinced.

"Don't trifle with us, monster. As long as that barrier remains in place, you are completely helpless! It peeves me to suggest this, but I'd say we should turn this into a battle of endurance!"

"G-Garde?!"

Renard was shocked. Garde was a man of reason, even if his anger sometimes got the best of him, but here he simply didn't know when to quit. As a paladin, that was perhaps the right choice, but it didn't seem at all like the Garde he knew.

But time had run out on that proposition. Shion's aura surged, projecting danger across the woods.

"Ha! You still refuse to accept it? I really *will* need to kill you now..."

Renard shuddered. *All—all that force...?! If this monster willed it, we would all be dead in an instant. Holy Field or not, we can't anger her...*

"We can't anger her! Stop with the provocation! Put your weapons down and—"

"You fool! A paladin never accepts defeat! Have you forgotten *that* as well?!"

Garde promptly shot him down. This display from him was unimaginable. If anything, he seemed like a different person.

"Y-you..."

But before Renard's confusion could fully transform itself into doubt, he was interrupted.

"Hngh!"

With that grunt of force—accompanied by a sharp *kreeeeen* echoing across the sky—Shion's blade cut through the barrier. The Holy Field, the source of confidence for all paladins, was shattered.

"N-no..."

"That is a holy barrier!!"

"Is this...some kind of nightmare?!"

"How can a monster destroy a Holy Field?! It blocks all magicules!"

The paladins murmured among themselves, their words and faces full of gloom. Shion, on the other hand, treated all of this as the obvious result.

"...I knew it. It's not a dense Multilayer Barrier at all; it's just a Special Barrier modified to change the rules a little bit. Modifying the laws of nature like that happens to be a specialty of mine. I'm good at cooking that up, you could say!"

Renard had no idea what any of that meant, but there was no doubting what she just did. Using Master Chef, she had modified the results the Holy Field projected on the world. Rewriting the cookbooks, in a way, overwriting the barrier with something more to her liking.

That was the Guarantee Results skill, the most valuable tool in the Master Chef arsenal and the main reason why her food had gotten much better as of late. It was perhaps a waste of such a powerful skill to reserve it for the kitchen primarily, the way that she did—but now, in dramatic fashion, she had just showed off its battle applications.

The final results: four paladins, plus two officers, struck dumb with fear. What possible way was there to defend against an opponent who was free to get the results she wanted just by *thinking* about them? It was useless. The only way to counter that was to overwrite her will with an even bigger one—but that assumed you could mess around with the laws of nature in the first place. If you didn't wield that kind of power, there was nothing to be done.

Renard, genius that he was, immediately realized what this meant. The fear was numbing to him. Just as Shion predicted, terror had overtaken his heart. But as the leader of this squad, he refused to give up hope. If fighting meant destruction, then best to surrender and find a way to stay alive.

"It can't be... It's ridiculous... How—how can this monster...?!"

As Garde babbled helplessly by his side, Renard made his decision, his voice wobbly, as if waking up from a dream.

"...We surrender. I only hope you will offer fair treatment to my forces."

Finally, mercifully, Shion gave him a broad grin. For the first time, Renard looked right at her. That firm, guileless grin.

Then, mulling over his own words, he regained his calm and reflected on the day's events.

It seemed certain that this monster Shion really wasn't interested in killing them. That wasn't Shion's will, but that of her master, the demon lord Rimuru. This made the story of Rimuru ordering a demon to kill Archbishop Reyhiem seem a little unnatural to him. And come to think of it, the whole reason Hinata traveled here was in hopes of building a friendly relationship with Rimuru. Why would the demon lord himself seek to interfere with that? If he was trying to plunge the world into war and chaos, it would make sense—but looking at Shion here, Renard could tell that wasn't the case.

Which meant:

Wait. Am I the one being used here...?

Hearing that the demon lord Valentine, the nemesis that snuffed out the lives of so many of his fellow classmates, was connected to Hinata had made him lose his critical thinking skills. Had that been used to trick him...? By who? The Seven Days Clergy, of course.

Reaching this point in his mind, Renard felt the blood drain from his head. Now, he realized, the force he captained was nothing but a hindrance to Hinata and her mission. Stealing a glance, he could see her facing off against Rimuru right now, and neither side seemed in the mood to talk. It was the calm before the storm.

This, this is... I am so sorry, Lady Hinata! Thanks to me, any attempt at negotiation was...

Now Renard knew the truth. But the truth arrived too late to do anything apart from watch the battle. There was no room for him to intervene.

And then the battle started, Hinata and Rimuru crossing swords before Renard's eyes...

●

It was a stroke of luck that Hinata Sakaguchi ran into Shizue Izawa. Even if it was just for an instant—a mere month—she was the only person that Hinata ever truly opened up to.

In that short period, Hinata had learned all of Shizue's sword skills, and when she was done, she left. Hinata was afraid of being rejected, and in the end, she was afraid she'd lose the warmth she had managed to gain this one time. She was fully aware of how awkward this was, and she did it anyway.

She had killed her father for the sake of her mother—but all it did was break her mother's heart. Despite it all, she loved her husband. Perhaps her mother got into religion because she needed prayer in order to deal with it. But there was no eradicating unhappiness from the world. That was the natural, obvious truth. Trying to make it all go away would accomplish nothing.

Hinata didn't want to admit that. She wailed at the unfairness of reality, dreaming of a world where everyone could live in peace.

What if her mother prayed to make up for her daughter's crimes? If that was the case, did her mother really hate her? Just imagining it racked Hinata with fear. That's why she saw coming to this world as such a fortunate thing. Her being here freed her mother from the pain, no doubt, and Hinata wouldn't have to go crazy any longer. She could just go on and on, like a machine, and not worry about anything.

Such were the kinds of fantasies Hinata lived with.

That was why Hinata could never accept Shizue. If she did, and wound up hated for it, Hinata would likely make an attempt on her life. She knew that full well, and it drove her to leave before it happened. *The only broken one here*, she thought, *is me*.

The power she gained allowed her to live in a world full of despair, one where people could take other people's lives all too easily. But in the midst of it, she came across a scene that proved a shock to her. One where a calamity-class monster attacked, killing many, while others fought to keep children safe. None of them fled, as they formed a human shield to protect them.

And here she thought the world was full of nothing but people who cared only to keep themselves alive. It left an impression on her.

In this world, those who fight were called paladins. Individuals who put their bodies on the line for other people, even it meant the ultimate sacrifice. People who patrolled the area around this city, shouldering the duty of protecting humankind.

That way of life resonated with Hinata. She decided to become a paladin herself, taking advantage of her own power. If she could devote herself fully to battle, there was no need to worry about anything else.

Thus, Hinata found a way to atone for her sins. And now, ten years later, Hinata was another protector of humankind.

✳

The days were packed with monster combat. She couldn't really say when these constant moments, the same thing happening over and over again, began to bore her.

Once she became captain of the Crusaders, the measures she enacted had reduced casualties down to astonishingly low levels. They could make accurate predictions of where monsters would appear, and how much damage they'd cause. They worked better as teams now, revising their patrols for optimum efficiency. Reworking the system had reduced the mayhem, producing results that were nothing short of impressive.

Hinata could point to that as the reason the knights trusted her so much. She had to laugh at the irony of her behind-the-scenes connection to the demon lord Valentine, but she could see that was the best, most rational way to keep the peace in this land.

She didn't let it bother her. She had no regrets. Under the god Luminus, all were equal—and only in a fully managed world can people enjoy true happiness.

*　　*　　*

Now, though, the situation was poor. Laughably poor. But it had also led to a breakthrough.

There was no longer any room for negotiation. She had to win, or else she wouldn't even have the chance to explain her actions. It didn't seem like he was willing to listen to her, perhaps as payback for ignoring him so willfully last time.

The shoe really is on the other foot this time around…

Hinata chuckled at herself. Things had changed so much that she began to miss those days of boredom.

There isn't a single shred of kindness in this world, is there?

She could whine about it all she wanted, but her mind was already made up. There was no point worrying, or even thinking, about it. Victory was the only way she could break out of this. Were her beliefs right or wrong? That hardly mattered any longer, as her mind shifted solely to how she could win this.

Hinata sized up Rimuru. Arnaud and the others had moved away with their own opponents; it was just the two of them now.

Silently, she invoked her Measurer unique skill to look him over. He may as well have been a different person from before. Rimuru was a demon lord, and there was no telling how deep these waters went.

Oh boy. Look at all that growth. The idea of him warring with humankind makes me shudder.

If not even Measurer could fully gauge him, it meant Rimuru was either at her level or higher. She moved on, invoking Usurper, her other unique skill and the one absolute advantage she could always enjoy over those superior to her. It let her effortlessly see through and steal the target's skills and arts—and while that didn't mean she could use them all to their full potential, taking away the skills her opponent worked so hard to obtain was, in its own way, a cruel and merciless gesture.

If the target was below Hinata in skill, the evaluation results provided were always "not applicable." It meant she couldn't take that target's skills, even though that had no effect on her eventual victory. If the target was better than her, Usurper could either "fail" or "succeed." Ending with one of those results meant this was a pretty strong foe—but success meant she knew all the target's skills and arts, and if it failed, she could just try again, as many times as she wanted. No matter how formidable the foe, she could always make the skill succeed given enough tries. It was just a matter of staying on guard, buying time, and waiting for the right moment. Pull it off right, and Hinata's victory was assured.

When she fought Rimuru for the first time, Usurper came back with a "not applicable" for her. It convinced Hinata that she had nothing to worry about. She totally downplayed his chances, and while having Ifrit summoned on her was a bit of a surprise, it still wasn't a serious problem. She had honed her skills to the point that she had Force Takeover, a rule-breaking skill that was fully effective against weaker foes.

Forcing her to turn to that, Hinata had thought, was impressive of Rimuru. But that was all.

Hinata thus invoked Usurper as a starter, just to see what kind of enemy she was dealing with. This time, though, it failed her. The skill went through the motions…and once it was done, the result it returned to her was "blocked."

That was the second time she had seen that. The first was against Luminus Valentine.

So you're in the same lofty heights as Luminus…?

Hinata was impressed. And in such a short time, too. Trickery wasn't going to achieve much here.

She took the hefty Dragonbuster sword off her back and tossed it aside, realizing it would be no help at all to her. Instead, she drew the weapon Luminus gave her—Moonlight, a legend-class blade. Protecting her was her Holy Spirit Armor, the "original" that was granted to her other paladins in spiritual form. It was one of the Western Holy Church's greatest countermeasures, an item wielded by the great Heroes of the past, built for tackling dragons and monsters. Only those truly beloved by the spirits could use it.

The light shrouded Hinata, settling itself into the shape of glowing armor over her form. Now she was free of all restrictions and stronger than an Enlightened—a Saint in terms of force. Now, it was a clash of power against power—and she was willing to put it all on the line.

The boring routine her life had become had just reached its end.

Waging war without any hope of winning was the work of a madman—but here, Hinata's heart was singing. She smiled a little. Rimuru asked if she had received the message, which meant he was ready to settle this with a duel.

I suppose I can absolve myself with a victory here...

Her mind and heart made up, she let it beat out its frenetic rhythm as she pointed her blade at Rimuru.

Hinata pointed her sword at me.

She heard the message, and she still decided to tangle with me? I thought she wanted to talk when she threw that weapon away, but I guess not—she just whipped out an even meaner-looking one, eyes boring down upon me.

Ah well. Let's win this and have her give me the story then.

Facing off against her like this, I couldn't help but remember that this lady had no weaknesses at all. Out of any existing weapons in this world (the ones I had seen anyway), this had to be a far cry above anything else.

I took out my katana to address it. If I knew it was gonna shake out like this, I should've had Kurobe finish up that katana I had cooking for my own personal use. One had been sitting in my Stomach for a while, steeping in a steady stream of magicules and now a healthy-looking shade of black from tip to handle, but it was in Kurobe's workshop right now. I had waited so long for it, I figured there was no major rush. Faced with Hinata's blade, though, this substitute I had in my hand seemed a little lacking. Better keep it within my aura for protection and try to avoid a lot of swordplay.

So I had Uriel take control of my Magic Aura skill, covering the blade in dark, thundering flame. *All set now. Let's see what Hinata does.*

We kicked off with a few ultra-high-speed exchanges. It had only just started, and she was going all out.

The speed of Hinata's sword was staggering. Mind Accelerate raised my brain's computational speed to a million times normal, and it still just barely let me react. It even reminded me of my fight against Milim. But I wasn't losing. I'd deflect the blow, then return with a slash of my own.

We had exchanged a few blows at this point, but none of us had landed a strike. No grazing blows to my body, either, which I was glad for. We were testing each other out, but I still couldn't fathom what she was capable of. Even with the support of Raphael and the power of a demon lord, nothing. She has to be some kinda monster. Frankly, I thought I was gonna overwhelm her a little more. I mean, yeah, she's strong, but as a true demon lord, I figured that'd give me a decisive bodily advantage—but we were even.

Hinata, apparently reading the path of my sword with robotic precision, always lunged in at just the right moment. There were no extraneous movements in her flow, and even when I slashed back, she'd just shrug it off and give me a flurry of sharpened blows, poking at me in search of weaknesses. The old me wouldn't have had a chance, I bet—meaning, in other words, that Hinata wasn't really trying last time. Lucky me, I suppose.

I couldn't hold anything back here, either, then.

●

Guess he's not playing around, Hinata thought.

She had hoped to overwhelm him with her sword, making him accept defeat at an early stage. But Rimuru was easily her equal. It had taken her ten years to polish her sword skills, and he was countering all of them.

The human body has its limits. Only by using magic and skills and arts to their fullest could you finally duke it out against monsters. And Rimuru didn't even need to breathe. His endurance would never wane, his muscles never ache, and no magic healing was required to ensure that.

Heh-heh... Standing in the same ring like this makes me realize all over again how unfair this is...

She understood the disadvantage she faced from the start,

dealing with monsters. Survival of the fittest was the rule of law in this world, making it vital to set up all the conditions you needed for victory in advance. She revved up Measurer, speeding her mind a thousand times, even pushing it past the limit as she gauged her surroundings. It placed maximum pressure on her brain, even bursting capillaries—something she handled with self-regenerative magic before the enemy could enjoy a single glimpse of weakness.

In this state, the world seemed to be frozen to her—but it still wasn't enough. She used Measurer's Compute Prediction skill to figure out the paths of Rimuru's attacks. That was how cornered she felt. Every arrow in the quiver needed to be used—but Rimuru still looked like he was taking it easy by comparison.

She wiped away the drop of blood that just dripped from her nose, ensuring it wasn't noticed by anyone, and gathered her breath. If this went on for too long, defeat was guaranteed. Even in her present Saint-level status, Hinata's human body limited her. If she wanted to become a demi-human spiritual body, she still had one more wall to overcome.

Usurper, her main lifeline, was blocked and useless. The one advantage she could always count on against stronger foes was gone. Instead, she had to overwhelm Rimuru with all the technical skills she had cultivated over the years—and *this* was the result?

The sword Luminus granted her housed a scary amount of power. Using her magic force to impart an aura into it let her pelt foes with the kind of lethal damage basic regeneration skills couldn't cope with. Even foes with Ultraspeed Regeneration could be cut in half with this thing.

If she could just take an arm off with it, Hinata thought, this would be over. No killing. If she could have Rimuru accept her victory, then it'd be settled. But she just couldn't land that strike. Rimuru's masterful grasp of the air around them, plus his honed physical skills, let him accurately predict every motion of her sword.

I can't get over his growth—but only in terms of physical ability. I'm not so sure his technical skill has kept up...

He had evolved, and greatly so, but his innate talents hadn't changed that much from before. Even if he could steal arts the way Hinata could, all that involved was grasping the fundamentals and having your body remember the moves. Making full, actual *use* of them took years of repetitive practice. That had to apply to Rimuru just as much as it applied to her—and she was counting on that for her victory.

This might come down to fighting experience, and Rimuru was sorely lacking there. Hinata could see that, and so she switched tactics, alternating her tempo to throw him off guard. Feinting, in other words. Taking full advantage of her polished skills, she did her best to lead Rimuru to his doom...

●

Suddenly, Hinata's sword began to speed up.

Her sword skills seemed to change gears every other moment. My brain was going a million times faster than normal, but it was like she'd have her blade here, then the next moment, *bam*, it's there, like a jittery online video.

This isn't funny, I thought as I did my darnedest to fend her off. It was Hinata Sakaguchi in full swing. I knew this already, but they didn't call her "defender of humankind" just to be nice.

So I kept watch over her as we continued to exchange flurries of blows. She had a bit of a smile on her face, watching me as if her victory was assured. She didn't need her eyes to pull off those moves. They were focused right on me, like sensors tuned to pick up on everything in the area, detecting attacks. The core of her body remained firm, keeping her in a natural position that could handle any advance or retreat. None of her moves were forced; she could pull off a variety of attacks from a relaxed neutral position without any windup required.

How she was reading all my attacks, I didn't know, but I was clearly an open book to her. Meanwhile, I was watching her attack motions, then using my physical gifts to find a way to dodge. It wasn't exactly smooth-looking, no. I was being toyed with, and if this kept up, I was guaranteed to lose.

I was pretty sure I was more physically gifted, but for some reason, she knew every attack before I unleashed it. As a technical fighter, she was clearly better. In *this* battle, she wasn't letting her guard down at all. Everything—the atmosphere, her personality—was different from last time. And those strikes, laden with as much force as they were, were bound to sorely damage me if they hit.

Understood. The blow would not be lethal, but it would drain a large amount of magical energy.

Yeah, see? And not being lethal was great and all, but one poorly parried strike, and I was gonna pay dearly for it. A few in a row, and I'd be in danger.

According to Professor Raphael, that sword of hers had some kind of special force as well. Its wavelengths could change the local laws of nature, letting it break through my Multilayer Barrier. *For real? It can't be.* But I doubted Professor Raphael was wrong.

...

Oh? Sorry? Something up?

Report. Next attack incoming.

Oops. No time to be lost in thought. Hinata had a sharp sword on her, and she worked it freely, moving from jabs to sweeps in a single, dance-like motion. She was nothing if not steady, shunning all magic or fancy moves and relying on textbook swordplay to engage me. To be honest, the only other person in this world who could take on Hinata in a swordfight was Hakuro—and unfortunately, Hakuro would probably lose. The difference in potential was just too great.

Looking at it like this, Hinata was truly a combat genius. No half-hearted attacks would ever work on her. For example, summoning a Replication of yourself to fight her was pointless, because ultimate skills could only be used by the original body, while Replications could only use up to unique skills. Hinata would just mow those clones down pronto. Even if you took Soei's approach and assigned each copy only the skills they needed, that gave you no freedom to change your tactics midway, which meant you'd never keep up with her.

Tricks like that could leave you open, which was taboo. Perhaps it wasn't the most exciting strategy, but it'd be wisest to wait Hinata out until she got fatigued. Fatigue never happened to *me*, after all. *But now look at her—she's speeding up her slashes!*

…Wait, no. Hang on. I can't read her anymore. I was watching her motion, taking evasive action, but now she was pursuing me with follow-up strikes, anticipating where I'd land each time. *Wait, this can't be right…*

Understood. You are being lured into the area she plans to attack.

Ah, that makes sense. Wherever I try to escape to, Hinata's always there with the perfect attack. In other words, she can make me go wherever she wants?

My clothing got ripped. The grazing blows were starting to pile up faster. *Oh, crap. This is really, really bad. Professor! Professor Raphael!!*

My only chance was to have Raphael bail me out. *Isn't there anything we can do?* Think, *dude!*

Report. Predict Future Attack learned. Use this skill?
  Yes
  No

…Whoa. Glad I asked. This guy's unstoppable. I always knew the prof would come through in a pinch. I had trouble figuring out what it said out of nowhere, but that sounded like one hell of a skill I just acquired, so…

Report. It was not acquired. It was learned.

Um, okay? *I don't care,* I grumbled to myself.

As the professor put it, observing Hinata's movements, it reasoned that she must be predicting my attacks in order to dodge them all so well. Meaning it had learned from watching her during our battle together.

…Wait, it can do that?!

Understood. Yes, it is possible.

* * *

Huh. Guess so. And I really did have the skill now, so it wasn't lying.

I immediately used that skill, and when I did, I could see streaks of light in my vision—printed into my brain, if you will—like any of my other senses.

One of them was glowing. I brought my sword up to block its trajectory, then marveled at how effortlessly it let me block Hinata's blade. Those light streaks must represent the slashes and thrusts currently possible from my adversary's position, with their projected paths. A few more repetitions, and I noticed that some of these streaks were black in color—this meant unpredictability and a more threatening strike down the road. In other words, I suppose, all her feints and low-level attacks could now be pre-calculated, but a master like Hinata couldn't be predicted all the time.

This pre-calculation wasn't even the scary part about this move. *That* lay in its accuracy. The streaks of light didn't represent possibilities; if the prediction was successful, there was a 100 percent chance of an attack coming down that way.

And if that was the case, Hinata was no longer a threat to me. Her feints were no longer feints; they were just another step down the road to perdition.

I won!

And with that newfound confidence, I let my body flow and followed Predict Future Attack's guidance, attempting to wrest Hinata's sword from her hand...

It was instinct, a baseless hunch in her mind, and it told her that letting her sword continue along this way would be a fatal mistake.

Hinata preferred a logical approach to battle. She never engaged in behavior that ran counter to the evidence at hand. But this time, she believed in her sixth sense. That saved her. It was only a feint, luckily enough, and she could force her blade away from its path—or really, she shoved her own body in the way, making contact with Rimuru and exiting to a safe distance.

Rimuru looked a little surprised at this but readied his blade once more, waiting for her. Hinata did the same—but something was different. Now, Rimuru seemed like a different fighter from before.

She attempted a feint. He ignored it, letting the sword whiz by like it didn't even register, and slashed at Hinata instead. There wasn't a moment's hesitation, as if he knew exactly what Hinata would do next.

...Was that a coincidence? No... It's even more accurate than my Compute Prediction...

It was disturbingly close to predicting the future. She felt like he was almost perfectly reading her thoughts.

The speed he's growing at is incredible. I may outclass him in sword skill, but his latent ability more than makes up for that. Nothing half-hearted will work against him. And if it doesn't...

Coldly, impartially, Hinata compared herself to Rimuru. At that point, she realized, her chances of victory plummeted a shocking amount. She had hoped for a quick resolution, as more time would just shore up her opponent's position, and here was the result. If she wanted to beat this guy, she now realized, she had to throw away all niceties, any effort to "go easy" or not actively kill him.

There was only one answer left. To break out a move she normally never showed in public and to grasp victory with it.

She kept her distance, aiming for a fresh start to work with.

It looked like things were largely settled around them. Everyone was stopped, as if time was frozen for them; they were all focused on Hinata and Rimuru's battle. The two of them couldn't even attack each other any longer—they could both read so far ahead in time, they could predict the results before they took action.

Time passed.

"...Rimuru, I have a proposal."

"What is it?"

"Let's settle this with the next strike. I have a finishing move, and I intend to put all my power into it. If you can withstand it, you win. If not..."

"I lose?"

Hinata nodded. "But let me warn you in advance—this move is dangerous. Are you willing to accept this?"

She thought he would. And now that Hinata had kindly provided this warning, Rimuru was no longer in danger of dying from the strike. It meant Hinata could use it without any regrets. If she did kill him, the high-level magic-born under him would turn into berserk menaces, striking at all humankind without prejudice. Hinata, her strength exhausted, would be killed at once, followed by all her weakened paladin fighters. To avoid that, Rimuru needed to be kept alive.

This move was called Meltslash, part of the Overblade family, and normally, she'd prepare it on the sly, not letting anyone notice it in advance. It was a combination of magic and swordplay, and its force was massive. There was no way to temper it in a feeble attempt to reduce its lethality. That's why she could only rarely use it.

Besides, if I showed this to you, you'd just copy it like it was the easiest thing in the world, wouldn't you?

She had reserved Meltslash only for foes she intended to kill. Revealing it to Rimuru, who could learn anything after a single repetition, frustrated her. But so be it. Nothing else was holding her back.

...I need to settle this here!

The only way to make Rimuru admit defeat was to show him just how overwhelmingly outclassed he was.

"But let me warn you in advance—this move is dangerous. Are you willing to accept this?"

She must've been pretty darn confident about this finisher of hers. But it didn't make sense to me. Why would she give me advance warning?

Understood. No desire can be detected on Hinata Sakaguchi's part to kill you. If she is cautioning you, it indicates just how dangerous a move it is.

I see. She doesn't want to kill me.

Wait, what? Didn't she come to do just that? I mean, yeah, something about this did seem kinda weird to me. Too late to stew over it now, though. There'd be a lot more time later—all the time in the world, in fact, once I win this.

"Sure. I accept your challenge."

Hinata smiled at me. "Heh-heh... I thought you would."

There was something really pure to that smile. It made her look younger than her years—in fact, she could almost pass for being in her teens. It felt much more natural than the usual, battle-hardened Hinata I was familiar with. This wasn't some grin of cruelty, no derisive snickering. Maybe this was the *real* Hinata.

"But no hard feelings after this, okay?" I warned her. "If you lose, promise me you won't mess around with this nation any longer."

Hinata gave me a quizzical look, then nodded, shaking off her indecision. "...All right. I promise. I agreed to this duel because you requested it; I want to discuss the future with you as well."

She seemed up to the thought, at least, but hang on. Something she said didn't seem quite right.

"You accepted it because I wanted it...?"

"Yes," she nodded. "I received your message."

My message had started with a few polite greetings, then moved on to the topic of Shizue and the children stranded on this planet, in an attempt to ease our misunderstandings. In addition, I offered her a forum where we could discuss our issues calmly with each other. In the end, I capped it off with this:

"So I hope you will agree to come to the bargaining table, but if I've failed to convince you, I'll take you on. It can be you and me, in a one-on-one duel, so nobody else will have to be involved. If possible, though, I'd like to end this with verbal discussion, not physical destruction. So give it all the thought you need, and I'll be waiting for what'll hopefully be a positive response. For now, see you later."

...Or something close to that anyway; I forgot the exact words. I definitely wasn't gunning for a duel; it's just that Hinata's so stubborn that I figured I should throw that in or else she'd tune the whole thing out.

"Here I go."

"Whoaaaa!!"

Oops. As I was pondering all this, Hinata had readied herself for the strike. We definitely still had some misunderstandings between us, but with things how they were, I could say nothing to stop her now. It was crazy, how focused she looked; no words would ever reach her brain.

Ah well. If I hold out, I win. Simple.

*　　*　　*

It appeared that Benimaru and the rest had secured victory while I was busy. Some of them were lying on the ground, some seated, and few had the energy to do much else. Only Benimaru and Soei looked like they had any gas left in the tank. Even the Three Lycanthropeers were as spent as the paladins; I guess they never got around to Animalizing for this fight.

Soei, though... What was he doing? The female knight he was engaged with seemed to be unhurt, but for some reason, she was looking at Soei and visibly blushing. I could see her fidgeting nervously on her feet, even, which only added to the mystery. It was like she had a crush on the guy or something. *What's up with that? Aren't we kind of all locked in combat right now? I'll need to inquire about that later.*

Then we had Shion. She must've totally stormed through her battle, and she even had paladins meekly following behind her. Prisoners? Some of them looked wounded, but none fatally. A little recovery potion, and we'd be all good. I'd need to dole out some praise for that performance.

That just left Hinata and me. And we were just one attack away from wrapping up.

"Benimaru."

"Yes?"

"If, by some chance, this fells me, you're taking my post."

"Ha. Surely you jest. Nobody here would ever doubt your victory, Sir Rimuru."

I shrugged at his cheerful evaluation. Yep. I had people here that really loved me. Unlike my stash of "special" videos I kept in a hidden directory on my computer back home, this was one treasure I couldn't afford to leave behind. I wasn't *that* irresponsible.

"All right. In that case, wait for my victory right there!"

"Yes sir! Be brave!"

I nodded and turned my gaze to Hinata.

Looking around, it seemed to Hinata like the stage was set. She could see her exhausted squadmates nearby, but they appeared to be receiving better treatment than she'd expected. Prisoner abuse must have been strictly prohibited.

As it would be, I imagine. Judging by your disposition, I suppose I should have believed you from the start.

The thought certainly took some time to occur to Hinata, but it was a sincere one. And it still wasn't too late. She could just win this fight, and they could build a new relationship.

She corralled her rising excitement, turning it into a prayer as she began to chant a spell in her clear voice. That wasn't strictly necessary, but she wanted to show it off to Rimuru. If he was going to steal it anyway, she wanted to be sure his copy was a perfect one. This was a Disintegration spell, and now its force was gathered around Hinata's left hand, letting out a blinding light. Glowing particles fluttered around it, creating an otherworldly sight, and then she imbued her Moonlight sword with this mystical force, as if gently caressing the blade with one hand.

Now everything was ready. Her sword contained the strongest magic possible now, and there was nothing it couldn't slash through.

"Are you ready for this?"

"Bring it!"

"Here we go... Meltslash!!"

Hinata, a glowing orb of light, lunged for Rimuru.

A bright light. Not the glint of a sword, but her entire body, with shiny particles shooting out of it, as she advanced at a superhuman speed that went way beyond what I expected.

The sword she wielded had the power to dispel and evaporate all types of evil.

Report. Unable to defend. Unable to evade...!

I had never heard Raphael sound legitimately panicked before. Even with my senses enhanced a millionfold, the light looked like it was going at regular speed—a sign of just how fast she was going.

Between the distance, the angle, and the timing, Hinata was aiming below my stomach. She must have figured I wouldn't die

if my head stayed intact, but even if she didn't intend to kill me, this move was way too dangerous. I couldn't evade it, Multilayer Barrier was meaningless, and that light was spiritual in nature, evil-dispelling, capable of tearing down anything it touched. The moment we made contact, it would sear through my body.

Report. It is suggested to sacrifice your ultimate skill Belzebuth, Lord of Gluttony, to cancel out this attack.

I *knew* I could rely on old Professor Raphael at a time like this.

As much as I hated to let go of Belzebuth, I didn't have much choice here. Out of all the suggestions it had, this was the most likely one to work, so there wasn't much point wavering on a decision. At *this* speed, besides, aiming practically didn't matter. It's not like I could adjust my trajectory midway.

Raphael used Predict Future Attack to calculate the point Hinata aimed at, activating Belzebuth at that exact spot. The moment her sword hit me, Belzebuth would swallow it all up—or so the plan went.

Pretty simple. No reason to waver. And in another few scant moments, Hinata's skill crossed paths with Belzebuth.

....

......

...

The result? Well, I survived. I thought I wasn't gonna for a second, but I did.

"Heh-heh-heh… Ah-ha-ha-ha-ha!"

I could hear Hinata's laughter ringing in my ears as I was lying there on the ground. All the magicules in the area had been purified; Universal Detect wasn't working for me, making this the first time in a while that I "heard" using my actual eardrums. It was more unnerving an experience than a nostalgic one.

My body couldn't move. Canceling out Hinata's strike consumed a vast amount of magicules—in terms of damage, it probably wiped out over 70 percent of my store. Which, hey, it's fine as long as I'm alive…but what a *scary* attack she had up her sleeve. If she busted that out without warning me… Well, just thinking about it made a chill run down my spine.

"I'm impressed. In the midst of that, you took the attack full-on? On purpose?"

Huh? What's Hinata talking about? What kind of idiot would intentionally take an attack like that?

...

Um, hold on...

Perplexed at Raphael's suddenly odd behavior, I decided to ask it a question. But the prof was silent. Hiding something, likely.

"Well, if you took it and lived, I lose. It's not like I can fight beyond this."

The protective light around Hinata disappeared...or fizzled out, really. She was spent. Even that amazing sword of hers was gone, gobbled up by Belzebuth. She could no longer offer any more resistance to anyone. Only her dignity was intact, her head held high, as she waited for my reply.

"Yeah. We'll call it a win for me..."

The battle was over. But the problem hadn't been solved.

As I attempted to declare victory over Hinata, I spotted something out the corner of my eye. Hinata noticed it, too, and turned toward it.

Up ahead, coming our way, was a large sword.

Report. Thought interference and magicule instability detected on target. It will explode soon.

The target was the great sword itself. If someone was interfering with it... Was it an attack aimed at us?!

"No! Are these the depths you'll sink to, Seven Days?!"

Hinata screamed out as she stood in front of me. I was still immobile. And then, the promised explosion. And then I could see Hinata's body slowly crumple.

LITUS

ARNAUD
BAUMAN

RENARD
JESTER

CHAPTER
6

GODS AND
DEMON LORDS

That Time I Got Reincarnated as a Slime

In the land of eternal night, within a burial chamber unknown to the world, encased in a casket of ice, there was a beautiful, dark-haired, naked girl. A figure was in front of her, also nude, as she embraced the casket with an eerie smile on her spellbound face. Her skin, as pale as the white-hot sun, burned a shade of red as she let out a satisfied sigh.

Ah... So beautiful... Ah...

Beholding this girl in the coffin, and showering her with love, was the secret delight of this charming silver-haired figure, her red-and-blue eyes flickering as they let out their ominous glow. They brought out her traditional beauty, enhancing it to another level. But what struck any observer of her the most were the two prominent white canines jutting out from both sides of her lips. Whenever she opened those lips, her bloodred tongue and milky-white fangs would bare themselves.

This was the demon lord Luminus Valentine, Queen of Nightmares and ruler of the night.

Whenever she touched this casket, it left a burn-like mark on her beautiful skin. It was an ark, a pure block of holy force, and thus damaging to Luminus. As a vampiric demon lord, this whole casket was like poison to her. But she didn't let it bother her. Even the bruising was bliss itself.

Even a demon lord with Luminus's powers was incapable of breaking the casket. So instead she lovingly caressed it, hoping for the day when she'd finally be able to release the girl sleeping inside...

*　　*　　*

One of her trusted associates made contact with her.

"I apologize for interrupting your fun, but there is something I wish to inform you of."

It was Louis, the one she had enlisted to be Holy Emperor of Lubelius. The sound of his voice annoyed her, but she put up with it. It was rare for him to speak up like this, and she could easily imagine it being an emergency.

"Oh. Louis? Did something happen?"

"Hinata has moved to defeat Rimuru, the root of all this evil. I tacitly allowed her to do so, but things have apparently grown complicated."

"...How do you mean?"

Louis gave her the truth, as revealed by his own investigations.

"Ah... No time to relax, then."

With a weary sigh, Luminus removed herself from the casket, left the burial chamber, and called for a servant.

"Gunther!"

"Yes, my lady?"

Gunther was an elderly vampire in Luminus's service, a butler who had joined her at Walpurgis. Now he emerged from the darkness, one of the Three Servants under her control and almost on her level of power. Louis was her point man on the emperor's throne, Gunther within the city of Nightgarden, and the late Roy her stand-in demon lord as a deterrent against outside propaganda. All three were also Luminus's bodyguards; Luminus was currently in a burial chamber situated deep inside Nightgarden, and Gunther was keeping watch over her nearby.

With a measured hand, Gunther assisted Luminus with her clothing. The fact that she preferred the ceremony of manually putting on her outfit over some instant magical transformation was a telling indicator of her form-over-function tastes.

"Honestly," Gunther griped at Louis as he helped her change, "bothering her with such trivial nonsense..."

"My apologies," Louis replied. "But if we leave things be for much longer, we run the risk of losing your beloved Hinata as well, I fear."

"Such silly concerns! Although, if it is the demon lord Rimuru she crosses swords with, prudence would certainly be in order…"

"I come to you both now because I don't *want* them to cross swords. If Hinata is killed, what would Luminus…?"

"Louis," Luminus grudgingly interrupted, "that's enough from you. You too, Gunther. A single appearance from me is all this needs, no? Then we can eliminate the source."

The Three Servants hated it when one of them horned in on the territory of another, which was a source of frustration for Luminus. Louis knew that, which was why he deferred to Gunther this time.

"Yes, my lady."

"I apologize…"

The two of them bowed their heads meekly. Luminus gave them a snort.

"With Roy gone, I'll need to rejuggle your assignments. Right now, though, I don't have the time for it. Both of you, follow me."

She began to walk, in all her solemn majesty. The two magic-born were ready to follow her.

"Yes, my lady."

"Allow me, my lady."

Then Luminus stopped for a moment, turning back toward the casket her beloved slept within.

Wait for me, all right…?

She then whispered the name of the precious girl inside, before grimly caressing the chamber's door and closing it behind her.

Soundlessly, shut away by Luminus's massive magic barrier, the chamber slipped down into true darkness.

Damrada the Gold, one of the leaders of the Cerberus secret society, had finally made it back to Farmus from his clandestine meeting with the Five Elders. He was now in Migam, out in the countryside, and given how well he knew the money-hungry Earl Nidol of Migam, he hadn't forgotten to placate him with enough presents to earn his trust.

This time, as well, a little bribe was all he needed to allow a protégé of his to reside within Migam. Edmaris, too, was there now in an undisclosed location, and Damrada knew this domain would become the eye of the storm before long. Edward, the new king, had dragged a force of twenty thousand toward this domain's borders—Damrada knew that, too.

His spreading the word that the hero Yohm was keeping the old king, Edmaris, safe was enough to convince Edward that the two were conspiring against him. That armistice, after all, was unilaterally signed by Edmaris. There was no need, Edward had made it very clear, for the new administration to honor it. And as Edward told his people, he had attempted to reason sincerely with them, only to have Edmaris and Yohm raid their royal coffers and steal away their money.

To Farmus's urban dwellers, far removed from the borderlands, a hero incapable of anything except combat wasn't *that* worthy of their appreciation. Being so safe in their cities, after all, made them underestimate the need for such stout defense. Some even questioned the need to keep people like Yohm and his force fed on the public dime. It was funny to see how such a large swath of people failed to realize that safety came at a price.

In the midst of this, the announcement that the hero Yohm and the old king, Edmaris, had embezzled the reparation funds infuriated Farmus's upper class. More and more of them volunteered their support for Edward; nobody doubted his moral superiority on this question. And with that support egging him on, Edward had deployed his troops.

If current trends continue, it wouldn't be long before Yohm and Edmaris were arrested on trumped-up charges and executed. They wouldn't be willing to accept that, of course, which meant war was on the horizon—just as Damrada drew it up.

Yohm had only about five thousand troops here in Migam, but they had been taking in reinforcements for the past three days.

Hmm... So Rimuru hasn't abandoned Yohm after all. How terribly naive of him. Now Hinata the Enlightened has a better chance of victory than ever before. Perhaps now is the time to move...

This, too, was within Damrada's realm of imagination. On a

wholly personal level, he would love it if Hinata could be taken out of the picture for good. It was likely that she knew she had been taken advantage of by her lies, so it was best to eliminate her before she got in the way. Damrada doubted she'd ever forgive him for it, and he needed to keep that in mind during his operations in the Western Nations.

For now, though, he would have to leave Hinata in the hands of the Five Elders. Any more direct intervention with her would be too dangerous.

Ah well. Not like this mission will end in failure…

The leader of Cerberus ordered him to trigger a war in this region. Nothing else. As far as Damrada was concerned, his job was already done, so it'd be a smarter bet to pull out before Hinata got back. But there was just a bit of unfinished business left. Damrada didn't care who won between the hero and the new king, but if he wanted to secure future profits, he had a promise with the Five Elders to fulfill. The demon had to be killed.

This, however, was where his plans began to go awry. Earl Nidol Migam had tipped Damrada off on an internal meeting held in his domain, and judging by the report, this demon was aiming for a quick end to the battle as well.

What would this mean to him? It meant that the new king and the demon wanted two completely different things for Farmus. Edward had no intention of hostilities against Rimuru. The monster forces clearly outclassed his, and there was no way Farmus could beat Tempest alone. But despite that, Rimuru had still sent reinforcements to the hero Yohm. That indicated to Damrada that he wasn't afraid of war, should it come to that. All that talk about a "just cause" was turned on its side the moment the demon lord sided with Edmaris. He had changed his mind, it seemed.

This gave Damrada some concern. In the midst of his investigations as he sought the demon, he had come to learn that the magic-born Razen was now serving the demon Damrada was trying to kill, not Edmaris. Which meant…

…Was it that demon who defeated Razen, not Rimuru himself? This is no Johnny-come-lately demon given physical form on this world, then. Perhaps an older demon has been revived…

The thought made him grimace. There wasn't enough intelligence to work with; not even the Cerberus leader provided any information about the demon. This adversary, he reasoned, would have to be considered at least an early-modern Arch Demon, possibly older. The strength of this type of demon depended greatly on their age, and while "modern" ones were one thing, early-modern Arch Demons—two or three hundred years old—were a calamity-class threat. A "medieval" one, pushing nearly a millennium in age, could be powerful enough to serve as a demon lord's aide. It was a completely different level of strength from some lower-level evolved demon. If an Arch Demon like that was on this world, it was devastating news, a threat to humankind as an ongoing concern.

It was worth noting that human beings had only successfully summoned demons up to the medieval level of age. That was as far as the records showed, and it made sense, because anything *more* powerful than that would mean the end of the summoners' souls. They'd be immediately consumed. That was why the Eastern Empire's latest research regularly called for limitations on demon summoning—although it took a hero-class summoner to make an Arch Demon do their bidding in the first place.

"The magic-born Razen, though...?" Damrada murmured.

Yes, Razen's name was known far and wide across the Empire. Power like his was easily the match for a medieval-aged demon. If there was a demon out there who could defeat the likes of him...

Plus, the Five Elders seemed to be fairly blatantly scheming with one another. That piqued his curiosity a bit as well, but his instincts told him this was one wasp's nest he was better off not prodding. *Best to make good my escape*, he thought, *before I am caught up in anything else.*

"Is something the matter, Sir Damrada?" his servant said, responding to the words he spoke to himself.

Damrada weakly smiled back. "Heh-heh-heh... This is too hot to touch. No more of this. We have word to lie low for now, and I'd consider it wise to heed that advice."

"Pardon...?"

"We are retreating. Leave two or so observers behind and order everyone else to leave this nation."

"Yes sir. What about you, Sir Damrada?"

"I will extend my formal greetings to King Edward, then pay a visit to Tempest."

"But I thought you were advised to lie low...?"

"Hmm? Heh-heh-heh... Oh, I will. For now, I will cease my behind-the-scenes maneuvering, in favor of other advances. There's no law against a proper merchant requesting an audience with the demon lord Rimuru, after all, in order to improve his business."

"I see. Very well. And what should we do with the six Contractors we brought over from our homeland?"

"We'll bring them to the new king. They will be a fine souvenir for him."

"So it'll all be pushed on King Edward's shoulders, then?"

"If you want to put it *that* rudely, yes. It'd be a favor to Edward, all while I fulfill my promise to the Five Elders."

These Contractors were an Eastern Empire organization that served roughly the same purpose as the Western Nations' Free Guild. They were a group that assigned work to specialist professions, including demon hunters who worked full-time pursuing the demons of the realm. Only the best, most experienced monster fighters would be granted a license for this profession, and Damrada had paid a princely sum to bring six of these demon hunters with him. He had hoped to use them as advertising for Contractors at large, but now he sensed that things were too dangerous even for them.

"But do we really need to be on our guard this much? We haven't fully made back our investment yet..."

"We'll see, we'll see. I may be overthinking it, but I like to trust in my instincts. I'm also not enough of a fool to lose my life when I should've been cutting my losses."

"Ah. Yes, my apologies for doubting you. In that case, I will begin preparing for our retreat."

"Good. And I will prepare another present for the new king."

The servant left the room. Preparations went quickly after that, and before much longer, Damrada had put Migam behind him. He was right to do so, for if he had dawdled any further, he might have had an angered demon trying to kill him.

Edward, newly crowned king of Farmus, was beside himself with excitement.

The nobility across the land was falling over themselves to pledge their support to him, expanding and strengthening his forces. It surprised him to see the hero Yohm side with Edmaris, his elder brother, and when Rimuru sided in turn with Yohm, he feared his entire plan would fail. But the heavens hadn't abandoned him.

With Archbishop Reyhiem dead, the wheels had begun turning. Hinata herself was off to slay Rimuru, he had been informed, with the Crusader forces in tow. Even better, the heroes of the Holy Empire of Lubelius—the Three Battlesages, the royal officers second only to Hinata in strength—had offered their support to Edward's cause, deploying the Temple Knights for the effort. The divine-enemy label hadn't been formally announced yet, but given this deployment, it had to be a matter of time.

The Temple Knights were assigned the task of defeating the demon who killed Reyhiem, but that was just a convenient excuse. In Edward's mind, they were actually aiming to mount a resistance against the demon lord Rimuru, armed with an enormous force that was essentially the federated armies of the Western Nations. That was why he granted them safe passage through his lands, as well as the right to engage in any military activity they saw fit.

He had no intention of tangling with Rimuru, but under the circumstances, that didn't matter. There was no way Hinata would lose to the demon lord, and with this large a force, he reasoned, defeating the Tempest forces wasn't an impossibility at all. Veldora remained a concern…but with a dragon that finicky, the combined forces of the Western Nations ought to be able to seal him up once again.

Now he needed a just cause to link all these efforts together, and that was already taken care of. A powerful merchant from the East had visited him, bringing a letter from Earl Nidol of Migam. It was a request for help, and it instantly solved all Edward's problems. It didn't take long for him to reach a conclusion.

With reinforcements flowing through the border from all sides, it might be best to use Migam's rescue as an excuse to deploy my own.

A full-on war wasn't in his plans, but deploying his force out-side the city walls should prove enough of a deterrent. There was nobody around Edward to warn him otherwise—which he would come to regret later—as he sent out the order.

●

In Glenda's eyes, the plan had gone seriously out of whack, but that sort of thing was a given on the battlefield. She just had to adjust her tactics, make things work more her way, and she'd be fine. Looking at it that way, things didn't seem so bad to her. A large number of nations were taking an interest in their moves, and a virtual army of journalists were here to see her in action.

Everything was set up just as she wanted it. Rimuru not focusing exclusively on Hinata was an unwanted surprise, but as Glenda saw it, it just meant he spread out his forces too wide for his own good. It wasn't a problem.

Damrada had fled the country, but he had left a team of anti-demon experts with King Edward as a symbol of goodwill, each one battle-steeled and ranking an A or better. She figured they could be trusted to do their job.

No reason not to sacrifice them, if we need to, Glenda idly thought. No matter how it turned out, she optimistically believed that the demon would be out of her hair. That breezy mood didn't last for long.

●

Heh-heh-heh-heh-heh...

Diablo, the demon in question, let out an evil laugh as he spread his batlike wings, looking like a sign of the apocalypse as he sur-veyed the land below. He was searching for the traitors who outed him, causing shame and embarrassment in front of his beloved Rimuru, and he wasn't in a forgiving mood.

Not once in his life had he ever felt anything resembling fear. But the mere thought of being relieved of his work duties made him quiver. Picturing Rimuru staring at him and saying "All right, you can go away now" sent shivers up his spine. The terror tore him apart.

Now Diablo had to pay back the people responsible for that feeling. He contemplated what he'd do once he tracked them down. It made the smile even broader.

Then he found Edward, the new king, at the rear of the forces. With him were several others who stood out of the crowd strength-wise, at least somewhat—enough so that they could at least go toe to toe with Diablo. Part of the Ten Great Saints, perhaps?

Rimuru instructed him not to kill anyone who wasn't involved. If they *were* involved, that didn't apply—at least that was how Diablo and Hakuro, his overseer, had interpreted the missive. Any troops not defending themselves would be let go, of course, but if they attempted to fight him, that was another matter—especially if they decided to initiate hostilities themselves. Then, there was no need for mercy.

Resisting the urge to greet this new king at once, Diablo sent a Thought Communication, reporting his findings to Hakuro.

(Sir Hakuro, I have found one standout among them headed your way. He should keep Sir Ranga occupied, I would imagine.)

(Hmm. Roger that. Is it better not to kill him?)

(Yes. I believe he is related to Lubelius, the origin of those rumors against me. Capturing him alive would make him a useful pawn in our negotiations.)

(Very well. I will inform Sir Ranga.)

(Also... This target is leading approximately five thousand troops. By the Free Guild's ranking, this includes several fighters graded at least an A.)

(Hmm. Perfect, then. Let's point Gobta and Gabil at them.)

(Yes, a fine idea. I am sure this is a battle they cannot lose, but...)

(No need to worry. I will be watching them, so feel free to do whatever you like.)

(It relieves me to hear that from you. Excuse me, then.)

(Don't overexert yourself.)

With his report given, there was now no need for restraint. He flew down toward his prey.

The sight of Diablo swooping in from out of nowhere froze the blood in Edward's veins. Saare, enjoying a cup of tea with him, was barely able to react at all.

"Hello there. I believe we have met before, King Edward? My name is Diablo."

He gave them an elegant bow. Before he could even finish his greeting, Edward's knight captain was barking out orders.

"Fan out! Take defensive positions! Protect King Edward!!"

The royal guard jumped into action, grabbing Edward and trundling him toward the rear. The guard instantly formed a line of defense to cover Edward and create a wall of humanity between the devil and the king. Diablo took his time to react, simply standing there while all these troops scurried around. As far as the demon was concerned, his target was in sight. The hard work was all done. There was no reason for undue haste.

In another instant, Diablo found himself surrounded by Saare and his forces, covering the large, opulent royal tent the demon had landed in front of. He looked at them all, enjoying the sight—but although nobody noticed it, his eyes were burning with rage.

Soon, a group of journalists was on the scene, curious to see what was going on. Diablo kept smiling.

"I will not harm any of you. Just stay over there for me, please."

Then, with a snap of his fingers, the press corps was covered in a barrier—a bit of helpful consideration on Diablo's part, to ensure against collateral damage. He also meant to suggest that exiting the barrier would be seen as hostility punishable by death, but the journalists (luckily for them) never even entertained that thought.

By the time the forces were all in position, Edward had regained some of his composure.

"Well, well! The agent of the demon lord Rimuru, then? May I ask what brings you here?"

The greeting may have lacked much in the way of royal majesty, but it certainly succeeded in sounding pompous.

"Heh-heh-heh-heh-heh… Oh, just a warning for you."

"A warning? What kind?"

"Send your troops back immediately and hold talks with Sir Yohm. Then you will not have to taste the kind of fear you are better off not knowing about."

For appearances, at least, he began by recommending talks. That, however, was not what Diablo really sought. If anything, it'd be a pain for Diablo if Edward actually agreed to them.

"Ha-ha-ha! What a strange proposal this is. Besides, all of this began when my brother embezzled the reparation money from our accounts. We are simply trying to recover these funds, in a gesture of sincerity toward your nation. I see no need for you to meddle in our affairs!"

"I see. So you're stating your intention to adhere to our peace accords?"

"Of course... Although I now see there was no need to. I was almost tricked myself!"

"Meaning...?"

"Hmph! Enough playing dumb! You are conspiring with my brother Edmaris to charge us for double the reparations, are you not? Don't think I haven't seen through your little schemes!"

"......"

"Nothing to defend yourself with, is there? Whether he calls himself a demon lord or not, this Rimuru fellow has already demonstrated just how shallow he is to me. He seeks to plunder us, by fair means or foul, and he's spreading the seeds of war across the land, is he not?"

"............"

"But what a pity, isn't it? You may have killed Archbishop Reyhiem in a bid to keep him quiet, but his words are recorded right here!"

Edward took Diablo's silence as an invitation to chatter on and on. The crystal ball he took out was held high above his head, ensuring the press on hand could see it. It depicted a very haggard-looking Reyhiem, perhaps after a torture session or two. "I had no intention of betraying you!" he shouted. "Please, please forgive me!" One could tell any viewer that this was footage of Reyhiem's final moments in this world, and they'd believe it.

"And what does this piece of evidence prove?" Diablo asked.

Edward laughed back, clearly considering it a foolish question. "Don't you see? Lady Glenda over there brought this to us. You infiltrated Lubelius and killed Sir Reyhiem, did you not? Perhaps you thought mere threats would cow him into doing your bidding, but his faith outclassed your terror! So you feared him telling the world about your crimes, and it led you to do *this*!"

He looked down at Diablo, all but daring him to respond. Diablo's smile remained intact.

"How impressive. A mere *human being* able to overcome his fear of me? That's a rather funny joke."

"Don't dodge the question! You've seen the evidence against you; you cannot merely talk your way out of it—"

"Enough. Silence."

Diablo's quiet voice cut off the new king as he was trying to show his full dignity to the press. For a single moment, his smile disappeared. Replacing it was a hideous, barren, unfathomable terror.

"This charade is over. I cannot enjoy a battle of wits if you neglect to bring any with you to the contest."

The words were enough to freeze Edward where he stood.

"I had thought about explaining the truth in detail to prove my innocence, but I see that would be a waste of time. Humans are wired, after all, to believe only what they want to believe. But there is an easier way to prove my case..."

"Wh-what are you saying...?"

The change in Diablo's attitude intimidated Edward. Only now did he realize that this approach of his might not have been the most intelligent idea.

"You would like me to prove my innocence," Diablo continued, "wouldn't you? If anybody here is able to overcome their fear of me, I will gladly admit defeat. But let me caution you: I have never been defeated before. If you seek to defy me, then be prepared to face the consequences."

His voice was just as calm as always. But within those golden eyes of his, a pair of crimson pupils burned with rage. If this were only for himself, Diablo could've still held himself in check, but Edward had decided to cruelly slander Rimuru as well. And at that moment, Edward's luck ran out.

"K-kill him!" the fear-stricken Edward shouted. "Engage this demon menace at once!"

The demon hunters mixed in with the soldiers guarding the king were waiting for this order. They all simultaneously leaped out and attacked Diablo.

"Overcome our fear of you? Too easy! You might think yourself invincible as an Arch Demon, but we stumble across demons like you in our homeland all the time!"

"No demon can survive for long if you pulverize their physical form! That applies just as much to an Arch Demon!"

"We've done our homework on how to handle demons like you. Don't count us humans out!"

The hunters worked in tandem as they shouted at him, going into a lethal formation. They had a laser focus on Diablo, despite what their bold insults would imply. Diablo, after all, had a name, and a named Arch Demon was a level above the norm threat-wise.

"What? No response, then?"

"All bark and no bite, eh?"

Swinging Special compound-alloy chains imbued with the holy element, they pinned Diablo down, binding his arms and legs. Their very first move had succeeded, and it made them let up on their caution just a bit.

The Eastern Empire, for better or for worse, had more experience with marauding demons than the Western Nations. This was supposedly because of a demon stronghold in the East that held sway over a gigantic amount of power, but either way, it also meant that demon hunters really *were* well-trained fighters in the art of anti-demon tactics. An Arch Demon was strictly the stuff of legend in the West, but eastward, they had conducted extensive research on demons, dividing them into categories and coming up with strategies for each type.

The leader of the demon hunters had pegged Diablo as a medieval-age demon, but considering his named status, it seemed sounder to treat him as an "ancient" one instead. A member of the demon nobility, gifted with massive power, intelligence, and perhaps even a vast army of kin. The threat could not be underestimated.

But the leader still believed in their chances at victory. He had experienced several Arch Demon fights himself, and he never doubted the decision-making skills he learned from those battles.

"Are you ready, then?"

That was why Diablo's question seemed so befuddling to him.

"Wh-what?"

"I mean, if you have made your preparations, I would appreciate a starting signal."

The leader failed to understand what the serene demon meant. "...Huh?" He hid his concern, trying to sound as defiant as possible. "Are you saying you won't get in our way, no matter what we do?"

"Why would I? With all the effort you are clearly putting in, I don't want to interfere, you see. This will just make the fear that much more vivid."

"Heh...heh-heh... Don't toy with us, demon. Your arrogance will be your end!"

Diablo's joking around sent a slight chill across the demon hunters' minds. Demons like him often looked down on people, overestimating their own skills. With that knowledge in mind, Diablo wasn't venturing far from the typical demon script. This time, though, he was delivering these lines while already chained to the ground. Even a seasoned demon hunter would be put off by *this* much confidence.

Still, these were professionals. They didn't delay a single beat, executing on the training routines they repeated day after day.

"...You shall regret your arrogance in hell! Vanquish him now! Thunderbolt!!"

As King Edward, journalists from nations worldwide, and Saare and the rest of the Lubelian royal guard looked on, Diablo was roasted by blinding flashes of electricity.

"How about that! What does natural, non-magicule-infused lightning taste like to you?!"

"A demon like you is protected by layers of barriers, we know. But too bad for you! With our Imperial technology, we can break right through your defenses!"

"Demons must be granted physical form to impose their will upon this world. With your body destroyed, there is nothing you can do!"

The demon hunters seemed to treat their victory as a given. Any magicule-driven force could be easily blocked by a barrier built for the purpose. In response, the Eastern Empire had researched weapons that didn't rely on magic to work. This lightning trick was one of them, the latest in anti-demon tech, and hearing that made Edward's terror ease a bit.

"Wonderful!" he shouted, relieved. "Truly, you are the heroes of the East! I must raise my reward for that merchant!"

His face was twisted in glee as he looked at Diablo. The lightning was roasting the demon alive... Or was it? The flashes of light had fully enveloped his body by now, but that smile was still on Diablo's lips.

Only Saare and Glenda picked up on this at first. It worried them. The demon hunters' leader, however, was puzzling over something else.

...*This shouldn't be happening. This shouldn't be happening! Why isn't there a single burn mark on his clothing?!*

Then he saw it. That evil, evil smile.

"Y-you...!!"

"Heh-heh-heh-heh-heh. A rather meager effort. Too meager, in fact. You thought this would suffice against me? After all that hard work, I can't help but call it a disappointment."

Diablo casually brought an arm up. The moment he did, the chains binding him shattered.

"Whoa!"

"Nngh!!"

With unbelievable force, Diablo ripped the reinforced-alloy chains off his body.

"Y-you monster!!"

He laughed at the words of shock from the leader's mouth. "Right, then," Diablo said, as if nothing had just happened. "Now for the selection test."

"W-wait! This is insanity! Why didn't the lightning work on you?!"

Out of disbelief, or perhaps to divert his impending terror, the leader had to ask the question. Diablo was kind enough to provide a detailed reply.

"Why, you ask? It's simple. I am equipped with a strong resistance to natural influences, electrical discharge included. Your attack just now was such a meager strike at me, it didn't even merit building a defensive barrier to counter it. Is that satisfactory?"

The leader began to visibly shake. If anything, that was brave of him. The rest of the hunters, realizing the portent behind Diablo's statement, had already fallen screaming to the ground.

"Aaaahhhhhhh!! Get away! Stop! Get away from me!!"

"Nnoooooooooo! H-help me!!"

These were first-class demon hunters, fearless, battle-trained warriors. And they weren't alone. Except for the protected journalists, everybody witnessing this scene felt their spines freeze solid. Edward fainted right where he stood, foaming at the mouth, and so did his royal guard.

What just happened? The leader could see it well enough—this overwhelming terror, the sheer pressure this demon was sending their way. To put it as simply as possible, all Diablo did was unleash the full brunt of his aura—but that aura was daunting enough in itself to kill.

"Oh? So only three of you passed the test? Well, I suppose you *do* deserve praise for withstanding my Lord's Ambition. You hereby have my permission to engage me."

Hearing this, even as he felt the terror closing around his throat, the leader turned around. There, just as Diablo promised, were the two others left standing—Saare and Glenda, the young man and the wild beauty.

The sight of them seemingly unfazed helped the leader rally his exhausted mind. *It's all right. It's still all right. The Battlesages didn't let us down—truly the heroes of the West. My hunters may be done for, but with these two on hand, victory could yet be ours...*

Encouraged, the leader turned back toward Diablo. "Heh... Heh-heh. Yes, you are every bit your demon lord's servant. You're just as good at bluffing as he no doubt is."

"Bluffing, you say?"

"I do! You called that Lord's Ambition just now, didn't you? It takes a demon lord–class monster to wield that skill—and if Arch Demon is the highest level of the demon races, it is impossible for you to become a demon lord! That proves you are a liar!"

In the East, this fact was considered highly classified research. Demons, he knew, had an upper limit to the amount of magicules their bodies could store. This was a set number across all of them, even though they could differ in other forms of strength. Older demons would have more experience in battle, allowing them to form better strategies for conserving their magic and squeezing everything they could from it. This was also one reason *not* to fear demons as much as people often did, for if you knew your enemy's magic limit, you could work with that, no matter how they tried to spin it. Knowledge is power, and having the right knowledge can keep an obvious bluff from clouding your mind.

"I see. That is both correct and incorrect. It is true that demons like myself are limited in our magicule count. However, it *is* possible to evolve to the next level, assuming the right conditions are met."

"Huh?"

"I think the Red would be an example famous enough for you to be aware of?"

"The Red? What do you...?"

And then a certain demon flashed across the leader's mind. One so famous, his entire existence was the exception that proved the rule.

"It would be simple enough to obtain the title of demon lord, you see. All it takes is for one of us to build our strength up to the maximum level, then live for at least two thousand years. One hardly needs to even work for it."

Diablo made it sound easy, but in reality, it was fiendishly difficult. As a spiritual life-form, demons naturally enjoyed combat. Even if they were never summoned to the physical realm, battle was a constant part of life in the spiritual one. Losing a fight over there would dock magicules off your upper limit, which meant that some demons actually *de*volved over time. Reaching one's maximum, then maintaining it for two millennia, basically meant evolving into an Arch Demon and building an unbeaten record that entire time—not even a single loss.

The demon hunters' leader wasn't aware of that per se, but even he had a hunch that Diablo was heavily downplaying the stakes involved. But the offhand reference to the Red was what attracted his attention—Diablo was speaking of that absolute ruler, the famous demon, as if they were casual buddies.

It couldn't be. Out of all the things, it couldn't be that...

Demon society worked in a strictly hierarchical relationship, according to a theory first advanced by Lord Gadora, the great sorcerer from the Eastern Empire. This hierarchy was punishingly strict in nature, applied equally both to the Primal Demons and the higher-level members of each demon type. A lower-level one referring to a higher-level one without some term of respect was as unthinkable as the end of the world.

"But perhaps the White would be more famous in the East, where you grew up? I observed her using Lord's Ambition over there just the other day..."

The remark cleared the haze from the leader's mind. He recalled the events of several years ago, just before Blanc, the fearsome Original White, took form in this world. They called the event the Bloody Shore, and if it had turned out the wrong way, it would've marked the birth of a second Guy Crimson, disrupting the balance of demon lords and dooming the planet to chaos. The Empire used its clout to bury the events of that day, ensuring the public didn't know about them.

The leader turned pale. Now he knew. The demon that casually called them Red and White had to be at least as powerful as the one that caused the Bloody Shore.

That, that, that just can't be...possible...! There... There's just no way for us to win! It's ridiculous. How could any of this happen?!

The leader screamed internally...and then, all too easily, something snapped. Demon hunters were professionals, not thrill seekers. They didn't risk their necks over a job unless the money was right. If it involved protecting their own family, that was one thing, but nobody wanted to die in a faraway foreign country like this. And now that the leader understood how desperately outclassed he was, he abandoned all resistance as futile.

"Please, save me!" He let go of all shame and honor, pleading with Diablo. "At least spare my life... Help me, please...!"

Diablo rewarded the display with a gentle smile. "Oh, what's wrong? You passed the test for me. Why don't we have some fun? Don't you want to find out whether I'm bluffing or not? You should see it for yourself."

The leader was desperate. There was no more doubting Diablo. He realized fully now that this was a supreme danger to himself and the rest of the world. Bluffing? Don't be ridiculous.

"P-please, forgive me! I only came here for the money. I swear I will never defy you again! I'll never do anything to interfere with you. If you order me to slit the king's throat while he's still unconscious, I'll do it for you right now! Please! Anything for my life!"

The pleading was taking on a pathetic tone. It turned out to be worth it.

"Hmm. In that case, you may leave. Go into the barrier the journalists are in, and take all the other people strewn around here with you."

The leader immediately obeyed. Without hesitation, he shook his fellow hunters awake, ordering them to fetch the fallen knights for him. The king, he personally hefted over his shoulder before fleeing into the barrier. None of the journalists chided him for it. They were too busy watching over this bizarre turn of events, holding their breath in anticipation.

✳

The area in front of the tent was much cleaner now, as Saare flashed a defiant smile at Diablo.

"Hmm... Impressive. I find it hard to believe you're merely a calamity-level Arch Demon."

"Oh? You weren't fleeing me?"

"Fleeing? Such an amusing remark. My name is Saare. I directly serve the Holy Emperor of Lubelius as part of his Imperial Guard, a member of both the Three Battlesages and the Ten Great Saints who stand in opposition to this demon lord of yours. But who are *you*?"

"As I stated earlier, I am called Diablo. That is my name, as granted to me by the great and powerful lord Rimuru."

"...And you still aren't going to reveal yourself?"

Saare attempted to keep himself friendly and at ease, even as the humiliation was making him reach his boiling point inside. All Diablo's talk about people failing to "overcome" his terror was a direct affront to him—but he kept his thoughts rational. He wasn't the kind to let pointless anger cloud his self-control, but in his mind, Diablo was acting far too disdainful with him.

Those demon hunters from the East were a joke, bragging about how professional they were but forced to beg for their lives at the end of it. Saare had let them keep up their act, since Glenda had suggested using them as sacrificial pawns, but this performance was far below his expectations.

Internally, he sneered at the demon before him. *I shouldn't have expected more from private citizens. We are tasked with guarding the Holy Emperor and the god Luminus herself. We are far more prepared to battle than they would ever be!*

Despite that, he kept himself on a higher alert than usual. *Grigori wanted to fight as well,* he recalled, *but it looks like the prey chose me instead. In which case...time to make him regret his arrogance.*

Diablo was an unknown name, not mentioned in any of the ancient texts he was familiar with. It meant this was no great demon, nothing to pose a threat to him. *Red, White—all that pretention. What's there to be so afraid of? If this was a still-unnamed Primal Demon, all bets are off, but...*

He could tell his foe was no regular Arch Demon, but to Saare, this didn't seem like much to be concerned about. It was the sort of confidence that only the truly ignorant could have. He just knew too little about demons.

In his eyes, if this one wasn't going to reveal his true nature, he'd just have to rip the disguise off by force. Saare, after all, had enough power to fight a demon lord alone. Valentine may have escaped at the end of their battle, but he was a hair's breadth away from slaying him. A mere Arch Demon wasn't cause for alarm at all.

That explained why Diablo's attitude irked Saare so badly...but Diablo's next statement made the Battlesage doubt his ears.

"...Reveal myself? Ah yes. I have so little interest in strength, I forgot to mention it. Indeed, as you say, I am not an Arch Demon. In fact, I have completed my evolution to Demon Peer. Rather similar, I think you'll see," he casually added, "but do try to remember the difference."

That much really didn't matter to Diablo—not as much as his name did. It was a trivial matter to him, but a massive crisis to Saare.

He couldn't believe it. He didn't *want* to believe it. What did the demon before him just say? A Demon Peer? That was...purely the stuff of legend, unofficially classified as a disaster-level threat, and its force far exceeded anything else in the demon family. Not even a higher-level spirit could hope to catch a whiff of that kind of power. It would take multiple elemental lord–class creatures to deal with it.

Only a few very old tomes had examples of one interfering with this world, but it proved that they did exist. Just look at the strongest demon lord that ever walked the earth...

Oh.

Now it made sense to Saare. A demon who had lived for millennia and become a demon lord–class presence, like Diablo mentioned, could evolve into a Demon Peer via some kind of trigger. Of *course* that evolution would boost his force to such dizzying levels. The Red's magicule count had ballooned to several times that of a regular Arch Demon, and he had all those extra years of experience, too. Truly, there was no limit to his strength.

The demon hunters' leader, warily eyeing these events, had fallen unconscious the moment he heard the words *Demon Peer*. He was overcome—not with fear, but with relief. If he had actually *fought* that demon... That was too much to even consider. And the joy he felt, avoiding that fate, literally knocked him unconscious.

Nobody could blame the guy. Even Saare was taken by an all-encompassing desire to run away. And the scariest part? Some fool out there was insane enough to give such a rare Arch Demon a name.

What in the name of Luminus could Rimuru have possibly been thinking?!

Saare could feel a cold sweat erupt from every pore in his body. His instincts were sounding the alarm bells, the easygoing attitude of a moment ago now barely a passing memory. He knew how impossible this was.

If Diablo had given his name without hesitation like that, it meant there really was someone out there who had granted it to him. A masterless named creature would never be so eager to share his name, since it would expose him to falling under the control of someone else. It proved that the demon lord Rimuru really *was* behind this.

But could Rimuru, freshly ordained as a demon lord, even have the energy needed to name an Arch Demon?

There wasn't much point pondering that question, but Saare

couldn't help but wonder. His mind was just attempting to escape reality at this point.

Then he felt something in motion next to him.

"What are you balking for, Saare?! Let's you and I take out that sexy-looking demon together!"

Glenda was virtually screaming at him.

"No! Glenda, wait!"

Saare was already too late to stop her. Like the wind, she strode forth, sneaking up to Diablo without a sound and thrusting her black-bladed knife at him. It plunged straight into Diablo's undefended heart.

"Ha! No threat at all!!"

Glenda laughed. She could tell that hit home. But sadly, Diablo had no intention of dodging that from the start.

"Heh-heh-heh-heh-heh… That is some commendable physical ability. Unfortunately," he flatly stated, "physical attacks do not work on me."

That was the truth. Diablo had acquired a trait known as Cancel Melee Attack.

Glenda quickly leaped back a safe distance. "Pfft! What a pain!" Then, ignoring Saare's warning, she launched a barrage of quick attacks. Even she could tell he was a formidable foe; she no longer openly berated him like before, and she was treating this like a battle against a full-bore demon lord.

But it was all mere sport to Diablo. He was in a realm of his own, power-wise, and nothing Glenda busted out could ever affect him.

Now Glenda realized this—or to be exact, she had sensed as much from the start. Her real goals lay elsewhere.

Saare, resigned to his fate, steeled himself. Unable to abandon Glenda, he joined the battle, unleashing his spiritual force and boosting his physical skills to the max. Wielding the Demonslayer, a Unique weapon obtained through massive amounts of capital, he slashed at Diablo. It didn't work.

"Dammit! Slashes don't work on him?! Glenda, buy me some time so I can unleash my holy magic…"

Reasoning that only his strongest magic would knock this menace out, Saare asked Glenda for a hand. Glenda had no response. Diablo spoke in her place.

"I believe your female companion just fled?"

Saare had trouble understanding this at first. Turning around, disbelieving his own ears, he couldn't find Glenda there. Diablo was right; she had fled the scene long ago.

"Damn herrrrrrr!!" he screamed at the top of his lungs. It didn't accomplish much. Glenda decided unilaterally to start this battle, and then she left Saare to deal with the fallout. It enraged him, but Diablo *was* right there, sporting his evil grin. It was time for Saare to worry about his own hide, not hers.

I can do this. I have to do this! I need to keep this going until Grigori returns!

With his hopes now pinned on his other stalwart companion, Saare roused his spirit. Grigori had gone to the city to lure the demon over to him. Their target was right here, and thus he should be back shortly. Believing in this, Saare plunged himself into this desperate battle—a fleeing wish that never had any hope of coming true.

As Saare faced these insurmountable odds, Grigori of the Three Battlesages was in a desperate situation of his own.

There, as he ran across the battlefield, he was greeted by a calamity from the skies. It was the mercenary force Yohm had brought on, seemingly fighting to protect the city gate. They were doing what seemed to be a fine job, fending off Farmus's vanguard force.

This wasn't the prey Grigori was supposed to be targeting. He had no interest in Farmus's internal strife; it had nothing to do with him. He was only after the demon who killed Archbishop Reyhiem, and his intelligence stated that he'd be found working undercover in this town.

King Edward was accompanied by those specialists from the East when I saw him, he had thought. *Unless they run off on him, I doubt I'll have much work to do...*

But now Grigori was faced with a much more present threat than a demon. It was a gigantic, fearsome wolf in his way.

*　　*　　*

The wolf, of course, was Ranga, wagging his tail with glee as he sprinted across the heavens. He was light, as light as a feather, and now his feet weren't kicking against the ground at all. This was Skywalk, a technique only a small handful of magical beasts could hope to learn, and he had acquired it all too naturally.

To Ranga, however, this was a trivial detail. The waves of power released from his body were bringing him pure joy as he whirled around, feeling himself fill up with magical energy. His legs, covered in jet-black fur, were crackling with gold-colored lightning—his aura releasing electricity into the air, whether Ranga meant to or not. It was being controlled by the shining gold horns on his head, radiating a force like a crown, even as the lightning-infused fur shone black like a robe of darkness. He was the king of wolves, and now he had every bit of the majesty that title entailed.

Now he approached the speed of sound in the air, as he instantly sighted the group Diablo tipped him off about. Another moment, and he was back on solid ground—right in front of Grigori.

Accompanying Grigori was a small handful of the Lubelius Imperial Guard. The other five thousand with them were the second wave of Farmus knights sent by Edward as reinforcements.

One of the Farmus generals, an inexperienced member of the nobility, nervously approached.

"S-Sir Grigori, your orders?"

Hell if I know, he thought.

All of Farmus's top-notch knights were long gone, erased from the world during the previous attempt to invade Tempest. What remained were the also-rans, the fighters whose skills and brainpower weren't enough to join in last time. None of them could think for themselves; they relied fully on Grigori, this wonder child from exotic lands, without even the slightest sense of shame.

"General Gaston, you tackle the forces lagging behind us. You saw them advancing from the ground and the sky, right?"

The observation made Gaston come to his senses. "Very well. What about you, Sir Grigori...?"

"Me? Isn't it obvious? I gotta take that guy on. Python, Garcia, you two join—"

Join Gaston and keep him guarded is what Grigori wanted to say, but he was interrupted by a dark gale-force wind rushing by.

"Wha...?!"

At a speed that only Grigori could react to, Ranga charged right into the forces Gaston led.

"Dammit!" Grigori shouted. "That stupid dog!!" He thrust his halberd forward with all his might; Ranga easily leaped out of harm's way, then began exercising free rein to wreck the whole troop. Leaping up and down, he kept attacking and attacking, piling up the casualties. Neither Python, nor Garcia, nor all of their many companions could avoid the feast of violence, sending them all crashing to the ground.

And before long, those fangs were being bared at Grigori himself.

Gobta and Gabil were chasing Ranga as fast as they could.

"Come onnnn, Ranga, you're too faaaast..."

"Indeed. I fear there will be no assignments left for us at the end of this."

"My brother," interjected Soka, "please, enough whining. Continue the chase."

They were all bickering at one another just like usual, but everyone knew they were good friends. Only the three of them thought they were hiding it.

"Right!" bellowed Gobta. "Here we go!"

"Got it!"

Gobta triggered Shadow Motion, accompanied by a hundred of his goblin riders. Gabil flew ahead, a hundred members of Team Hiryu joining him. Soka, meanwhile, returned to Hakuro to give the field commander her report.

As the first person on the battlefield, Gobta was greeted by the sight of heaps of soldiers lying in what felt like a single spot. The knights still in the fray were in a loose circle around Ranga, keeping a prudent distance and praying that Grigori could defeat this beast. The downed knights were all the talented ones—or at least, those courageous enough to engage Ranga and keep Grigori guarded. They paid for that dearly, all gathered together in a heap because Ranga was using his front paws to toss them over there, ensuring he didn't accidentally trample them to death.

The faces of all the praying knights were strained with despair. Their cheers, loud and enthusiastic at first, were now replaced with stony silence. Grigori was already covered from head to toe in wounds. Victory, at this point, would be a dream wrapped within a dream. Even with Impervious, the steel-like protection covering Grigori, in Ranga's eye he was just a slightly tougher chew toy than usual. The fact that he couldn't be knocked out simply meant he had to endure the pain that much longer.

"Whoa!" The sight half panicked Gobta. "That's, uh, that's a bad wolf, Ranga! He's gonna die if you do any more of that!"

"Yes," Gabil agreed, "we must heal him at once!"

The order made Ranga freeze in place. Noticing the sorry sight around him, he hunched over, tail pointed straight down, shrinking down in size.

"Um... Right. But doesn't this human wish to play for a while longer...?"

Grigori was unconscious, a broken halberd still in his hand, as Ranga ruefully prodded him with a paw. It was just too pitiful a sight for Gobta and Gabil to stand. Just imagining themselves in his place...

"Um, no, no, I don't think so, Ranga..."

"No, indeed! Best stop this for now, or else Sir Rimuru will never let you hear the end of it!"

The mention of Rimuru's name forced Ranga to give. Looking at the two of them with his sad eyes, he finally gave up.

"Oh no. He'll be angry at me..."

The freed Grigori's face was caked with drool, his limbs going off in assorted slightly off-kilter directions. Just slightly, mind you, but still in no angle the human body was designed for. He was pretty seriously banged up, in other words, and it was a wonder he continued to draw breath.

But Grigori survived it all. And with the healing potion Gobta provided, he made a full recovery before the sun set on the day. His body may not have paid the price for the experience...but his self-esteem certainly did. In later years, he came to be known in his homeland as the Canophobe Crusader, for reasons he refused to divulge to the general public.

*   *   *

For the remaining forces, Gabil promised not to pursue them further if they retreated, an offer that General Gaston immediately accepted. Word was quickly sent to the battered and bruised forces still attacking the town gate.

So ended the siege of Migam before it really began. And as he left the scene, Gaston could be heard shouting "Beat *them*? How could we *possibly* beat them?!"—a quote that became far more famous worldwide than he probably intended.

Come on, Grigori...! Come on! Get over here!!

Saare couldn't have wished that any harder for himself. But he was in luck—Grigori *was* coming, draped over Ranga's back. In fact, Saare's wish was about to come true in just a few more moments. Grigori probably wasn't going to provide the services he was looking for, but for Saare right now, ignorance was bliss.

Besides, he reasoned, this Diablo was just too ridiculous a demon to deal with. Here he was, one of the most powerful human beings on the planet, and not even he could fully plumb the depths of this guy's force. There was no doubting Diablo now. He really *was* more powerful than the demon lord Valentine. Why would he bother going out of his way to kill Archbishop Reyhiem? A few well-planted threats from Diablo, and he could get literally anyone to worship the ground he walked on.

So why did I even have to deal with this...?

Saare was still expending every effort possible to fend off Diablo's barrage, but he knew the end was near. His endurance, and his mental acuity, were about to be exhausted.

"Heh-heh-heh-heh-heh... Come on. Put in some more effort. Show me an interesting skill or two."

And the demon was gleefully enjoying the sight, too. Saare just wanted to cry. From the bottom of his heart, he wanted to go home.

He had been praised as a genius. He was long-lived, thanks to his elven blood, and his dauntless effort helped him sharpen his fighting style to a fine point. His reward for this was the unique skill All-Rounder, which let him fully understand and acquire an opponent's art after seeing it only once. It worked on the same principle as Hinata's Usurper, just geared specifically toward arts.

It went without saying that actually using these arts required superior physical ability. Saare knew that well, and thanks to that, he had mastered a wide variety of skills, including complex magic/arts combinations that were among the trickiest moves out there to perform. Adding magical effects like that to his own aura unlocked access to some incredibly powerful sword slashes. Thus he preferred to use Spiritslash, a basic Battlewill move and also the ultimate way to enhance one's physical ability. To this he would add whatever element his current foe was weakest against, letting him unleash a strike that could rip through almost any enemy.

That was a source of pride to Saare—and none of that worked here. Before he could even deploy the magic, Diablo analyzed its structure and disassembled it. It robbed Saare of his ability to bend the laws of nature—and without that, there would be no miracles today. Instead, giving up on magic, he opted instead to just fight with the Battlewill art Aura Sword.

"Dammit," he bitterly whispered.

The most frustrating thing about all this was how Diablo wasn't even seriously trying yet. He could tell. The difference in magical skill alone was like comparing a grown adult to a newborn. The same was true in physical strength. Only in tactical skill, something that could be learned on the battlefield and nowhere else, could Saare safely consider himself close—but even then, Diablo was already closing the gap within the space of this fight. The speed of his growth was dizzying. If he wanted to, Diablo could've easily killed Saare right now.

And if he's not, that must mean…

Diablo had no intention of ending his life. Which meant that someone else out there must have killed Reyhiem. But who?

Yes. Hinata never wanted to be involved with all this, and the incident occurred after she left—as if aiming for that exact moment. It's so…

…so suspicious. Wait. Not even suspicious. It *had* to be the Seven Days Clergy behind this. Saare was sure of it. And just then:

(Saare, we've come to give you aid.)

(Rejoice! We shall destroy this demon together!)

(Hold the demon back for us. Our magic will take care of him.)

The air warped behind him as Saare felt a new presence, one bearing a stupefying amount of force. They were the members of the Seven Days Clergy—three of them in all—and despite the way they put it, the magic they were attempting to cast was far too dangerous to use in this space.

A good criminal always knows how to destroy the evidence. And in this case, the "evidence" was anyone who knew that Diablo didn't kill Reyhiem. Which included the journalists on hand. They weren't idiots—many of them had come to the same realization as Saare by now. It was the whole reason Diablo kept them around.

So if the Clergy wasn't aiming for Diablo at all...

"Run! Get away!!"

Just as Saare turned toward the press and gave that warning, a massive fireball engulfed the entire area.

A white-hot bolt of force penetrated Hinata's chest.

Hurriedly, I came over to help her up.

"Hey, you all right?"

"Ngh... Gaaah!"

She was coughing up blood. But through the pain, she still brought a hand to her chest, attempting to cast a spell. It failed—as it would, given that she couldn't speak any longer. Instead she eased herself down, lying limp in my arms. The blood from her began to stain my clothes a bright shade of crimson.

Unless I did something, Hinata was going to die without ever knowing what happened. We could work out the timeline that led to this later. I took a potion out of my Stomach and sprinkled it over her chest. But while this would normally begin the healing process immediately, now—of all times—nothing happened.

Understood. The subject Hinata Sakaguchi possesses high resistance to magic. Her body automatically disassembles magicules, neutralizing their effects.

It cancels out magic?

"M-magic won't work on Lady Hinata," her assistant Arnaud said, shaking his head as he ran up to me. "Any recovery magic has to be holy in its alignment, or else it will be neutralized on contact..."

Ah. So holy magic, which didn't work through magicules, was okay? A lot of good that did me. These potions were useless, then. In that case...

"In that case, don't just stand there. Cast some holy magic on her!"

We needed something more effective. Hinata was still alive. If we used holy magic to heal her, she ought to be able to recover.

After I shouted at them, Arnaud and the other paladins began to act. But they couldn't move. Something was blocking them—a ring of light, binding all the paladins. A group of people, each bearing a huge amount of power, had used a high-level teleportation spell to jump into our area, restraining Arnaud and the rest.

The two mystery visitors kneeled before me.

(Demon Lord Rimuru, it is a pleasure to meet you. We are members of the Seven Days Clergy, and we have come here to punish Hinata Sakaguchi for violating our orders...)

It sure was brazen of them.

Hinata was on the ground, barely conscious; Arnaud and the other paladins were all tied up; and then these guys show up. And I had heard of the Seven Days Clergy before. Adalmann didn't seem to appreciate them too much. *Very* suspicious. I wanted to learn more from them, but things were kind of urgent right now.

"I don't know what's going on with you guys," I said, trying to sound as annoyed as possible, "but don't get between Hinata and me. We already settled things between ourselves, so I'm not gonna let her die."

The Clergy raised their arms up high, making their disagreement clear. (Unfortunately, we must insist. Hinata, the woman there, has ignored the will of the god Luminus. This is blasphemy, and we must issue divine punishment in response.)

The gall of these guys. They teleport right into my backyard and think they can just say anything they want.

"B-but...!"

"Please, forgive Lady Hinata! She had her own motivations for this..."

The Clergy had no interests in the pleadings of the paladins.

"Don't give me that crap!" one of them suddenly shouted. "You tricked all of us, didn't you?! You wanted Lady Hinata dead from the start!"

This was the captain of that band of a hundred, the one who'd faced off against Shion. Then, suddenly, things began to get a little hectic...by which I mean, the paladin standing next to him took out his sword and plunged it into that captain's body.

"Wha—? Garde, y-you..." the captain gasped.

"Such insolence, Renard. I refuse to allow you to speak so ill of the Seven Days. You were conspiring with the rebel Hinata all along, weren't you? You're the one who tricked us!"

The shouted accusation created a stir among the rest of the paladins. They had no idea who was telling the truth, I figured. That was how much political power this Clergy must've had over them. But that wasn't true, was it? I mean, that heat beam or whatever came from Garde's direction. Which meant...

...Well, it meant I had no idea what to do next. Things were so chaotic, there was no hope of putting them back in order. I wanted to take Hinata back from the brink of death, but the Clergy was in my way—and now Renard was betrayed by his own men and in mortal danger himself. And then the Clergy says they want Hinata dead for defying them, although they don't seem to be hostile to me.

So now what...?

Job one was to save Hinata. Shizue asked me to, for one, but beyond that, I think we were just a few steps away from working everything out with each other. If we could make up, I figured that could lead to friendlier relations with both the Western Holy Church and the nation of Lubelius. Abandoning her was never an option for me.

"Look, I'll hear all of you guys out later. This is my nation, and you need to follow my laws while you're here. Um, you're Arnaud, right? Cast your healing magic on Hinata now."

My nation didn't have laws, really, but I still had executive power, and I meant to wield it. But the Seven Days Clergy wasn't impressed.

(We cannot allow that. The followers of Luminism have sworn absolute allegiance to the god Luminus. Even if the demon lord Rimuru wishes it, no one here will execute your request.)

They were keeping all the paladins from doing anything. It was *so* annoying. There was no time to try reasoning with them. I thought about forcing the issue—but just as I did, Diablo sent me a Thought Communication.

(Sir Rimuru, I have an emergency report—)

(What is it? Keep it short; I'm kind of busy.)

(Pardon me. I have discovered Reyhiem's killer. It is a group known as the Seven Days Clergy; they appear to have devised all these events behind the scenes.)

(Hohh…)

(I am faced with three of them right now, and I fear that leaving them alive might cause harm for us later—)

(Can you provide evidence that they're the killers?)

(We have a press corps full of journalists from around the world here as eyewitnesses, my lord.)

(…All right. Permission granted. Rub 'em out.)

(Yes sir!!)

What impeccable timing! Diablo definitely earned a nomination for Most Valuable Butler with that show. I had no idea how he had engineered this to work out so well, but I guess I had the right man for the job.

This solved a lot of riddles on my end. So the Seven Days Clergy were the bad guys here? Their motives were unclear to me, but I guess they were after Hinata, not me. They wanted her dead, presumably because she'd be trouble for them alive—and since she'd be too formidable a foe for them, they had hatched a scheme to turn the rest of the world against her.

The dude who just stabbed the paladin Renard must have been connected to them, too—or maybe he was a Seven Days member himself—but either way, this Garde guy was the real hit man here. He must've wanted a clean kill, but performing the crime right in front of me was a mistake. My Universal Detect was in operation, so doing the deed with me around was like shouting "I'm the killer!" as you pulled the trigger.

I suppose these were the guys who fiddled around with my

message for Hinata, and I had to assume they interfered with Diablo's plans, too. These were the culprits, and no one else—and now that I knew that, I didn't have to worry about hurting my relationship with Lubelius.

This was *my* nation.

Originally, I had thought it best to leave them alive, but they had been a thorn in *my* side as well. I didn't see much need for that now. If they were going to run on me, let's just kill 'em off instead.

So leaving Diablo to take care of his own business, I began to take matters into my own hands. Time to let off a little steam.

"Benimaru! Soei!"

""Sir!"" they both shouted.

"Capture those two. If they resist, take any measures you deem necessary."

"Just what I was waiting for!"

"As you wish, Sir Rimuru."

Benimaru and Soei came for the Clergy, who immediately shot me a pair of dirty looks. I didn't let it bother me.

"Shion!"

"Yes, my lord!"

"You take care of Garde over there for me."

"...!"

"Watch out. He might be a Seven Days guy in disguise."

"I see! Then let me show him the deepest pit in hell and expose him for what he is!"

She gleefully readied her massive sword. This time, I didn't stop her. Hell, I was *hoping* to see that sucker.

(Heh...heh-heh... Well, look at this!)

(Are you quite sure? It will mean all-out war against us.)

Those two could babble all they wanted. If I let them be, it'd be even more trouble for us later— And if I was gonna take action here, better make it count.

"Sorry, guys, but you went too far. I guess you tried pinning the blame for Archbishop Reyhiem's murder on me, but I've seen right through all that. If you're picking a fight with me, I assume you know what's coming for you, yeah?"

The paladins exchanged confused looks. A few of them, at least, seemed to see things my way. Arnaud, meanwhile, with an enraged expression, already had his sword pointed at the Clergy. But the pair didn't look daunted. In fact, they were laughing in our faces.

(Heh-heh-heh! I didn't think we would be found out.)

(Wah-ha-ha-ha-ha! But the Saint is already dead! Demon Lord Rimuru, you and Hinata both exhausted your strength in that battle, didn't you?)

(We wouldn't dream of missing this golden opportunity!)

(And if all of you know the truth as well, you will die with your demon lord!)

At least they weren't making any more excuses. The Seven Days Clergy fully admitted to it, laughing the whole way. Such a vulgar display. It almost made me sick. There was no value in keeping them alive at all.

Benimaru, Soei, and Shion each sized up their prey. But it turns out the Clergy was craftier than I thought.

(Fools! I commend you for exposing us, but everything has already been accounted for.)

(We planned to kill all of you from the beginning!)

(Heh-heh-heh… Let us begin!)

With that, the two of them leaped back and floated into the air. Garde joined them, revealing his true colors before Shion could reach him. Then, with the three of them grouped together, they constructed a large-scale magic circle on the ground. This was dangerous—certainly beyond what a human of regular intelligence could handle, and certainly something that required advance preparation. Inside this circle was us, two of the Three Lycanthropeers, and the paladins. They intended to kill us all and make sure no evidence ever saw the light of day.

"Hellflare!!"

"Demonwire Slash."

Dark pyres of flame shot out toward the trio, accompanied by a torrent of Sticky Steel Thread powerful enough to break through sheet metal. But the only sound anyone could hear was high-pitched laughter.

(Ridiculous! You waste your time! This magic circle deflects all non-holy strikes! Any magical attacks from evil creatures like yourselves could never penetrate it!)

(Wah-ha-ha! Such utter fools. Our knowledge has been built and refined over centuries. It will never lose out to the brute force of some arrogant monster horde!)

The laughter echoed above us, but I was too busy keeping Hinata alive. She had a temporary heart, made from my own body, but it took up a ton of magicules. I wasn't used to pulling this off, and it wasn't exactly a very compatible donor organ for her, so it wasn't working as well as what I concocted for Mjurran.

Then Shion charged forward, ready to push all my concerns away.

"Shut up! That means nothing in the face of my Goriki-maru Version 2!!"

She wasn't making much sense, but she made a mad dash for the Clergy, muscle memory winning out over her brain. It would have struck most people as idiotic. But Shion was on another level today.

(Ha-ha-ha-ha-ha! You imbecile! What could that sword possibly—?!)

There was an audible ripping sound, out from the air in front of the sneering Clergy.

(N-no!)

(She's going to break down the magic circle?!)

(So be it! We must release it now!!)

Shion's nonsensical attack was pure brute force, something that didn't care much about elements or attributes at all. In addition...

Understood. She appears to be using Guarantee Results, part of her Master Chef skill, to alter the space around her.

This is just crazy. I can only hope she doesn't start using that stuff on me.

Report. While the possibility is slim, the subject Shion's attack might be effective against you as well.

Aw, crap, really? Better make sure I never piss her off again.

This had taught me all over again how amazing she was, but sadly, even that couldn't stop the Seven Days Clergy's attack.

Report. Attack incoming.

*　　*　　*

Their broad-range annihilation attack was complete. *Crap. What should I—?*

Report. It is not a problem. The magic circle has already been analyzed.

The cool, refreshing voice of Raphael calmed my frayed nerves. Okay, uh, great. No problem at all, then. This magic circle looked kind of complex to me...but ah, I guess it was child's play to the wise master here. I hated to dent the Clergy's confidence and all, but I guess a riled Raphael could still outwit them.

((((Prepare to meet your doom! Trinity Break!!)))

Three voices chanted in unison to launch the spell. But all that effort was already in vain.

Report. Relaunching the ultimate skill Belzebuth.

Just as the professor reported that to me, Belzebuth swallowed up all the droplets of murderous light raining down from above. In a moment, they were all gone. Yikes. Set this thing to full blast, and it was a real monster. Even the paladins stared wide-eyed at me, shocked at the sight of all those missile blasts disappearing before their eyes.

But...wait a second. Didn't I "sacrifice" Belzebuth when I fought Hinata just now?

Understood. The ultimate skill Belzebuth, Lord of Gluttony, was indeed sacrificed, but a copy had been backed up, so it was not a problem to reactivate.

Huhhh? Backed up? And why was Raphael using the past tense there? You gotta *tell* me about this crap, man! I thought I had lost that thing forever. The professor acted like this was all settled history, but I wasn't sure I was willing to accept that.

Report. Rise in holy force detected. Main attack incoming.

*　　*　　*

Oops. That last strike wasn't the main one?

(((Face your ruinous end, demon lord! Trinity Disintegration!!)))

Whoa, crap! Belzebuth ain't gonna cut it now.

Report. It is not a problem. Invoke Absolute Defense from the ultimate skill Uriel, Lord of Vows?

> Yes
>
> No

Hey, hey! There's the professor I know. That's another yes, but... Hang on. Again, something didn't seem right.

But even as I pondered this, the first Absolute Defense wave activated—a single, thin, transparent layer covering my skin. This was all it was—and this was all it took to perfectly disable Trinity Disintegration.

✳

Right. Yeah. That's the thing. That was definitely the first time I used that move. I had been using Multilayer Barrier up to now, not Absolute Defense.

Taking advantage of my Mind Accelerate speedup, I finally asked Raphael the question on my mind. *Hey. Why didn't you activate that earlier? I could've blocked that strike on Hinata with that thing!*

The response was enough to push my frustration to the brink.

Understood. This is because the ultimate skill Uriel's Absolute Defense may still be penetrated by spiritual particles on occasion. As a result, it was determined that invoking it would be meaningless.

Raphael made it sound like common sense. *I swear, you don't have to be such a perfectionist about this stuff...*

The behavior of the spiritual particles that magicules were made of was apparently difficult to predict. They ignored time and space as they moved around, cutting straight through well near any barrier. The near-random elements that controlled their movements—the forces of nature that governed over these particles—made it impossible for Absolute Defense to handle them, unless you knew how they worked.

And yet, here I was, perfectly safe after that barrier just trounced Trinity Disintegration. What's up with that? Did Raphael fully predict things this time?

Understood. In the previous Meltslash attack, Belzebuth both canceled out the strike and invoked Predation on it. This made it possible to gather enough information to successfully recognize the random elements involved. As a result, it became possible to predict and defend against holy attacks. In addition, you have also obtained the holy sword skill Meltslash.

Hmm...

What? Wait. Waaaaaaaaaaiiiit. Huh? So you mean you sucked up Hinata's sword on purpose back there?

......

Dude, don't clam up on me, you bastard! I can totally picture you reacting like "Oh no, Rimuru got me" just now! Your silence is telling me everything I need to know!

Although... Wait a second. I know Raphael isn't the type to take dangerous risks, but...could I have, like, survived a Meltslash blow without having to cancel it out with Belzebuth?

Understood. Of course. You lost a great deal of magical energy, but your material body could have been instantly reconstructed with Infinite Regeneration.

...So what were you so freaked out about? You didn't just want to consume Meltslash so you could analyze it, did you?

......

Oh, more of that, huh? Bastard's getting better and better at dodging my questions. More...malicious, you could say, or human-like. You could tell me the guy was a living being, and I think I'd believe you.

But...I dunno, I suppose I would've wanted it, yeah. Wanted to withstand that attack, wanted to use it myself... Did it take that moment of desire to act upon it that quickly? What a crazy ability I had. It almost felt like it was going to waste on a bum like me.

Negative. I exist only for the sake of my master.

Pretty fast replying to that one, huh? Pfft. Thanks. Keep up the good work, partner! Just try not to keep any secrets from me.

Thus, within the dilated time Raphael and I bickered with each other, our entire conversation ended in a single real-world instant.

✳

(No! That couldn't... No!!)

(It is impossible. Such a ridiculous feat should never happen!)

(There could be no creature in this world who could withstand a direct blast of Disintegration...)

And so on and so forth.

All three of them were mightily confused, and...y'know, I could see why. Even *I* thought it was kind of freaky, and I allegedly cast it. The ultimate in holy magic, cast in triplicate no less, and I blocked it like a spit wad. If I were them, I probably wouldn't want to accept it, either.

But that's reality for you. It's what you get for making me—or, I guess, Raphael—your enemy.

"All right. Now it's our turn."

Benimaru, Soei, and Shion nodded.

"Your fancy magic circle seems to have disappeared," Benimaru said, a ball of flickering black flame in his hand. "Think you can withstand this a second time?"

The Seven Days Clergy visibly recoiled at the sight of this. Their hand was fully played, and they had nothing left to counter with.

Shion flashed a fearsome smile as she sized up her prey. "You can't escape us, you pile of garbage. Prepare to die!"

Soei was silent, watching the Clergy's movements with an unblinking eye. Alvis and Sufia, the Lycanthropeers, were watching over the paladins, making sure none of them stepped out of line. There were unlikely to be any more real threats among them, but no harm in being sure. Not like any would-be assassin among them could do much of anything now.

(Ngh...)

The Seven Days trio had now been herded into a single location. But they still refused to give up.

(Think this over carefully! We are the guardians of humankind! If you kill us, the followers of the god Luminus will not take it sitting down!)

(Exactly! Luminus's rage will burn all of you to ashes!!)

(We will step back this time. Now that we know you are not evil, I am sure talks will proceed smoothly with the Western Nations. You will be good neighbors to each other...)

With a mix of intimidation and flattery, they deigned to negotiate with us. This was really starting to piss me off. It was time, I thought, to end this—

"...I seem to have caused quite a lot of trouble for you, Demon Lord Rimuru."

—but then a cold, bracing voice echoed over us as a massive gate appeared, cutting through the air. The door opened, revealing a beautiful young woman. Between her unique silver hair and her heterochromatic eyes, there was no mistaking it—she was the demon lord Valentine herself, and I probably didn't need to ask why she came.

(Gahh!)
(My... My lady...?!)
(What are you doing in a place like this...?)

The Clergy visibly withered in her presence, cowering in fear. Then they kneeled before her.

Well, then. I guess Valentine was actually the god Luminus this whole time. The realization struck me dumb.

Diablo, almost shaking with glee, let out an evil laugh.

(...All right. Permission granted. Rub 'em out.)

With those simple words from Rimuru, he had full permission to do as he pleased. He wanted these fools eliminated as quickly as possible, yes, but before that, there was some business to take care of.

He turned toward the press corps. "Now, everyone, are you all right?"

The fireball was blocked by the barrier Diablo built, keeping all the journalists unscathed. This barrier also kept all the demon hunters, as well as King Edward and his knights, safe from injury. Nothing based on magicules, including aspectual and spiritual magic, could penetrate it.

(Tch. Annoying little demon. You are capable of that much...?)

(A fearsome foe, indeed. It is time to show off our own holy force...)

(Prepare to launch!)

The Clergy, expecting to wrap this whole thing up in a matter of seconds, had to be surprised. No matter how powerful this demon was, destroying his physical body would eliminate any influence of his on this world. The moment he could no longer maintain his magical form, it was back to the spiritual realm for him.

Anticipating this, the Seven Days Clergy launched an ultimate-class magic the moment they arrived—Nuclear Flame, part of the nuclear family of aspectual magic. Three people were required to carry it out, the force of it being too much for one, and it rained unquenchable hellfire upon its target. Against Diablo, however, it was powerless.

Overwhelmed, the Clergy quickly opted for their final weapon. Defeating someone as powerful as Diablo required holy force, and nothing else. Their minds made up, they decided to bring out their finisher—Trinity Break. It was the same move their compatriots tried against Rimuru, and while it took some time to prepare, they could be protected by a barrier during casting, keeping them safe. What's more, the Trinity Disintegration launched at the end of this spell was the most powerful of all holy magic, capable of reducing anyone and anything to its composite cells. No matter how great the monster or magic-born, from demon lords on down, this attack could never be resisted.

It was thus with total confidence that the Clergy uncorked this spell...just as Diablo began negotiating. Not with Seven Days, but with the press.

"Did you see that attack?" he gently asked. "It seems clear to me that they made an attempt on your lives, didn't they?"

Even Saare, enemies with Diablo until a moment ago, couldn't deny it. The journalists certainly didn't. They all nodded their understanding. The guardians of humankind, the great heroes, the Seven Days Clergy of legend—everyone there knew of them. Diablo was telling the truth; they were sure a moment ago that they'd be breathing their last. The Clergy would bury them all, Diablo included, and then they'd pin the blame for it on the demon.

"But there is no need for alarm. I will protect you all."

To the crowd, Diablo's smile looked like the reassuring countenance of a benevolent god. They believed him. If he was powerful enough to shrug off a Battlesage like Saare that easily, beating the legendary Seven Days didn't seem so fantastical, either.

"What, what do you want from us...?"

"Oh, money?"

Some among the press worried about what Diablo would desire in return. Demons never work for free—they always demand something back, and Diablo was no different. He'd never provide a service for no reason, unless he was doing it for Rimuru.

"Heh-heh-heh-heh-heh... I appreciate your understanding. I seek only one thing from all of you..."

His demand, given with a smile, was this: Report his innocence to the world. The journalists, hearing this, breathed a sigh of relief. They were expecting a cruel, merciless demon, but the truth was something else entirely.

If Saare, one of the chief officers in the Holy Empire of Lubelius, was caught up in the Clergy's dragnet, it meant that group had to be conspiring on an impossibly high level behind the scenes. The journalists were being used, too, and once they knew that, there was no reason to turn down Diablo's request.

"Of course! Let us spread the word far and wide!"

"Yes, we will write whatever you want! All about your glorious deeds!"

"That we will. So please! Please, help us!!"

There were nearly a hundred members of the press there, and all of them promised their loyalty. The unique skill Tempter was faithfully doing its work on them. Betrayal would not be forgiven. The pact had been forged.

"Heh-heh-heh-heh-heh... Very well. Then I promise to save all of you...but *not* you."

The demon pointed at Edward, only now recovering from his fainting spell.

"Wh-why?! What did I ever do—?"

"Silence!" he spat out. "You openly mocked the great Sir Rimuru, a crime worth a thousand deaths. It is time for you to realize that saving you is worthless."

Edward racked his hazy mind for some way out, but none came. The only thing for certain was that, if things kept up, he was going to die. He looked toward his knights; they averted their eyes. Defying the will of a monster like that, or the heroes of legend, was not conducive to their health.

"Please... Please, if you could, allow me to live..."

All that remained was to attempt a teary-eyed round of begging. It failed to bend Diablo's heart.

"Heh-heh-heh-heh-heh... Feel free to continue lamenting your foolishness as you depart this realm."

None of the press lifted a finger to help Edward. What could they do? Edward was the cause of all this in the first place; nobody was going to step in for him now and face that demon's wrath.

The king, realizing this, started crying. "I'll give you everything. My money, my position... My, my throne! I'll abdicate and give you everything..."

Diablo paused, apparently giving this offer some serious thought.

"Come to think of it," he said, lightening his tone, "the hero Yohm is guarding Edmaris at the moment, is he not? I believe he is the only one qualified to truly lead the land of Farmus, but what do you think of that?"

Edward knew that. His mind, racing at speeds higher than he ever felt in his life, was sure of that.

"I—I agree with you! He has great potential. I would gladly announce him as my successor..."

The answer was a source of great satisfaction for Diablo. The journalists could sense it as well. A couple of them even began to laugh.

"Ha-ha-ha... The birth of a hero king, is it?"

"This is the news of the century..."

Diablo nodded contentedly. Now the table was set perfectly. A few of the details had gone awry in his plan, but the results wound up more than satisfactory.

Now all that remained was to sweep up the garbage.

The time had come.

(Hmph. Are you ready for this?)

(In just a few more moments, a rain of light will cleanse this realm of evil.)

(Enjoy what few remaining seconds you have left to—)

The Clergy had been watching these events from afar, assured that their upcoming spell would win the day for them. What arrived instead was a single moment of despair.

"Am I ready for what, exactly? Don't make me laugh, you scum. You meddled with my plans and shamed me in front of Sir Rimuru—both serious crimes. You will taste the fear and despair I felt many, *many* times over."

There wasn't a trace of a smile on Diablo as he regarded the Seven Days. His face was expressionless, the beauty to it only adding to the fear factor.

(Wh-what...?)

(What are you saying?)

(Have you lost your mind? This spell could never—)

The Clergy was cut off by a snap of the fingers—and then the world was enveloped in horror.

"Enjoy the sensation of powerlessness in a crumbling world! ...Moment of Despair!!"

This was Diablo's power, taking advantage of Tempting World—one skill in the Tempter repertory. Normally, it worked directly on the target's subconscious to affect their mental state, but Diablo had improved on it. It let him materialize a virtual world for its hapless victim, then exercise absolute control over that world. Diablo could even dictate who lived and died in this virtual realm—and then, with the help of the Truth Twist skill, he could switch out that pretend world for the real one. The phantoms and monsters crafted by him would take on real form in the physical plane.

It was as unfair a skill as it was inhumane. Breaking out of it could only be done with sheer willpower and a well-trained spiritual body—but almost nobody could defeat the spiritual life-form of Diablo in that contest, and not even the Seven Days Clergy was an exception.

(What, what is this?!)

(Our, our magic is disappearing?!)

(N-no...)

The three of them struggled in abject surprise, but there was nothing they could do. The clock ticked on their personal hell—and after a short while, their world collapsed.

"Enjoy reflecting upon your foolishness in the deepest pit of hell..."

It was time for the final flourish—End of the World, the final snuffing out of the Tempting World he created, taking everything inside with it. It swallowed up the Seven Days Clergy's full despair, taking it all the way to the final second...

...and then the promises made in this battlefield were safely carried out.

Having the demon lord Valentine, er, Luminus show up was kind of a surprise, but now someone else was coming through the door. This was the so-called Valentine from Walpurgis, right? The stand-in for Luminus?

The three Clergy members here paled in his presence as they kept kneeling before Luminus. They had no interest in fighting any longer, trembling like lambs waiting for their judgment. So what would Luminus do? The way she apologized for causing me trouble, I suppose she wasn't here for a fight, either.

But then the former stand-in opened his mouth. "Stand back," he commanded, his voice projecting far and wide. "I am Louis, the Holy Emperor, and the presence you see here is our god—Lady Luminus!"

The paladins promptly fell to their knees. It reminded me of a certain retired lieutenant general—not that I said that to anyone. Instead, we decided to watch what would unfold, as confused as we all were about it.

But...a demon lord serving as a god? What kind of a joke is that? And that stand-in was the Holy Emperor? The propaganda getting thrown around was so ridiculous, I hardly knew what to make of it. Thinking about it, though, maybe this was the most effective way for her to position herself...

Affirmative. It would allow you to create the most efficient environment for ruling over the species of humanity.

Hmm. Yeah. But I wasn't suggesting we copy that, all right? Don't let me be misunderstood on that. Otherwise, I was scared of what Raphael might decide to try next.

"...Hinata," Luminus said as she approached her knight, still cradled in my arms. "I told you to restrain yourself, but you decided to venture here anyway..."

She lifted a hand into the air.

"May your heart be revived. Resurrection!"

This was Resurrection, the miracle of god, in action. Before my eyes, the hole from Hinata's back to the left side of her chest began to close up. This was even faster than my own recovery potion. Which...

...Wait a sec. Why did a "demon lord" wield holy energy like this?!

Understood. The "miracle of god" refers to the efficient utilization of spiritual particles. These particles cannot be intervened with normally, but I have discovered a way to do this. This will be analyzed later...

I didn't really get Raphael, but I guess the wise master had a nice new project to tackle. That guy's so helpful. Let's leave the job to it for now.

"Nn-nnhg... Master...?"

Oops. Hinata's back awake.

"Hey. Quit babbling," I said. "What's this 'master' talk? Who—?"

I couldn't help but needle Hinata a little. It was funny to me. None of her usual grimness. She looked almost innocent now. *She got summoned to this world during her high school years, right, and now she's spent the past decade or so here? That put her at around—*

—but before I could finish the thought, her eyes bored into me, just as icy as I remembered.

"...You."

"Yes ma'am."

"You weren't thinking something rude just now, were you?"

"No, not at all."

"Oh. All right. So how long do you plan to cling to me?"

Cling? She makes it sound so dirty. I was helping her this whole time, too. But now didn't seem like the right time to complain about it, so I better just shut up and apologize. Sometimes, as you learned over time, losing was the best way to win.

"Oh, excuse me! Not that I minded it particularly!"

Hinata jumped away from me. Then she looked down at her chest. There was a hole in her clothing, revealing the pale skin below.

"...Huh?"

Crap. She wanted to kill me with every fiber of her body now. Did I step on a landmine there?

"Has anyone ever told you," she asked as she glowered at me, "that you're completely tactless?"

"*You're* the one staring daggers into me right now. Why do you have to be so stubborn? You never listen to people!"

I didn't mean to mouth off like that. *That* was a mistake. Hinata's beauty turned into a mask of angry rage. I could hear her give me an exasperated *tch*. But she simply took a breath, bottling it up, and flashed me a smile—which was scarier, in a way.

"…Look. I'm just shortsighted sometimes, that's all. You *are* tact-less, aren't you? I bet you had trouble getting dates your whole life."

Her words pierced straight through my heart. A critical hit! *Shut up, lady! Quit making me remember my forgotten past!*

"I—I did not! People thought I was considerate and reliable!"

"Oh? Well, great," she replied, giving me a look of pity as she chuckled. *God, I hate her. Right at the end, she beat me good.* I won the battle, but now I felt like such a loser. And, oh, wait, I never declared victory anyway…

Leaving me to deal with my shock alone, Hinata used her own healing magic to take care of Renard. *Her* spell did a hell of a job as well. I thought Luminus might've helped him out, but she couldn't have cared less. I guess she's the type to pretend people didn't exist if she wasn't interested in them. *Hang in there, Renard. Guess he's got it worse than I do, in a way.*

By healing Hinata, Luminus had restored the paladins' confidence in her. Some of them knew the Holy Emperor Louis's name, too, and none seemed to question his presence here. Seeing Renard come back to life sent up a cheer among the troops, many shouting "Lady Hinata!" and crying their eyes out.

She punched out one dude she caught staring at her chest, though. *That's Hinata for you. Can't let your guard down. What's she talking about, being shortsighted? It's not like she didn't have Magic Sense on all the time. But I guess she was particularly sensitive to the wandering eyes of men, huh? Better be careful. Kinda too late for me, but…*

After the commotion calmed down a bit, Luminus slowly opened her mouth.

"Now… Seven Days Clergy, what excuse do you intend to make for this?"

We all looked on, wondering how she was going to handle this. Then I got another message from Diablo.

(…The job is complete, Sir Rimuru.)

(Good. How did it go?)

(Heh-heh-heh-heh-heh! All according to plan.)

He sounded pretty happy with himself. Guess there were no more problems on his end.

(Excellent. Report back here to me once things settle down.)

(Yes, my lord. I look forward to it.)

Diablo closed the Thought Communication and went back to work. I guess he was no longer blamed for that murder, then—which meant I didn't need to intervene in how Luminus decided to handle these Clergy guys. They were certainly a pain in the ass, but she had just apologized to me for it. Any further meddling would just complicate matters. Better just sit here and think about how to improve our future relations.

As I thought that, Luminus made her decision. She was judge, jury, and (as it turned out) executioner.

"I sentence all of you to death. At least allow me to guide you to your end by my own hand..."

(Have—have pity on us!)

(It was only for your sake, Lady Luminus...)

(I swear by our years of faith to you, please...)

They clung to her in the most pathetic way. She didn't let them for long.

"...Death Blessing!!"

She spread her arms wide, and then the hand of an unseen god wrapped itself around the Clergy. It was, I suppose, one final act of pity for her servants.

A warm embrace of pity is all I could call it, but apparently it was much crueler than that, turning the living into the dead as it did. It was my first glimpse of the extent of Luminus's power.

Thus, painlessly and all too easily, the Seven Days Clergy, who had attempted to trap us all in their cruel schemes, met their end. It came so quickly, I have to say. And here I was bracing myself for full war against the Holy Empire. Instead, it was now time to negotiate our future relations.

*

It wouldn't do to stand around outside like this, so I decided to change locations, staging a sort of victory march back to town as I guided Luminus, Louis, and Hinata along.

Soon, I spotted Veldora back in town—and then I remembered.

"Oh, uh, sorry, the final defense line turned out to be unnecessary."

"Aw, dammit! I was waiting here with bated breath, all this time..."

The news didn't exactly thrill him, but he'd have to deal with it. Thus, everything was settled—or so I hoped. But the moment Veldora laid eyes on Luminus, he dropped another bombshell.

"Whoa...!! You! I remember you! I know I do! You're Luminus, the *demon lord* Luminus! That vampire whose castle I blew to splinters! Wow, I'm glad I remembered! Otherwise, it'd be bothering me all day—"

He was stopped by the tip of a sword Luminus produced out of nowhere tapping against his neck. But, like, too late now, huh? He just went and proved to the world that the god Luminus was the demon lord Luminus Valentine.

The paladins were, uh, nonplussed. They fell silent, unable to parse this all at once. Hinata, apparently aware of this before now, put a hand to her forehead and sighed, while Louis just stood there like he was above it all.

Hoo boy. Time and time again, Veldora proved himself the biggest troublemaker I ever knew.

We all had to team up to restrain the enraged Luminus after that—"This accursed lizard! Getting in my hair every single damned time!!"—but that's a story for another day.

EPILOGUE

A NEW
RELATIONSHIP

That Time I Got Reincarnated as a Slime

Deep inside the Inner Cloister, Gren, the Sunday Priest of the Seven Days Clergy, was waiting for his comrades to return from their mission. There had been some complications with the elimination of Hinata, leading to an emergency request from Arze. Failure wasn't an option here, so Dena and Vena went out to join them.

That woman has too keen a mind for her own good. We need her out of the picture before she obstructs our plans any further. We must use that demon lord, that god Luminus, if we wish to become the true rulers…

Gren had served Luminus for several hundred years with that secret ambition in his mind, weeding out anyone too talented (and therefore dangerous) for his liking. The fellow Clergy under him did their jobs well, portraying him as a loyal servant to the faith, and it was easy to make them move on his behalf. Luminus liked him, and if he could appeal to people's sense of jealousy about that, they did whatever he wanted them to do—just as he knew they would this time.

Arze was on his way to assassinate Hinata, disguising himself as the paladin Garde after the original one had been "dealt with" on the sly. Everything was in place. The disguise was the product of Dena's own sorcery; nobody could see through it.

The Dragonbuster he gifted Hinata was equipped with a device that caused it to self-destruct anytime he wanted. If it broke right when the demon lord Rimuru attacked her, that would be enough to ensure her defeat. But she didn't use it—and even worse, she started with a leg up in the fight.

Hearing that, Gren decided a change of plans was in order. If Rimuru killed Hinata, then great. If he didn't, Arze could seal the deal instead. Then the Clergy could move to kill any eyewitnesses and assuage Rimuru, earning his trust and ensuring things would go in the right direction.

But the problems just kept piling up. The demon in the Farmus province of Migam proved much stronger, and craftier, than predicted. Throwing that strength around—that forceful, almost unfair strength—had planted doubts in the minds of the journalists Gren went through the trouble of assembling for the event.

A frantic report from the Saturday Priest, Zaus, who was observing the fray, convinced him to send out the Wednesday Priest, Melis, and the Thursday Priest, Thalun. The witnesses all needed to be killed, and the entire crime had to be pinned on the demon. Framing it as divine punishment for the demon's unspeakably cruel actions would be enough to paint the Seven Days as the just side of this conflict. Just put it all on the demon, not on the demon lord Rimuru, and all was well.

If negotiations proved difficult, that's where the god Luminus would come in. Rimuru was keen on establishing a foothold in the Western Nations—if he was declared a divine enemy, he'd be effectively shut off from that. The Clergy had more than enough bargaining chips to work with.

Gren had the situation read perfectly. There was no doubting the success of his plan. If there was any loose end to it, it lay in that demon Diablo's insane amount of power...but Thalun was second only to Gren himself in force, and with him on the scene, "Sunday" was positive that victory was theirs.

But none of them had come back yet.

What could they be doing? he asked himself, the question appearing on his lips. Nobody was around to answer...except someone was.

"Whatever is the matter? You look very peeved about something."

(You... Why are you here...?)

Surprised, Gren turned around. Cardinal Nicolaus, Hinata's close confidant, had entered the room without permission.

"Well, I've made quite an interesting discovery, you see."

(A discovery?)

"Yes. This."

Nicolaus took out the crystal ball containing Rimuru's message.

(And what—?)

"I've found evidence this has been tampered with," he replied. Interrupting a legendary hero was frightfully rude of him, but Nicolaus didn't seem to care at all. A visibly annoyed Gren looked at the crystal; it was playing the full message, including the parts he thought he deleted.

(...?!)

Picking up on Gren's disturbed reaction, Nicolaus continued. "I have to say, I don't care very much about what your objectives are. I don't even care if you use the favor you enjoy from our god Luminus for your own aims..."

(What are you talking about? Our god is a concept. A concept that lies in the hearts of us all—)

"Don't try to trick me. I realized ages ago that the god Luminus exists. Lady Hinata kept it a secret, so I simply followed her lead. But as I said, I truly didn't care."

Nor did I care about how you tried using this god, Gren could almost hear Nicolaus saying to himself. He opened his eyes wide; Nicolaus returned the gaze with a thoughtful-looking expression, his eyes as eerie and his emotions as opaque as the waters of a marsh.

(You...)

"Elders as destructive as you have no place in this world. Disintegration!!"

(No—?!)

Gren had no time to say anything else, his face frozen in surprise as he disappeared into the storm of light particles and faded from sight.

"Accursed insect. You thought I'd let you do harm to Lady Hinata?"

With those parting words, Nicolaus returned to his study as if nothing was amiss.

The good cardinal was more than just Hinata's confidant. He

was also her biggest fan in the world. And to him, all this religion was another way for him to stay connected to her. This made him a heretic, a nonbeliever at the highest echelons of the Papacy. His faith was directed toward no god at all, but a single mortal woman.

*

Inside a warm, firelit room, Granville Rozzo sat on a heavy, padded chair and meditated.

"Nicolaus... Curse you..."

He opened his eyes, the blinding light of the Disintegration burned into his mind. As well it should. For Granville Rozzo was none other than Gren himself, the Sunday Priest and leader of the Seven Days Clergy. He had the ability to send his spiritual power into other people, possessing their bodies, and he had just transferred himself to another host the other day. Now all that effort was wasted.

Today's experience was a chilling one, even for him. If that had been his *actual* body, the cardinal really could've ended his life. That only added to Granville's rage.

But perhaps the time was ripe to pull out anyway.

As he opened his eyes, he sensed Glenda approaching his mansion. It meant things had not gone according to plan. It was all a failure.

The moment she stormed into the room and saw Granville, Glenda began shouting.

"Sir Granville, we couldn't do it! There's no way I could handle that monster! It's crazy!"

She looked exhausted, like she ran all the way here from the battlefield. There was no doubting her. It was the truth.

"What about the other Battlesages? If you took him on as a team..."

"No, I tell you, he's just not on that level. In battle, you know, my nose is highly sensitive to the smell of death. I decided this was all trouble for me, so I pushed the battle on Saare's shoulders and ran off. That guy's a demon lord–class foe—maybe even stronger, for all I know."

It sounded like an exaggeration to Granville, but he had still received no contact from his Seven Days companions. He even sought out their presences, somewhere in the battle over there, and found nothing.

"No..."

As much as it shocked Granville, it was the incontrovertible truth.

Several days later, the spies he had deployed across the land informed him that King Edward had been deposed. The journalists on the scene were all safe at home, reporting their accounts far and wide. There were even rumors from Blumund that Tempest was planning a grand festival for themselves.

Putting all these reports together, the only conclusion to make was that Granville's plan had failed. The Seven Days Clergy, Granville included, were no more; the good name of the god Luminus could no longer be leveraged.

Then his beloved Maribel gave another prediction:

"It's dangerous. Too dangerous. That town is too dangerous!"

Granville failed to understand what this meant.

"You mean the angels' attack?"

"No. No, Grandfather. That demon lord seeks to rule the world through economic policy."

Ruling the human realms through their finances—that was the aim of the Rozzo family, the exact plan Granville had underway this very moment.

"He couldn't be..."

"It's true. It's really going to happen. That's why...we need to crush him."

Maribel wasn't one for lying—at least, not up to now. It made her suggestions worth listening to all the more.

"I see. Well, if that's what you say, I'm sure it shall be so."

After all, Maribel was both Granville's direct descendant...

"It will. Next time, for sure, it will happen. I swear it on my name as Maribel the Greedy!"

...and a reincarnated girl. The future hope of the Rozzos, gifted with knowledge of the "other" world and an uncommon amount of power. As long as she lived, Granville thought as the flames of ambition began to burn anew, the family would never be defeated.

●

It didn't exactly come easy, but I patched things up with Luminus and cleared up the drama between myself and Hinata. In exchange, as a sort of apology, they agreed to send out a Western Holy Church missive declaring us to be harmless.

All this came about because of how hard it was for us to understand each other. I'm sure it wouldn't be the last time, either. But I think this was also a lesson for both sides, a trial we should strive to overcome and improve ourselves with.

The occasion also led us to reconsider the relationship between Tempest and the Holy Empire of Lubelius. For the time being, we agreed to sign a nonaggression treaty and give tacit consent not to meddle in each other's affairs. The whole, uh, "thing" with Veldora was an outstanding issue, but it was no skin off my nose, really. More of a personal problem. Veldora's, that is. Not a Tempest matter— That's my story, and I'm sticking to it.

Luminus was clearly reluctant to leave it at that, but I promised her that I wouldn't intervene in anything involving the guy, and she grudgingly agreed to that. Besides, I had the ultimate skill Veldora, Lord of the Storm, on me, and as long as I did, Veldora was de facto immortal. Even if something popped up, I didn't expect any problems.

Understood. There will be no problems.

Good.

So yeah, it was pretty much selling off my best friend, but I served Veldora up as a sacrificial pawn to quell Luminus's rage. I thought I heard something along the lines of "Nraaahhh! Are you abandoning me?!" from him, but I'm sure I was just imagining things. It was kind of his fault, besides, and I can't babysit him through every little thing. Kind of sad, maybe, but it's all part of growing up.

Thus, with a small sacrifice on my part, we had regained our peace. I had no idea how this got worked out so fast, but Yohm was even ascending to the throne. That whole bit was going along great, I heard; all that remained was to wait for the big coronation day. It felt nice, seeing every one of these problems fall all at once like dominoes.

And from that day forward, we were formally accepted by the Western Nations.

ROUGH SKETCHES

BACCHUS

FRITZ

GARDE

GRIGORI

GLENDA

SAARE

AFTERWORD

Thanks for your patience! *That Time I Got Reincarnated as a Slime,* Vol. 7 is finally here, and as you can see, this one also wound up on the lengthy side.

I think my conversation with my editor went something like this:

"I'm going to keep this one more compact!"

"Oh, you will? But it's going to run long anyway, isn't it?"

"No, no, there are a lot of parts I'm cutting out from the Web version, so it's gonna turn out shorter!"

"You don't have to force it, you know. I've already given up on that."

And of course, right on schedule, the manuscript began to grow into a tome.

"Um... As I write this, I think it's looking just a bit longer..."

"You say that every time, don't you? I'd assumed as much."

I suppose you could say we've built a relationship of trust by this point. Mr. I, my editor, could see through everything. Was it that way from the start? I better not overthink it.

So let's talk a bit about the content. As those of you who've been with me up to now are aware, I often include spoilers in my afterwords. Not that this warning matters by now. You don't see many people picking up a series at Volume 7, so I assume I don't need to recommend that you should read the actual novel first.

✳

If you've read the Web version, I can't blame you for thinking this is an entirely different story. To be frank, the content doesn't match at all.

My claim that the "overall plot is the same" is *really* starting to ring hollow, I know. That's because, as I change the story's developments here and there, it's becoming impossible to keep everything connected the way it used to be. Thus, at around this point in the story, I decided to rewrite things a fair bit so we could get back to the main plot. An even bigger reason, however, is because the background for a certain character has changed extensively. I won't say who, but while the personality may be much the same, the motivations and skills that character comes with aren't the same any longer.

Hinata, the star of this volume, was probably influenced the most by this. She might seem like a different person from the Web version by now, but this is how she originally was. I'd suggest comparing her between the Web and novel versions, but really, if you've gone this far and not read the Web one, perhaps you'd enjoy sticking to the novels more by now. Take it the way *you* like it!

The people engaged in that foreboding conversation at the start of this volume sure didn't show up again, did they? Don't worry—I haven't forgotten about them. Be on the lookout for the next volume!

Although by now, I think something's begun to dawn on most readers. What? "The author's got no clue what's going on"? No, not that. More like "The author has no intention whatsoever of writing out the Web version over again."

Admittedly, it's true that sticking to the Web version is probably a lost cause. However, with Volume 7, I'd like to think I succeeded at righting the ship and helping it sail back to its original route. As I write this, I'm thinking that maybe, with luck, I could keep Volume 8's content pretty close to the Web version. I mean it. A lot depends on how I feel about it when I start writing, but still.

So yeah, maybe I'm not the most careful planner with stuff like this, but hopefully you'll still want to keep up with me. See you all in the next volume!

Taiki Kawakami : Art

←READ FROM RIGHT TO LEFT!